and other tales of mystery

Ten Thousand Blunt Instruments

and other tales of mystery

Philip Wylie

Edited by Bill Pronzini

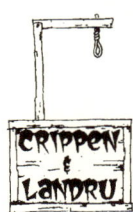

Crippen & Landru   Norfolk, VA   2010

Cover painting and design by Tom Roberts

Lost Classics design by Deborah Miller

Crippen & Landru logo by Eric D. Greene

Lost Classics design based on a drawing by Ike Morgan, ca. 1895

ISBN: 978-1-932009-83-5 (cloth)

ISBN: 978-1-93200984-2 (trade softcover)

FIRST EDITION

July 2010

10 9 8 7 6 5 4 3 2 1

Printed in the United States of America
on recycled acid-free paper

Crippen & Landru Publishers
P. O. Box 9315
Norfolk, VA 23505
USA

Email: info@crippenlandru.com
Web: www.crippenlandru.com

CONTENTS

INTRODUCTION

PHILIP WYLIE: WRITER
IN RENAISSANCE

A writer's writer, a renaissance man of letters, a hugely prolific author of limitless versatility and imagination, one of the most popular and influential writers of his time, a profoundly original thinker, an unflinching critic of American morals and mores; controversial, provocative, inconoclastic — these are just a few of the many laudatory descriptions of Philip Wylie by critics, scholars, and aficionados of his work. His amazingly broad range of interests and expertise included but was not limited to: psychology, philosophy, biology, ethnology, technology, physics, atomic energy, modern education, women's rights, environmental issues, engineering, UFOs, deep-sea fishing, orchid growing, Hollywood filmmaking, mainstream science fiction, and mystery and detective fiction.

Wylie was born in Massachusetts in 1902, grew up in Ohio and in Montclair, New Jersey, where at the age of ten he survived a near-death experience from a burst appendix. Intense, introspective, and a voracious reader, especially of the works of H.G. Wells and Jules Verne, he began writing at an early age and published verse in school and church newspapers. After entering Princeton in 1920, he contributed frequent columns under the pseudonym Philip Speyce to the *Princetonian*.

Disenchanted with academia, he left the university before graduation and spent four years on the staff of *The New Yorker* before taking on numerous other full and part-time jobs: writer of pulp science fiction stories, deckhand on a cargo boat, salesman of dress goods for a New York department store, press agent, editor with Farrar & Rinehart, and syndicated newspaper columnist. His eventual success as a novelist and slick-magazine writer led to such honors as vice-president of the

International Game Fish Association, director of the Lerner Marine Laboratory, and as a result of his civil defense work during World War II, special adviser to the chairman of the Atomic Energy Committee.

He was married twice, first to Sally Grant in 1928, then to Frederica Ballard in 1938. The first union produced his only child, a daughter, Karen (who under her married name, Karen Pryor, is a celebrated author and expert in the fields of marine mammal biology and behavioral psychology, founder of Hawaii's Sea Life Park and Oceanic Institute, and pioneer of "clicker" training of dolphins). Wylie died of a stress-related heart attack in October of 1971.

The list of his literary endeavors is as richly varied as his interests and his personal resume. Astonishingly prolific (he once dictated a 100,000 word novel in nine days while on a ship crossing the Atlantic), he produced, by his own estimation, forty-eight million words of fiction and nonfiction over a period of more than forty years and saw a third of that number in print. His published works include:

Poetry. *Dormitory Ditties* (1923), his first book, privately published while he was a student at Princeton.

Mainstream novels. More than a dozen, including *Heavy Laden* (1928), *Babes and Sucklings* (1929), the heavily autobiographical *Finnley Wren* (1934), *Night Unto Night* (1944), *Opus 21* (1949), *Triumph* (1963), and *The End of the Dream* (1972).

Nonfiction books. Several, the most famous being his 1942 collection of essays, *A Generation of Vipers*, a no-holds-barred assault on "momism" and other then considered sacred attitudes of American life and culture, which caused a firestorm of criticism both favorable and vilifying and was a huge bestseller. Of his equally mordant and controversial *An Essay on Morals* (1947), a review in the *Chicago Sun* stated that "copies will be snitched from libraries by people determined to keep the book out of circulation [and] undoubtedly a few at least will be burned."

Articles and essays. Dozens for literary, popular, and scientific publications on topics ranging from sex and censorship to medievialism and the MacArthurian legend to "The Crime of Mickey Spillane."

Mainstream short stories. Many for diverse publications, several of which deal with the misuses and potentially destructive forces of atomic power.

Screenplays. A handful for feature films, including *Island of Lost Souls* (1932), based on H.G. Wells' *The Island of Dr. Moreau*; he also wrote portions of the classic horror tale, *The Invisible Man* (1933, uncredited).

Several other films were produced based on his novels, short fiction, and screen treatments, notably *Charlie Chan in Reno* (1939) and *When Worlds Collide* (1951). One of his last works was a 1971 script for the television series *The Name of the Game*, entitled "Los Angeles: AD 2017," which concerns a dystopic future in which deadly smog forces everyone in southern California to live underground.

Fantasy and science fiction. In collaboration with Edwin Balmer, two seminal novels in the field, *When Worlds Collide* (1933) and *After Worlds Collide* (1934); the former inspired Alex Raymond's Flash Gordon comic strip. Other of Wylie's s-f novels: *Gladiator* (1930), which is said to have been a partial influence on the creation of the *Action Comics* hero Superman; *The Murderer Invisible* (1931), elements of which were incorporated into the film version of *The Invisible Man*; and *The Disappearance* (1951). His contributions to this field have been called "formidable" for their innovative concepts, intellectual perspective, and sharp wit.

Romance novel. *Blondy's Boy Friend* (1930), published under the pseudonym Leatrice Homesley.

Adventure fiction. *The Savage Gentleman* (1931) is widely believed to have been the inspiration for the pulp magazine superhero Doc Savage. Wylie also wrote more than one hundred fishing tales for *The Saturday Evening Post* featuring Crunch and Des, a Florida charter boat captain and his mate. These stories, several of which had criminous elements, were so popular that they inspired a syndicated TV series featuring Forrest Tucker and Sandy Kenyon that ran for 37 episodes in 1955-56.

Spy fiction. *The Smuggled Atom Bomb*, a short novel which first appeared in his 1951 collection *Three to be Read* and was later issued in a separate paperback edition, and *The Spy Who Spoke Porpoise* (1969).

Mystery and detective fiction. Several novels and many short stories, long novelettes, and serials for *American Magazine*, *American Weekly*, *Collier's*, *Blue Book*, and other publications. With Edwin Balmer: *Five Fatal Words* (1932), *The Golden Hoard* (1934), and *Shield of Silence* (1936). With Bernard A. Bergman, published anonymously: *The Smiling Corpse* (1935). Solo mysteries: *Corpses at Indian Stones* (1943), featuring mild-mannered anthropology professor Agamemnon Telemachus Plum and his feisty aunt Agatha (praised by Anthony Boucher as "slick and smooth") and two short novels issued in paperback, *Danger Mansion* (1940), originally published as a magazine serial, and *Experiment in Crime* (1956), from *Three to be Read*.

Wylie's ingenuity and grasp of the elements of successful detective fiction are evident in the stories collected in these pages. "Murder at Galleon Key" is a tense tale of mystery and mayhem set in the Florida keys, featuring a unique method of body disposal and a hurricane as an added menace. "In a Hole" was the first of a miniseries of stories published in *Collier's* in the early 1930s, about amateur sleuth Willis Perkins who here uses his wits and knowledge of criminology to expose a gang of bank robbers. "It Couldn't Be Murder" is a clever impossible crime story in which a young artist and his model prove that a series of seemingly natural deaths by heart attack in the same family are in fact cold-blooded murder. "The Paradise Canyon Mystery" pits a former Olympic swimming champion against a ruthless murderer in and around an exclusive hotel in the southwestern desert country. "Death Whispers" combines a newspaper editorial writer's temporary blindness with elements of *Rear Window* to create a satisfying blend of detection and mounting suspense. The halls and galleries of New York's Museum of Natural History form the unusual setting of "Ten Thousand Blunt Instruments," in which the weapon used to bludgeon a man to death is as surprising as the motives behind this and other crimes perpetrated among the skeletons of man's remote ancestors.

Although these stories occasionally show the haste with which they were written for magazine deadlines, their overall quality and entertainment value remains as high today as when they were first published in the 1930s and 1940s. It's a pleasure to bring them back into print for the enjoyment of contemporary readers.

BILL PRONZINI

MURDER AT GALLEON KEY

I

At this particular moment, a hundred detectives, policemen, reporters, newsreel cameramen, and others are after me. I've evaded them as long as possible. And I want to have a statement prepared for the first of them who overtakes me. So here is my side of what just happened at Galleon Key.

My name is James Thomas Martin. After graduating from Northwestern University and taking a postgraduate business course at Harvard, I was hired by Douglas Lee, the mining engineer, as private secretary. I became thoroughly familiar with Lee's complicated affairs.

I met Lee's daughter Diana two years later, when she returned to her home in Boston after a year abroad. I fell in love with her. Her mother, Beatrice Lee, became my friend. But when I asked her father to allow me to marry his daughter, he refused. Lee was a stern, dictatorial, uncompromising man. He was in a sense ruthless. He was ambitious. He fought steadily to increase his fortune. He coveted social position. He looked upon my suit—the suit of a mere secretary—as insubordinate and impertinent. He said so.

I eloped with Diana.

That is to say, I started to elope with her.

By a mere coincidence—an appalling one for me—Lee was waiting in the station for a local train when Diana and I bought tickets to New York.

He summoned the police. I won't describe the scene. I did take a swing at Lee in the early part of it, and I blacked his eye. But the elopement was a fizzle.

Lee, of course, fired me.

That was four months ago.

He sent Diana and her mother away. He used his influence and several private detectives to make sure I wouldn't follow them.

11

Early in February I learned, however, that Diana and her mother were going to spend some time fishing at Galleon Key. Lee owns the island, a small one set out two or three miles from the curve of keys south of Florida. He maintains an elaborate fishing camp all winter on Galleon Key, for his use and the entertainment of various friends, some of whom contribute to its running expenses.

I had saved and made about eight thousand dollars during my two years with Lee. But there was no chance of weaseling into the camp as a guest.

I know the place—Lee had taken me there twice. I was reasonably sure that the people on the island would not have heard of my trouble with Lee. I went down there before any guests arrived, and found that my belief was correct.

Two captains had hitherto regularly kept their boats at Galleon Key—Pepper, a native of the district, and Brothers, a Long Islander. A third had arrived this year, a Yankee named Graham. I knew him.

During September and October of the past autumn Lee had managed to get Graham well out on a limb in the real estate business. Then Lee had chopped off the limb. After taking Graham's property and leaving him pretty nearly flat, Lee had done a thing rather typical of him. Knowing that Graham was a passionate fisherman and a good sailor, he had sold him his cruiser for a song and offered him a berth at Galleon Key as a charter boat captain.

If I had been Graham, I would have refused as violently as I could, but Lee apparently knew his man, for Graham accepted the whole arrangement. He even said that he had always preferred fishing to business and that he was glad Lee had "taken" him, because now he'd have a good time all his life instead of only for a few weeks each year.

I wired Graham, and he met me at the train, which stopped on another key. I told him why Lee had fired me and that I was looking for a job. He asked me if I thought Lee would object to my working on the key and I told him no—which was a lie. So he offered me the position of roustabout—handy man—general crew—on his boat, the *Neptune*.

I took it.

For two weeks nothing much happened. A few parties came and fished and went away. The weather was marvelous—Florida winter days are blue and bright and balmy. The fishing was fair. Most of the sailfish were being taken farther north, off Palm Beach, but reef fishing was fine.

We also caught, one day, a sunfish that weighed 906 pounds, and we harpooned a seven-foot ray. Big amber jack, grouper, yellowtail, barracuda, king mackerel, bonito, and dolphin were taken on every cruise.

Five nights ago Douglas Lee, his wife, Diana, and about a dozen guests arrived.

My plan had been to lie low until I could see Diana, persuade her to elope if I could, and get away in a car. A plank bridge led from Galleon Key to the next island. It was the only connection with the main road, the only access to the trains except by boat, and it also carried the telephone wire. I had even figured that if Di was game, we could cut the phone wires and burn out a section of the bridge, and get a start that would adequately foil her irate pop. Romantic—maybe. But Diana was the kind of girl to start the mind working in romantic channels.

I stayed on the boat and the dock that evening. I didn't meet anybody. There were three buildings on the key—a dining hall, a long dormitory, and a lounge and game-room. They were laid out on three sides of a square lawn. The open end faced the cove and dock. I kept watch—on the chance that Diana might decide to come down to the pier—people often did at night, sometimes to watch the water and sometimes to harpoon sharks. There was gear on the dock for that— harpoons and rope—but the sharks usually got away, pulling out the barbs or breaking the ropes on their first dash for deep water. But Di didn't come.

I'd made Graham promise not to mention my presence to Lee that night.

"He may be a little sore," I had said, "and I want to talk to him about it myself first."

Graham agreed. He was a very decent guy.

But Pepper told Lee. Not for any reason—just to make conversation.

He told him late that night. Lee had been on the dock two or three times, and so had a dozen other people. When they'd come down, I'd go below on the *Neptune*. I ducked again when Lee appeared, but he hopped aboard the cruiser and yelled for me.

He was wild. "I told you," he said, "that you couldn't see her again. I meant it. I'll have you locked up—"

"It isn't any crime to love your daughter."

"For you, it is. Now—I'll give you half an hour to get off the island."

I asked how. There was no train that night. There would be no cars on the road from Key West to Miami, because that road was broken by a three-hour ferry trip, and the ferry didn't run at night.

He said, "Walk."

I refused. "Mr. Graham hired me," I said. "I don't want to be responsible for his embarrassment. He didn't know about your attitude toward me. If he wants me to go, I shall. You own the island. You can kick me out of my room ashore. But—"

Graham showed up, then. He was annoyed at me for not telling the truth to him, but he was sorer still at Lee. He was going to quit on the spot and move to some other base, partly on my account and partly, no doubt, because he owed Lee one beating. That stymied me.

So I agreed to make the trip on the next day with Graham and then head out. A helper could be hired in Miami or Key West to take my place on the *Neptune*.

Lee left, swearing at me loudly all the way up the pier.

I went to my room; the camp help had a wing in the building that housed the dining-room and kitchens. I knew I couldn't get to Diana that night. I figured that I'd leave and then return, unannounced. I was sore, too.

Graham woke me several minutes before six o'clock the next morning.

"You get below on board and cut bait," he said. "I don't know yet who will fish in our party. A guy named Morelli is signed for the *Neptune*. New York lawyer. Morelli and party."

I heard them arrive.

And then, for a change, I had a break.

Diana was in that party.

I stayed below. Graham cast off. We were out first. Captain Pepper's *Dorothy* was second. The *Marlin*, Brothers' boat, was last. It's a fine sight to see the fishing boats start out from those green and white keys. I watched through the porthole, pretty excited by my luck. The feather dusters of the palms blurred. Mist hung over the coral headlands. The water became bluer with every minute of sailing. There was a slow swell.

I noticed a few clouds, went and looked at the barometer, and realized that this weather would not hold. We might have to put back before evening. But I wanted to be well out to sea before I showed myself to Diana.

Graham turned the wheel over to her and came down after half an hour. He picked up the bait, and gave me one of his fling-eyed stares. You could never tell by his eyes whether he was amused or angry. He said, "Your girl's here."

I looked at Graham. "Look," I said; "it was decent of you to defend me last night. I don't want to make any trouble for you, but I'm going to see Diana."

"Good." He stared at me for another moment. "I haven't the slightest objection to seeing Douglas Lee take a fall for once in his life."

I asked him about the rest of the party. "Antonio Morelli's a smart man," he said. "Criminal lawyer. Been talking about his cases to Melville."

"Melville!"

"Of course. You know Dan Melville."

I did know him. He'd been a friend of Lee's since their early childhood in Salem. He and Lee had been in a good many business deals together. I knew vaguely that both of them had been in love with Beatrice, and that when she became Mrs. Lee, and not Mrs. Melville, even that had failed to break the friendship. More than that, Melville had interceded for me and my suit of Diana, and, after Lee had fired me, he had offered me a job.

I was glad he was aboard the *Neptune*. My fortunes were turning.

Graham, still answering my question about the party, said, "Mrs. Morelli is about forty-five, but a handsome woman." Then he went back on deck.

I looked over the two motors. I heard the reels click as they were tested and lines were let out. I heard the pandemonium as Melville, sitting in the starboard chair, hooked a good 'cuda and brought it in.

After that I began to be pressed for patience. When Diana yelled, "I've got one!" I went up.

Di's legs were propped stiffly against the stern. Her short gold-brown hair was whipping in the wind. Her rod was bent and line was running out against a hard drag. She looked like the ancient huntress, herself, at that moment.

Melville saw me and was startled. Then he began to grin.

Mrs. Morelli was reeling in from the other chair. Her husband stood beside her—a queer bird even at a quick glance. Short, plump, bald, dressed like a fashion magazine's idea of the deep-sea fisherman, he looked at the same time comical and dangerous, foppish and clever.

Diana suddenly said, "There!" Line stopped screaming from the reel. She began to "pump" in her fish.

Then she caught sight of me.

She slowly let go of her rod. Melville jumped with extraordinary speed and caught it. She said, "Jim."

My wait was over. I'd had months of it. Waiting and trouble.

We kissed each other without reservation, consideration of time, or feeling for our audience. Then I whispered. "Let's go below and talk it over," and we went.

I suppose that the pursuit of a rich girl, whose father has detectives chase you, and your past inspected, and your mail read, is funny. I didn't care whether Di had ten millions or a dime.

We sat together on a bunk and planned how to swing an elopement this time that wouldn't fail.

We may have talked for two hours. Or one hour. I don't know. I do know, however, that no one bothered us—which was considerate. Melville explained the situation to the Morellis. Morelli wanted to interfere on Lee's behalf, but Melville wouldn't let him.

Morelli didn't know Lee at all. He had come to the camp because Mrs. Morelli, who had been an old and good friend of Lee's in his college days, had met Mrs. Lee at a party. That encounter had led to the Florida invitation.

They fished, and gossiped about us.

We were about ready to come out on deck when I heard Graham yell, "Jim!"

There was a note in his voice—the note which makes you realize at once that something is seriously wrong.

I shot up the companionway.

A couple of hundred feet off the starboard bow was a buoy.

Everyone was looking toward it.

I saw it a second later—somebody in the water. Floating. Dead, I realized.

"Get a line around it, Jim," Graham said, "and haul it aboard up forward."

"I'll give you a hand," Melville said.

We went up. I tied a running bowline in a manila rope and, as Graham warped up to the body, I made a couple of throws. It was a man, and

I caught the feet on my second toss. Melville, looking pale, pulled with me. The body came up a bit, but it didn't come clear. We hadn't looked at it attentively. Now we did.

There was a rope leading from the body to the buoy. We came in between the body and the buoy and cut that rope. Melville and I knew what had happened.

There was a harpoon in the corpse, and the rope from the harpoon had fouled the chain of the buoy. The whole thing was horrible.

We got the body aboard, then. I turned him over.

It was Douglas Lee—Diana's father.

I think we dried ourselves on a piece of canvas and lighted cigarettes.

I said, "He must have been killed late last night. I saw him myself after twelve."

Melville looked at me then in a curious way. "So you did," he muttered. "I heard Doug swearing at you."

I said, "Listen, Melville. That sounds as if you thought I did this. I didn't; see!"

He said, "Will you tell the others?"

"I'll tell Diana."

I told her—down in the cabin. She looked at me. "Did you do it, Jim?" I shook her. She cried.

Then, afterward, she said, "Poor Dad! I never really loved him—but—dying like that—"

I said that it must have been quick. The harpoon had been driven through his heart and out between his shoulder blades.

"I think I'll ask Dan Melville to tell Mother," she said.

II

I was introduced to Morelli and his wife. I'd already noticed his odd characteristics—his foppishness and the sharp look of his eyes. Mrs. Morelli was middle-aged, but she still had raven-black hair and clear skin. Her mouth was large and expressive of many desires. She looked not only handsome, but strong and passionate and hard to get along with.

Morelli said, "We're putting back to Galleon Key, of course. I was on the point of sending for you."

He cleared his throat and turned toward me: "You quarreled with Lee late last night?"

"Yes."

"What time?"

"I don't know."

"You hated him?"

"No."

"Then why did you quarrel?"

"You know damn well why. Melville's been telling you."

He nodded. "If Lee had come back on that dock later, it would have been easy to kill him. There were harpoons there."

"I went to my room right after the quarrel."

"Can you prove you stayed there? Can you prove you didn't kill him and throw him into the sea?"

I answered, "Mr. Morelli, I'll talk to the police, but why should I talk to you?"

Graham turned toward us and held the wheel with one hand. "I'd like to ask this, Mr. Morelli: Before we get up any theories of who did it—how did the body get out on that buoy?"

"Tide," Morelli snapped. "Current."

Graham's narrow, Yankee eyes fixed on the New York lawyer. "If you draw an imaginary line from that buoy to the cove on the key where, presumably, the thing happened, you'll find this: The current runs at right angles to that line. The tide was coming in from midnight till after dawn—in the opposite direction from that in which the body moved."

Morelli's wife then murmured, "Somebody must have taken the body out in a boat to deep water."

Graham was still staring. "No. We have three fishing boats, one rowboat, and two outboards at the camp. We all know the big boats were in. There wasn't any gas in the outboards. And I had part of the bottom open on the rowboat. I was fixing it."

"Well, then, what's the explanation?" Morelli asked.

Graham replied solemnly, "As far as I can see, it was simply impossible for the body to get out there."

Mrs. Morelli said, "A swimmer?"

"Nobody swam that body out—in these waters. Too many barracudas."

The sky was overcast when we reached the key. After Graham cut the motors, you could hear people laughing in the camp.

I made the boat fast.

We all stepped on the dock.

Melville took Diana's arm and said, "I'll take Miss Lee to her mother." To her he added, "Let me break the news."

Morelli and his wife stood by. He began to give Graham instructions about what to do. "Leave the body where it is. It shouldn't be touched. Then—arrange to notify the *Dorothy* and the *Marlin*."

Graham replied, "I'm going to send the body up to camp. There's a room behind the office in the dining-hall building where it can be put. It won't be necessary to send for the other boats."

"Why not?"

Graham pointed toward the horizon. It looked black out there. "They'll put in—fast."

I went up to the camp and got some of the help. We improvised a stretcher, and moved the body. We didn't touch the harpoon.

I was on my way back to the boat when I saw Diana come out of the dormitory. She seemed frantic.

"Mother's gone," she said.

"Gone? Maybe she's out on one of the other boats."

"She's not, though. Mr. Blantz says she isn't. He thought she was sleeping."

Blantz was the camp manager. At that moment he ran out from the office and hailed us: "I've got the master keys."

We followed him. The dormitory was a one-story building with a long porch. Inside was a hall which ran its length, and off the hall were numbered bedrooms. Morelli was in the hall, and so were several other guests. They were in a state of chattering excitement.

"We knocked, and Mother didn't answer," Diana said. "She's not in there—" her face lost color—"or else—!"

Blantz opened the door. Diana and I went in first.

Beatrice Lee wasn't there. Her bed hadn't been used, but a satin nightdress lay across it. Her suitcases were open and the fittings of a weekend bag were laid out on the vanity. All the rooms had French doors which gave on a path behind the building. The doors here were open.

Diana said, "Oh, no!"

Morelli pushed in. "Went out those doors, eh?" He grabbed Diana's shoulder. "When did your mother go to bed?"

It made me mad. "Get out," I said.

He ignored me.

"Look," I went on loudly. "This girl's shot to pieces. Let her alone. You have no authority—"

"I'm a criminal lawyer," he said. "I consider myself in charge."

A lot of people were gaping at the door. Morelli shook Diana hard and said, "Your mother! When did she go to bed?"

Diana was crying.

Morelli tried another: "Your mother's been fishing for years. She can throw a harpoon, can't she? And hasn't she had trouble with your father?"

Maybe he thought that star-chamber stuff would work on a person under strain. Maybe he believed that Diana would spill something through fright and hysteria. I didn't stop to reason. I was tired of Mr. Morelli.

I smacked him.

I weigh a hundred and seventy-six. I once held the intercollegiate record for the javelin throw. I'm tough.

Morelli went out like a light.

I picked him up, pushed back the people who were crowding in and starting to get sore, handed Morelli to them, slammed the door, and locked it.

Diana was terrified. "Why did you do that?"

"My nerves are lousy this morning," I said. "And besides, I hate that guy."

"What shall we do?"

"Nothing. The idea that your mother might have done that to your father made me boil. And shooting it at you—I wish I'd hit him harder."

People were banging on the door.

I took Diana through the French window. We followed the path down toward the dock, behind the buildings. I was beginning to wish I hadn't socked Morelli. I wanted to cool off before I faced everybody again.

You can't see the cove from the buildings. A fringe of hibiscus and about six tall palms—the only big ones on the island—growing at the water's edge, cut off the view. We pushed into the shrubbery. Diana picked up something that had been lying just off the path: three gardenias tied into a corsage with cellophane ribbon.

"They were Mother's," she whispered.

She handed them to me. There was a brownish blot on the ribbon. Old blood.

She was in that glassy state which makes possible thinking and saying and doing anything. She gazed at me. "Then Mother was here last night. And she got blood on her corsage. She must have had something to do with—it."

"We'll hide this," I said, "till the cops come. I wouldn't want Morelli to get it."

We put the corsage in a cranny under the shore end of the pier.

Then we saw that the Neptune had put out again.

"Graham's gone," Di whispered. There was relief in her voice. "He did it! Father ruined him and then pensioned him off with this job. He probably accepted it so that some day he'd have a chance to take his revenge."

I hadn't thought of that. You simply don't think of people you know as murderers. Particularly as brutal murderers.

We just stood on the dock for a while. Then the wind hit Galleon Key. It blew hard and abruptly. The day grew dark.

With the wind, the *Dorothy* came in.

A woman passenger hailed us: "Hello, Diana! Isn't it beastly! Driven in so early in the day!"

I called Pepper up from his boat when it was moored. The others were crowded around Diana. We'd already seen that her mother wasn't aboard the *Dorothy*.

Pepper was a small, scrawny man with no chin and an accent so broad that you had to spend time on the keys before you could get half of what he said. A native. "Conches," they were called, an unbred, parlous bunch of people whose blood was that of the pirates and convicts who escaped to Florida when it was Spanish.

"Somebody murdered Lee last night," I said in a low tone.

Pepper was holding a boat hook. It dropped. "Can't be!"

I told him how.

"Body out on that whistler," he said slowly. "Funny." He jumped back on his boat and got up the fish. I followed.

"What do you make of it?"

He ignored me. He threw the fish up on the dock and then said, "Where's Graham?"

"Gone out again."

"What for?"

"Don't know."

Pepper screwed up his eyes. "He done it, eh? Well—can't blame him. Lee was a hard man. Too hard a man."

"What makes you think that?"

He peered at me for a long time, a crusty, antagonistic expression on his face. "Nothing—only except what he done to Graham. Smashed him. And bought him off with a boat and a job."

I had an idea, but I didn't want to get onto that eternally hostile ground which exists between "natives" and urban people. Diana had left the dock. Pepper's one-man crew—Tate—was fumbling around on the foredeck. The horny "conch" decided to go ashore and listen in on the gossip. That suited me.

I shoved forward and sat on an anchor looking at Tate. He didn't yet know about the murder.

"What's Pepper got against Lee?" I said.

The young bird, a seedy but less bleached copy of the older one, did his pull-up too fast. "Nothing."

"Meaning plenty." I shrugged. "I know about it, anyway. And I have been getting to understand you guys. You're right. Rich men from the North haven't any right coming down here and breaking into your affairs."

"They're a bunch of bums and racketeers, themselves," Tate muttered.

That wasn't definite. I said, "I've had trouble enough with Lee myself—"

I reeled off a song and dance about my happy but interrupted love affair.

"Just like him," said Tate. He scrubbed his oyster-colored hair with a knobby hand, and went into one of his native silences. Close-mouthed people.

III

Slowly, I moved up on the dock, thinking that Lee might have been killed there. Things were in their usual order. Harpoons in the rack—I counted them—six: but I didn't know whether there had been seven or not. I was ready to bet there wasn't a man who knew how many there had been.

I stuck around.

When the *Marlin* came in, Beatrice wasn't aboard. I took aside the *Marlin's* captain—Brothers—and told him.

Brothers was calm about it.

He was an unusual man, one who had educated himself. He had fished professionally, so to speak, off the Grand Banks for twenty years, moved to Long Island when he quit, and taken up the winter charter-boat business some years later when his savings were washed out. He was about sixty now. Tall, well built, silent, an excellent man to fish with.

"A lot of people were down here last night with Lee," I said.

"Only place to go—outdoors—at night."

I speculated out loud on the possible motives for killing Lee.

Brothers surprised me. "Motives?" he said. "Scores of people must have had what would pass as motives." He sat down in the stern of his boat and I sat beside him. "You had a motive," he said, smiling at me. "A powerful one. Pepper had that sour, native, hate-nourishing disposition—and he at least resented Lee. Graham had a fine motive. Dan Melville might have had. Remember—he loved Beatrice and lost her. That's common knowledge. Men sometimes harbor things like that for years—and then blow up. Lee told me last night that he used to be crazy about that Mrs. Morelli—twenty-five years ago. Hadn't seen her in more than twenty years. Now, that might conceivably give Mrs. Lee the motive of jealously—or Mr. Morelli the same motive—or Mrs. Morelli might have carried the long grudge."

I shrugged. "If you draw things that fine," I said, "you can suspect everybody. I've got to go up now. I don't want Di left alone."

Lee's guests were all in the lounge. It was my first good look at them. Most of them were middle-aged. All of them were wealthy, and if they didn't have the patrician elegance of European nobility, they had what corresponds to it in the American elect of the rich: snootiness, vigor, health, and any amount of self-confidence. Even a murder and a disappearance hadn't materially diminished that. There were a couple of fine-looking girls and two or three youngish men. Sons.

Morelli was holding court again—Morelli with a first-degree shiner.

I saw Diana with Melville. A fire had been built in the room and occasionally the rising wind outside whooped it out from under a copper hood.

The lawyer stopped when I came in. "There," he said, "is the man who interfered with me."

I grinned.

Morelli went on with his cross-questioning. As I remember it, he established that Mrs. Lee had been last seen at about twelve, on her way to her room. Mr. Lee had gone down to the dock at least six times on various errands. Eleven other people had been alone or alone with Lee on the dock, and none of them could definitely state the time. The lawyer got nowhere—as I had expected. I must say for him, however, that he handled the whole affair in a competent manner.

When he finished proving that you couldn't prove who killed Lee by checking the time element, he said, "I now suggest that we search the island for Mrs. Lee."

A lot of people protested. They didn't want to go out in that storm and get wet.

A few volunteered.

I was among them. Morelli asked me some questions, then, and added me to the list of people who had been with Lee. He brought out my private war with the old man, too.

I suggested, maliciously, that when we had looked for Mrs. Lee, we might look for the *Neptune* and Captain Graham. Diana hadn't said anything at that time about the missing boat. Morelli hadn't heard of it. Now he became angry—angry, I suppose, because it complicated his case. It was all very muddled.

More so, when, before we went out in the rain to look over the island, he asked me, "When are the police to arrive?"

I said, "What?" Just—"What?"

He shouted. "You don't mean to tell me you haven't sent for them yet?"

I shook my head. "I presumed you would. You were taking charge."

He swore. "I told you to phone."

He hadn't. And the emphasis with which he said it made me wonder. "Did you tell anyone else that I had called the cops?" I asked.

"Certainly. I told everybody."

That was a hot one. If Morelli had wanted to gain an hour on the police, he'd done it neatly. And if he'd just been confused, he had been badly confused. But I'd done the same thing. I'd taken it for granted that the police were on their way—from Key West, or Miami, or both.

Morelli now charged to the phone extension in the room and clicked it. He put it back on a little tabouret slowly. "Dead."

Blantz apologized: "I'm sorry. But the phone here often goes dead in storms."

"You take a car and drive to the nearest phone that's working," Morelli ordered.

Blantz went out. It was hard work closing the door after him against the wind. The room was growing very dark. The lights were switched on.

Then Graham came in.

A good, dramatic entrance. He was half naked, soaked, and he had a rope in his hand which he threw on the floor.

Morelli rushed up to him. "Where have you been, Graham?"

"I ran my boat back to that buoy."

"Why?"

"To get that rope."

"What rope?"

Graham said, "I'm sorry to appear half dressed. But I knew you'd all be wondering about me." He strode to the fire. He was shivering. "I wanted to know how the rope from the harpoon in Douglas Lee's body had become fastened to the buoy. I had to hurry because it was getting rough."

"And how was it fastened?"

"I moored my boat to the buoy," Graham continued, in his customarily dry voice, "and dived down."

I wasn't the only one who shuddered. He had nerve.

"Well?" said Morelli.

"The rope Martin had cut to free the body was still there. About four feet under water. Wound three times around the buoy chain. The cut end — and the other end — which you can see was broken — were standing out fairly straight in the current."

There was a silence.

"And what do you make of that?" Morelli asked.

Graham shrugged. "I can't understand it. There aren't any eddies around the buoy. Current's straight and strong. Couldn't have wound up the rope." He looked at everybody. "To my way of thinking, it's the damnedest thing I've ever seen in my life. An impossible thing. Contrary to fact, contrary to sense. If you don't mind, I'll change."

Morelli stopped him for a moment and asked more questions. Graham readily admitted that he had been smashed in business by Lee a few months before, and that he had not seen Lee in the intervening months.

He was also the twelfth person who had been alone on the deck with Lee, "Late last night—I can't say when."

Then he departed.

We went out to hunt for Mrs. Lee.

Morelli had sent three men to watch at the bridge to keep anybody from leaving the island. I took the northeast shore.

The rain was by that time a diagonal, blinding, suffocating torrent. The wind was a full gale.

It was rough country—coral rock, palmetto, creepers, and thorns. I pushed along gingerly. The wind kept throwing me off balance.

I found out why the telephone wouldn't work. A fair-sized tree at the water's edge had fallen and brought down the wire. I looked at the broken ends, and the break appeared to be natural and not a cut.

IV

After about twenty minutes I reached the bridge. There were several people and two cars on it—the men Morelli had sent and Blantz, among others.

I hailed them. "Can't get across!" they shouted in my ear.

It was a long, plank bridge. The wind had taken hold under a span somewhere in its middle and ripped up about thirty feet of plank. The denuded stringers had been collapsed by wind and wave.

"Might throw a rope over and send a man on foot," I yelled.

"In that wind?" Blantz, rain-streaked and worried, motioned the cars to turn back. "We may be here for days!" he howled. "Nobody on the mainland knows about the murder. Boats can't make it."

I went on.

We were marooned.

I began to think about Beatrice Lee. She had been on the dock path— and dropped her gardenias. There was blood on them—consequently, it was at least logical to infer that she had been close to her murdered husband. Had she done it? I couldn't think so. She was too fine a person. And she couldn't have thrown a harpoon that hard.

Had she seen it done—and fled because she was hysterical, or because she hadn't wanted to give away the murderer?

Was she secretly in love with Melville, for example?

I did a little unconscious reconstructing: Beatrice in love with Melville all those years. Lee finding it out; accusing Melville on the dock, where he had gone to have some sport harpooning a shark; Melville, holding the harpoon, losing his temper, and throwing it. Beatrice an accidental witness—rushing in terror over the bridge and out of our ken. Well? How had Melville then arranged to have the body magically wafted miles out to sea and anchored to a buoy?

That was the tough part.

Then I saw Mrs. Morelli. She had been one of the volunteer searchers. She was standing now, a hundred yards away, on a high coral rock. The sea roared on three sides of her. She swayed in the heavy wind and with difficulty turned to see, apparently, if there was anyone watching.

I thought that she was going to commit suicide by jumping into the sea.

I yelled, and started toward her.

She didn't hear me, and she didn't see me. The rain was driving from my angle. She took something from her dress and flung it as far as she could into the water. Then she lost her balance. She teetered for a split second, whirling her arms.

Then she gave a tremendous leap. It took her over the water and she came up, like a trapeze acrobat, with the limb of a tough scrub tree in both hands. Her feet raced around. She scrambled from that little tree to safety—and that was that.

I was stumbling toward her. I had thoughts—lots of them. What she threw was white and it seemed to sink at once. Her jump had been spectacular, but unimaginably horrid, because I had involuntarily thought that a woman with so much power and energy could easily drive a harpoon through a man.

I scared her, because she didn't see me until I was almost touching her. We had to yell to converse at all.

"What did you throw in there?" I yelled.

"Nothing!"

"I saw you."

"I threw nothing. I merely flung my arms to keep my balance. I almost fell."

That was no lie. "Why did you climb up on that rock?"

"I was looking for Beatrice."

"In the ocean?"

She didn't answer that.

I left her and carried on alone around the edge of the island. I didn't see anything of Beatrice Lee or any tracks of a woman's feet anywhere between the camp and the bridge.

I was about the last to come back to camp. People were changing. Food was being carried from the kitchen to the lounge in big containers. I went in. Diana wasn't there—still looking for her mother. I'd wanted to go with her, but Morelli had insisted on each person's taking a beat of his or her own.

They had in the lounge a personnel list of everyone on the island, and they checked me in as I appeared.

The people were low. It was a cinch that they'd spend at least twenty-four hours in this isolation, with a corpse in one building, with Beatrice Lee missing, with a murderer in their midst.

I ate.

Diana came in finally. "Mother must have crossed the bridge last night," she said. "Oh, Jimmie, she certainly knew something or did something— but—"

I got Di into a corner in the game-room and talked to her for a while. I kissed her a couple of times. She was holding herself together in a way that made me proud.

I had changed when Morelli started his show again. The island had been pretty well covered, considering the weather, and nobody had a thing to report.

Morelli got me on the carpet. "I've been going through your rooms," he said.

I thanked him.

"I found something of interest."

Everybody listened. The Italian addressed the crowd: "Mr. Martin is a champion javelin thrower. He has medals for it. A javelin thrower, my friends, could also throw a harpoon—"

I cut in on him: "So I could. So could half the men here. As a matter of fact, I'm good with a harpoon. Lee was. Melville is. Graham is. And Pepper and Brothers. Blantz harpooned a big shark a week ago."

Morelli considered. He took the men in turn. "True, Melville?"

"Certainly."

"Graham?"

"Of course."

"Pepper—naturally, you—being a native—"

Pepper stood up. "That's right. But, as a matter of fact I couldn't of done it yesterday."

"Why not?"

"I'm cramped up with arthritis. Get nearly paralyzed by it. Had to have my boy—Tate—do everything today."

Morelli was immediately assured by people who had gone out on the Dorothy that such was the case. And Brothers stood up.

"Last night," he said, "and the night before, I rubbed Pepper's back and arms with snake oil. He was in bad shape. But there are plenty of us who can throw a harpoon—and I'm one. In fact, I'm reasonably celebrated in these waters and around Montauk for my accuracy. I never tried it on a man, though."

There, again, we were getting nowhere. I gave a hard stare at Mrs. Morelli, who'd put on a tailored suit and dried her hair. I said, "I think that most men—and even a strong woman—your wife, for example—could have thrown that thing."

Morelli whirled around. "That's an insinuation I won't stand for, Martin!"

So I spilled the anecdote of Mrs. Morelli and the white package hurled into the water.

Morelli was wild. He stamped up to his wife and said in a loud sarcastic, courtroom voice, "Well, my dear?"

She got to her feet and put down a plate of lunch. She was calm and sure of herself.

She made a speech—a honey. "Mr. Martin," she began, "has evidently resented my husband's actions concerning Douglas Lee's murder from the very first. My husband has a black eye in token of that resentment. It is true that I went as far as the north end of the island. It is true that Mr. Martin and I met there. But I did not go out on the rock. It was I who spotted him on the rock. And it was he who threw something into the water. The visibility was poor, but I am reasonably sure that what he threw away was a revolver. I saw the glint of metal. It sank at once. I'm a little bit flabbergasted at the twist he has given the incident. He begged me not to mention it. When I refused, he was very angry. I was frightened. I ran. I'm a good runner—I've done a lot of mountain climbing. I managed to lose him."

For one second I was insane with rage. Then I thought I'd better calm down. Morelli, vastly relieved, was regarding me: "What have you to say?"

I shrugged. "It's her word against mine. I say your wife is as cool a liar as I've ever heard of. I can't prove my story. She can't prove hers. You won't be able to show I had a gun, because I never owned one in my life. And, another thing: You have just made an issue of the fact that I was a javelin thrower. I was also a half-miler. Mrs. Morelli may be a good mountain climber, but she's a woman. A strong woman, as I pointed out. But I'm a strong man. You carry proof of that." Somebody laughed. I went on: "The idea that Mrs. Morelli could have gotten away from me in a storm is the feeble part of her lie. She should have left it out. If you don't believe me, I'll chase her around out there now—and prove it."

That obfuscated the issue. People who had probably braced themselves to jump on my neck now merely fidgeted in their seats. There was something to my logic. If I'd murdered Lee, and Mrs. Morelli had caught me with a gun, presumably I wouldn't mind murdering her also, and certainly it did seem that I could have caught up with her.

What would have come of things at that moment will never be known.

The wind, which had been increasing in fierceness all day, notched itself up twenty or thirty miles an hour more in one blast. The building began to quiver, and there was a noise—a howl—outside which curdled my blood.

People jumped up—Graham, Pepper, Melville, Diana, Mrs. Morelli, and others—thinking in unison that the roof was coming off.

There was outside in the uproar a louder clamor—a ripping crash—and through the windows we could see what had happened. One of the high, thickly fronded palms down near the water had been overthrown and lay with its top on the lawn between the dining and recreation buildings.

The wind sagged back to gale force. We all stood there in appalled silence.

The tree-top was pouring its fanlike leaves along the wind. And, out beyond those hissing leaves, lying on the grass, bound by rope, was the body of a woman in a white dress. We knew who it was.

I took a look around. Morelli's face was maniacally tense. Melville was gray and trembling. Graham had been playing Canfield and had brought his cards to the window. His face was angry, I thought, and the cards were spilling from his hand. Brothers was there, looking without expression. Pepper, at his side, said, "It's her!" and yanked open the door.

We all dove fast into our second soaking.

V

Anybody could see what had happened. Mrs. Lee had been hit once with something large and heavy which had made a terrific wound on her head and killed her. That wasn't the thing, however. Her body had been hauled up into that treetop and hidden there among the leaves and lashed tight. The crashing fall of the tree had loosened the body and thrown it free.

Blantz, Brothers, Morelli, and I carried her into the back room adjoining the office.

The people in the lounge, when we went back, were too scared to press us for information. I took Diana out of the room and told her what I'd seen.

She'd said, "Mother!" just as all of us went out through the door.

She let me hold her, although I wasn't much comfort. "I knew she was dead," she whispered over and over.

I told her not to talk.

It didn't stop her. "I knew it," she repeated. "And because we've found her, I don't feel any more wretched than I did. In a way—it's better. At least—people will give up the idea that Mother had anything to do with—"

Then she cried.

After a while we went back to the lounge. She wanted to go to her room alone, but I persuaded her not to. This was no time to be alone.

Morelli had finished his discourse. He'd told the facts to everyone.

Graham and Brothers and Pepper came in a little while later. They were soaked, but so were most of us.

Brothers spoke for the three captains. "Mr. Morelli," he said, "asked us to look over the tree—and the ropes. We did. We can say what was done to get her there, but—" He looked at Diana.

"Go ahead," Di said.

He spoke, then, as if to her alone: "Whoever killed your mother got a rope from the dock. Plenty there. They tied a noose in one end and threw the other over the treetop. Then they hauled up the body. After that they went up the tree—on the rope, probably—because the body would have caught on the underside of the branches. They moved the body to the top of the tree where it was out of sight, lashed it there, cut off the end of rope, and came down the tree."

"Why would—somebody do that?" Diana asked.

Graham said abruptly. "That's what I don't understand. Why? We'd have found the body sooner or later. Because—" He stopped.

Melville said bitterly, "They could have thrown her off the dock just as easily. The sharks—"

Pepper answered that: "Not safe. Sharks don't always make away with things—"

Then Mrs. Morelli became hysterical. She got up, saying, "I can't stand listening to such a conversation! You're all beasts—"

Her husband said in a loud and stern voice, "Murder has been done here! We've got to consider the facts! Sit down!"

But she went on moaning. One of the women took her out of the lounge into the sedan Blantz had used for moving people from the porch through the rain. They drove across to the dormitory.

People, in private conversation, had winnowed out the fact that a lot of the guests didn't especially like Lee. But Morelli, after seeing his wife to the door, put the basic questions.

"How did that body get out to the buoy?" he asked, almost of himself. "And why was she put in that tree?"

The rest of the afternoon was a jittering stalemate.

I say stalemate. It wasn't quite that. You cannot keep men like Melville and Morelli and Graham, and even Brothers, inactive for long hours under such circumstances. Obviously, we all had the run of the island. Nobody could get off, and the wind outside showed no sign of dying out. The rain, however, stopped entirely for several hours during the afternoon.

I did a lot of things.

I took Diana for a walk. We talked over everybody. It was tough— because some of the people we liked.

We got this:

The Morellis had acted strangely, Mrs. Morelli chucking away something that must have been incriminating; Mr. Morelli not calling the police and blaming the delay on me; Mr. Morelli taking charge and, being an Italian, at least possibly violently jealous of his wife, who had once been in love with Lee.

Captain Pepper had a grudge of unknown origin against Lee, but Pepper had been too crippled to do any dirty work.

Melville had loved Mrs. Lee—"A lot," Diana said. "I remember one Christmas a couple of years ago when Father was away and he asked her if he could kiss her. She laughed and said he could. I had to make a scene to stop him and Mother cried afterward. Also, he often felt Father was too much interested in business and too matter-of-fact with Mother. One night last fall I heard him raising the devil with Father for ignoring Beatrice."

"Did he ignore her?"

Di sighed. "Not more than other husbands who have been married for twenty-odd years."

"Any other woman in your father's life?"

She didn't answer for a while, and then said, "A few. Not very serious. He was wild when he was young. But Mother understood him—his temperament, his interests, and his emotional limitations."

We discussed Graham. I told what I knew. Di said, "I saw him in the middle of the days when Dad was selling him out. He came to Mother—to ask her to get Dad to let up. He's been philosophical about it ever since, but he wasn't then. He was so furious, he scared Mother."

"Did your mother intercede for him?"

"She couldn't. Nobody could budge Father when his mind was made up."

We looked at each other. We knew about that.

"I hate to think anybody I know had anything to do with it," Di said. And so did I.

After our walk, I sluiced around the camp.

I went through Melville's room—I pried open the French door—and I took all his papers over to my room to read. I found that he traveled with some pretty fast people, fast and sharp. Mr. Melville had a revolver, loaded, which he kept under his mattress, and inside the stiff bosom of a dress shirt in a suitcase he had twenty-five one-thousand-dollar bills.

That looked as if he had come to Galleon Key with plans. Running off with Beatrice, for example.

I got out of his room when he walked down the hall.

I went around to the front door and knocked. He was shaving.

I sat down on his bed and said, "Why do you have a gun and why do you carry twenty-five thousand bucks in cash?" I was safe enough, because I was sitting over the revolver.

He came up in the wind quietly, but sarcastically: "You're a nice boy, Martin."

"I'm in a mess here, myself. I'm trying to find all the 'out' I can. I like you. I've considered working for you. I ruffled through your room. Now I'm asking."

"I'll tell you," he said, "and I don't care whether you believe me or not. I left my office in a rush—winding up to get here on the Special. A bird who owed me twenty-five thousand brought it in cash. A gesture on his part. I had fifteen minutes to make the station. I had to take the dough. So I borrowed my night watchman's gun—in case—and came along. Okay?"

"Okay—for now," I said.

Then I looked up Tate. I got tough with him. I told him I was really a secret service agent investigating the funny business on the keys. I told him that if he didn't come through with his side, I'd have him arrested. I showed him my authority—an item I'd made out on the chef's typewriter and signed in two inks. And I learned why Pepper had a grudge. It seems that in the slack summer season Pepper had used the *Dorothy* to run West Indians and Cubans into the U.S.—at a fancy price. Ladies and gentlemen, mostly, who were on the wrong sides of the minor revolutions and who couldn't make the quota. Lee had found out about it, and didn't like it, but, as far as Tate knew, he had reserved action.

I did that work on board the *Dorothy*. Tate was staying there to see that she rode out the storm without being staved in against the pier. I swore him to secrecy.

When I went ashore, he followed me up on deck. I don't know why I turned. I did. Young Mr. Tate was moving up behind me with a large gaff and a calm, deadly expression. He pretended he was making the gaff fast on the cabin wall, and the expression faded.

I went along.

Mr. Tate was a sour apple. I suppose that he'd have put a few dozen big sinkers in my pockets and dropped me over. I don't know.

I pretended to go up to camp, but I sneaked back and made a minute study of Captain Graham's *Neptune*. My boat. The only thing I found on board her was a rifle, rolling in the aft cockpit. The tip of a shoe lace. Just on the chance, I went up and barged into the office. Nobody was there. I took a look at Lee's shoes—and a lace tip was missing. The one I'd found matched. Of course, it only meant that Lee had been on Graham's boat, which we knew, anyway. But it helped my state of mind later when I was in a worse spot.

I went back to the lounge. I joined the crowd. I was thinking that it was anybody's murder — so far. I became absorbed again in the problem of how the thing had been done — a problem that had driven everyone into so depressed and irritable a state of mind as to be almost insupportable. And, since we all repeated to each other that no hope could be held for the discovery of the killer until the method of the killings was understood, we made no progress either individually or collectively.

Blantz had dinner cooked and served in the lounge. It was pitch-dark and there was still a terrific wind outdoors. It began to rain again.

VI

Somewhere in the middle of a tense and quiet effort to eat, a Mrs. Willis put a coup de grace on the emotions of all of us. She screamed sharply and dropped her knife. She was staring into space, but at first we all thought she'd seen something.

Melville said, "What is it!"

Mrs. Willis shuddered. "I think I've got it!"

"Got it?" several people echoed.

"A fiend —" Mrs. Willis said. She was a fleshy, scary woman.

Melville said, with an only fair assumption of calm, "What do you mean — a fiend?"

Mrs. Willis looked at us with wild eyes and held out her hand in a very disturbing gesture. "I can feel his presence," she said hoarsely. "And I understand all this. It is not one of us. Not one of the help. It is another, stalking this island. A maniac killer, who may strike again tonight —"

Diana, cold as ice and as firm, shut her off with a wrenching voice: "I don't think, Mrs. Willis, that this is the proper time for any pseudo-seance."

This seance quality of the woman's proposition wouldn't have affected any of us, ordinarily. But behind the gesture was a terrible possibility.

Hurt feelings shut up Mrs. Willis.

But the idea was there. Somebody of imponderable malice out in that night. Somebody.

People at that time were agreeing to sit up all night together in the lounge.

The guests had clung throughout most of the early afternoon to the pompous idiocies of their stations in life. There wasn't any more of that now. They were cowed.

I except, in a sense, the Morellis, Graham, Melville and Brothers. I might include Captain Pepper, the conch. I could say also, I think, that I still had control of myself.

We sat around the fire for an hour, trying to change the subject, and trying to get a new approach to it.

Finally, and rather abruptly, Morelli slapped his thigh lightly and said, "I've got an idea. Come with me, anyone? Pepper? Brothers? Graham?"

Brothers went.

Morelli crossed the room. He took a long look at me. I was sitting quietly with Diana. When the two men got the door closed against the wind, I whispered, "I'm going to see what's up."

I went out, alone. I wore a slicker. The two men had an electric torch. I didn't. I followed them. They went down to the dock. I began to get excited. They boarded Graham's boat and sluiced around in the rain on the deck. I could see that they were handling ropes.

They came back.

I beat them into the lounge and sat down again. My shoes were wet. People had watched those exits and entrances, but hadn't questioned them.

Morelli came back with his fattish face glistening and smiling. He woke up the general inertia by getting in front of the fireplace and saying, "I have a few questions to ask Mr. Martin."

People got out of huddles and put down magazines they were pretending to read. The inquiry went this way:

"Mr. Martin, I presume you can tie a running bowline?"

"I can."

"Correctly?"

"I think so. Captain Graham has been teaching me knots. A running bowline is a hard one to learn."

"Exactly. You might make a mistake?"

"I might."

"But, still—the knot would work—it would make a slip noose?"

"It might."

"In fact, you tied just such a knot in the line you used to pull Lee's body from the water?"

I thought. "I did."

"But Brothers, who has just examined it, tells me that the knot wasn't tied right."

I said, "So what?"

Morelli gave me the fish eye. "A running bowline was used to haul Mrs. Lee's body up into the palm, Martin. It wasn't tied correctly, either."

People made that wicked mutter which must be the beginning of a mob sound. I was in a jam. I pondered before saying, "Most of us are amateur mariners here. A good many people would try that knot and muff it—besides me."

"You saw Lee alone," Morelli began meditatively. "You quarreled— lots of people heard him swear at you. You had an excellent motive for getting him out of the way: his rich and lovely daughter. You had a motive for killing Mrs. Lee: the daughter would inherit at once. The daughter is infatuated with you. Now. You were also seen throwing a gun into the sea. That means you came here ready for business. Now— these knots."

I was speechless.

Diana got up. "Mr. Morelli," she said, "you're not empowered to do this. It's monstrous. You're my guest—I forbid it."

Morelli shrugged.

Graham said, "Where are the knots?"

Captain Pepper answered, "I had to untie the one around Mrs. Lee to get her loose. Rope was wet. The other is down on your ship. I noticed the mistake in the rope around Mrs. Lee when I took the knot out. Mentioned it to Mr. Morelli."

Trying to bluff something, I asked, "When was Lee killed?"

Morelli replied, "We don't know. Some time last night. He had prepared his pajamas, but he never undressed."

"All right," I replied. "I went up to the help's quarters and said 'good night' to a couple of the men there, around one. I went to bed. Nobody heard me go out—although the floor squeaks and the door squeaks and there are screens nailed on the window. I told you about being seen there. I'm telling you now that I couldn't have left." I took another flyer. "The whole thing is insane. I could accuse you as easily, Morelli! And where's the other knot? You haven't any proof—"

Connel, a gray-headed banker, cut in, "This looks mighty bad for you, Martin."

Diana said, "Stop it." She was shaking with rage and grief.

Brothers walked over to Pepper. "Sure about that knot?"

"Positive."

They discussed the error and illustrated with string.

The Long Islander turned and addressed everyone: "Graham or Pepper or myself could tie that knot in our sleep."

Connel wanted the floor. "I say—let's lock up Martin. We've got reason enough. And we don't want even a possible killer loose tonight!"

Melville got up then. He smiled at me in a decent way and spoke calmly: "Evidence is too flimsy, in my opinion. Take me. I used to sail constantly when I was a kid. I knew every knot and splice in the book. But I'm rusty. I don't think I could tie a running bowline now—not properly—at the first crack."

I was amazed, but Melville hadn't finished. He hadn't even begun. He was still smiling. . . . "I had a motive for killing Lee, too—if you like. I loved his wife. I never kept it a secret from her—or from Doug. I saw Doug alone last night. I, also, had an argument about the proper way to harpoon a shark. I illustrated it with a harpoon. I didn't kill him, but if I were you, Morelli—with your great criminal prosecutor's brain—I'd let people alone and try to figure out first what happened. That's the line I'm taking."

It was a swell speech. Connel took a seat quickly. The people were stunned.

I should have thanked him. But I just stood there. I was thinking: *"Suppose he did kill them, then wouldn't this speech be the finest disclaimer ever made? He's a cool, logical, controlled person—and reckless in spite of that. Or was he defending me as an impromptu bargain to keep me from mentioning the gun and twenty-five thousand?"*

Morelli stopped picking on me and stared at Melville. Maybe Morelli was thinking along the same line I had thought.

That brought us up to ten o'clock, when Morelli suddenly realized that he had forgotten to search the dead man's clothing.

We got over to the office and went through Lee's pockets.

We found two hundred and sixty-eight dollars in a wallet that also contained a number of club cards and so on. We found a cigar case, three cigars, a lighter—and that was all.

We had a bug for searching, then. A lot of people had looked into the rooms of Mr. and Mrs. Lee, but they'd been left undisturbed because we had expected the police to arrive. So we searched them now.

We opened suitcases—Graham, Melville, Morelli, Connel, Pepper, and I—all of us watching each other closely. We looked under beds. We dumped things out of closets. I found a crumpled piece of paper in Lee's wastebasket and snared it. But I didn't have a chance to read it, and I was darned if I would hand it over.

We went through Diana's room, although I protested, and then through mine.

I wanted to break away and look at the paper I'd snagged out of Lee's wastebasket but I didn't get a chance.

VII

It was after eleven when we reached the lounge. The big overstuffed chairs in the place had been put in pairs, face to face, and the divans were all confiscated. Blankets and quilts had been brought. People were getting ready to try to sleep.

I talked to Diana.

I persuaded her to take a couple of bromides. "It'll be tougher tomorrow. Tougher if the storm breaks and the police come. Tougher still if they don't."

She asked me if I would stay in the lounge. I said I couldn't.

"Why?"

I told her that I was going to stooge around all night. I wanted to be on hand if anything broke, or if anything odd happened. I was in deep enough.

Diana kissed me goodnight, publicly. Then she put her lips close to my ear. She whispered, "I love you. You know I'll never doubt you. All day I've been thinking how infinitely more terrible this would be if you weren't here."

I told her to go to sleep. She shut her eyes, grayed lids over those liquid eyes.

I moped out into the uproar.

Melville? Graham? Mrs. Morelli? Mr. Morelli? Pepper? A stranger on the island?

Who?

Why?

I went to my room. A bare room, one of many, in a one-story wooden wing. Clean. A good bed. I locked the door. I fished out the crumpled paper.

Then somebody knocked.

I hid the paper, thinking I might be searched again. There was a washbowl in my room. I stuffed the screed up the hot water faucet. Even if a searcher took a drink of water—

It was Morelli.

"I want to talk to you."

I had one chair. I took the bed.

Morelli's red cheeks were a bit drawn now. He looked worried. And, for the first time, he looked rather decent. Like a smart guy but a good one. Maybe he was all right.

"What did my wife throw in the sea?" he said.

"I don't know. It was too far away. Something white. It sank—I think."

He jerked his head. "You know, of course, that I realize your innocence? I thought by making my suspicion of you obvious, someone else might tip their hand."

I said nothing.

He talked: "I love my wife. She's a passionate, somewhat irresponsible woman. I believe that she was once desperately in love with Lee."

"That's too bad."

He shrugged. "I'm sorry I came here. I realized that she was more than normally excited about seeing Lee again." He was staring at me, a perplexed, unhappy man. Just a martinet. Just a guy. "She wouldn't kill—without a great reason. And never a woman. So—" He stopped talking.

"Why tell me?" I asked.

"Because you can think, and you're the only one I know positively is innocent."

Now I got up and ambled around the room. "Listen, Morelli, you're wasting your time and a lot of talent trying to make me confess something I didn't do by buttering me up."

He laughed.

He took my shoulder and pushed me down again. He talked straight and fast: "Son, I'm a lawyer. Smart. Rich. Able. I know men. I'm worried about my wife. I need help badly. I'll tell you why I know you didn't do it: If you had killed the Lees, you'd think hard before every move you made. Fast, perhaps, but hard. For instance, you might have been bright enough to figure out that by socking me this morning you'd make people think you had nothing to worry about—that is, if you had had something. You might have figured it, but the sock would have been a masterpiece of subtlety—and the subtlety would have taken time. You didn't. Yours was, if I may say so, the impulsive sock of a young man whose girl is being pestered."

I grinned, myself, at that.

He nodded. "You wouldn't have told about my wife until a time when the telling would help you to ease out of a tougher spot. Besides—I know her. I knew at once that her story was a phony."

"What do you need help on?"

"Who do you think killed the Lees?"

"I don't know."

"My wife?"

"She's strong enough," I said.

"Yes. Strong. I thought of that. She's a real sportswoman. She could have hoisted Mrs. Lee. And she can probably tie a bowline. Or a knot like it."

"Graham had a reason," I said, because his line of thought was hard for him to express. "But he really seems glad to be free of his office and out in a boat—even without his dough.

"Pepper?" he asked.

"The conch?" I pondered. "Maybe."

"He's a crafty man. And a born grudge carrier. All these local people are."

I spread my hands. "How about Melville?"

Morelli nodded. "I know. But when a man murders his best friend he generally does it in a refined way. This is a barbaric thing. Brutal. Fierce."

"How about you?" I said.

He looked up and smiled. "That's right. How about me?"

We didn't talk for a long time. He walked around a little.

"How could a body, with a harpoon in it trailing a long rope, get from a dock 'way out to sea against current and tide in a matter of seven or eight hours?"

He said it pensively.

And something in the relationship of the facts he murmured made me see the way it could have happened. I said, "I know."

My voice must have been curious. He flinched. "How, Martin?"

"Plenty of harpoons on the dock," I said, blowing smoke. "Plenty of rope. A rope on one of them. All right. The killer slammed it through Lee. Then he had a harpooned body to dispose of. He thought of throwing it to the sharks in the cove—but they might not touch it. A slim and yet a serious chance. But that made him think of sharks. The murderer ties another harpoon on the rope that leads to the one rammed through Lee's heart. He waits for a big fin—lots of sharks out there—"

Morelli pounded me on the back. "—and harpoons a shark and throws the line overboard until the harpoon at the other end of the line yanks Lee's body into the water!"

"That's it. Hit sharks and they head to sea. They'll drag boats for miles. This one drags Lee's body out. But it fouls the line on the anchor chain of the buoy—"

"Bass do that deliberately to get loose," Morelli put in excitedly.

"Deliberately or accidentally—the shark either winds up the rope or, being pulled up, tries to swim straight and succeeds only in making circles around the chain till the line breaks."

"We—you've got it!"

"We've got how," I said, "but not who."

"No."

I said that it was a slick job. And I added that the chances had been a thousand to one that the body would ever have been recovered.

"Maybe. Maybe sharks will always snag a line like bass. Anyway—a fine idea. But how about Mrs. Lee? That wasn't a good hiding place. Bound to be found—"

We thought.

Possibly we thought for ten minutes.

"If the same person had killed Lee," I said, "it stands to reason that he—or she—would have used the same means to get rid of the body. It would work any number of times."

"Yes—unless people had come down on the dock in the meantime."

"There were plenty of people on the dock last night, all right," I said. "Going and coming all the evening."

"In that case," Morelli continued, "her murderer would have been forced to dispose of her some other way. But not in a tree."

"Darn good temporary hiding place," I said, almost without thinking.

"Right! Right! How right!" He sagged. "Lots of others—though. She could have been buried anywhere."

"Not anywhere at all," I answered. "The island's coral. Rock. Soft—but you can't dig it. I doubt if you'd find dirt enough to cover the body in any one spot on the whole key."

"Let's be sane about this," he said slowly. "We may have an inkling. We may not. Now. Where could you stow a body for a few hours—or over a day until another night?"

"Under the palmetto anywhere on the north end."

"A long way to carry her. And a long way back. Suppose our hypothetical 'he' killed her near the dock. People prevented his immediate use of the fine scheme he had worked on Lee. He'd want the body near by so he could work his system again late at night—using the dock was out, until late. Buildings and grounds—absolutely out. No sand to bury her in. Water—unsafe. People might see—something. How high was that tree?"

"Say twenty-five feet. Or less."

"And how long," Morelli asked, "to throw the rope, haul, climb, lash the body, cut the rope, and get down?"

I thought. "There was heavy under-brush at the base of that palm. He'd be all right with the body in that shrubbery, and on top of the tree. It was dark."

"So his danger intervals were going up and coming down?"

"Yes—and throwing the rope."

"Then—he could do it all without taking much chance. And plan to come back later—that night—but why didn't he? Obviously either someone was around until you early birds got up this morning or the man lost his nerve and decided that even when they found the body in the tree they couldn't pin it on him." He swore absently. "Now. What about Lee's blood? There'd have been a lot on the dock—if he was struck there."

VIII

That one was easy. "Sure. We bring in our fish there. Often they made stains. We had a hose on the dock to wash it down. A minute's work."

"Excellent. Superb! What a murder! But why Mrs. Lee, also?"

"Probably planned to get both."

The lawyer shook his head. "I doubt it. Neither killing looked planned. Especially hers. She was clubbed. That's a spontaneous method."

We were both tense with excitement.

"I know," Morelli said presently. "She saw something. Maybe she started through that hibiscus tangle and saw what was happening to her husband. Or something suspicious. Then hid to see more. And the murderer spotted her. And he saw that he was licked—so he killed her."

"He did," I said then. "Right beside the path. That's where I found her corsage." I told him about that.

He whistled. "Boy, we're getting closer than I even hoped."

I carried on. "But why didn't she scream, yell for help?"

We worked on this. We decided that if she had known she was going to be attacked she surely would have tried to get aid. So we assumed that she didn't know. We assumed that the murderer spotted her and pretended that he had not. That he walked up the path—and suddenly struck her.

It all fitted. We checked back, as best we could, by trying to think of other ways to explain the existing facts. And we couldn't think of a way. We were sure about Lee's body on the buoy. And why else would a body be put up in a tree?

When we had carried the discussion to that point, Morelli said suddenly, "Well, I think I'll get some rest now."

It startled me, because we were still under full steam. I had been planning to tell him all I knew. I said, "Why? We've just started here—"

"All in," he answered. And he went.

Leaving me to think that he had hit upon some angle which he wanted to work out by himself or that he still believed I was the harpooner, or that he thought things were getting warm for himself. Perhaps for his wife.

I sat on my bed a while listening to the booming in the blackness outside.

Then I remembered the trophy in the faucet. I fished it out. It was a note from Mrs. Morelli to Lee.

It said: "Douglas darling—you haven't changed. Seeing you recalled—everything. I know it may sound silly and I know we're growing old—but why not relive a few of the hours we once spent together? The very fact that we are not as young as we were ought to make the idea desirable and both of us wise enough to appreciate the full flavor and value of—Indian summer. Yours—E. P. S. I shall be waiting—at the dock—late. Very late."

I wasn't exactly surprised. Mrs. Morelli. And yet—

I sat down, wondering.

A little while later there was another knock—and Morelli announced himself again. I let him in. He said, "I decided we'd better go on working together."

"Yes."

He shut the door, pulled a gun, and said, "I want that paper."

My wits, such as they are, foundered.

"I saw you pick it up," he said. "I watched just now around the edge of your blind. I recognized my wife's handwriting. Hand it over."

That paper was my best exhibit. I went in under the gun—hard and fast. He sidestepped, and I got the gun under the ear.

My next conscious intellectual effort showed me that I was bound, gagged, and locked in a pantry. My head hurt. I was weak and dizzy. I spent about twenty minutes shaking it off.

I went to work. The rope cut both of my wrists some, but when I stood up—quietly—I mustered my circulation. Then I shut my mouth and made desperate noises through my nose.

A guy outside, the chef, hollered, "Lie still, you!"

I tried to make the noises pleading—then strangling—as if the gag were too much for me. Finally, as my gasps tapered off to simulate suffocation, he came in. I clipped him.

I gave him my gag and my ropes and locked the pantry.

I went out into the gray, sickly dawn.

The shortest way into the scrub was the one I took. And I found out that everybody in the place was down near the dock. I made my way there, circuitously, through the wet brush.

A dandy little scene was going on, a scene conducted by Morelli. He was taking the entire populace over the grounds, showing them exactly how I had done both murders! And they were drinking it in. He had finished the harpoon explanation, and had evidently illustrated it. From my cover, I could see a rope with a harpoon tied to each end of the pier.

He had about wound up the tree episode. I couldn't see all of his audience—forty-odd spellbound people—but most. Diana wasn't in my line of vision, and I wanted desperately to glimpse her face, but I was dangerously close, as it was.

Morelli wound up: "So last night, after figuring it out, I accused him. He attacked me. That is why he lies now, bound and guarded."

Connel said, "I knew it! We should have grabbed him earlier. I advised it."

Graham said, "I can't believe it."

Melville gave me another epitaph: "He certainly wasn't that kind of guy originally. He must have been driven insane by Lee."

Pepper grunted, "You never can tell."

Morelli had one more act in his charade of what I'd done. He had recovered the gardenias from under the dock. He held them up. "These were the unfortunate woman's flowers. There is blood on them. It dropped on them when she was hit by the rock which I've demonstrated is missing from the path border." That, I reflected, was his work—and good. "But," he went on, "there is more than just blood. There are fingerprints—a man's fingerprints! Martin's fingerprints. When these prints are checked with our prisoner's the case will be complete."

That astounded me. I knew there had been no fingerprints on those gardenias.

Graham walked up, stared at the cellophane and said, "Sure enough!"

I couldn't see the prints. I was too far away. I couldn't have heard, except that they talked loudly, as the sea was still noisy. I was sick. Morelli had brought up those flowers while I was unconscious and daubed blood on my fingers, printed the ribbon, washed my hands, and now he was going to nail me for what his wife had done. . . . Or had she?

I was trying to think what to do next. The crowd was moving weakly toward the lounge. Morelli was being congratulated. They'd soon find I was gone.

I looked at the sea. Too rough, still, to try to swim. But if I was seen running loose, now, I'd probably be shot.

Then I saw Diana. She was casting off the *Neptune*. Working fast. She started the engines. I ran out on the dock. I got aboard as the water opened up. People charged from the lounge. The boat bucked high. Di saw me—and threw in the gears. We started.

A lot of men reached the dock. I pushed Di below. A bullet chipped things around me. But we made it.

Di said she'd gotten ready to take out the boat when she saw that Morelli had framed me. She said, "Framed." She said that she was on

her way to the best detectives and lawyers money could hire—
for me.

All the time, we were shipping green water. Barrels of it.

We made port above the ferry in about three hours. They gave us a
big start on the people at Galleon Key.

It was calm and clearing.

Being very rich means something in a crisis like that. We had New
York on the wire in short order.

We ate breakfast while a plane was coming. It landed in a lagoon.
It shot us to Miami.

By that time detectives were flying from New York, and lawyers.

A hotel manager and a girl clerk at the cigar store shopped for dry
clothes for us. We were trying to get my defense set up before Morelli
and the others came through from Galleon Key and had me behind
bars.

Toward evening of that day the phone rang. "It's for you," Di said,
and she looked scared. I took up the receiver.

"This is Morelli."

My heart popped. "Yes."

"At Galleon Key. Wire's been fixed."

"Yes." I wondered why Morelli had called instead of sending police
for me.

"We got the murderer," he said. "That is, we identified him."

He said that they'd located Di and me by calling her father's offices in
New York.

He said, "When I hit you last night, I did it to get that note. I wanted
to protect the name of—" he whispered—"Mrs. Morelli. See?"

"How about pinning the fingerprints on me?"

Morelli chuckled. "You were present for that? Well—I thought this:
I thought that since I'd knocked you down I'd pin it all on you. Then
I'd tell everyone—everyone in the place—that you did it and that we
had proof which would be absolute when the police arrived. That we
could swear to the murderer when we checked those fingerprints. Then,
so I believed, the person who really did it would think that his period
of grace would end as soon as the fingerprints failed to check with
yours, and as soon as everyone else was printed. I assumed that I could
make the murderer believe that he had left his bloody mark on that
cellophane ribbon."

That was something. I was in a fever.

"Who did it?" I asked.

"I'm coming to that, my boy. But you get the setup? So—what would the murderer do?"

"Scram," I said.

"Well—yes—eventually. But first he'd try to get that corsage with what he thought were his fingerprints. That was my idea. I got everybody in the lounge for breakfast and I ostentatiously put the flowers under a big dish on a table."

"Well?"

"Melville looked them over and Graham paced the floor near them—but Pepper took them."

"No!"

"I was surprised, believe me. I'd never thought much about him. But he did—started sidling when I sounded off and got everybody's interest. Picked up the corsage—and nobody saw him but me. Went out. I told the other men in the lounge what had happened. We started after him. I had a gun—as you know. Melville got one from somewhere. Graham and Blantz took camp rifles. Pepper beat us by a considerable distance to his boat. He was under way when we got there. We started shooting, but the *Dorothy* was dancing like a cork—even in the channel. Brothers wouldn't take a chance. Pepper went out about a mile, and got crossed up in a big comber—and foundered. We got his body this afternoon—it washed ashore."

"How can you be sure—even so?"

"Two reasons. One was that he hollered back he did it and we'd never get him. The other is Tate. Tate knew a lot. Pepper smuggled aliens into the country. Lee had discovered it—"

"I know about that."

"Why didn't you say something?" Morelli laughed. "Still—it would only have added to the general confusion. . . . Look. The police are here. They'll want to talk to both of you—matter of form. Well—that's the *finis*. Pepper should have been considered sooner. Lee could have put him in prison for years, and Pepper thought he would. It was the sort of job one of those low, degenerate birds would do. He'd planned it for weeks— maybe months—and faked his arthritis well ahead. He told me that the bowline around Mrs. Lee was wrong, but it couldn't have been, because he tied it himself. And untied it. And then, according to Tate, he went aboard Graham's boat, where he must have retied incorrectly the knot you made to pull in Lee's body. Putting the buck on you. Tate said Pepper hung around the dock all night the night before last, but Tate was there and so was Blantz, with a waitress, till four. So he couldn't get the other body down. Of course, he never did plan to kill Mrs. Lee—we must have been right about her watching."

That left very little to say. I asked Morelli what his wife had thrown into the sea.

He answered rather sadly, "Letters Lee had written her. They were old letters, but she was afraid to be caught with them after Lee was murdered. She was excited about the prospect of seeing him again, but—well, Martin—a man's wife—you can't drag her in . . . You won't mention her when you see the police, will you?"

"Of course not."

"Thanks. And—say—I'm sorry I hit you last night."

"You owed me that—for the shiner on your eye."

He laughed.

Then I said, "Say! Whose fingerprints did you put on that cellophane ribbon?"

"My own, of course."

"Suppose Pepper hadn't given himself away and the police had found your prints?"

He laughed again. "Chance I had to take. Cost me a bad hour."

I swore—but I meant it to be congratulation and thanks.

I hung up. I told Di.

And that was the beginning of another trouble. She was jittery. She refused to see the police. She made me leave the hotel with her and go to another. We took two rooms under different names. But she wouldn't desert mine that evening. And the house detective came up and was rather unpleasant. So we moved again. The next day she seemed perfectly well, but she wouldn't see the police, and she insisted on getting a car and driving.

I told her that I couldn't go running around the state compromising her.

She said, "Well!"

So we went through a lot of rigmarole, and now we're married.

The newspapers found out about our wedding. So they're after us. So are the newsreel men. And the cops. They want to question us to round out the case. They have no respect for the nerves of a girl who is trying to forget a horrible tragedy and at the same time trying to adjust herself to being married to an oaf like me.

IN A HOLE

The newspaper-reading public never learned the details of the Manhattan Commercial Bank and Trust Company robbery. The story was made a secret for a variety of reasons, not the least of which was the humiliating part played in it by the police.

In missing the inside story of this robbery, the public also missed a glimpse of one of the strangest persons living in Manhattan. The brilliant sleuth and silent avenger of the bank disaster was himself a former bank clerk. His name was Willis Perkins. There are a great many people like Willis Perkins, but few of them, because of their very nature, attain to a parallel success.

Perkins, a thin, frail, prematurely aged and almost childlike man of forty-odd years, lived alone on the top floor of a brownstone apartment house in the Chelsea district. He was familiar to most of the people in the environs of his lodgings because he had dwelt there for more than twenty years. However, he was so shy that few of them had acquired even a casual acquaintance with him. Early in his childhood his consuming passion had been born, and two decades spent over the ledgers of a downtown bank in no way served to dim his purpose. Willis Perkins had decided at the age of twelve that he was created to be a detective.

If he had applied for a position on the New York police force, his application would certainly have been greeted with laughter. The departmental concept of a detective is far removed from vague gray eyes, stooped shoulders, and thin trembling hands, so Perkins' course was necessarily different. He joined six libraries. He had read almost every mystery story produced by publishing houses since 1905. He had devoured textbooks on criminology and he had devoted many of his evenings to a study of psychology and to chemistry in the Extension Courses of Columbia University.

Perkins had also saved his money, so that after twenty years of arduous labor and careful investment his accumulated pittance had become a sum sufficient to afford him an income for the rest of his life. He had then resigned from the bank and embarked upon the serious business of being a detective.

Needless to say, his career thereafter was partly fantastic, partly absurd, and almost wholly pathetic. The front room in his apartment in Chelsea was crammed to the ceiling with his books. In the back room was his chemical laboratory and there he lived, waiting, watching, and hoping for the occurrence of a crime. It is a matter of record that in the vicinity a crime did occur and that, although Perkins devoted to it the full benefit of his self-training, his clues were unreadable and his conclusions worthless. The solution of that particular crime was arrived at by accident, and the part Perkins played in it gave him an introduction if not an entrée to the local branch of the police department, but after the few stirring days surrounding that single sordid misdeed, Perkins relapsed to his old manner of living.

Perkins kept a private file of all crimes recorded in the newspapers. He might occasionally be seen on the fringe of a crowd that gaped at the comings and goings of the police and reporters near a scene of violence. At other times, in dead hours of night, Perkins might have been observed slinking through mid-downtown streets, his eyes prying suspiciously into every dark corner and his nose almost sniffing the air in the hope of detecting sinister maneuvers. . . .

On a hot evening in August Perkins was on his way home from an investigation of some suspicious-looking boxes he had noticed in the subway station at Times Square, when he joined with several other loungers to observe an excavation which was being conducted on a twenty-four-hour-a-day schedule. The excavation was deep—driving toward bedrock to make a foundation for a future skyscraper, and it furnished a rather handsome spectacle. Some of the steel work had already been put in place, and the last blasting and drilling was being done under floodlights.

For a long time Perkins watched these pygmies who worked in the gloom, but of all the bystanders he was the only one who noticed that the excavation was being made next door to the Manhattan Commercial Bank and Trust Company. It was natural that he should do so; Perkins was a safeguarder of the public. His first observation was that the actual physical stability of the bank might be in some measure endangered by the propinquity and depth of the excavation. His next observation was that in the intricate tiers of rock and machinery a nice chance would be afforded to pierce the wall of the bank and enter it from a subterranean point.

That thought captivated Perkins's mind to such an extent that he allowed himself to elaborate it. The tools were at hand—it would be necessary only to organize the men. Sufficient cover was furnished by the steel work and the skeleton floors laid across it. Perkins became so enamored of the idea that he converted it into one of his myriad suspicions and determined to report it to the police.

Hence, on the following morning he appeared rather smugly before the local precinct captain and produced his card, which read, "Willis Perkins—Private Investigations."

The captain said, "Well, what do you want?"

"Did you ever notice," Perkins half whispered, "how close the excavation for the Seward Building is to the Manhattan Commercial Bank and Trust Company?"

"Yeah. What about it?"

"That's all," Perkins said mysteriously.

"Huh?" The captain looked blank.

Perkins vouchsafed a little more information. "Of course I have no proof, but if I were a police officer I would give the greatest attention to such items as excavations that are made in juxtaposition to banks."

Perkins was rather rudely informed that the captain's time was valuable; and the request that he depart immediately was in no way polite.

Undaunted, Perkins supervised the excavation for the foundations of the Seward Building. He watched the drills go deeper, he listened to the blasts, he saw the growth of the steel work, and in all that he saw nothing amiss. The walls of the bank had been shored up. The excavation went vertically downward beside the bank. Perkins also inspected the bank and again found nothing to appeal to his imagination.

If he had carried his investigations further, he might have discovered that the bank's vaults were on the same side of the building as the excavation; he might have discovered that, owing to the continual bombardment of steel-bitted tools and dynamiting in the large hole next door, the burglar-alarm devices had been disconnected so that they would not register false alarms. On a particular day he might also have discovered that a rumor of mysterious origin had led the Manhattan Commercial Bank and Trust Company to anticipate the possibility of a run, so that into the bank's vault was hastily placed an additional three million dollars. But Perkins missed all those facts.

He was quietly preparing his breakfast of dry cereal and boiled eggs when the police came for him. He was ushered into the presence of the captain of the local precinct and was greeted with a mysterious sentence:

"Well, Mr. Perkins, we got the goods on you all right, so you might as well come clean."

"Goods on me — come clean — what about?"

"Come on," the captain said, "what about this bank business?"

Perkins was a little bit relieved. "Oh, you have turned up something on it?"

The captain was more explicit. "Listen, Mr. Perkins. You knew something about that. What was it?"

Perkins was now very much frightened and he could not understand why his willingness to assist the police had involved him in such a vigorous questioning, especially since he had acted on no more than a whim.

"Put him in the cooler," the captain said, "and maybe it'll improve his memory."

Perkins spent twenty-four perplexed and almost tearful hours in a cell which was supposed to improve his memory, but since his memory was as free from guilt as a child's, it merely acted as a source of further alarm. Twice he was taken out and twice he was questioned. His entire life was investigated by the authorities. Finally the captain was compelled to conclude that Willis Perkins's warning had been what Perkins would consider a brilliant deduction, and what the police department knew was but mere outlandish chance.

The truth was self-evident. On the night of August 26th a great many things had happened in the vicinity of the Manhattan Commercial Bank and Trust Company. The protective devices in the vaults had been disconnected because of the noise of excavation. A large sum of cash had been stored in those vaults in anticipation of a run. The excavation beside the vaults had reached its maximum depth and was screened from public gaze by the flooring on the steel work. The policeman on that beat, shortly after midnight, was attracted to a vociferous street fight. The night watchman and the protection agency operative had been slugged. There had been several heavy explosions beside the bank. Laborers had bored under the vaults. With dynamite and oxyacetylene torches they made their way through the wall. Thereafter they removed the small inner vault of the Manhattan Commercial Bank and Trust Company and withdrew through the hole.

From that moment on the inner vault and its contents disappeared. The explosions had wrecked part of the side of the bank. They had also extinguished the floodlights and turned the excavation into a pit of intense darkness.

Actual entrance to the vaults, together with the heavy explosions, had set off the few alarms that remained connected, and in a few minutes, from all sides, both police and private detectives rushed toward the Manhattan Commercial Bank and Trust Company. The thieves apparently made their getaway in four vehicles. The police arrived in time to follow two of them, but, while one—a truck—was overtaken, nothing of any value was retrieved.

The truck was driven by a youth who insisted that he had been hired to sit outside of the bank until a certain instant and then to drive as rapidly as possible toward Albany. A protracted grueling produced no further information. The young man had no knowledge of his employers' names; the description he gave of them was worthless; and he was the sole individual whom the police could capture who was directly connected with the disappearance of a little less than three and a half million dollars.

Naturally the police had remembered Perkins and his warning. In their feverish desire to present the public with a victim they had hastily arrested him. He was released only when they realized that the presentation of him as their victim would be more ridiculous than having no victim at all.

The entire city was frantic. The steady ground-fire of police criticism increased in volume to a public uproar. If millions of dollars could be bodily exhumed from strong bank vaults, then nothing was safe. All private property was at the mercy of diabolic fiends. The press alternately sneered and bellowed. Little by little the ingenuity of the scheme became apparent. In the first few minutes it was thought that an accidental explosion had merely damaged the bank wall, and pursuit of the fleeing automobiles was a matter of routine, but when the crumbling and riddled vaults were discovered, and when it was found that the entire night shift of the excavating crew had vanished, it became all too clear that the explosion was part of a robbery.

In the morning the caved-in borings were uncovered, and the place where the floodlights had been cut off was found. Connection was made between the cutting off of the burglar alarms in the vaults and the tunneling, and by afternoon of the first day the whole world knew that the rumor of a run on the Manhattan Commercial Bank and Trust Company had been deliberately started to insure the presence in the vaults of a large sum of money.

It was not until twenty-four hours later, upon his release from jail, that Willis Perkins learned of the affair. Then he went home to think.

Meanwhile the police were frantically working on the case with the information, or rather the lack of information, at their disposal. It was easy for them to learn what had been done. Almost the entire force which had been hired by the contractor to do his rock and steel work had either belonged to the gang or had been bought by the gang.

Various other clues were presented in due time. The borings that led into the bank had been ingeniously hidden so that any chance inspection would not reveal them. There was no evidence of collusion with superiors but only of an extreme foresight and cleverness. Three of the four vehicles which had left the scene at the time of the last and largest explosion had been discovered and two of them proved to be stolen cars. Some hours after the explosion a plane had landed at a Newark field. Two men carrying large suitcases had stepped into it, taken off, and disappeared. Since one of the stolen cars had been recovered in Newark it was thought that the thieves possibly made their getaway by airplane, after opening the stolen inner strong-box and removing the contents.

Precautions against dissemination of the money were taken internationally. In every police headquarters in the world the numbers of the bills of large denomination were made known. Thousands of gunmen and yeggs everywhere were apprehended and questioned. Detectives visited innumerable dives and offered quietly a variety of bribes and trades to the criminal world if it would only divulge a single piece of information, but the regular criminal world did not seem to have this information.

Even Willis Perkins—he sometimes thought of himself as "The Great Perkins"—was unable to evolve a theory. He might have admitted defeat—for did not even Sherlock Holmes have his little volume of cases unconcluded?—had it not been for his accidental meeting with a former friend.

For twelve of his twenty banking years Perkins had occupied a desk side by side with Milo DeMar. The meeting point of the two men had been figures, and only the most conventional friendship had existed between them. DeMar had used his funds to support a large family, while Perkins had saved his for his future as a detective. DeMar had been moved to considerable awe when Perkins resigned from the bank, and it was DeMar whom Perkins met while he was making his regular monthly withdrawal from his account, which he kept at the place where once he had been an employee. DeMar wore an old felt hat and a somewhat shabby coat over a shiny suit, and DeMar was on his way to lunch. He saw Perkins in line at the window and he greeted him warmly.

"How are tricks, old man?"

Perkins started and recognized his one-time co-laborer. "Oh, hello, DeMar," he said. "Fine, fine."

"Why not have lunch with me?"

Perkins considered. He looked critically at his watch and then sharply at DeMar. "Can we get through in thirty minutes?" He wished he had said twenty-eight minutes. It would have sounded more effective.

"Sure."

DeMar waited until Perkins's turn at the window had come. Then, together, they went to a cafeteria. They took an inconspicuous table in a corner of the room and began to eat. Perkins ate in a preoccupied manner and he was pleased to notice that DeMar was watching him curiously. Finally DeMar spoke.

"What do you do with yourself these days, old man?"

That was the question for which Perkins had waited. "My work is of a rather private nature," he said. "I am a detective."

"No!" DeMar said. "No!"

Perkins nodded silently and rested his hand on DeMar's arm. "At the moment—and this is in strict confidence—I am making a separate and personal investigation of the robbery of the Manhattan Commercial Bank and Trust Company."

Only then did Perkins notice that DeMar's prodigious emotion was not occasioned by amazement. A singular color had come into DeMar's face. His little eyes were almost shut. His fork had been dropped on the table. He exploded. He roared with laughter. "Oh, that's the funniest thing I ever heard in my life. Wait till I tell the old gang; it'll paralyze them."

He paid his check and staggered from the cafeteria, leaving Perkins rooted to the spot. His heart had turned to ice, his feet were unable to move, and two actual tears flooded the rims of his eyes.

Back in his room he sadly surveyed the two chambers which he had prepared as the background for his world-shaking career. There were his books—shelves that reached to the ceiling—and there in the other room, his microscope and his test tubes, his beakers and his retorts.

A sort of frenzy gripped him. "If I could only have gone through the tunnel on my hands and knees, if I only had some clue. A squashed stub of a cigarette, or even its ash. A hairpin at this time would be worth a fortune."

He threw himself listlessly into an armchair. On the table beside the armchair was a meerschaum pipe, and on a hook within easy reach was a fore-and-after tweed cap. On the table was a humidor filled with shag tobacco. Even these props of greatness were no use to him in his time of travail.

For half an hour Perkins did not move. He was thinking. Then slowly and painfully he spread out his collections of newspaper clippings; beside them he set the notes on his investigations. For the thousandth time he began a course of reasoning, and he talked aloud.

"We deduce," he mumbled, "the theft of three million four hundred thousand dollars, by an organized gang. Now—" and at that point Perkins was illuminated by divine fire. "Now, since this sum of money was so intelligently attracted to the vaults, and since the vaults were so ingeniously rifled, may we not also deduce that the eventual concealment and disposition of the money would be conducted on the same intellectual plane?" At this point Perkins stopped. It was a step in logic which he had not hitherto taken, a step in logic which the police would doubtless overlook. Whoever had stolen the money would certainly cover their tracks and conceal the money as ingeniously as they had taken it. Once more Perkins spoke aloud to himself:

"Would it be as clever to sling that inner vault into a waiting truck as it had been to mine beneath the building? It would not. An automobile might be wrecked. It might be arrested for speeding. Anything might happen to it." Perkins's brain, driven by desolation, worked with redoubled energy. They had actually arrested the driver of one of the vehicles and a veritable inquisition had adduced no information except that the driver had been hired to wait near the bank until a certain instant and then to flee precipitately toward Albany. Suppose the driver's story was true. It would mean that the escaping automobile had been merely a blind. Three other automobiles had escaped. Suppose they, too, had been blinds. An airplane had left Newark field with mysterious passengers some time after the robbery. Suppose that also had been a blind.

Perkins was pale as death. He rose and strode back and forth across his room. "Ruses," he murmured. "Blinds," he shouted. "Eureka," he said, and finally, "Hot ziggity!"

Another fact had pressed upon his intelligence. Immediately after the explosion the lights which flooded the excavation had been cut off. What did that mean? It meant that the bank's inner vault was disposed of in the darkness that followed. It was not sent away in the fleeing trucks. It was moved somewhere in the small area of that darkness during its short duration. "Where?" Perkins spoke the word aloud while he stared at the chandelier. "Where?" He pulled the end of his nose. He took the meerschaum pipe. He filled it with shag. He paced the room. "Where?" He sank his chin upon his chest. "Where?" He gripped the bowl of his pipe in his fist. Not across the street, for the street was lighted. Not over the back of the excavation, for it was cut off by a brick building. "Where?" To one side. And how? The inner vault was enormously heavy. It could not have been handled like a trunk. Cranes! Donkey engines! Windows! If—and Perkins was staggered by the thought—if the prize had not been sent away in the rapidly departing automobiles, it surely must have disappeared through one of the windows of the tall building on the side of the excavation opposite the bank!

Ten minutes later Perkins was on his way to the scene of the crime. With a little judicious questioning he elicited the fact that a short while before the excavation had started, a new firm had rented the offices on the third floor of that building.

One of the facts most frequently alluded to by the newspapers was that the small inner vault containing the money was exceedingly heavy and to move it in a few moments was no mean undertaking, but Perkins saw how it could have been accomplished—how it had been accomplished. The great blast, then darkness, then the slow, downward reaching of one of the powerful steam shovels.

He concluded his investigations and once more went to the local police station. He would speak only to the captain, and his very persistence at last gained him an interview.

"I suppose," the captain said, "you want to tell me that they're going to bomb Grand Central Station."

Perkins shook his head. "No. It's about that bank robbery."

"Listen—" the captain began savagely, for the bank robbery was the sorest point in his life.

It was Perkins who interrupted him. It was Perkins now who was master of the situation, Perkins who with a quiet indomitability compelled the other's attention. "It'll just take a minute," he said. "Please don't interrupt me. I'll sketch at first a few details of the robbery."

He proceeded to do so. Then to the increasingly irritated captain he said, "I presume you have never read a story entitled 'The Purloined Letter.' "

"Get to your point," the captain said.

"In 'The Purloined Letter,' " Perkins continued pleasantly, "a valuable document is hidden by being put in the regular letter box with other letters. Detectives search the house, probe pillows and so on without finding it, because, so to speak, it was before their very eyes. I think" — and Perkins made his conclusion very dramatically — "that you will find the same condition applies to some three million four hundred thousand dollars for which you're searching."

The captain spoke quickly. "Is that all you have to say? If it is, get out of here, and the next time you show up I'm going to send you over to the Island as a public nuisance."

Perkins explained the rest of his theory; that the automobiles and trucks were merely to put the police on the wrong scent, and that the loot was not in the automobiles; and since it weighed so much, it could not have been disposed of very easily, and certainly could not have been moved even from the excavation unless it had been moved in the first few moments after the big vault had been entered. Hence it must be concealed somewhere in the same block as the excavation. Perkins then demonstrated that the windows opposite the bank could easily be reached by the steam shovels, and that the steel cargo in question would be nothing to those powerful arms.

When he finished, the captain leaned forward. "Listen, guy," he said. "That's the craziest thing I ever heard in my life, but it makes sense. If you're right, well—" He rapped on his desk.

The recovery of the entire sum stolen from the Manhattan Commercial Bank and Trust Company is a matter of record, and of somewhat dramatic record, for, when the police investigated the two-months-old offices of the firm of North & Griggson, which overlooked the Seward excavation, they were met with a hostile reception. Two policemen were wounded and it was necessary to toss tear-gas bombs through the transom to subdue the defenders of the bank's funds.

It was midnight when, flushed and triumphant, the police captain knocked on the door of Perkins's apartment.

Perkins had expected the call. He was smoking his meerschaum and wearing his fore-and-after cap. He looked up from a thick tome, the title of which was criminology, recognized the police captain and said, "Ah."

The captain was voluble. "I have been expecting you to come into the station all afternoon," he said. "Listen, guy. This is just about the greatest thing that ever happened to you. I haven't told the Commissioner who tipped me off yet, but I'm going down to see him tonight, and I want you to come with me. I suppose you know that there's a reward on this thing big enough to set you up for the rest of your life? Get your coat and come on."

Perkins shook his head. "Thanks," he said, "but you'll excuse me, Captain O'Hara."

"Huh?"

Perkins stretched and yawned in a slightly bored manner. His moment had arrived, and from a thousand mystery novels he had learned how to wait. "The fanfare, the publicity, of such a thing is scarcely in my province. I'm a private investigator, and I prefer to remain in the shadow." Now Perkins frowned. "I can conduct my operations more easily if I'm unknown. I hope and trust that you will not mention my name publicly."

The police captain was flabbergasted. "But what'll I tell them, then?"

Perkins's smile was austere. "My dear O'Hara, the simple chain of deduction which led to the location of that money was for me a most elementary process. Elementary, my dear O'Hara, elementary. Even you, under certain conditions, would be capable of it. You're young, life stretches before you. I insist that you assume the authorship of the discovery."

"You mean—" O'Hara said stumblingly.

"Tell the public you did it. Give the police credit. Of course I'd appreciate the mention of my name privately to the Commissioner inasmuch as I am very anxious to obtain a slight favor from him."

"Favor?" repeated the startled O'Hara. "He'll give you the City Hall for a skating rink tonight if you ask."

Perkins shook his head. "No," he said, "I don't skate. But I would very much appreciate a police card which would allow me to pass unhindered through fire lines and the like."

It was a blow that staggered O'Hara. But some Irish intuition told him that he had come upon a rare and magnificent character. With a flourish he unpinned his gold badge and placed it on Perkins's lapel.

"If that's what you want," he said, "I'll see that you get it from the Commissioner; and the reward too."

"One other thing," Perkins said, as an afterthought. "I'd appreciate it if the Commissioner would write a letter for me."

"A letter?" O'Hara said.

"Yes. A brief note to the effect that my services had not been without value to the department. A personal letter, you understand, to a man named DeMar, a friend of mine. A rather skeptical friend, I regret to say."

It is not a matter of public record, but it is a fact that the check for the reward was given to Timothy O'Hara, that he promptly endorsed it and mailed it to Willis Perkins, that Willis Perkins returned it, that finally they divided it in equal parts, after many hours of harangue and argument, and that, at present, one Timothy O'Hara now an Inspector in the New York police force and one Willis Perkins, Private Investigator, regard each other with an almost infinite mutual esteem—as two gentlemen of such high caliber should.

IT COULDN'T BE MURDER

I

When the police are confronted by that ugly evidence which is proof positive of premeditated murder they do not first "cherchez la femme." They look immediately, rather, for any persons who might profit by the evil deed. Lust, envy, spite—all these yield place to greed in forming the mental flaw which sets one being cogitating on how to destroy another.

And the horror which accompanies those patient, relentless, often imaginative steps toward homicide is sometimes accentuated by improper setting. For not all sinister human behavior is cloaked in darkness. Not all hellish footsteps echo through murky corridors, empty garrets, abandoned buildings, crypts, caverns, and the tree tunnels of lonely lanes. Sometimes the roaring city, the dazzling street, and white sunlight form the incongruous background for slinking assassins as terrible as any on a storm-swept castle roof or a fog-wrapped moor . . .

It was hot.

Two men walked side by side into the great departure chamber of the Grand Central Station in New York. One was in his early forties. He carried a brief case. His free hand blotted his damp, heavy face. The other was rather more than half his age. He looked exhausted by some inner experience more arduous than the heat.

He was talking urgently as they came down the stairs. "Look here, John! It's silly to forbid Betty and me to see each other! She's twenty-two, after all. Grown—"

John—John Stanton—stalked toward the ticket windows, bumping people as he went. His voice was rasping. "I thought I settled that last night! Or more accurately," he added, "at three a.m. today."

"You didn't. I love her. She loves me. What more . . .?"

The older man butted into a line at a ticket window and tramped impatiently on one spot while a chauffeur ahead of him bought Pullman reservations for somebody named Poremann. "Once and for all, Jerry! It's out! Frank doesn't want her to marry you. Paul's more dead set than I am. If even one of her brothers was for it . . ."

Jerry flushed and perspired. "It's so darn narrow, John! So Victorian! For you three to cut her off if she keeps on with me — golly! It's in the dime novel tradition!"

John looked immeasurably weary. "You asked for it again, remember! I'll repeat. The Stantons have held a certain position in society — even, you might say, in the nation — for a good many generations. We've lived carefully, married carefully, kept our place. There haven't been any chorus girls in the line — any Stanton girls marrying grooms or butlers. There isn't going to be any Greenwich Village artist — "

"Illustrator," Jerry corrected.

" — illustrator. Your father was a grocer in Iowa — "

"Kansas."

" — your mother taught school. Even your name — Jenks! That's enough. I like you all right. Paul does. Frank does. We wish you luck — even. I hope you fill every magazine in the country with pictures of pretty girls. But you can't have Betty — and that's that!"

Jerry's face was crimson now. People in the line at the window and people standing over their luggage were listening and grinning. An entrance across the room disgorged a crowd of commuters that fanned out and hunted exits to the blistering morning street.

The young man opened his mouth to speak and closed it. He felt lost. He'd met Betty Stanton at the Illustrators' Ball. That wasn't his fault. He'd fallen in love with her. That too, he felt, was not a fault but something inexorable.

He looked up on the balcony at the vast lithograph display urging the public to visit New England. There were pictures of cool lakes and people swimming and fishing. His gaze went back to John Stanton. He had been on the verge of conceding. But now, inexplicably, his mind changed. "You can't stop us!"

And John yawned. He yawned with deliberate insult. The eavesdroppers grinned more widely. Anger seemed then to seize him. He interrupted his own yawn, cleared his throat vigorously and raised his voice. "We'll see, Jenks! I'll wire from the train and we'll find out how Betty likes a boycott. Now — beat it! I've listened to you all night! You had the consummate nerve to catch me this morning! Against you as a person I have nothing! Against you as a member of the family . . .!"

He stopped talking. He coughed uncertainly. His eyes showed puzzlement. He took a deep breath and swayed. The color changed in his cheeks.

Jerry realized that he had been taken ill. Suddenly and violently. The heat. His futile rage vanished. "John! Take my arm! We'll head for a bench in the waiting room!"

"Yes!" John was panting. "Please! Ah—it's my heart!"

Expression faded swiftly from his eyes. He fell toward the floor. Jerry caught him and yelled fiercely for a porter. There was a sort of quiet pandemonium in the great chamber.

Sickness and collapse occur in all public gathering places. Provision is usually made for the emergencies thereby incurred. They took John to a room where he could lie down. There were two doctors—one who appeared from the throng of commuters when John was seized, another supplied automatically by the station authorities. There was a nurse. A policeman came along with the stretcher.

The doctor who volunteered to aid opened John's shirt and produced a stethoscope. Jerry stood beside him, waiting. The doctor's face was tense and blank. He listened and frowned. The man on the bed seemed to Jerry to be breathing weakly. But it might have been an optical illusion—a wishful self-deceit.

Presently the doctor took away his instrument and folded it. "He's gone," he said quietly. "There were faint fibrillations for a moment. My name is MacCarrister. Rye. Are you a relative?"

"No," Jerry replied. "A friend. You're sure?"

The official doctor hurried in then. He said a few words and he listened. He looked at John's eyeball. He nodded.

"What's the name?"

"John Stanton."

"You mean the John Stanton."

"Yes," Jerry replied.

The doctor sat on the bed. "Heart. Been bad?"

"I don't know. He was quite an athlete in college."

Dr. MacCarrister described what had happened in technical words. He gave his card to the official medical man. "You can reach me if you need me." He was gone.

"I suppose," Jerry said slowly, "I'd better tell the family."

"Yes." The doctor who had remained was offhand. "The heat, of course . . ."

Jerry went to a telephone booth. He felt frightened. With cold foreboding he dialed a number which always before he had dialed happily.

"Hello?"

"Oh—Haynes," Jerry said to the butler. "This is Jerry Jenks. I want to speak to Paul." Jerry would rather have broken the news to Frank, who was thoughtful and fairly understanding, but Paul was the next oldest of the three brothers.

"I'm afraid you cannot speak to Mr. Paul Stanton," the butler answered with a kind of incisive relish. "He has forbidden it."

"Get him, please, Haynes. This has to do with John. It is serious."

"I shall try to get him, sir."

Jerry waited. Finally he heard Paul's voice. Usually it was ingratiating, although loud and resonant. Now it was only loud. "Well, Jenks? What about John?"

"He's dead." Better tell that first. It would avoid noisy quibbling over any effort made to soften the blow.

"What! How? Accident?"

"No. Heart failure. He keeled over in the station. I was talking to him."

"I'll be right down. Grand Central?"

Jerry told him where his brother could be found. Then he went back to the little room.

Paul came in with Betty about fifteen minutes later. Jerry was sitting on a straight chair. There were cigarette stubs, crushed flat, around his feet. Betty had not been crying—then. She still had most of her color. The heat had curled stray strands of her shining hair. They made golden circles on her forehead. There was anxiety in her eyes. When she saw Jerry she smiled a little and the dark blue of her irises became lighter and more lustrous.

Paul walked toward the bed, nodding to the doctor and the station agent as he went. He turned back the sheet. He frowned—perhaps sadly, perhaps speculatively. He was as heavy a man as John had been—but more handsome. He had dark eyes, thick white eyebrows, hair combed smoothly in a mingling of black and white. His premature grayness was arresting and it gave strength to features otherwise ordinary and complacent.

Betty sat down beside Jerry and took his hand. They stared at each other searchingly, longingly.

"How soon did you get here, doctor?" Paul asked.

"My name's Lane. Almost immediately, Mr. Stanton. Another medical man—I have his card—accompanied your brother here. Mr. Jenks was with him when he collapsed."

Paul turned. "You were baiting him, I presume?" His tone was not precisely threatening. It was one of level condemnation. "Going over the grounds we all covered last night?"

Jerry sat still. "I wasn't baiting him. I was—begging maybe."

"Put it any way you like. You made him angry enough yesterday. That and the heat—"

Dr. Lane intervened. Jerry was grateful to him—and surprised, because his respect for the Stanton name had been obvious. "You cannot blame another person for an accident of that sort. Emotion is not enough. Our hearts are intended to stand it. Heat. Indigestion. And an organic condition. I presume he had a record of trouble . . ."

Paul put back the sheet. He thought while he spoke. "Nothing really serious. He expected this, I suppose, more or less—but not for twenty years more!" He put in words the notion that had been in his mind while he had talked. "It couldn't have been anything else?"

"Anything else?" Dr. Lane was perplexed.

"Anything else!" Paul snapped the words. "Isn't that clear?"

"Oh!" The doctor's small and studious face drew minutely more taut. "No. Classic case. We'll have more of them—if this heat wave turns out to be a real one. Dr. MacCarrister agreed. I'm very, very sorry, Mr. Stanton. For you and for the family. I would like to speak to you of course about the disposition to be made . . ."

He took Paul into another room.

Tears ran down Betty's cheeks then. She pressed Jerry's hand. "Gee," she said softly. "This is terrible—for us."

"I know, dear."

The policeman was listening. "But you mustn't give up, Jerry! I can see what you're thinking! And you mustn't! I love you!"

He looked away. "What can I do—say—now? Paul blames me for this—in a way. He can't help it. Frank will. So will Maude and Les. Everybody!"

"But me."

He took courage with that. "Yes. But you—darling you! All right. They can have Haynes toss me out bodily. I'll come back. They can sic Rex on me. They can—but what they'll do to you!"

"Never mind, dear. Here's Paul again."

That was the way they had fallen in love.

The same courage and vitality that had sent a banished nobleman to America in the eighteenth century to found the Stanton family had sent the Jenkses across the Atlantic—fleeing persecution—westward to Kansas. They were still, behind differences of fortune and class, the same people. Brave and determined people. And if those early fires had dwindled in some of the members of those families—in people like Paul and Frank—they burned nonetheless in a thousand Bettys—in thousands of Jerrys.

"You will come with me," Paul said to his sister. He glanced briefly at Jerry. "I don't believe, under the circumstances, that even you will fail to see you will be no longer tolerated by the family."

They went away . . .

II

Jerry started for the subway from habit, but his feelings recoiled from the crowds, the pressure, the noise and the steaming suffocation of the place that morning. So he hailed a cab. It took him downtown by way of Fifth Avenue. When he stepped out in front of the large and not very new apartment building in which he lived and held out a dollar bill to the driver, he saw that his hand was shaking. He tipped the man fifteen cents and went up two flights of stairs. He let himself in and a voice greeted him cheerfully.

"Hyah, boy!"

"Hello, Holly!" He walked back toward the end room in his quarters—his studio. Holly was sitting in a chair, reading a magazine. She looked, as usual, young and fresh and very pretty—for a girl who was as seriously determined to become a famous illustrator as was Jerry himself.

He had forgotten that she had agreed that morning to come over and act as his model. Sometimes the situation was reversed. When Holly Barker obtained one of her rare orders for a drawing and when the order demanded "a typical young American with a good chin, straightforward gray eyes and a pair of shoulders," she would telephone for Jerry. It didn't cost her anything that way.

He had forgotten Holly.

She tossed back her luxurious rust-colored hair and started to say something. What she did say was obviously different from what she had intended. "What's the matter? You said nine o'clock and I barged over. You weren't here, so I got the janitor to let me in. You look as if you'd just seen your great, great grandfather not in the flesh!"

Jerry stared at the half-finished oil on his easel before he answered. "I went up to the Stanton house this morning."

"I thought you were going to have that out last night."

"We did. Fireworks enough for a world's fair. But we didn't get any place."

"You mean you didn't get any place."

"Listen!" He spoke with the rude vehemence permissible among old and very good friends. "John was going to catch a train for Chicago this morning. He said so last night. So I made him let me ride down to the station with him this morning. I thought maybe he would have cooled off."

"Not on a day like this he wouldn't!"

"Can't you let me finish? Sorry. My nerves are roaring around just now. I argued some more and it didn't do any good. I followed him right up to the ticket window. He practically laughed in my face—or yawned in it—and then he got sore and started to tell me where to get off all over again. He never finished. He dropped dead."

"He what!" Holly instantly shared his mood.

Jerry had been walking around the room. He sat down—hard. "I don't think that he died right away. There was a lot of excitement. People rushed up. They got a stretcher. Some doctor came along and helped out. But anyway he didn't live long. By the time they got him in an emergency room he was all through."

"That's awful, Jerry!"

"Isn't it? Betty and Paul came down later on, and she was terribly decent about it, even though she must have realized that I had probably worked him up to the point where his heart quit."

"Maybe it was a stroke. On a day like this . . ."

"What's the difference? But it was heart failure. All those Stantons hated me before. You'd think I'd done something indecent and illegal to Betty. But now—well, Paul told me in so many words to stay away—for good."

Holly nodded. For a time they were silent.

"The whole family will say that I murdered John—or as much as murdered him."

"Yeah," Holly answered softly. "Nice people! I don't suppose you feel much like work this morning."

"I'll say I don't!" He sat still, considering that. He compressed his lips unconsciously and narrowed his eyes. "But, by golly, I think I will! It's better than brooding. It's the only way I'm ever going to get anywhere in my business. Dammit, Holly, I'll marry that girl yet! I'll work so hard and get such a reputation that even the Stantons will have to give an inch for the mile I took. Come on! You know the pose."

She didn't say, "Nice going!" out loud. She said it with her eyes.

Jerry squeezed flake white on his palette. He picked up a brush. He began to paint. "Fingers none too steady." He grinned at her.

"I can imagine." Holly was lying on the floor with her head propped up on three books. The three books were supposed to be the roots of a tree. Where the drafting board stood was presumably an old mossy rock. Beyond it, by the heap of picture frames, was an imaginary brook. The caption which would eventually appear under the finished picture was to be "Daisy used to lie there, chewing a long stem of grass, dreaming."

The grass stem was a soda straw from a milk-shake carton.

She knew he liked to talk when he worked. She knew that he would like to talk now and she knew the subject which was on his mind. He was keeping silent out of deference to some complex code of his own. Her eyes wandered around the familiar room—to the piles of magazines on the floor, the fantastic theatrical masks he had made, the portraits, the bust of a child he had carved.

"How were things last night?" she inquired after awhile.

Jerry snorted. "The less said the better!" Having relieved himself of that dictum, he proceeded to say a great deal. "Well, of course you don't know the people . . ."

"I feel as if I do, from all you've told me about them."

"I guess. The whole famdamily was there. John and Paul, Frank, Maude and even Les—paring his fingernails as usual, grinning like a billikin and not saying much. Though when John asked him what he thought, he looked at me as if I were something splashed on his windshield and said, 'He's out. But definitely.' Then he cut off another fingernail. That goat—"

"Didn't anybody help you out?"

"Oh, sure, more or less. In fact Maude got pretty sore. Said it wasn't sporting of the family. Said that her opinion was the solitary intelligent and unprejudiced one in the crowd. Which was correct. She told them she was all for us.

"But John read her a lecture about not being a Stanton. He told Les that he ought to manage his wife better. Les flared up—he's got a honey of a temper although it seldom shows—and tried to tell John to mind his own business. That was a rather nifty little squabble in itself."

"I can imagine."

"Yeah. I suppose that since Les is only a cousin he feels out on the rim of the family. Anyway Maude fought for me and Les fought for Maude. I think Frank would have been on my side if he'd had the nerve to say anything at all. But you know—or rather you don't know—how John yells. I should have said, yelled. He yelled habitually about everything. About what's for breakfast and why doesn't somebody fix the taillight on the Rolls and why doesn't the Republican Party do something sensible.

"Well, finally Paul stood up and made one of his courteous skin-you-alive political addresses on the subject of me and who was I. Where did I come from? What chance was there that I would ever succeed? What stupidity it would be to entrust Betty's share of the millions to a man who had never had a thousand dollars in a lump in his life! How would Betty feel five years from now, not being in the social register any more—not having her old friends?

"Oh, it was lovely! I felt like a specimen in a bell jar. When Paul finished John took up the reins again, pacing around in his dam' dinner jacket and winding up his little address by saying it was 'virtually miscegenation.' "

"Didn't Betty do anything, even at that point?" Holly asked quietly.

"I was going to tell you. Betty slapped John right square on the kisser. A beaut. Then she started to cry and she beat it for her room. That was the last I was allowed to see of her. Miscegenation! I can't say I'm glad to see anybody dead but I will say one thing. John Stanton's heart probably failed because it was too small to take care of his carcass!

"My God! They go around telling you how cultured they are and how refined, and how old and dignified their family is, and then they scream and squabble like a bunch of chimpanzees dividing up a bamboo shoot!"

Holly grinned evanescently. "Well, Jerry. You wanted the gal. You knew what you were getting into. I guess you got in plenty."

"Sure. And I'm going to stay in."

At that point there was a knock at the door. Jerry sauntered down the short dark hall and opened it. A man came in at once—talking as he entered.

"I'm Malloy, of the *Dispatch*. You're Mr. Jenks, aren't you? I understand you were with Mr. Stanton when he died this morning."

Jerry hadn't thought about reporters. There were seven of them that morning.

When the papers appeared Jerry was thrown into a fresh panic. The reporters who had come to his house had made every possible effort both by direct questioning and subtle implication to cause him to admit that he and the "Stanton heiress" were in love, "secretly engaged" or "on the verge of eloping." To protect Betty he had denied it as strongly as he could.

That was difficult, because he had been seen with her at various places for one thing. For another two or three Park Avenue columnists had printed airy meaningful squibs about them. Such things as, "What bonded blueblood is making eyes around town at what struggling-but-promising young illustrator?" Such things as, "What three elite brothers are huffing and puffing because their sister has gone in for oils?"

He had insisted that they were not engaged—only friends. He had said that his reason for accompanying John Stanton to the station had been casual.

But he had not reckoned with the stupid vanity of a great segment of mankind—that particular vanity which assures its dimwitted possessor that nothing is sweeter than your name in the papers, regardless of how it comes to be there.

The *Dispatch* had located such a person—or rather—such a person had doubtless rushed to the offices of the *Dispatch*. A woman. Mrs. Myrtle Darbulony Simmons of Long Island. Mrs. Simmons, from her published photograph, was a middle-aged fleshy baby-faced woman who wore busybody pince-nez glasses and doubtless had a voice that sounded like scratching a blackboard. Jerry vaguely remembered that face.

It appeared that she had been just behind John in the line at the ticket window that morning. She had heard everything. And she had a phonographic memory as well as a scandalous imagination. Her sense of justice was, however, biased.

Perhaps she felt that by showing a prejudice she would earn the gratitude of the Stantons and maybe even an opportunity to meet them. In that estimate of higher society, if such indeed had been her appraisal, she was woefully wrong. The Stantons would have wished Mrs. Simmons on Mars rather than at the station.

"I was waiting to buy a ticket to Greenwich," she said in her dictated interview with an editor of the Dispatch, "right behind the poor deceased magnate. This young person was harrying him from the first. Harrying him about Miss Betty Stanton, whom he had managed somehow to meet and whom he insisted he would marry.

"Mr. Stanton bore up very well and behaved throughout like a gentleman, which is more than I can say for Mr. Jenks. I, myself, burned with outraged indignation as this young Greenwich Village Bohemian swung his fists incessantly and talked in a tone that was alarmingly violent.

"No doubt Mr. Jenks is a radical and believes that all of us should work in mines under whips. In my opinion it was the supreme effort at self-control which finally burst the great heart of Mr. Stanton. He did not want his sister Betty exposed on the altar of communism."

It went on and on. Mrs. Simmons had drawn liberally from her imagination. She had been, no doubt, subtly coached by a fiendishly delighted reporter. But she had put in her monstrous declaration enough actual quotation to make it impossible for Jerry to defend himself. He would have had to admit that certain things ascribed to him were true—and to admit that would have made things only worse for Betty.

He read the story in a seething frenzy—read it aloud to Holly. "There ought to be some way," he said violently, "to keep newspapers from doing this sort of stuff! I could sue them for libel."

Holly nodded sadly. "Sure. And admit you did fight with John about Betty. Make a worse mess to clear a mess. If you sued the paper would drag in the Stantons to prove their side."

"But it says I swung my fists! I didn't!"

"They'd maintain you had your hands clenched—in court."

"It says I'm a Communist! Why—why, I voted for Landon! My father knows him!"

"Sure, Jerry. But they'd say that you have models alone here. That I come in when I please. That you're an artist and Bohemian."

"If I knew who prodded that female devil into such frightful nonsense, I'd get that guy—"

"Hey! Wait a minute! It's Mrs. Simmons who poured gasoline on the fire! And the world is crammed with those self-righteous creatures—full of incendiary platitudes—creeping around interfering! The mistake you made was to get mad in public."

"Yeah." He thought for a moment and then went to the phone.

Holly was alarmed. "Whom are you calling?"

"The Stantons."

"What for?"

"They've got to know that most of this is rubbish. They've got to!"

"Probably they do."

She waited.

He said, "Hello, Haynes. I'd like to speak to Mr. Paul Stanton. This is important. Yes, it's Mr. Jenks." There was a pause. Jerry put back the phone. "Hung up," he said. "Well, let's finish the rest of these feeble-minded stories."

She shook her head dubiously. "Why bother? It's just the usual newspaper rubbish. They're bound to go to town on the Stantons. Bradstreet's and the Blue Book. Old family. Leading citizen stuff. They're like all other rich people. They've lived down the undoubted pirate who founded the fortune and now whenever they have a cold it's news. When they die—it's the works. I'd skip it."

"Nix. We read—every word. John's great works—gifts to charity—companies directed—committees chairmanned—all of it."

He was correct in saying "stories" for there was more than a mere obituary for John Stanton. Besides the recitation of his biography—in every paper a somewhat cut-and-dried account of the head of a large and snobbish family—many other items pertaining to the Stantons were called to the view. If the death had occurred on a day when there had been important foreign news or a sporting event of national interest, a major catastrophe or a sensational shift in the stock market, it would have received less attention.

They read them back and forth.

"Here," Jerry said, "is the old familiar feature about Maude— 'Mrs. Leslie Stanton, wife of a cousin of the deceased, is the well known sportswoman and African big game hunter. Not only are some of Mrs. Stanton's specimens on display at the Smithsonian Institute in Washington, D. C., but she brought back from the Congo a film of her exploits, *Jungle Jeopardy*, which proved popular last year.' "

Jerry grunted. "Maude is all right. Listen to what they say about Frank and his wife. She wasn't there last night by the way. 'Mr. Frank Stanton, youngest brother of the dead man, has what is said to be the largest postage stamp collection in America. He has lived a retiring life and, except for his marriage to winsome Molly Evans, the musical comedy star, in nineteen twenty-seven, has been less in the public eye than his brothers . . .' "

Holly interrupted him at that point. "Anyway the tragedy hasn't stopped Paul's ambition. It says here that he intends to go right ahead with his campaign for Congress. The funeral is going to be held at the Old Stone Church day after tomorrow but tomorrow our Paul apparently is going to speak. Lousy taste, I call it. Listen. 'Asked whether or not he would now abandon his campaign for Congress in the silk-hat district, Mr. Paul Stanton, who was scheduled to make several outdoor addresses tomorrow, replied, "Sad and shocking although the death of my brother is, I am determined to an even greater degree to hew to the line of duty. In spite of my bereavement I shall fufill all planned speaking engagements." ' "

Holly executed a ladylike equivalent of the snort. "I'll bet your friend Paul is secretly pleased at the publicity coming his way right now. What does he want to go to Congress for anyway?"

Jerry shrugged. "Same reason Mrs. Simmons told all she heard and more to the reporters—to get in the public eye." He turned a page. "My God, they've even got to Betty!"

He stared for a minute at a picture of the blonde girl he loved. She was dressed as she had been that morning at the station. She looked very worn and miserable.

Holly glanced at the picture, murmured, "She's certainly lovely," and continued her researches. "Even the servants!" she said after a long silence. " 'Albert Haynes, for eleven years butler in the elaborate Stanton ménage, expressed his sorrow over the untimely death of the head of the family. "Mr. Stanton was a stern but just man." To those words were added similar expressions by other servants, among them Marcel Peltz, the chef who has for years been celebrated by New York gastronomes for his unusual practice of growing his own herbs and spices in the garden and hothouse attached to the Seventy-sixth Street Stanton residence.' "

Holly threw down the newspaper. "Well, he's gone in all his glory. Relatives that hunt lions and cooks that grow sassafras. The light's too weak to paint now, Leonardo, and I could do with a bit of food. Afterward I think we ought to go to a movie—an air-conditioned one. In my opinion it's getting hotter."

Jerry put down the paper.

As they started out of the apartment the telephone rang.

He went back to it.

It was Betty. She spoke rapidly. "I'm calling from the drugstore on Madison Avenue and I haven't got much time. How are you, darling?"

"I'm fair."

"Look. Did you see the papers?"

"Sure. They're terrible. I'm thinking of going out to Long Island personally and strangling Mrs. Simmons."

"That's what I called up about. Paul is furious. The whole house is in an uproar. You'd think with John dead that at least until the funeral was over they'd try to act decent about things. But Paul's been awfully nasty. When the reporters were here just now he practically blamed you for what happened to John. I wish you'd go and see him about it."

"He won't talk to me."

"Then break in on him somewhere. He's going to speak up at Cabot Park tomorrow noon. And I happen to know he hasn't anything to do for lunch. Maybe, if you catch him after the speech. . ."

"I'll try."

"That's one thing. The other is I'm going to go away for a few days. I'll write you where when I get there. So maybe you can come and see me wherever it is. It's a cinch you couldn't see me here. I'll leave right after the funeral."

"Good." Jerry's voice was unsteady with emotion. "Are you doing all right?"

"You bet I'm doing all right."

"Keep your chin up!"

"Goodbye, darling."

"Goodbye, honey."

Jerry and Holly started for some early supper and an air-cooled movie . . .

III

There wasn't a cloud in the sky. Even the smoke umbrella over the city seemed to have been baked out of existence by the sun. It was late in the season for such a hot spell but New York had escaped its customary siege of excessive temperature so far that summer.

Jerry came up from the steaming cavern of the subway and blinked in the blistering sunlight. He looked at his watch—eleven-fifty. He walked four blocks east—through a shabby section where elevated trains roared and fat women in kimonos leaned on pillows placed to prevent iron fire escapes from burning them. Then past a block of smart moderne apartment buildings, and into Cabot Park.

A loudspeaker was giving vent to a radio recording. It was Paul Stanton's theme song "Anchors Aweigh." The raucous music, together with posters on the speaker's truck, had already gathered a hundred-odd citizens. They waited in the baking shade of a group of wilted sycamores—nurses with babies, elderly gentlemen from the smart apartments, a colored cook or two, janitors in their shirtsleeves, exhausted pedestrians, park bums, a man selling balloons. It was not a heartening crowd but every word Paul would speak had already been forwarded to the newspapers "For immediate release."

Jerry joined the crowd, wondering why Paul had picked on "Anchors Aweigh" for his song and then remembering that one of the planks in his campaign platform was a bigger navy. Ten minutes passed while more records were played. Then Jerry saw Paul coming briskly from his limousine. His attitude of vitality was marred by the fact that he was mopping his forehead with a large linen handkerchief.

He stepped on the open end of the truck, faced the crowd and the apartments across the street and began to talk. Jerry paid little attention to what he said. It was the usual political jargon, couched now in an elite accent. Democracy must be preserved . . . Democracy must be protected . . . The enemies of the people lurk at every hand . . .

The sound of a human voice haranguing in authoritative tones will always collect a crowd. The hundred-odd slowly became three or four hundred. Paul warmed to his oration and Jerry waited in stultified sweating discomfort for the finish.

But Paul Stanton never finished his appeal to the people of New York City. He reached a climax of eloquence—"Shall we longer permit this perfidious continuum? Ahhh! We shall not!"

He stopped. The vague and rolling expression of the orator's eyes became a sudden sharp look of pain. He swallowed hard. He licked his lips. He seized the railing of the truck.

Jerry watched with mounting horror as Paul half-staggered, drew himself up and said in a choked tone, "I'm sorry, my friends. I've been taken suddenly ill. The heat—my heart . . ."

He put one hand over his chest and with the other seized his throat. His campaign manager, who had been sitting beside him, grabbed his arm and helped him down from the truck. They started toward Paul's limousine.

Jerry followed them. When Paul's steps grew weak and very uncertain, he aided. But before they reached the car Paul's feet failed altogether and his head fell forward.

With the help of the campaign manager and a bystander they lifted the stricken man into the automobile and started down the street in search of a doctor's office. Jerry rode on the running board and yelled when he saw a shingle. It said, "A. M. Black, M.D."

Dr. Black was in—a thin redheaded Scotchman with deep-set eyes, who hurried to the car at his curb. He bent over, examined hastily, then said, "You'd better bring him to the office. I'm afraid he's in bad shape!"

For sometime, in the offices of the unknown physician, there was a frenzied almost wordless activity. Unlike the two doctors who had attended John, Dr. Black did not resign himself to the inevitability of death. He worked with a fierce dexterity, whispering commands to his nurse. "Amyl nitrite!" He shook his head. "We'll try adrenalin!" "Yes, that needle!" "Take off his coat, young man!" "Iodine, please." "Hold his shirt back!"

It was no use.

Paul Stanton was gone beyond recall. Dr. Black exhausted his resources. Only then did he ask, "Who is this man?"

The campaign manager told him and added, "My name is Collins. I suppose I better go down and break the news to his family. It's going to be tough. You see, yesterday his brother died—the same way."

Jerry heard himself speaking. "Let me do it." He didn't know quite why he had said that. It was largely because he wanted to be with Betty—somewhat because he wanted to help her family. And perhaps, in a small and unconscious degree, because he hoped that the Stantons might now receive him. It had been John and Paul who had most violently disliked him.

"Who are you?" Collins asked.

"A friend. I was expecting to have lunch with Paul. I'll hop in a cab— it isn't far. You stay here with—the body."

He went.

As he closed the door the doctor was saying, ". . . sometimes—like an occasional appendicitis. Psychic effect. One member of the family gets it and then another—as if it were catching."

The blinding blocks passed quickly. The brakes ground. There was the house, the walled garden with the glittering glass of the conservatory behind it. Jerry clanged the gate. An elevated on Third Avenue rumbled and was still.

Haynes opened the door widely.

"I want to see anybody in the family. Everybody."

Haynes was ice. "I'm sorry, sir. Nobody is in, sir. I might add that I think it was impertinent of you to come here at this time, sir." His mouth moved almost as if he intended to smile.

"I'm sorry, Haynes, but you're going to let me in."

"As it happens," the butler answered, "I am speaking the truth. Not a single member of the family is in. Not that it matters, sir. Mr. Paul Stanton has given me orders concerning you."

"Mr. Paul Stanton," Jerry answered quietly, "is dead."

The butler stared. His jaw dropped. He did not sway but balanced back and forth agitatedly on his feet. Jerry was sure afterward that there came into his eyes an expression of fear and conjecture.

Then the gate clanged. Betty was coming hurriedly up the walk. "Oh, darling," she cried, "you shouldn't have come here! I don't think Haynes will let even me let you in."

She was on the steps, beautiful, distraught, affectionate. He told her. He made his account lucid but brief.

She stood numbly for a while and then unconsciously moved out of the sunlight. "That's awful!" she said softly. "Awful! Come in."

Haynes stood aside.

The drawing room was vast, Victorian and gloomy. If any place could have been cool without artificial refrigeration that day it would have been the Stanton drawing room. The two huge chandeliers that hung above its ornate furniture were like ice carvings. No sun penetrated the heavily draped front windows and only a quiet mélange of dull color descended from three stained-glass side windows to the dark mahogany and the thick Persian carpet.

Betty was not crying. She spoke her random thoughts slowly and quietly. "It'll be strange without either one of them. I couldn't agree with them always—but I was fond of them. I sent you there, didn't I, Jerry? You say you helped him to the car?"

"I don't think he knew who was helping him."

She nodded her head several times. "I see. He was foolish to go out on a day like this. He was foolish to run for Congress anyway, I think. But it doesn't matter now—does it? You say Mr. Collins is up there?"

"Yes."

"What are you supposed to do, Jerry? I don't really know. I never had to . . ." Her lip quivered.

He took her hand. "Neither did I but I'll do it. We ought to call the undertaker. Where's Frank?"

She shook her head. She led him to the hall and he made the necessary phone call. Afterwards she tugged a red velvet bell pull and Haynes appeared.

"Wasn't Frank coming here for lunch with Molly?" she asked.

"Yes, Miss Betty. At one o'clock."

"It's one now, isn't it?"

"Two minutes past."

"And Les was coming too? With Maude?"

"Yes, Miss Betty."

"Please set a place for Mr. Jenks."

"But—"

"I said, Haynes, a place for Mr. Jenks."

"Yes, Miss Betty."

Jerry's impressions after that were confused. Too little happened—too much was thought and felt.

Maude and Leslie Stanton arrived first. As she came through the door she quenched a laugh but she said to Betty, "I can't be too reverent about these things. I liked John well enough but he was a dreadful grouch. Maybe if Paul goes to Washington we can invest this mausoleum with a little cheer."

Then Betty told her.

Maude reacted violently and simply. "Great heavens, child, why didn't you throttle me when I came in? That's frightful!"

Leslie Stanton ran his fingers through his hair over and over and over and kept repeating, "Two of them. Both of them. Two of them. It's ghastly!"

He was their cousin, a chemical engineer by profession—a nervous saturnine man—tall and rather good-looking.

Molly—Frank's wife—was the least readable of them all.

Molly wept. Perhaps it was partly play-acting but perhaps the abandonment of a glamorous career on Broadway for an unexciting and even stuffy life with Frank Stanton had given her too little opportunity to express any emotion whatever. Certainly it had faded her rather overt good looks to near-dowdiness. And yet, in spite of all that, she seemed to think first and with relief that it had not been her husband.

Frank turned his back on them. He walked gravely toward the stained-glass windows, lifted his head and looked up into their browns and crimsons. They saw his hands clench together behind his back, tight and shaking a little. By and by he said, "It has to come for all of us."

Then he voiced a thought which must have been in the mind of everyone. "But good Lord! There wasn't anything the matter with Paul's heart—he had the constitution of an ox! He took care of himself as if he were cut glass. I can't understand it."

Haynes frightened them by clearing his throat. "Luncheon is served."

On the way in Betty took Jerry's arm. She hugged it a little and whispered, "I'm so glad you're here! So glad!"

Then they sat down and pretended to eat.

Afterward he and Betty went out into the garden together. A high wall shielded it from the street. Jerry had never seen it before. It seemed to contain a thousand different sorts of flowers. She watched him as he looked at it—and smiled sweetly and forlornly. "It is lovely, isn't it? I can imagine that under other circumstances we'd have enjoyed it—you and I."

"Yes." He looked back at her. "I didn't know that the Stantons—I mean John or Paul—cared for things like this."

She seated herself on a stone bench. "I don't suppose Paul ever noticed what grew here. John liked to show it off because it is impressive. But it's really Marcel's hobby."

He remembered. "In the papers—of course."

"Yes. They had even that, didn't they? But Marcel's quite famous for his cooking. People who love to eat love to eat here. I wonder . . ."

"Wonder what?"

"If it'll ever make any difference to me any more whether I eat spinach or lima beans—squab or hamburgers?"

"You bet it will! Someday, Betty. Someday . . ."

"Someday." She went on talking about the garden for the mere sake of talking. "Marcel raises all his herbs and spices and things out here—and yonder in the greenhouse. He grows the flowers just because he likes them. When John realized how good he was at it he put on an assistant gardener to help him. I used to come out here when I was a little girl and hide in the plants and pretend I was in some distant country. It was fun!"

They smiled at each other. Footsteps coming along the gravel walk stopped that half-sad and half-romantic reminiscence. They saw that it was Molly.

She looked at them and smiled diffidently. "Not disturbing . . . ?"

They said, "Not at all," in unison.

"It's hot everywhere. I thought I'd try it here." She sat down on the bench beside Betty. Jerry measured her—her exquisite and still-young profile the aspect, or maybe it was only a feeling, of something faded—the slow way in which she moved and the careful way in which she spoke.

Behind all that was more—a concealed energy—a camouflaged and leashed violence. Repressions from her lost career, probably. Regrets, impatience, hates, maybe. She went on talking softly. "I know how you must feel, Betty. And I thought it was very brave of you to insist on having your young man stay here for luncheon."

"Not brave, Molly. I needed help."

"Yes. It's terrible. John—and then Paul. It's worried me dreadfully about Frank's health. I've just been thinking that I must see to it that he has a thorough check-over. At once. Paul seemed so strong. And Frank seems weakest of the three . . ."

"I wouldn't worry," Betty answered. "Frank's well enough. Paul just overdid things. And probably John's death not only put an unendurable strain on him—but frightened him, in a way."

Jerry entered the conversation then, because it had languished. "That's what Dr. Black said. Told us it was psychologically catching—or something of the sort."

"I wonder?" Molly's china-blue eyes met his and moved away, not in avoidance but in ever-traveling and never-fulfilled search. "It's going to be arduous for some time. The publicity. The photographers." For an instant her expression brightened.

"They were at our house early this morning! I was really forced to pose for an hour. It reminded me of the times when—but I shouldn't think of them in this connection." She turned to Betty. "Now you and Frank will have the responsibility for the whole estate. You and Frank—and Leslie."

Betty did not respond to that until she saw a frown on Jerry's face. "Molly means—that we've had a system for dividing inheritance in the family for generations. A system of pro-rating. I hadn't thought about that."

Jerry was still frowning. He hadn't thought about it either. Perhaps ever since he had met Betty his most passionate wish had been that by magic she might have changed from a wealthy girl to a poor one. In the last analysis it was riches and riches alone which stood between them. The two tragedies had now vastly increased that barrier. He still did not speak.

Betty thought he wanted an explanation. "I forget just how it goes. Frank and I will receive most of what Paul and John possessed. Les gets a certain specified part. There will be quite large sums for Haynes and Marcel. It's always like that. If it had happened to me, then they—but let's not talk about such things."

"No," he said slowly. "Let's not. It only makes—me being here, caring for you—seem more impossible."

Then she understood why he had been silent. "Jerry," she said gently. "I'm sorry! It was stupid of me to go into sordid matters. It's just that—a custom among us—everybody knows about it, I mean."

IV

Jerry wanted to put his arms around her then and tell her not to talk about anything. But Molly sat there, watching them vaguely. And deep inside himself was the bitter realization that now his Betty would be rich in her own right. Worth millions, sought after, courted. Valuable for something besides her own self. That was uncomplicated and unaffected—emotional and yet sensible. But millions—millions made her both more and less than a charming girl.

So he stood there.

And then Maude came into the garden—briskly with long strides. Her skirts swished. Her wide-set eyes were quickly appraising, quick to be friendly. She looked like what she had been so often—a huntress. Not like a predatory huntress but a Diana—a woman who thought like a man, acted like one and who, in her most feminine moods, was doubtless never less than regal. Had an imaginary superman searched for an ideal comrade and pal he might have decided to end his quest upon meeting Maude.

She talked coolly, helpfully. "I've done everything I promised at lunch. Seen about Paul. We—Reverend Daniels and I—thought it would be best to postpone John's funeral—for Paul's. The family wanted it. They would have wanted it that way, too. I had a long talk with Dr. Black. He's very intelligent man. I . . ." She looked at Molly.

Betty said, "That was swell of you, Maude."

"I—hate to discuss these things."

Molly shrugged delicately. "We must, I suppose . . ."

"Well—" Maude decided to go ahead. "I suggested an autopsy."

Betty stared. Molly swallowed and gasped, "Oh! You couldn't!"

"I did, though. Dr. Black thought it was unnecessary. Said it was clearly heart failure. Paul's own doctor—Schmidt—thought it couldn't have been organic. Something sudden—shock. He said Paul had a fair heart for his age."

Betty was quite pale. She licked her lips. "But an autopsy . . . !"

Maude took her arm in a sisterly way. "Oh! I see what you're thinking! That wasn't in my mind. Heavens, no! I just felt that for our own satisfaction we ought to know exactly what was the matter. And I thought too that medical science is interested in sudden things like this. Dr. Black agreed with me there."

Betty had somewhat recovered her poise. "For a minute I thought that you suspected somebody had—had—never mind. I can't bear to think of an—autopsy!"

Maude nodded. "Neither could Les—or Frank when I put it up to him. I'm too matter-of-fact and I know it. But I didn't mean to hurt you, Betty. You either, Molly. You just don't do autopsies in this family out of mere medical curiosity. I shouldn't have suggested it. Anyway—everything's arranged. We'll have the service day after tomorrow." She said the last sentence gently. "And then we'll try to get over it all the best we can."

Betty nodded. "You make me feel pretty uncourageous—and grateful besides. I guess I need something in the nature of an older sister right now."

"Sure you do!" Maude turned then to Jerry. She studied him for a moment—a very faint smile on her lips. "And in that capacity I'd like to speak to you, Jerry. Betty's tired and shot. She ought to go to bed. And you ought to beat it. If any good comes out of all this catastrophe you can bring it to Betty.

"I know you feel frightfully sorry for her—but it isn't good taste or good sense to barge in constantly now, just because you can. I'm for you, and Frank will be, and in the end you'll be all right. Just—let her alone more or less for awhile, hunh?"

Jerry flushed and his answering smile was warm. "You're right. I'll go now, Betty. And call tomorrow. If you want me in between—you know my number." He touched her hand and she nodded. He turned to Maude. "Thanks—lots. You're a dear."

Maude shook her head. "I just know a good kid when I see one."

Haynes opened the door for him when he went out and said a grudging, "Good afternoon."

And Jerry walked toward the subway, feeling happier than he had felt for many weeks. The deaths of Betty's brothers had shocked him. But he was too honest with himself to pretend that they had brought to him a deep sorrow. Both men had been superficial and overbearing. The world would not miss them much or for long. Betty had loved neither one profoundly — dutifully, rather. He was on a train when he realized that he too was exhausted.

It came to him in the night, waking him up. A mere thought. Of course — Betty had held it in her mind fearfully for a moment also when Maude had considered autopsy.

Supposing it had been —

Murder.

He sat up in bed. Perspiration burst out upon him. He switched on the light. He saw his face in a mirror and it was pale. He walked into his studio and found a cigarette. The light, the city sounds, the familiar curl of smoke drove away that nightmarish idea. Maybe he had been dreaming.

He was calm again when he extinguished the cigarette and put out the light. Maybe he had dreamed something. A hangover from the alarming instant Betty had experienced when she had assumed that by mentioning autopsy Maude had been thinking of — murder.

Foolish. It couldn't be murder. Both men had died in broad daylight in the middle of crowds. He'd actually seen both of them die — and nobody had even touched them. The doctors would have noticed any signs of violence. But poison — he thought about poison. Suppose they had both swallowed something — John at breakfast, Paul sometime before his speech? He wondered what poison would act that way.

By and by he went back to sleep. But in the morning the fantastic speculation returned. It clouded his mind as he worked. For he was working again — with Holly as his model. Working feverishly as an anodyne to last until Betty phoned for him.

This time Holly sat on a bookcase and her hands clung to its edge. The bookcase was, by hypothesis, the cabin of a small cruiser and she was talking to an imaginary youth in the cockpit below. The white wall behind her was part of a sail. The green top of a tree, in the court between the wing where Jerry lived and the wing beyond, was a wave.

He painted steadily and told her about the day before. Only one reporter called — there had been a siege of them late the previous afternoon — and that one was speedily dispatched.

"So you see, Holly, things could be worse!"

"I'm glad. Look. Shall I put one knee up? People like pretty knees in magazine illustrations—and mine are mighty pretty."

"You're on a boat, lug! You can't take a pose that throws you off balance!"

"On a boat—but no sea breeze! When I walked over this morning two kids were trying to fry an egg on the walk. And believe it or not the egg was frying fine!"

Ten minutes passed. His brush made small slapping sounds. "Say," he muttered finally.

His tone made her break her pose. "Something, Raphael?"

"A thing occurred to me last night. You'd think I was crazy if I told you . . ."

"Put your mind at ease. I think so anyway."

He failed to grin. "Not a funny thing—a stupid one. But it sticks in my craw. Maybe, if I did tell, I'd shake it off."

"Shoot."

He hesitated. "It's about the Stantons . . ."

"Naturally, my love-struck Leonardo." Her words were flippant. Her eyes, however, were alert and sober.

"About John and Paul. John apparently had a bum heart. But Paul didn't. Kind of funny, their dying a day apart. And the thing that came into my dim brain was—"

"—that they didn't die naturally."

His eyes raced from the canvas. "Why—yes! Had you thought of that?"

"Just idly—as a girl will. Plenty of people will think of it before the ashes are cold. Why not? But what of it? They're probably wrong. And nobody is going to be able to investigate. It looks like a simple coincidence and the doctors say it is. The odds at Lloyds are probably a thousand to one it's a simple coincidence. Paul probably ate diamond-backed terrapin and coupe Jacque the night before. I don't think the tragic demise of his brother spoiled his celebrated appetite."

"Sure. But it gave me a chill."

"I should think it would give you a chill," Holly exclaimed.

He stared. "Me? Why me particularly?"

Holly then looked flabbergasted. "Having thought so far, didn't you pursue your ghoulish speculation one more step? Why you indeed! Because you were right beside John and right in front of Paul when it happened! And because you had three beautiful possible motives for wishing those two men not to be. You disliked them to put it mildly. You love their sister and they stood between you and her. Then—if they were disposed of and you married the girl—you would be in the way of taking over some twenty million dollars."

He gazed at her a moment longer and then began to laugh. "It's a conviction! Sure I poisoned them. I did it with an invisible trained tarantula I keep secreted in my ear! Golly! What minds women have!"

"Usually you deny they have any!" Holly was laughing too then. She resumed her pose.

And Jerry recommenced to paint. "You can smoke if you like. I'll fool with this sail. It looks as if it were starched. Well, tomorrow my victims will be ashes and the evidence destroyed. I still wonder, though, if there is any kind of poison that could do a job like that?"

"Why?"

"Why what?"

"Why do you wonder?"

"Oh." He gestured with his brush. "Just idly—as men do. Something in a capsule that would melt after being swallowed and make a collapse look like heart failure."

"I dunno," she answered. "Be kind of interesting to look up."

He said, "Yeah—would." Then he became lost in the problem of painting a sail so that it would fairly push the boat off the page of a certain popular magazine.

That night he and Holly went to another picture.

The next day he worked without her. A whole day on waves and sky. With the thermometer at ninety. No reporters bothered him. They were sitting unwillingly in the sepulchral gloom and tedious heat of the Old Stone Church and following the Stantons and their myriad friends to the crematory—pursuing step by step the liturgy and last rites for John and Paul—listening to the organ music and the grossly flamboyant encomiums and noting how the women wore their mourning. How they wore it and what couturier had hastily made it—Betty and Maude and Molly.

Holly dropped in at six. She was carrying a book. "Haloo, Matisse! Finished yet?"

"For the moment. Haloo-haloo! Reading? Didn't know you could."

She held up the back of the book. He perceived its title—*Poisons and Their Antidotes*. He whistled. "Still pursuing the sinister?"

"Just curious. So I bought this. You ought to read it. All sorts of useful information—in the event that you get bothered by your companions."

He nodded. "Think I will. I may want to get rid of a pretty egregious model I occasionally use."

"Really? But she knows all the antidotes! Seriously—I've been perusing this thing all day. It's remarkable. You can get stuff out of common weeds and ordinary flowers, if you know how, that'll tie your Aunt Ella in knots in no time."

"And you discovered that John and Paul were unmistakably the victims of—"

"—of about twenty different ones if they were. Pretty nearly half of these little things make you gasp and waver and choke and collapse."

"Pleasant."

She grinned. "You're still eating?"

"If I don't get these pictures in—or if Mr. Joselyn happens not to like them—I won't be eating much longer."

"He'll like them. They're swell."

Jerry gazed at her for a moment. "Say! In all the hurly-burly, I've forgotten to ask about your affairs. You got that book to illustrate, didn't you?"

She smiled and tossed back the rusty luxury of her hair. "An etcher named Miller go it."

His whistle, if a whistle can be emotional, contained both sympathy and affection. "Say! That's tough. Look! I could lend you fifty bucks till *Household Magazine* kicks through for these."

Holly grinned. "The Barkers don't borrow until the sheriff is breathing down their necks. But you might buy me some chop suey."

They went out together . . .

V

The following morning was somewhat cooler. Clouds covered the sky. Here and there in Manhattan quick unsatisfactory showers steamed on the pavements. During the afternoon thunder rolled steadily over toward New Jersey. Fewer urchins splashed and floundered around open fire hydrants. The day's toll of prostrations dropped. But the weather report was not reassuring and by noon the breeze dropped and the abnormal heat returned with sullen emphasis.

People are restive in such weather. Jerry had been almost unable to work. He should have completed the last of his three canvases that day, but he did not.

He took two showers.

He tried painting in the altogether for a while.

He phoned Holly but her room-mate said she had gone to the beach.

He wanted, of course, to call Betty. He had not heard from her since the afternoon he had spent with her in the garden. He fought the impulse but he began to worry. Perhaps, in spite of Paul's death, she had carried out her original plan of going away.

He fidgeted around his room. He read for a while in the book about poison which Holly had left. It was a bizarre and morbid book but it failed to hold his attention.

At one-thirty he made coffee for himself. At two Mr. Peck of the *Woman's Review* called to ask him to come up in a day or so to discuss illustrating a serial by a famous author. Ordinarily that would have made him turn handsprings across his studio. It was roomy and bare enough for handsprings. But now, with his biggest opportunity in sight, he was unable to rejoice.

It was a little after two when he decided he would call. He dialed the Stanton number and asked Haynes for Betty.

Her voice reassured him greatly. "Oh, darling! I was just going to call you! Must be telepathy. I want you to come for dinner tomorrow night. The whole family will be here. And it won't be very gay. But they're all willing that you join us. Practically as a member."

"That's wonderful!"

"Isn't it! I tried to get you yesterday evening."

"Did you! I was out."

She laughed. "So I discovered. With another girl, I bet!"

"I was not!" There was a ring of candor in his voice. He meant it. Then he reflected that he had been out with another girl. Holly. But she was so old and familiar a friend that he hadn't counted her as a girl. The error was amusing—and he did not bother to rectify his statement. It was both exhilarating and reassuring to talk with Betty.

He remembered the offer that had just come. "I have a surprise for you. I don't suppose there's a chance of dropping in—or meeting you anywhere—today?"

"I wish there were. But I'm taking Frank over to see my dentist at three. Dr. Burdeckl."

"Can't Frank go to the dentist alone?"

She laughed again. "I guess so. Though he has a phobia about his teeth. Molly has been pretty frightened over his health. I can understand that. She made him see two doctors and they said all he needed was some dentistry. He was so sunk that I took pity on him. Said I'd take him to my man—he's marvelous—and wait for him. Frank's been drinking highballs all morning to get his nerve up."

"All right. It'll be tomorrow then."

"At seven. 'Bye, darling."

"Good-bye, gal!"

The call elevated his spirits. Betty was still in town, still as fond of him as ever. An important magazine was considering the use of his work for an important serial. It was stupendous! And he realized, with all those blessings then apparent, that he was hungry.

He went down to the corner drugstore and had two lemonades and two club sandwiches.

Afterward he started on a walk. The skies threatened rain and occasional big drops fell. Trees turned up the silver undersides of their branches. But the imminent storm did not break. He walked at random, downtown, over to the river, back through the Italian section and into Washington Square, which was not far from his home. He had taken no exercise for days and the promenade made him feel better at every step. In the Park he sat down for a full half hour, smoking and day-dreaming.

When he rose to return the clouds had broken and the promising gusts of wind had died down. The heat, tense and humid, stifled his breath. He walked slowly through exhausted and straggling crowds to his apartment and up the stairs.

When he opened the door he smelled fresh tobacco smoke. He thought it was Holly and called, "Hi, gal!"

But it wasn't. Sitting in the only good chair in his studio was a man in a blue serge suit. A tall sinewy man with an affable Irish face. A man of about forty-five—a total stranger—who grinned at Jerry cryptically and said in an amiable bass, "Sorry to startle you, Jenks. But I've been waiting here since half-past four."

Jerry had two feelings—one of irritation at the man's composure, another of undefined alarm. "Who—what . . . ?"

"Just dropped in," said the man, "to ask you where you've been since two o'clock."

"Walking. But—"

"Walking where?"

"Around. Down to the River. But—" Then Jerry's color faded.

The stranger frowned and watched him. "You get it, I see. Yeah. I'm a cop. I'm Riley. My job is homicide. I came over here to arrest you for murder—three murders."

Jerry sank slowly on a battered chest. Then his head snapped up. "Three? What three?"

"The three Stanton brothers." The detective became an image of pure concentration. He leaned toward Jerry. His eyes were sharp stars. His hands were limp in his lap.

And Jerry said nothing for a moment. His face blanched. His chin began to quiver. His eyes misfocussed. "Has—did—something happen to Frank? It's—impossible! Betty told me not three hours ago that she was taking him to the dentist."

"What dentist?"

"I don't know." Jerry was nearly incoherent. "Bleekel or some such name. Is she all right?"

"Yeah. Look, Jenks, can you prove where you went on this walk?"

"Prove it? How? I just wandered around—everywhere."

Riley shook his head. He sat there thinking for a full minute. Finally he said, "That business about arresting you was bunk. I haven't a warrant. I just wanted to know how you'd take it. You see—Frank Stanton dropped dead in the dentist's chair at a quarter past three this afternoon.

"Heart failure—apparently. His sister was in the waiting room and the dentist was in his laboratory getting a tool or something. Miss Stanton herself called us. She was frantic. Two people can possibly drop dead in a family. But not three. Not unless there's been some tampering with the laws of chance. Right now we're not saying anything. The papers are going to get a story of natural causes. But the chief sent me out to talk to you. And here I am."

Jerry was staring. "God, that's awful!"

"Murder usually is. I'm not saying it's murder. We're having a post mortem done right now. Then we'll know more. But if you can't prove what you did this afternoon—and if it was dirty work—you're going to be in a spot."

"Yes," Jerry answered softly. "I can see that."

The detective crossed his legs. "Cigarette?"

"Thanks."

He smiled in a friendly manner at Jerry. "Personally, I'd bet a year's wages your bill of health is clean."

Jerry was startled. "Why?"

"Because—if you'd done it and found me here and I accused you—you being, if I may say so, an emotional if brainy guy—you'd have either raised hell denying it or gotten clever on me. You merely acted like a kid finding out about Santa Claus.

"Now look, Jenks. I'm a cop. I'm not a fool or a softy. When this third death breaks in the papers everybody on earth is going to yell at the Department. But I'm as much a human being as you. And from where you sit you might help us more than all the flat-feet and savvy guys on our payroll. I'd like you to throw in with me."

Life was returning to the young artist. "You bet I will!"

"Don't be too excited about the idea. It may be tough for you. Suppose we prove Frank Stanton was knocked off. And suppose things begin to point to the girl. Would you turn her in?"

"Betty? It couldn't be! Besides—she phoned for you."

Riley shrugged. "Maybe—maybe not. Though more than one murderer has called the cops. She had the same motives you have. Opportunity—until she can prove she didn't. And who knows what a dame in love will do if she thinks she's going to miss out?"

Jerry didn't answer.

The detective watched him. Finally he said, "See here. I've read lots about these people—besides everything that was printed in the last few days. I talked to Betty Stanton for awhile before I came over here. The way the family fortune gets split up makes everyone a possible candidate until we rule them out.

"For instance, Leslie Stanton isn't especially wealthy. He will be now. That includes his wife. Molly is going to be worth millions now. Betty, we've mentioned. The net coming to the butler and the chef will be a decent sum. The Stantons' wills always pensioned off favorite servants. Those two birds may be in for fifty or even a hundred thousand apiece.

"Besides that plenty of outsiders disliked the Stantons. I haven't got a list in my memory right now—but there are a few birds and maybe a few women who would have enjoyed doing the job. John and Paul were bachelors. Their private lives will stand a lot of poking around in.

"What I mean is—this may prove to be one of the trickiest jobs the Department ever under-took. And there will be dough and influence and pride to block us at every turn. I can guarantee that you'll be let alone at least for now. I don't know what I want you to do. You were invited up there for dinner tomorrow?"

"Yes."

"Well, I asked Betty—nice kid by the way—to stick to that bid. The family'll be huddling together anyhow. Go up. And just see whatever there is to see—see and hear. All right?"

"I'll do it," Jerry said after a moment, "but you can't expect me to be unprejudiced. If somebody killed those three men it was undoubtedly somebody outside the family. And as for Betty . . ."

Riley stood up. His face was troubled and at the same time paternal. "I never get used to the things people do. And in my business, you see a good many of the worst ones. I can't even understand why a bird like you falls for one of those Park Avenue debs."

"It just happened."

"Sure. I suppose so. Anyway, I must say she's better than the run-of-the-mill heiress. I probably ought to congratulate you." He chuckled. "Maybe I envy you." He picked up his hat. "By the way, who's Holly Barker?"

Jerry smiled slightly. "Do you know everything?"

"Everything I can find out."

"Holly is another artist. We went to the Art Students' League together five years ago. I've known her ever since. She's a hell of a good gal."

"You aren't two-timing the Stanton girl by any chance?"

"Good Lord, no. Holly's around here a lot but she's—why, she's practically a sister."

"I get it." Jerry followed Riley to the door. The detective held out his hand. "I'll be over late tomorrow night. Around one o'clock, I'd say."

"All right."

"Lousy weather, isn't it?"

"I'll say it is."

The detective sauntered toward the elevator. Jerry closed his door. He walked to the window of his studio and looked out. The trees in the courtyard below were limp. Lights were going on in the wing of the building that faced his rooms. The heavy slowly scattering clouds bore the last dun hues of the setting sun. Jerry felt sick and weak. He spun the tassel on the window curtain and tried to think.

If they had all been killed it could only have been by poison. There was no other possibility. He had seen two of them die. He thought of the book Holly had brought to his apartment and he started to look for it.

It was gone.

VI

Riley must have taken it—smuggled it out. Jerry wondered frantically if that book, so innocently purchased, would someday be the necessary evidence to convict its innocent possessor.

It was eight o'clock and Jerry was still sitting in his studio when the phone rang.

"This is Riley."

For an instant, he couldn't think who Riley was. But the voice had registered on his mind. "Oh. Yes."

"I'm assuming that I didn't need to tell you that our conversation this afternoon was strictly on the q.t."

"I haven't seen anybody since. And I wouldn't talk about it anyway—of course."

"Right. We've just had a preliminary report from the Medical Examiner. It doesn't get us anywhere at all. There was nothing the matter with the guy's heart—but the guy had heart failure. Of course something may come to light before they're finished. I have a hunch it may not. But regardless of whether or not they find anything I'm going ahead quietly. They've gone over him inch-by-inch with magnifying glasses. There isn't a puncture on his skin—not a spot."

"What does that mean?" Jerry asked agitatedly.

"You tell me. I don't know. If somebody didn't slip him poison in his food, if he wasn't pricked or stabbed with something poisonous, but if he was poisoned nevertheless—"

"Maybe it was something he breathed."

"Maybe. I just wanted you to know so that when you go up there tomorrow night you'll watch for any kind of a lead—any kind. For the time being we're giving out to the papers that he died of natural causes. The family is getting the same story. Meanwhile we're checking up about ten thousand necessary details." And with that the detective hung up.

Jerry had been feeling for hours that Riley, in spite of his pretense of friendliness, had actually been trying to trip him. He did not relish that feeling. He did not relish the idea of becoming a sort of spy in Betty's home. But there was no way to avoid that—and Riley had seemed likeable. Over the phone now he sounded friendly.

Jerry decided to investigate one source of his multiple anxieties. "You took my book."

"Yeah," Riley replied easily. "I was wondering if you'd notice that. What were you doing with it anyway?"

It was only then that he realized telling the truth would involve Holly. He hesitated and decided the exact truth at all times would be best. "Well, after John and Paul Stanton died that girl you spoke about—Holly Parker—suggested it might be poison. We sort of kidded about it and the next day she brought over the book."

"I told the chief it was probably something like that. Will Miss Parker be able to prove where and when she bought it?"

"Search me."

Riley laughed. "It's a lucky thing they assigned me to look into your particular activities, Jenks. There are plenty of fellows down here at headquarters who would have you behind bars by now. Well—see you tomorrow night. If the Parker girl hasn't anything to do you might invite her in. I'd like to have a look at her. And she seems to know more about what you're doing than you do yourself."

"I'll ask her."

"So long."

Jerry went back to the window. It was dark now.

After dinner the next evening, with half a dozen other fatigued Villagers, he stepped from the last bus downtown and walked across Washington Square to Waverly Place. Holly was waiting for him. Together they went up to his apartment. Riley was sitting there. He didn't explain how he had gotten in. He hadn't explained before.

His attention was concentrated on Holly, and a detached person watching the detective might easily have deduced that what he saw further relieved his mind. After a moment of introductions and general conversation Riley became relaxed and affable. Holly obviously liked him from the first. And he was indeed more like a friend—a shrewd detached friend—than a detective. Jerry surely hoped he'd prove to be a friend.

They all sat down. And they lighted cigarettes before Riley said, "You look as if you'd spent a bad evening, Jerry."

"I did."

"How were the Stantons?"

"What would you expect? They've been told Frank died naturally. But every one of them knew he was in perfect health. They suspect they're being kidded by the police. I understand you spent the morning up there."

Riley grinned. "I don't believe I told them my name."

Jerry's answering grin was very slight. "The description they gave fitted. What did you make of it?"

Riley chuckled.

Holly said, "Why, Jerry, you can't ask an officer of the law that question! He wants to know what you saw."

"Well—not much. I can't really say I saw anything. Betty was all broken up and I felt so darned badly about it that most of the time I just moped around her. Still—well, look! I might as well give you the whole thing in a job lot. I don't believe any of them did anything. Or the servants either. But when your assignment is to be suspicious, apparently you suspect everybody you see."

He rubbed his face with his hands. Riley prompted him. "As for instance?"

"As for instance the butler—Haynes. He was as nervous as a cat all evening and he isn't the type that gets jittery easily either. Cold as a dead fish. But tonight when he announced me in the drawing room, he said 'Mr. Jenky Jares' or something like that—messed my name up.

"At dinner he fumbled a plate and tried to grab it and knocked it halfway across the room. After dinner Betty's maid served coffee because Haynes had gone to bed with a headache. Well? That's Haynes. If you can assume that he had a chance to poison all three of them . . ."

"We can assume it for the time being," Riley said offhandedly, "since we don't know how the poison was given—if poison was given at all—or whether the servants have good alibis. All the others say they were in bed the morning John was killed—or died. But they can't prove it. They don't seem to remember what they were doing the day Paul made his last speech.

"And yesterday"—he thought a moment—"Betty was in the dentist's office, Leslie says he was home alone in his apartment, Maude was driving her own car—shopping, she says—and Molly was in a movie. Haynes was taking his afternoon off and says he was riding on a ferry boat to get cool, which, God knows, he may have been doing. Marcel, that dizzy frog chef, maintains he was in the garden for four hours but he can't prove it.

"Sometimes people have good alibis and sometimes they don't. Sometimes a good alibi is more suspicious than a bad one. Proving an alibi is about the easiest and oldest dodge a deliberate murderer ever uses. Personally I don't pay much attention to them. If somebody gets bumped off I just assume for the sake of argument that everybody who might have done it could have been on the spot—whether it looks like it or not.

"Of course, if somebody can prove, say, that he was locked up in a bank vault or that she was clamped to a permanent-wave machine, I'm willing to rule that person out more or less. But this gang is hazy in the first place and snooty in the second. They resent questions and they don't have good memories." He wiggled his thumb at Jerry. "Go ahead. Shoot."

"Well, we went in to dinner like a bunch of mummies. Nobody ate much. It even occurred to me that they were scared to eat. Maybe you told them that Frank's death was natural but they all have a pretty good idea it wasn't. The feeling that swallowing a spoonful of soup may result in laying you low isn't a comfortable one. I had it myself up there."

"Did they talk about it?"

"Not directly. Maude did say that they were all behaving foolishly. She tried to cheer them up At least to make them talk about something. For a couple of courses she gave everything a whirl from the weather to the World Series. Finally she said that in her opinion the doctors would probably discover nothing unpleasant and everybody could carry on. That's as close as they ever came to mentioning what they felt."

Riley nodded. "Maude was the only one who was really decent to me this morning. She seems like a pretty level dame."

"Yes." Jerry paused. "What did you make out of Molly Stanton?"

Riley smiled. "What did you? She was just this side of hysterics when I saw her. Of course I told her what I told everybody—in a sudden and unexplainable death the M.E. and the police have to ask a few questions— but she seemed so upset that I didn't push anything very far."

"She wasn't upset tonight," Jerry said. "At least she wasn't hysterical. She was very quiet. She didn't pay much attention to what anybody said. All through the meal she had a faraway look in her eyes. I thought at first that maybe she was cracking up, losing her senses. But the more I watched her the less I believed that. She's got something on her mind that nobody else in the family knows about. It's something big and absorbing and it isn't grief over Frank's death."

"No kidding?" Riley drummed on the arm of his chair. "That's something I didn't get a slant on. I'll have to see what Molly Stanton's tail reports."

"Tail?"

"Sure. Everybody in the family is being tailed, including your Betty. All right. Molly has something on her mind. What about Leslie?"

Jerry leaned forward and frowned. "You saw him this morning. Was he pale? Shaking? Scared to death? Did he say anything about planning to go away?"

"Go away?"

"Right. Just as soon as Frank's funeral is over. Somebody from a travel agency called him up during dinner. I heard him say over the phone that he didn't care where just so long as it was a good ship and a restful voyage. He told us that he was planning to take a cruise because he had been through about as much as he could stand.

"Maude argued with him. Said it was no time to desert the family. Said she didn't want to go on a cruise this summer—things being the way they were. But he kept insisting with a sort of tormented determination. I can tell you for a fact that Les Stanton is scared of something, plenty scared."

Riley's voice was dry. "I got that when I talked to him."

"And another thing." Jerry halted uncomfortably. "I mean—when you get suspicious it does peculiar things to your brain. But look—I take it you're going on the assumption Frank was poisoned. Presumably Paul and John were also. It must have been a pretty clever job."

"It was—maybe too clever."

"So think of this. Leslie Stanton is an engineer—a chemical engineer."

"I already have thought of it." Riley was grinning. "And it's something to think about. But I I should have told you kids the final report from the medical department."

Jerry unconsciously stood up. "What was it?"

Riley made a rueful gesture. "A complete blank."

"They didn't find anything?"

"Not a thing."

"Then," Jerry asked, "why do the police go ahead?"

"Several reasons. Three brothers don't die of heart failure in a row when one had a fairly good heart, another a sound heart and the third had just been checked by a first-rate doctor. That's one thing. Another is that every time a Stanton dies a good many people benefit largely and directly. A third is that the newspapers are going to town on the story. And we're not entirely licked."

He studied them as if he were pondering whether or not to say what was on his mind. "Assuming they were killed, I can't see any other method than by poison. There are several poisons that don't show up in an autopsy. If they were murdered and their murderer used one of those poisons I'd have a pretty good case if I could even prove the existence of such a poison in the house or in anybody's house."

"What kind of poisons work that way?" Jerry asked.

The detective turned to Holly and his eyes twinkled. "You ought to know, Holly, if you read that book I swiped. The most effective one would be aconite, I think."

A similar gleam came in Holly's eyes. "Wouldn't aconitine be better?"

He laughed. "It would. A few drops in the bloodstream are enough. It's quick—it's sure—and your autopsy shows nothing. Just the regular post mortem picture of suffocation due to heart failure."

"Can you buy aconite or aconitine without a prescription?" she asked.

"Lord, no!"

"Then can't you trace who bought it?" She spoke agitatedly.

Riley yawned and stretched. "It seems to be a general belief that if somebody is poisoned all the homicide squad has to do is find the phony prescription. That presumably leads directly to the guilty person. "Trace the poison' is just like cherchez la femme in the public mind.

"Now, no kidding, is that sensible? Suppose you, Holly, want to put something in Jerry's coffee. Are you going to get a prescription and buy it at a pharmacy? Would you be that stupid? You would not! You'd figure out what poison would do the job"—he grinned—"maybe even buy a book on poisons first. Then what would you do?

"Within fifty miles of this very spot there are literally hundreds of one-man drugstores. Hundreds of places where a single druggist is on duty alone. You could walk into one or sneak into one. While the druggist was busy—making a milk shake or out in the street looking at an accident—you could easily step into his little back room, help yourself to enough poison to knock over a regiment and sneak out. Or maybe even buy a magazine or some aspirin as you left."

"I never thought of that," Jerry said slowly.

Riley yawned again. "No? But lots of other people have. Why, hell, I'd lay you ten dollars to ten cents that I could go out of this apartment for an hour and come back with a bottle of almost anything you could name. It's a cinch. It's such a cinch that it's a wonder the mother-in-law mortality isn't ten times as high as it is.

"The dumbest shop-lifter could swipe a bottle of aconite. And yet, if this story breaks in the newspapers, they'll be screaming at us to trace the poison. If somebody bought it—we could. If somebody swiped it—we might just as well try to trace a bumble bee by the trail he leaves in the air. For that matter . . ." He shrugged.

"For that matter what?" Jerry asked.

"For that matter, if it was aconite or aconitine, anybody who knew how could make the stuff out of plants. Aconite comes from the roots of monkshood or wolfbane. You can grow them in your garden. Aconitine is merely a sort of super-essence of it. Our friend Leslie could have extracted the stuff, for instance. What's the matter with you?"

Jerry was staring at the detective. When he spoke his voice was hoarse. "Matter? Plenty! I forgot to tell you one thing. After dinner Betty and I went out in the garden. That chef was fooling around there. He usually is. Come to think of it, though, people don't do gardening at night! And he didn't seem to be any too pleased that we had come out there and found him."

"What was he doing?"

"He said something about transplanting some stuff. Anyway he was pulling up a whole lot of flowers."

"Pulling them up?"

Holly broke in. "You don't pull up things you're going to transplant. You dig them. And you don't transplant things this time of year, anyway."

Riley was already at the telephone, dialing furiously. When he got his number he gave his name and asked for Willis. His voice was quick and commanding. "Oh, Willis. Riley! This evening the Stanton chef pulled up a lot of plants in the garden. Yeah, plants. See if you can get them.

"I don't want anybody up there to know you're working on that angle. Sure. They might be lying in a pile or in a basket somewhere. You might look in the furnace in the cellar. If you find anything newly burned— bring the ashes. That's it. Yep. Check."

He turned around and looked at Jerry. "I had a hunch yesterday that it wouldn't do any harm to send you up there for dinner tonight. If we don't find wolfbane or monkshood in that bunch of plants I'll be surprised. That is—if we find the plants. I'll see you tomorrow and thanks a lot—an awful lot."

He was gone.

VII

After Riley had left Jerry took Holly to the drugstore on the corner. They were quite excited. "I'll bet," she whispered to him over a frosted chocolate, "they find that Frenchman has a roomful of different poisons he made from his plants. I'll bet they also find he owed a lot of money—or needed a lot desperately for some reason. Maybe a woman. He knew he'd get it if any of the Stantons died—so he did it."

Jerry shrugged. But it was not an especially convincing shrug. He more than half believed that theory himself. Artists have never been known as cold logicians. And he was no exception. He lived by impulses—good impulses, generally well controlled—but impulses nevertheless. A coldly logical person would never have allowed himself to fall in love with a girl as remote socially as Betty was from himself. He shrugged, therefore, and said, "Maybe."

Her eyes shone. "And the police will owe the whole thing to you. Imagine! Imagine what the papers will say—'Shrewd Observation of Young Artist Leads to Conviction of Murderer!' "

"I hate to wish anybody hard luck," he answered in an effort to seem modest. "But if he's the guy—I hope they get him."

"Me too. It is exciting—even if it's terrifying! Just think, for example, what Riley was saying about drug stores. And we're in one!"

She looked around—at the bottles of perfume, the magazine rack, the candy counter, the soda fountain, back toward the cubbyhole where prescriptions were compounded. "I've always thought of drug stores as pretty prosaic places. But Riley's right! Why—even I could sneak in there and help myself to anything I pleased!"

She shuddered ecstatically.

Jerry grinned and answered, "Tomorrow will tell." He tried to sound nonchalant. But there was a quiver in his voice.

He was mistaken.

He stayed all day in his apartment—and nothing happened. No one called. There was no news from Riley.

The next day was the same. He bought every paper and found no hint of new developments. He telephoned twice to the Stanton home but Haynes told him Betty was not there. Both times he left messages for her to call but for some reason she did not. He tried to work but that was useless. He walked over to Holly's apartment but only her roommate was there—a mousy girl for whom he did not particularly care.

By ten o'clock that evening he was desperate. He had decided to go to Police Headquarters and try to find Riley when there was a knock on the door—and Riley came in. A very dejected Riley indeed.

"I've gone three quarters out of my mind," Jerry said, "wondering what the news was."

"And in the same time," the detective answered, dropping into a chair, "I've gone completely out of mine. About this time last night I thought you were one bright boy. They got those plants—every damn one that Frenchman pulled up. And by the way he isn't French. Alsatian, or something of the sort.

"Well—the plants were as predicted. Monkshood and wolfbane and hellebore. Deadly nightshade and purple foxglove. The works. Enough poison could have been brewed out of the mess to knock over a small town. Well—enough, anyhow. You can see how I felt."

Jerry's eyes were wide. "You bet I can!"

"We got the chef all right, too. Took him to Headquarters yesterday morning. And this was his story. He raised herbs and spices for his kitchen—which he's famous for doing—and those poisonous flowers for fun. Some of them are common in many gardens. Some aren't. It amused him, he said, to see what decent-looking flowers had such indecent characteristics.

"Obviously he was a crackpot, a morbid bird anyhow. He said he was poetic. Said all chefs are poets. Well, next we asked him why he was pulling up his little garden on that particular night. Because this morning there wasn't a harmful plant in the whole place. And he had a pretty good answer."

Riley paused to light a cigar. Jerry asked, "Where'd you find the stuff by the way?"

"It was easy. He left out two ashcans full of dead shrubs and flowers for the D.S.C. to pick up in the morning. He didn't think we'd be on to him so quickly. Nobody had ever paid much attention to his posies. A good thing too. Well, he said that the deaths of the three brothers and especially the way they died made him think that perhaps they had been poisoned.

"That scared him because he had a gardenful of poison—and it was possible that if the Stantons had been poisoned it might have been by a kind of drug he grew for amusement. So he pulled them up to get them out of the way. That was his story—and he's stuck to it for thirty-six hours."

"Maybe he'll break down."

Riley gazed at Jerry sympathetically. "It's important for us to figure this thing out," he said slowly. "When things are important we work hard. Very few people hold out for thirty-six hours—unless they're innocent."

"You mean you used the third degree?"

Riley lifted a shoulder. "Depends. There was a bright light and the boys shouting. And he was allowed to get pretty thirsty. We didn't rubber hose him. We don't—in my department. Nope. He acted straight. I'll say that."

"Did you search his rooms?"

"Search? Son, that's the wrong word. We put a microscope on that guy's whole life—and not a thing turned up. He had a good war record—a beaut. He has about eleven thousand dollars tucked away in banks and in bonds. He has a wife and two kids in Astoria—all of which the Stantons knew, of course. He has written a little book in French about cooking sea food that's supposed to be tops on the subject.

"His friends are other chefs and a Columbia professor, who is an authority on herbs, and a few Frenchmen he plays cards with. Everybody gave him a clean bill. Wife's nice—kids bright and progressive as sin. Wish my own did as well. No sir, I'd be ready to swear Marcel's as innocent as I think you are. How do you like that?"

Jerry thought for awhile. "What did you do with him?"

"Turned him loose. Nothing else to do."

"Could you have gotten aconite or aconitine, for example, from those plants?"

"You bet—if you knew how. It's something of a trick, chemically, to produce pure stuff."

"Then someone else could have used Marcel's garden."

"Sure. But who? How do we prove it? The answer is, Jerry, my boy, we don't. The Medical Examiner wouldn't play with us any longer. The certificate says 'natural causes.' The funeral is going to be in two days—and a quiet one. I've had cases like this before—plenty of them. I hate 'em—but there they are. Maybe the guy did die naturally. Shock following shock topped off by the dentist's chair. He hated dentists. Could be. And we haven't got a thing."

"You don't believe it was natural."

Riley chewed hard on his cigar. "We get plenty of dead bodies with murder written all over them—and catch nobody. There are far more that we never get. Somebody kills them and they're marked 'natural causes' and buried. I don't mind telling you that this business is hard to bear because I hoped to be an inspector soon and the papers are making that 'soon' pretty unlikely.

"I've seen everybody I can think of. Done everything I can think of. Asked every question that has popped into my mind. Even held you in partial candidacy till now. And now—we have no evidence, no body even, no chief suspect. I guess the guy must have corked off!"

"You aren't going to close the case?" Jerry asked with astonishment.

Riley spread his large hands. "There was never a case. We won't forget what happened—if that's what you mean. But while I've been wasting my inadequate talents on the Stantons other people in other parts of town have been going haywire. There's a stack of stuff on my desk. There are three or four assignments the Chief wants me to start on. I came down here to say so long." He smoked a moment and stood. "Like to see you again—but people like me haven't very much opportunity to fool around."

Jerry shook his hand. They went to the door. In the hall the detective turned. "Look," he said. "I told the old lady I'd met you. She's noticed your name in some magazine. Say, if you happen to have one of those drawings you don't want to keep—I mean after it's been printed— would you—that is—she'd about burst with pride—if you see what I mean?"

Jerry realized that he had found his first true fan. "I'll send her one— one I was doing last week—as soon as it's returned."

"Elegant," said Riley. "Swell! She made me promise to ask. It's just twenty-two East Belliman Street, Brooklyn. Well . . ."

He was gone.

Jerry sat down alone in his studio. He couldn't believe it. All over, abandoned, nothing. Three men were dead—probably murdered—and nobody would try to find out any more about it. He wondered for a moment if money had silenced the inquiry. He decided that that was impossible. People like Riley, for example, were not for sale.

He went to bed at one o'clock—but it took him a long time to go to sleep. He felt deflated—disappointed almost. He had lived for a short time in a very unreal but extravagantly exciting world. Now the doors of that world were closed.

In the morning, he reflected, he ought really to go up to see Mr. Peck at the *Woman's Review*.

But he did not go that morning. When he rose there was a letter waiting in front of his door—a letter from Betty. She wrote:

Dear Jerry,

When you receive this I shall have left for Newport. We have decided to go to our place there—although summer is about ended. The whole family is coming up. We all feel we want to be together and we want rest and privacy. It's been terrible for all of us, of course. I feel for myself that I want time alone to think.

So I'm asking you not to come up—at least unless I write again. All that has happened has changed me somehow. The love I thought I had for you seemed all-important ten days ago. Now in the face of everything it seems sometimes strangely trivial. Please don't be angry with me. I just want to get to understand that. And please don't try to see me till I do. Good-bye.

Betty.

He read the note and read it over. Still standing in his hall, he tried reading it out loud. It continued to say the same incomprehensible things—in the same unfamiliar tone. He closed his door and carried the letter into his bedroom. He sat down on the bed and read it once more. Tears filled his eyes.

He thought he ought to rush to her at once. He thought the strain of the past days had been too much for her nature. Then bitterness crept into his mind and sullied it. Maybe the vast changes in her fortune had changed her personality. Maybe she felt free and no longer wanted him. Maybe she had used him only as a way of tormenting her brothers—as a tangible rebellion. At that stage, he cursed all women for being fickle and faithless. He cursed them with the aching savagery of a young man disillusioned in his first consuming love.

In that short hour he became a cynic. He would face the world and hide his hurt. By and by he dressed. He would work. Paint his head off. Someday she would see his masterpieces everywhere. In museums. She would remember. She would be saddened. She would regret.

And when he reached that decision he decided also to have some breakfast. He went to the restaurant where Holly usually ate and she was there. He said to her with cynical bluntness, "You look like sin this morning."

And Holly answered with the wanton perspicuity of woman-kind, "What's the matter? Fight with Betty?"

Then he sat down and told her everything. . . .

For three weeks he did work. Three long, arduous weeks.

Mr. Peck saw to that. He worked bitterly but successfully. The serial became his to illustrate. But in the same period his cynicism gradually thawed. He began to long for Betty. To recall scores of precious moments they had spent together. Kisses—promises—smiles shared. He grew to believe that the shock of those tragic August days had temporarily unbalanced her. He hit upon the idea that he was entitled to one last interview with her, whatever its consequences might be.

Thus, when his cynicism had thoroughly ebbed and his love had largely returned, he came to the day when it became obvious he must go.

VIII

It was a beautiful blue and golden day in early September. He packed a bag and took the train with elation.

Newport was magnificent.

The entrance to the Stanton estate, although forbidding, made his heart beat happily. His cab wound through a quarter mile of trees and shrubbery and he came upon Betty before he reached the house.

She and Molly and Leslie and Maude were playing darts in what was meant to be a badminton court. When the cab stopped, they halted the game and Betty came toward him slowly. A changed Betty—a Betty who used careful politeness to hide whatever her feelings were.

"Why—Jerry! Hello! This is a surprise! You know everybody. We're playing darts. Come on!"

"What'll I do with my things?"

"Things?" Betty asked him.

He was disconcerted—but he tried to grin. "Aren't you going to ask me to spend the night?"

"Well, as a matter of fact . . ." She looked at the others and then changed her mind. "Why, of course—do! Have the driver deliver them to Haynes at the house. And join us here. I'll find you a room when we're through."

So he found himself playing darts with them under a benevolent sky in the midst of a vast and exquisite lawn. Only Betty seemed changed. Maude accepted his arrival pleasantly. Les was quite genial. "After all we've been through, old man—great!" And Molly, as usual, didn't seem to notice the addition to their party.

Betty repeated, "This is a surprise!" She gave him darts with orange feathers. "Leslie's champion," she said, "and Maude's runner-up. Let's see what you can do! Stand here. How are things in town?"

He said they were fine. The tone of his welcome had disconcerted him. He had expected to be taken for a long and private walk by Betty. Now—he had to throw darts.

Jerry's manual skill was considerable. He hefted his dart and threw a bull's-eye. Then another. Maude was delighted. The game continued for a considerable time.

Then Betty suggested a swim.

The Stantons had a pool. Molly refused to swim but Leslie and his wife joined them. After the swim there were cocktails—an innovation in the Stanton family. After cocktails they sat around, trying to talk. Ordinarily they would have dressed. But Jerry had neglected to bring his dinner clothes. When dinner was finally served he discovered that Marcel still prepared the Stanton food. And he learned very little else.

Some people came in for bridge after that.

It was past ten o'clock when Betty suggested that Jerry might like to take a stroll with her. At that his spirits bounded.

They went out into the evening together. As always before, he felt the nearness of her, and her loveliness. He was on the verge of trying to take her in his arms when she said rather flatly, "You got my note, of course?"

"Yes. And obeyed it—till now."

"Jerry. You shouldn't have come."

"Why—darling?"

She walked a step from him and stood still. "It's hard to explain—if you don't understand. Impossible, I guess. But after Frank died—after all that—I just wasn't the same. Even about you. I felt as if I could never love anyone—with that dreadful shadow in my life. Don't you see even a little?"

And abruptly he did see—or at least he thought he saw. Betty believed her brothers had been murdered. She believed the murderer was still unpunished. She could not feel free to love or even to live while the assassin, whoever it was, went unknown and unpunished. That was like Betty as he had always pictured her! That made the tone of her wounding note not cold—but pitiful.

When he answered, his voice shook. "Sure. I do see—now, Betty!"

She turned hopefully. Her eyes shone strangely. "Then—you'll go away tomorrow? And you won't come back? Because it only makes me unhappy!"

He swallowed. He had expected a torrent of confidences. But she was too proud and too brave to divide her wretchedness even with him. Well, he would go away. But he would not rest now until the case which Riley had abandoned was laid bare to the light of day. He would do something—anything—to take the burden from the shoulders of the girl at his side.

He spoke gravely. "Yes. I'll go. But I love you, Betty. I can't bear to let you stay this way. I won't."

She didn't speak.

So he said sturdily and gallantly, "Shall we go back?"

"Yes—please let's."

It was when they reached the broad brick terrace which served as a porch for the mansion that the idea came to him. He was startled by its simplicity—astonished that no one had thought of it. It meant he would have to work fast. But it could be done. The thing amazed him. As Betty went through the door he said softly, "In fact, dear, I think I can promise to remove that shadow."

She looked at him queerly and walked toward her guests in the card room.

Jerry refused to play. He wanted to perfect his plan. It was psychological in essence. The Stantons had not seen him for some time. They could not know what he had been doing. He would find some little chance to tell each of them alone that he knew the truth about the murder. Then he would leave.

Thereafter Riley could arrange to have all the Stantons—and Haynes and Marcel—carefully watched. The first one to make a break would be caught. He would put his threat in such a way that the guilty person would be sure to make some kind of significant move.

It was eleven o'clock. He had at best only twelve hours. And yet he managed.

Haynes was first. He found Haynes alone in the hall, tinkering with a lampshade. "I don't suppose you ever knew," Jerry began, "that I've been closely connected with the police?"

Haynes certainly started. "What, sir?"

"Just that, Haynes. And the police know everything. I'm telling you—simply because I've just fought with the Chief. I want to spoil the plans he has made for next Monday."

Jerry went away, leaving Haynes shaken.

The pretext of wanting a glass of milk brought him in touch with Marcel. He led up gradually to the point at which he said, "The police know, Marcel, where the stuff was made and by whom. I needn't say what stuff. I mean—and I'll skip my reasons for telling you this."

The news reduced Marcel's face to ashes.

Maude he found pouring a drink at a sideboard while she was dummy. He explained that he had been connected with the police and she laughed. "Good heavens! How exciting!"

He stared at her. "I hate to have shame brought on this family," he continued gravely. "But in my official capacity I know enough about one member to bring shame on all of them."

Maude stared and spilled her highball. And Maude was the most composed of all.

When, in the upstairs hall he found Les that night and when he had made his fateful implication, he was afraid that Les was going to faint. But he didn't. He just staggered and finally whispered, "What has to be—has to be, I suppose!"

Molly turned gray and wiped her lips. She had been first down to breakfast—except for Jerry.

And when the chauffeur drove Jerry to his train he left behind him a stricken family. Their reactions had been so violent, in fact, that Jerry wondered if it weren't possible they all knew the truth—and if whatever had happened was not the result of conspiracy.

He was impatient to get back to New York—impatient to tell Riley what he had done. He was positive his stratagem would result in action of some sort—overt action—an attempt at escape—a signed confession.

Even a suicide.

He had not thought of that. It disconcerted him. Riley wouldn't approve of a suicide. Maybe it would be better to wait awhile before telling Riley—to see what happened first. Possibly he could find some way of checking up on the comings and goings of the Stantons and their servants without informing Riley. Then—when somebody departed, he could tell—and the police could take up the trail. That wasn't perfect, either.

The closer he came to New York the more perturbed he became. He decided to talk it over with Holly before he went any further.

The recklessness of what he had done seemed thoroughly appalling by the time his cab drew up in front of his own door. If, for instance, no one was guilty and someone nevertheless became so frightened he or she did something rash—the entire responsibility for the deed would be his.

Being an artist he thought in pictures and seldom from cause to effect. That characteristic came near to undoing him. Ultimately it saved him. But on the day of his return from Newport he was approaching panic. He could see the Stantons in various dire situations—all the result of his mad idea.

He dropped his suitcase and called Holly. Nobody answered her phone. He sat down and tried to think. He had been impelled to his drastic effort by sympathy for Betty—by an urge to remove the incubus which was wrecking her life. His own motive was clearly altruistic. Even, he reflected, if he had known that he would never see her again, he would undoubtedly have proceeded with his dubious scheme for her benefit. But now the likelihood of smoking out the guilty person with no further complications seemed to be less. Anything could happen.

When Holly did call—on the chance that he had returned—he made no effort to hide his feelings. "Come over here right away! I've done something terrible!"

She came. Her very appearance was comforting. She was wearing slacks and her heavy hair dropping occasionally over her dark blue eyes made her toss her head in an old and familiar way. Holly was solid stuff. She sat and listened without interrupting.

But as she listened something happened to Holly. The sturdy youthfulness inherent in her was gradually shattered. She began to grow anxious. She lighted a cigarette and walked around the room. She shot quick expectant glances at him. Her behavior brought back his anxiety.

He finished as quickly as he could. "So I told them all—in different ways. I let Marcel and Haynes think I was doing it because I had quarreled with the police. I intimated to the various members of the family that I was telling them to prevent further scandal."

Holly gulped. "You told—everybody?"

"Haynes—Marcel—Maude—Les—Molly."

"But not Betty?"

He jumped. "Betty! Lord, no!"

"Didn't it ever occur to you that she had the same motives you did—at least insofar as John and Paul were concerned?" She hesitated and watched him closely. "As for Frank—maybe he found out too much—so that was why he died. Frank was the nicest of the three.

"Then look at all the money that came to her. And finally—she was with Frank when it happened—and for all you know she could have been up early on the morning John died. She knew where Paul was going to speak and probably saw him before he left. She—"

Jerry was shaking his head. "It couldn't have been Betty—"

Holly put out her cigarette and then lighted another immediately. "I hope," she said slowly, "I hope with all my heart it wasn't anybody in the family! Or Marcel. Or Haynes. I hope—they just died!"

"Why?" He sounded dull and uncomprehending.

She turned to face him—quickly and almost angrily. "Because, you idiot, don't you see what you've done? Can't you think at all! If one of those people to whom you gave that little message of yours really is a murderer—is that person going to run away? Hardly! He—or she—feels safe. There's no evidence. All three of the dead men have been cremated. The only real threat now—is you!"

He felt as if he had been struck in the pit of the stomach. He knew his scalp tingled—but it was a second before he realized that his hair was slowly rising. His eyes bulged.

Holly went on talking. "If you happened to connect with a guilty individual he'll know the police aren't after him. Because when the police have something to act on—boy, they act! He'll think, though, that you have gotten on to something he forgot or overlooked."

She bent toward him. "Jerry! Do you realize what a spot you're in? Do you remember that those three men died in the midst of crowds—and in a dentist's private office—with people all around? Dropped dead! And they were autopsied—or one was—and the medical examiner himself couldn't prove anything. Don't you see that whatever was done—if anything was—was fearfully clever? And if the person who killed those three—supposing they were killed—wants now to kill you—it would be a cinch!"

He nodded. He was breathing heavily. "Yeah."

"Where'd you ever get a cockeyed idea like that, anyhow!"

"It just came to me."

"Maybe you read it. Maybe cops do things like that sometimes. But cops are in that business. They know how to protect themselves. What are we going to do?"

"Tell Riley right away!"

She paused. "Maybe that would be a good idea. I'll get him on the phone."

And she did. "This is Holly Parker," she said. "And my boyfriend has just done something dreadfully dumb." There was a pause. "Yes, I know you've been called off the Stanton business. But listen . . ." She talked swiftly and earnestly. When she had finished she listened awhile. Then she hung up. Her hand was shaking. She looked as if she were going to burst into tears.

"Is he coming right away?" Jerry asked feebly.

"Not coming at all, Jerry. He said that in the first place he had come to believe the three Stantons just died. In the second he said you had no business to pull a gag like that. He gave me the devil on your account. Said, think of what you'd done to the people who were innocent. And he said finally, that whatever the Stanton business was, it was too fancy for the police. He told me — Jerry, he laughed and told me that if you dropped dead playing pinball in a drug store he'd believe in the murder theory again and re-open the case!"

He stared at her pallidly and said nothing.

That was the beginning of the worst two days in Jerry's life. They would have been bad days in the life of any man, however adventurous, however accustomed to danger.

Because he did not know, in the first place, whether or not he was in any danger.

In the second place, there was no way of guessing the nature of his peril — if indeed there were peril. A man who expects to be shot can stay under cover. A man afraid of being poisoned can select his own food. But a man afraid of sudden and agonizing death that comes mysteriously — in a crowd or in the privacy of an office — in a public railroad station even — has no means of protecting himself.

The first day he stayed in. Holly went out and bought his food — eggs and things in cans. On the second day his apartment began to seem a more lethal region than the street. He went walking alone — because Holly was compelled to do some work.

He strolled up Fifth Avenue in the bright sunlight. He sat for a little while near the Library lions. He came downtown on Sixth — walking all the way. And all the time, in the heart of the familiar city, he felt that death might come suddenly upon him.

He was so badly frightened that he was barely able to get back into his house. When he unlocked his own door he swung it open, stepped back and ducked. No one was there. Nothing happened.

"I can't go out," he told Holly that evening. "I can't stand it. When a car backfired beside me today I had to hang onto a lamppost for five minutes to pull myself together. A man popped out from behind an elevated pillar down by Twenty-third Street. I thought he was popping at me—and I almost socked him before I realized that he hadn't even seen me. It's awful!"

Holly nodded. She pulled down the blinds in the studio. She could readily understand that it was awful. For horror, whether real or imaginary, was stalking him not by night, not in the lonely places but by the blinding light of day and in the tumult of the city. It was a nameless horror—swift, explicit. A deadly horror.

Familiarity with it might make it wear off in time. It might break him down utterly instead. Holly shared some of that incredible feeling. The secret killer they had hypothecated might assume that she also knew whatever he was supposed to know. When she walked the public streets and when she lay down on her bed the fear of death was her constant companion too.

"If we only knew what to expect," she said for the hundredth time. "If we could only guess! I wouldn't mind waiting for bullets—or a stab. I wouldn't mind worrying about my food. But this is so . . . !"

He sighed. "The police gave up. They couldn't find anything. Not a capsule in his stomach—or a wound on his body. Even supposing he had been stuck, by somebody dexterous and accurate, with any kind of a weapon that could . . ."

And then he stopped talking. For Jerry's mind had suddenly reeled off a new set of pictures. It had been overworking during the past days, presenting dramatic cinemas of his own collapse and speedy death. But now other scenes flooded his imagination and some inner resource of his mind connected them up—pictures of the darts game he had reluctantly played at Newport and pictures of the three men in the instant before their seizures. Maybe darts were wrong but . . . !

He straggled across the room. He dropped limply into a chair. Holly thought for an instant that it had happened. She cried out and ran toward him.

"I've got it!" he whispered. "I've got it!"

"Darling!"

"I know how they did it!"

"Oh." Her sanity came back slowly. Her abject fright turned into excitement. "You mean you've figured out—"

Strength was shooting into his veins. "Have I! I'll say so! My God—it's the grimmest idea I ever dreamed of! An accident the first time! After that a deliberate scheme! And they'll never prove it now! Never! Only if—hey! Let's get Riley! He'll believe me! He's got a lot of brains—for a cop! Maybe we can figure out some way . . ."

Holly shook him. "Are you nuts? Or are you going to quit babbling and tell me what you're thinking?"

"Yeah. Get Riley, though."

And he told her.

IX

When Riley came, after much argument, and sat sardonically in the good chair, Jerry talked hard and fast for several minutes. Riley's amused skepticism slowly vanished. He became less a genial Irishman and increasingly a taut scowling vengeful human engine.

When Jerry finished he said, "Kid, I think you've hit it! But by all the saints and devils—it's a terrifying hunch! Look! If you're right you may be in danger—real danger!"

Jerry was relaxing for the first time in two days. "Sure. But if I'm right I know what not to do."

"Mmm, yeah. Say—how's your nerve?"

"Shot."

"I can believe it! But I'm serious! I want you to do—just what you ought not to do."

"Are you crazy?"

"We'll take precautions. Let's see . . ." Riley's eyes traveled around the room in speculation. "Plate glass—might show." He fastened his gaze on the theatrical masks which Jerry had made long ago and now used to decorate his rooms. "Holy mackerel! Boy—if this comes out, Jenks, I'll nab that inspectorship!"

They went to work.

It didn't "come out" the first night. They tried their experiment at twelve—and again at two. Holly and Jerry alone in the apartment—she peering cautiously from behind the front window blinds and he waiting tremulously in the bedroom.

Nothing happened on the second night.

On the third Riley said, "We'll give it one more whirl. If we draw a blank, then we'll have to quit. I can't waste my life on a trick I think is more rattle-brained every day!"

"I can't stand it much longer either," Jerry replied nervously.

At midnight it failed.

At one Holly made another of her countless verbal reports from the window to the bedroom. "Taxi stopping. Man getting out." A new note crept into her voice. "He's got a violin case!" Jerry waited feverishly. "He's going into the next entry! He just looked up and down the street! Now the cab's driving away. Jerry—do you think . . . ?"

She came quickly into the bedroom. He was sitting on the bed, shaking. His window was wide open. "I don't think. I'll do it again. But get out of the way!"

She stepped back into the hall. He sat still for about ten minutes. Then he muttered, "Time enough?"

She nodded.

Squatting on the bed he made his final preparations and checked them in a hand mirror. He was as white as paper and trembling violently. Holly, watching from the door, could feel her heart hammering painfully. He stood up on his bed. He took off his coat and vest and tossed them across the open window on to a chair.

After that he turned out the bright light in his room, which left burning only a small lamp on the window sill. Next, giving the appearance of casual ease, he stepped down from his bed, walked over toward the window, stood in front of it and stretched. As he walked and as he stood there, his mouth was open in a wide yawn.

When it came—it was almost nothing—a faint whizz, a soft minute thump.

Holly screamed.

Jerry fell back on the bed, away from the window, and ripped the mask from his face.

From across the courtyard in the wing of the building which faced Jerry's bedroom there came three rapid pistol shots. After that fusillade there was an instant of dead quiet. It seemed as if everybody in the building—everybody in the block—had stopped breathing.

Holly crawled across the room under the window sill on her hands and knees to Jerry's side. "Are you all right? Jerry!"

His eyes reassured her.

She reached for the mask.

"Don't touch it," he said.

There was an uproar then—in the courtyard and in the building. Windows were being shoved up. People were shouting.

Holly looked at the mask with hysterical concentration.

It lay on the bed. It had been made of metal—carefully painted by Jerry to duplicate his own cheeks, cheekbones, ears, mouth and jaws. The mouth of the mask was wide open and the teeth bared. But the mouth was not a mere hole. Behind it was a cup of heavy metal—a cup which fitted exactly over the backs of the teeth and which Jerry had taken into his own mouth when he put it on. Thus the cup had held his mouth wide open and the mask itself had given him the appearance of yawning.

For that was what Jerry had realized when he had shouted that he understood the mystery.

On the balcony at the station above John Stanton had been the huge lithographs advertising New England. A good shot, concealed behind the display, could easily have discharged the missile into John's mouth. It would have penetrated the back of his throat.

Paul had been shouting his speech as he faced a row of apartment buildings. Jerry had even remembered that almost his last word had been, "Ahhh." A syllable that had opened his mouth widely. And there were buildings across the street. Hiding places.

Frank had been in the dentist's chair—with his mouth propped wide—on a hot day when undoubtedly the window had been open.

Jerry's habit of thinking in pictures had solved the problem. No doubt the murderer had first intended merely to hit his victim with a missile containing poison. But John's yawn had been an unforeseen opportunity. The wound made by the missile would have been small. Perhaps it had not even bled.

The victim would have felt a twinge of pain and swallowed or coughed. And no doctor would have found the place unless he were looking for it. After that first lucky opportunity the murderer had waited for—open mouths.

Now Holly stared into the bottom of the cup in the mask, where there was a large wad of absorbent material. "It's wet," she whispered, "and there are little bits of broken glass. Thank heaven he was a good shot! If he had hit your eyes or forehead . . . !"

Jerry was too frightened to say anything.

A minute later Riley burst into the apartment. His face was gray and sweating.

"Are you all right, Jerry?" he yelled.

"Yeah. I caught it in that cup!"

Riley grinned weakly, swayed and flopped on the bed. He patted Jerry's back. He panted, "Thank heaven for that! If she'd missed I'd never have forgiven myself! I guess I wouldn't have been a party to this if I'd really believed it was coming off."

Holly was staring. "She?"

Riley had picked up the mask and looked at the fragment of glass and the wet spot. "She's dead. I had to shoot. I was standing in the dark, one flight above her, when she came up the stairs. She took her rifle out of a violin case. It was an old-fashioned German air gun."

He tipped the mask to throw more light into its cup. "She must have made these glass bullets herself. When I saw she was actually going to do it I covered her and called to her to drop her gun. I could see you standing over there. But she shot and turned at me and said as coldly as I ever heard anybody speak, 'It's a repeater.' I didn't wait after that."

Holly had been struggling for words—or a word. Now she found it. Her voice was ghastly. "Betty . . . ?"

Only then did Riley realize they didn't know. "Maude," he answered quietly. "Who else? She was the hunter of the family. A swell shot with a rifle. I don't know." He looked down at the floor, as stunned as they were. "Greed—those millions. Her husband was the poorest of the Stantons. She was a bold extraverted person. Probably she hated the snide and snooty family she had married. Despised her husband's cousins. Maybe she was insane."

Other people were banging on the door now. A policeman came down the hall, calling, "You in there, Captain Riley?"

"Yeah. I got to beat it now, kids." He stood up and looked at Jerry. "All the rest of my life, Jenks, whenever I hear anybody talk about guts, I'll think of you." He started away with the policeman. "I imagine you fellows won't sleep tonight. Want one of my men to keep you company?"

Jerry tried to keep on being brave. "We'll make out all right."

"I'll detail one anyhow. Help keep the reporters in line. And anyway you need a chaperon."

The reporters weren't finished until four. Then Jerry had coffee sent up from an all-night restaurant. At five it began to grow light. At seven they heard the ebullient voice of a newsboy—"Young artist traps century's cleverest murderess!"

They were almost the very headlines Holly had imagined in a flight of fancy some days before.

At eight the telephone rang. He recognized the voice—a voice frantic and ecstatic. "Darling! It's Betty! Molly just woke me up and told me! I had to call you right away! It's so wonderful! You see, I've thought all this time that you had done it. That's why I didn't want to see you—why I acted so funny! I'll get dressed and catch the first train to town! Oh—you don't know how relieved I feel!"

Jerry was staring into space. His voice was flat. "Don't bother."

"What?"

"I'll be busy this morning."

"Then let me know the first minute I can see you!"

He hung up. He looked at Holly and his blank expression slowly became angry. "She thought all the time I did it! I can't believe it! I must have been crazy! Can you imagine wanting to marry a girl who would go along for weeks actually believing you'd murdered her three brothers. And all the time I thought we were both in love."

Holly didn't say anything.

Jerry shook his head. "We'd never have been happy—never!"

She walked to the window.

The phone rang again, loudly.

"Oh, Jerry—this is Riley. Can you come down to Headquarters? The Commissioner wants to meet you. And by the way it was aconitine."

"Where did she get it?"

"We'll never know. Possibly swiped it from the laboratory of one of her husband's friends. I've just been talking to her husband, incidentally. He knew it—or suspected it. That's why he was so frightened. Why he wanted to take her away. Les had spent most of the money he inherited from his father and grandfather. His income as an engineer wasn't anywhere near big enough for Maude's ambitions. She had been riding him about it for years.

"Besides, Les was the only member of the family who knew what was behind that woman's good-natured exterior." A chill came in Riley's voice. "You see, Les had gone hunting with her once in Africa. He said a few things about the way she went out to make a kill—well, if I'd seen 'em I'd have gotten a divorce and bodyguard."

Jerry whistled.

"I found out what Molly had on her mind too. She's just announced that she's going back on the stage—producing her own play. With Frank dead and all that dough she realized she could return to the only life she ever cared about. There's another thing. A couple of weeks before John died Maude had engaged the whole family in conversation about poison. She had plenty of brass! Of course everybody remembered that talk—even Haynes. It's no wonder they were scared of each other.

"And look! Bring that Holly girl along with you when you come! It's none of my business—but I can't see why you looked twice at a pale thin blonde like Betty when all day, every day, you've got nature's own gift to a young man practically sitting in your lap!"

He hung up.

Jerry put down the phone.

Holly was perplexed by his expression. It seemed to be concentrated on her. "What did he say?" she asked. "What makes you look at me like that, Jerry?"

"Something," Jerry replied, "that just simply hadn't crossed my mind until now. Something perfectly obvious. Something that's beginning to make me feel very strange all over, and realize what a fool I've been."

"What are you talking about?"

He stood up. "Remember when I figured out how this was done? Didn't you, in the heat of excitement, call me darling?"

Then she understood his expression. She blushed. "Oh!" she said.

Jerry was beginning to grin. He was becoming his old self for the first time in weeks. "One pace closer, nature's gift," he said enigmatically.

Holly came a step closer and the enigma was solved.

THE PARADISE CANYON MYSTERY

I

It was three-twenty a.m. Jim heaved his battered suitcases from beneath the day coach seats and walked past sleeping passengers to the vestibule. A solitary red light slid through the blackness, and the train stopped.

"Paradise Canyon!" a distant voice shouted.

He descended to the lowest step and jumped. He gazed toward the station. A pale lamp made one window yellow. Somebody else was getting off the train. He looked at the sky, where the Dippers swung in dim tandem around the Polar Star. That was familiar—but not the sky's rim: jagged, lofty perimeter of mountains, from the summits of which snow and ice cast ghostly reflections down upon the desert where he stood.

The desert! Jim took a long inhalation of sharper air than he had ever breathed before and smelled dust and mesquite and cactus blossoms invisible in the enshrouding night. Then, carrying his luggage, he walked toward the lamps of the one car parked beside the station. Its driver followed the other nocturnal arrival, pushing a trunk and several bags in a handcart. The other arrival was a woman.

"Mr. Preston?"

"Right!" Jim called to the driver.

"I'll unload your stuff in the trunk in the rear." He turned to the woman. "You don't mind another person? It's Mr. Preston, the new swimming instructor."

"I don't mind a bit. How do you do, Mr. Preston?"

"Thanks," Jim said. He grinned to himself. They had told him in New York that the Paradise Canyon Hotel was snooty. But having to ask a guest if she would ride in the same car with the swimming director certainly was snootiness of the foremost rank. Ed finished loading the luggage and handed them a lap robe. He started the car.

For ten lengthy minutes they drove through the darkness, and the girl did not speak. Jim had perceived that she wore a fur coat, had a tilted nose, wasn't tall, and used a bittersweet perfume that smelled like the desert. Then his attention wandered from an imaginary reconstruction of the girl at his side to an examination of the fascinating objects which he glimpsed in the beam of the headlights: cacti, palms, poinsettias, adobe walls, dunes.

At the end of ten minutes he said, almost involuntarily, "It's grand!"

He could tell that the girl was smiling.

"The desert?" she asked. "Never seen it before?"

"No."

"It's fun. My stepfather enjoys it because of the hunting. Mother likes to be where she can see movie stars in the flesh."

"Where's your home?"

"Cleveland." She was silent for a time. Then she said, "You aren't Jimmy Preston, the Olympic champion, by any chance, are you?"

"Yes."

"You sound as if you resented being an Olympic champion," she said.

Jim pondered that. In a way, he did resent it. The whole world could get excited about his time for swimming fifty yards and about the way he dived. But nobody was interested in a scrappy, red-headed kid who augmented his mother's pitiful wages by hawking newspapers, worked his way through school and college, and earned a degree in engineering, with honors.

The desert road unrolled beneath the wheels of the car. Athletic ability had made his undergraduate days easier. But he had always felt it unfair that his full twist dive interested more people than the engineering degree he had earned. And, after graduation, though no one had wanted hydroelectric plants designed by him, a great many people had desired his services as a coach. He had fought against it for four years, but finally had accepted the offer of the Paradise Canyon Hotel to be pool tender and coach to its guests. He had wanted from boyhood to be an engineer. Now he was a professional athlete.

He said, "On the contrary. Can you imagine an easier life?"

"It must be swell!" She was trying to be nice, and make him understand that she did not mind the social and cultural gap between them.

"Just dandy! Following the sun. Miami and the desert in the winter. Northern resorts in summer. Making a living by playing!"

"Elegant!"

This, he thought, was to be his due all winter—the patronage of the rich. A good many of them wouldn't even try to flatter his feelings. They'd just order him about like a servant: "I want my water wings inflated and ready at ten, Mr. Preston!"

The car turned under an arch, swept through a double row of tall palms, and stopped in front of an immense hotel, where only the elevator shafts, the lobby, and fire exits showed lights.

When their eyes were accustomed to the brightness of the lobby they faced each other in common curiosity. Frankie Bailey laughed. "You've got red hair and blue eyes. I thought you were dark."

He grinned. "And you've got black hair. I'd have bet you were a blonde."

"Why?"

"Can't say. The perfume, maybe."

Her eyes were surprised, as if swimming coaches should not know the difference between the proper perfume for blondes and brunettes. Gray eyes, she had, set wide apart.

The night clerk came forward. "Miss Bailey! I'm delighted! Your mother and father are in bungalow fifteen. Same one you had last year."

"I'll sneak in, and go to sleep. I'm dead! Good night, Mr. Preston."

"Oh, Preston," the clerk said. "Your quarters are on the top floor—Room 611. I haven't a boy to help you with your things—"

Jim looked pleasantly at the clerk. "I can manage." He watched Frankie Bailey cross the lobby and go through a rear door into a garden. He stared for a moment at the luxurious furniture in the vast room, at the paintings of the mountains, at the embers in the huge stone fireplace. Then he started toward the elevators.

His room was larger than the clammy manner of the clerk had predicted. It had four windows, and Navaho rugs on the floors, a comfortable bed with wool blankets, three chairs, a desk, prints of desert flowers, and a private bath. He looked at his watch. Half past four. Soon be light. He didn't feel sleepy. The new universe he was to inhabit lay unknown all around him. So he took a shower and shaved. Not knowing the conventional desert costume, he put on the clothes he had worn on the train. Then he went down to the main floor.

The clerk was still at his desk.

"I'm going out for a stroll," Jim said. "Just to look the land over. Where can I get some breakfast?"

"At six, here. Any time, downtown." The clerk yawned at him.

Jim walked down the palm avenue in the dark. Beyond it was a street that led to the radiance of neon signs. He turned toward them and found an all-night restaurant, where he had coffee and eggs. Then he continued his walk. Forty or fifty stores, three hotels, a couple of hundred homes, a golf course, a movie theater, a half-dozen tearooms and cafes—and, surrounding it all, the desert.

It became lighter. He found a trail that led toward the base of the overhanging peaks. He followed it.

Soon the world through which he walked became very silent. The trail underfoot was stony. It meandered through a dry, light undergrowth of stuff he didn't know—bushes and plants and leafless trees and cacti that were like barrels and others that were like octopuses, and still others that were like railway semaphores—grotesque, impossible, meaningless in the murky light. Then he began to climb, and realized that he was on the mountainside. Beyond the town the gray desert floor rolled toward invisibility. He climbed up the path through boulders and slabs of rock. Finally he sat down on one of them. He remembered that there were rattlesnakes in the desert, and hopped up to examine his environment, but it was untenanted.

Then dawn began to break. Lemon light hovered in the east. Behind him the snow fields became blue, then salmon, then gold, and finally, blazing white. Colors surged across the desert floor—here a greenish carpet, there a pink dune, far away an abyss of cobalt blue. Whole mountains of purple and red shot up in the distance. When the first warm rays of the sun touched him he took off his coat. The cool and moving air before sunrise stood still. Warmth became heat. The colors were bleached out before his gaze. He did not budge until the full and majestic ritual was finished, until the dye was gone from the scenery and only a furnacelike radiance remained. Then he looked at his watch. It was after six.

As he made the movement there was a remote but sharp crack, and his tie flickered. He looked down, alarmed, thinking of snakes. A gash had appeared in his tie, cutting it almost in half. Someone had shot at him.

He started toward the direction of the sound for a split second, and then jumped down behind the boulder on which he had been sitting.

A voice floated unreally to his ears. "Hey!" it said.

"Hey!" Jim yelled back, half in fright and half in anger.

What had happened? Jim peered around his refuge. Far away, along the side of the mountain, he saw a man scrambling toward him. The man was calling, "Are you hurt?"

"No!" Jim bellowed back, across the gulf between them.

"Wait there!"

Minute by minute the man came nearer. He was obviously moving fast, but for a long time he looked like a fly crawling on a wall. Finally, he was near.

"I'm sorry!" he called.

He wore breeches, puttees and a flannel shirt. He had a goatee. His face was very white. He was middle-aged, but he moved with a hard alacrity.

"You're not hit?" the man said, as he came up.

"Nope. Only my necktie. But what's—"

The man stared at Jim. His eyes were not exactly frightened. Excited, rather. "It's that brown shirt. Just the right color. Faded, isn't it?"

Jim ignored the slight upon his haberdashery. "Right color for what?"

"A lion. Panther. Light was poor. I was using my telescopic sight. Your back looked just like a lion's when you moved. You're lucky. Astonishing you aren't dead. Can't understand missing. Must be a strong air eddy up the hillside . . . Oh. My name's Dr. Galt. I'm a guest at the Paradise Canyon Hotel.

"Mine's Preston. I'm the new swimming coach there. Where's your rifle?"

The doctor was by then quite calm. He smiled. "Left it, to expedite getting here. Thought you'd fallen back, hit. Don't bother about the gun. I'll send some of the boys out to find it. What do you say we go back?"

"Thanks," Jim answered, "but I'm going to walk a bit farther."

"Right. By the way—bill me for a new tie—eh?"

"Sure," Jim said.

The doctor started down the path. Jim stared at his back. Funny bird. Any normal person would have been frightened nearly to death by so close an approach to manslaughter. Bill me for the tie! Jim climbed back on the rock. "Shaking like a leaf." he said to himself. Then he began to laugh. "Some place," he said to nothing. "Been here three hours and I see the handsomest girl ever made, and the best sunrise, and the biggest jackass."

He started back.

II

He had crossed about half of the desert floor that lay between the mountain's precipitous foot and the village, when there was a crackling in the brush along the trail. He was frightened again. He thought, now, not of snakes, but of the lions the doctor had mentioned. What did one do for lions? He grabbed up a large rock, and waited.

A horse walked easily from the bushes, saw him, and stopped.

Jim greeted it with relief. "Hello, horse." He dropped the rock. The horse moved a step nearer, looking at Jim. There was a saddle on it, but nobody in the saddle. This desert, he thought, is thick with people. He raised his voice so that it would canvass the adjoining acres:

"Hey! Anybody lost a horse?"

Nobody replied. Jim chuckled. Doubtless somebody taking an early ride had been thrown. The rider was walking back—and so was the horse. So, gently calling, "Whoa boy!" he started toward it. The horse was big and handsome. There was silver filigree on the saddle.

Jim caught the bridle. He started to lead the horse. And then he stopped.

Why not ride? He went round the horse. The left stirrup was gone. "Well!" Jim exclaimed. He looked at its attachment. It was the sort that comes free if a fallen rider catches his foot and is in danger of being dragged. Someone had taken a really nasty spill. Jim's exploratory hand came away from the saddle with blood on it. Then he observed that on the off side blood had trickled down the cinch. The saddle, in front, was soggy with blood. But where the horseman had sat, it was clean. That meant the rider had started to bleed on his horse, fallen, caught his foot, and pulled the stirrup free.

Jim tied the horse to a bush and hurried off in the direction from which the animal had come. He followed the tracks for a hundred yards and then lost them in the record made by other desert riders. He called, but was not answered.

Running back to the trail, he untied the horse, and started leading it toward town. He was within sight of the spot where the paved street began when he saw a man coming toward him. It was Dr. Galt.

"I thought," the doctor said, as he approached, "I'd come back and intercept you. See you've captured somebody's mount. Why didn't you ride in?"

Jim was going to tell him, and then checked himself.

"Want you to do me a favor." Dr. Galt tugged at his black goatee. "If you will. Say nothing about the little—accident—we had this morning. I'd hate to have it known that my carelessness with a firearm—you understand how I feel?"

"I'm afraid I'll have to say something about it. Look."

The other man followed Jim's finger. While he examined the bloodstains, Jim scrutinized him. Dr. Galt lost color. That was all.

"Somebody's had a bad fall."

"You think so?"

"I imagine so. Fallen—cut himself—mounted again—and perhaps fainted from loss of blood."

"Or been shot."

The doctor's face sagged. "Good heavens! But that's absurd! Preposterous!" Then he caught Jim's shoulders in strong fingers. "Look here. I must recover the rifle at once! That'll be my insurance against any suspicion. See here, young man, if you implicate me by telling of our misadventure this morning, you'll only confuse the issue and give—but why presume?"

"That's what I was wondering," Jim answered. "Did you by any chance hear a shot this morning?"

The doctor did not reply. He started rapidly toward the mountain. "Be back in an hour," he called.

The man was either crazy, or guilty, or both. Jim considered chasing him. Instead, he hurried into town.

In fifteen minutes he learned that the horse belonged to the hotel riding master, a man named Poling, and that Poling had gone out at five, alone. In the same fifteen minutes the two policemen of Paradise Canyon had organized a posse, on horses and in cars, to look for Poling.

Jim went into the hotel. There was life there now, and for the first time, he saw it completely. Besides the six-story building, with its lobby-lounge and vast dining room, there was, on the side toward the mountain, a series of landscaped streets lined with Spanish bungalows. There were gardens and fountains. A brook meandered through the private village. There were three tennis courts. In the distance was the swimming pool. From the rear veranda of the building he could see the diving platforms and the bathhouses. At one corner, down the farthest of the short streets, were stables and a riding ring, all in all a sumptuous and charming arrangement for living healthfully, if expensively, in the sun. A man in white flannels approached Jim.

"Mr. Preston?"

"Yes."

"I'm Howard, the manager. Glad you're here. Had breakfast yet?"

"Not yet. That is—I had some very early."

The man was tall and blond. He had a wide, pleasant face built over-amply around a wide and not so pleasant mouth.

In a few words Jim described his adventures. The shock Jim's narrative made on Mr. Howard was only less noticeable than his effort to accept the story casually. His big face became absolutely bloodless.

He said, "Very strange that Poling should get hurt while riding. He was an expert. But you can never tell—"

"I suppose not."

Howard seemed anxious to be rid of Jim.

He waved his arm.

"I'll show you around when you've eaten. Go to the rear dining-room, near the kitchen. Ask for Sam."

"Thanks." Jim walked through the dining-room, thinking to himself that Howard had a hunch and it had frightened him.

He pushed open the kitchen door and yelled for Sam.

A jovial, rugged-looking man in a waiter's coat hurried up. Jim identified himself, and for the first time, he was made to feel that his advent to Paradise Canyon was not an intrusion.

"Oh—yes. Mr. Preston. I'll hustle you some breakfast. Just ask for anything. I'm the person to get it for you." He hurried into the kitchen and returned with oatmeal and silverware. "Hear you had a narrow squeak this morning."

"You did? What did you think of it?"

"I don't ever think—just listen." Sam laughed. "And you found Poling's horse."

"Yeah." Jim ate.

"He'll be the maddest man in the country. He used to be a cowboy. Came here from Texas. Why, that bird could ride standing on one hand!"

Sam went out laughing. He returned very quietly—with Jim's eggs. "They just brought Poling in," he said.

Jim looked up, startled.

"Shot—through the heart."

"Oh," Jim said.

Sam was very serious. "I guess Dr. Galt'll have a lot of explaining to do."

"Did they know each other?"

"Yeah, they did. And didn't like each other. Poling has made a joke around here of the way Galt rode. And last year Poling took two thousand dollars from the doctor at a bridge game."

"Still—" Jim said.

Sam shrugged. "You never know how far a razzing can get under a guy's skin."

Jim went back to the lobby, after thanking Sam for serving his breakfast. Mr. Howard took him to the pool and showed him the system for keeping records, the water-heating plant, the filter, and the chlorinator. When that was finished Jim was summoned by the two local cops and the mayor. He repeated his story. He didn't learn much. Poling had been popular. They had found him in the mesquite, with a 30-40 rifle bullet lodged against his backbone. He'd kept in the saddle for fifty feet, trailing blood. Then he'd fallen. And, lying there, he'd tried, with his last drop of consciousness, to write something in the sand. His finger had scrawled a letter "G". That was all. "G" was Galt's initial. And Galt was still missing.

Afterward, Jim returned to the pool, to his new duties. It was ten o'clock. He sat down in a canvas chair. He couldn't get his mind off the red saddle.

A handsome brunette girl came to the pool. Her face was so familiar that Jim said, "Hello!" and then racked his brain in an effort to place her. She smiled, and said, "Hello," and dived. She dived neatly, and it was only when she came up that Jim realized he did not know her at all, personally. She was Arlina McKay, of Diamond Pictures.

He was still blushing when another girl said "Good morning!"

He turned. Frankie Bailey was approaching with an older woman who looked like her and a man about thirty, tall, bony, and bespectacled.

"My mother, Mrs. Farnham," she said. "Mr. Preston. We drove here together last night. And, Mr. Willet, my fiance."

Jim was surprised that Frankie was engaged to such a person. She looked, in the bright daylight, like a calm and quiet person with a good sense of humor and a love of life. Willet was apparently humorless, irascible, silly, and fond, if not of books, at least of chairs.

She walked out on the diving board, looked up, made her four-step run, and did a competent half gainer.

Willet began to talk as if he seldom stopped. "Nice diver. Loves sports. Fine girl. Told me about your ride up here last night. Said you were a champion, or something. Can't go in for such things myself. Weak constitution. Why not get out and show her up? She needs discipline. I can't do anything with her. Not even make her marry me, after four years of steady effort."

"Herb!" Mrs. Farnham said. "Maybe Mr. Preston isn't interested in your troubles with Frankie."

"Should be," Herb answered. "All the gossip columnists are. Print the whole sad story annually. Where's Galt, Mother? Always around here putting the evil eye on Frankie. Probably taking one of his morning walks." He looked at Jim as if soliciting sympathy. "This fellow Galt has been chasing Frankie here on the desert every winter. Though I don't think Frankie likes him especially."

"Herb!" Mrs. Farnham said again. "I think I'll knit. Do you mind running back to my cottage for my knitting bag?"

"Not a bit." He started limply toward the bungalows.

"Mr. Preston," Mrs. Farnham said, "I presume Herb will be here at the pool a lot. Don't mind him."

Jim, who had been completely flabbergasted by the man's self-abnegatory, intimate, rambling discourse, answered earnestly, "I won't."

"But don't pity him, either. He's really quite bright."

"Sometimes," Frankie called, climbing out of the pool.

Jim walked to meet her.

"Look," he said, "you'll hear about this any minute, so I'm going to tell you." And, in a few sentences, he gave her the high points of the morning's tragedy.

"It's too terrible to seem real," she said when he had finished. "But, look. I know Henry Galt well—"

"So your fiance said."

She regarded him harshly. "Mr. Preston, you're new here. You don't know the people. Somebody may have shot Ted Poling, but it wasn't the doctor."

"But where—"

"Probably out walking—and worrying over what he almost did to you."

Jim climbed out of the water. "You don't happen to know what kind of rifle he had, do you?"

"I should. I gave it to him. It was a .30–40."

The swimmers had commenced to emerge from the dressing-rooms. Jim turned toward them, but he said to the girl, "That's what killed the riding master. A .30-40 rifle."

She lost all her color. "Of course—he might have had two accidents—but—"

Jim assumed that under normal conditions the afternoon would be very gay. People would crowd the pool and the tennis courts. The orchestra would play at four on the veranda. But, on this day, few people engaged in sports, and the grounds were dotted with small clusters of persons deep in conversation. Mr. Howard, the manager, had told Jim that on warm evenings he was to keep the pool open, with floodlights on, till ten o'clock. He did so, although no one came to swim.

Sam brought his supper in containers. He had little information. "They're having the coroner's jury tomorrow. Hundred people out hunting for Galt. Some detectives from Los Angeles flew in at noon. But I don't think they'll get anywhere."

"Why?"

"Because Galt was smart. He probably figured a getaway before he shot the guy."

Sam left. Jim heard him walking through the orange trees toward the main building. He pulled a table up to the wall around the pool and spread his supper on it. He sat down, out of the glare of the lights and began to eat.

Something fell with a splash into the pool near where he sat. Puzzled, Jim rose and went over to see what it was. He bent over the illuminated water and caught the flash of a sinking object. Then he was shoved hard from behind. He sank, pushed on the bottom, swam a few strokes, and surged up on the deck. There was nobody. He ran into the dark, dripping and tried to see who had crept up to duck him. He observed nobody. Then he hurried back to the pool and looked along its bottom. He saw something shiny there. Plunging in again, he came up with it. A half-dollar.

Someone had tossed a half-dollar into the water and, when he'd gone to investigate the splash, shoved him in. That was absurd. Senseless. Maybe somebody—Frankie's dopey fiance, for example—was trying to kid him. A poor time for practical jokes.

He called the desk on the pool phone. Mr. Howard heard his report. "Change your clothes, Preston," he said, "and come over here. I'll have men search the grounds."

Jim changed into slacks and a jersey. That, he had observed, was the prevailing costume. He did not turn out the lights around the pool and, as he left, he looked rather ruefully at his untouched supper.

He felt his scalp prickle. His meal was untouched no longer. The plate, on which had been steak and vegetables, was gone! He'd been ducked so his meal could be swiped, by someone who had no other access to food. That meant—Galt.

He ran to the mail office.

The grounds of the hotel were quietly ransacked. But hunting in the night was fairly useless.

III

When Jim came out of Howard's office he saw Frankie and her mother and Mr. Willet and a dozen others playing Bingo at a long oak table on the porch. Frankie was wearing a pale-green evening dress. She looked, he thought, like a daffodil. He paused, involuntarily.

She read numbers: "Seventy-one." She dropped the ticket in a bowl. The players put down counters on their cards. "Eight." "Fifteen."

"Bingo!" an elderly man called. He read off his numbers, and another girl handed him a dishful of silver.

Frankie beckoned to Jim. "Want to play?"

He shook his head slightly. She came to his side. "Come on! It's all right—if I invite you." She gestured toward a man with gray hair. "This is Mr. Farnham, my stepfather—Mr. Preston."

The man turned. Jim estimated that he weighed two hundred and fifty pounds. He had slaty eyes. Farnham, Jim later learned, was a steel manufacturer with a reputation for hardness and violence.

"How do you do?" he mumbled.

Jim sat down and bought a card. He had feared that the stakes would be too high. But the people at the table—all of them rich—were playing for dimes. Mr. Willet, across the table, gave a caricature of a salute. "Good evening, champ!"

Jim played for an hour, and lost twenty cents. Then the game broke up. He had enjoyed himself. It was only when he reached his own room that he remembered he had not slept at all on the previous night. He undressed and went to bed, and did not waken until the telephone operator called to tell him that it was six-thirty.

The inquest was held in the moving-picture theater at ten. Jim gave his testimony first. Next, Mr. Farnham gave a brief biographical sketch of Dr. Galt. Frankie described the rifle she had presented to him on Christmas. Three cowboys from the riding stables told about the feud between Poling and Galt. One of them said that Mr. Farnham had made an appointment to meet Poling at the riding master's ranch on the afternoon of his death. Farnham readily admitted it. He was going to plan a hunting trip, he said. A verdict was withheld, pending the finding of Galt. Search parties were organized. A special effort was made to cover the vicinity in which Galt had hidden when he shot at Jim. Jim, himself, with detectives, went over every step of his walk. But the rifle was not found, although a score of men tramped all day in the fiery sun.

Late that afternoon Jim went to the post office to collect a shipment of bathing suits and shoes he was to sell at the pool. On the way back he met Frankie coming out of a dress shop. She invited him to play Bingo again that night, and they strolled to the hotel together. He asked where Herb Willet was.

"Working on the case," she answered.

He grinned. "What does he expect to uncover?"

Frankie was almost indignant. "I wouldn't laugh too much at Herb. He's chattery, a silly man—if you like. But he's an authority on ligulae."

"Ligulae?"

"What the dictionary calls 'a genus of mollusks.' "

"Oh. Oh, I see."

"And that's not funny, either. To be an authority on that you have to wade in the Everglades in Florida. Fight snakes, panthers, swamps."

"And what has he found out about—Poling?"

"He hasn't said."

"I'll ask him."

"Do. But don't come to play Bingo unless you have the proper respect for Herb. I like him."

He smiled at her. "That," he said, "makes him okay with me."

The orchestra played again that evening. Mr. Howard wanted to revive the morale of his clientele. Poling's body had been taken ten miles away to his ranch. He was to be buried in another town. The bar was busy again. When Jim closed the pool for the evening and strolled over to the hotel he was aware of the effort to dissipate the miasma that had hung over the community.

He was wearing gray flannels and a blue coat, the best his wardrobe afforded. He had whitened his shoes. He might have been one of the sons of the heavy, assured hotel guests rather than an employee. He was introduced to several people.

A Mrs. Voight, sleek and past forty, was especially interested in Jim. She held his hand for so long that Frankie winked at him. "I had no idea there was a swimming master!" she said. Diamonds glittered on her fingers. "I must take some lessons. I'm terrified of water. I have a splendid idea! Won't you join my panning expedition next Friday?"

Jim grinned uncomfortably. "Panning expedition?" he echoed.

"Gold panning. There are places here where you can really pan it out. A few cents' worth. And I'm getting up a party —"

"If I can get away —" Jim answered. "Can you really —?"

Mr. Farnham spoke. "Pan gold here? Not enough to pay. But it's a stunt."

Down the table, Herb said, "If you knew the right spot maybe you wouldn't have to pan. Right around here, in the early days, they used to take out fortunes."

"How interesting," said a mousy lady.

Herb immediately agreed with her and with himself. "It is," he went on with trivial enthusiasm. "Absorbing. Romantic. Talk to one of the old hermits who come into town for grub occasionally. You've seen 'em. Some of them are the sons of Forty-niners, still poking around on the desert for millions their fathers found and lost. Not altogether absurdly, either. Ten years ago one of those old desert rats struck a pocket with half a million in it. Right outside Paradise Canyon. And legends, Mrs. Vandermahlen! The lost Cosset claim. The lost Golden Gregg. Supposed to have been a cavern. Fabulous country —"

"Let's play," Mr. Farnham said impatiently.

"Let's." Frankie handed the bowl of numbers to Miss Waite, the pretty hostess of the hotel. She collected the dimes and began to draw numbers. Jim started to fill his board, as did Frankie, sitting beside him. After a few minutes she whispered, "I've only got one place on two rows to put me out."

"I'll bet I win," Jim answered. "I have three rows ready to shoot."

"Thirty-seven." Miss Waite called.

"Bingo!" Frankie and Jim spoke simultaneously.

"You'll have to split the pot," the hostess said. "Read your numbers. Miss Bailey?"

Before she checked her count, Frankie held out her hand to Jim. "The winnahs!" she said. They shook. And from the downward glance to her hand, Jim's eyes traveled to his newly whitened shoes. He pulled one foot toward his chair leg. There was henna stain upon it, a stain like partly dried varnish. He bent farther down. Frankie's attention was attracted to the movement. He touched the stuff and looked at his fingers. He glanced around the table. No one was noticing him. Frankie was reading off her score. He stretched back so that he could see the long board running the length of the table and the wider centerboard beneath its top. He raised an edge of the cloth cover. He could see the legs of the people across from him, the baseboard, upon which was a lot of the stuff that marked his shoe, and a section of the shelf-like reinforcement under the top. On it, was a form. There was not enough light to identify it. Frankie glanced down, faltered, and went on. He realized that she also had seen.

Then Herb dropped one of his game boards on the floor. He ducked and groped for it for several seconds.

Frankie finished counting, and the prize money was handed to her.

People began to talk in preparation for the next game. Frankie whispered frantically to Jim, "What is it?"

Herb, white-faced, leaned toward them and whispered. "It's Galt. There's a knife in his back." His voice barely reached Jim. "We've got to break up the game before anyone else finds him."

Frankie looked at Jim with agonized eyes. "I—I—can't play now—" she whispered to him.

Jim caught her hand. "You've got to." He addressed the table. "I'm going to play three boards, and then quit."

Farnham said, "What the deuce are you young people scheming?"

"To beat you again," Herb said amiably. "This is going to be my last tonight, too. Getting late." He yawned delicately.

Of the three people who knew about the thing beneath the table, only Herb Willet was able to put his counters on the proper numbers. In fact, he won. "Bingo!" he cried finally. "Well! Victory at last! I'm going to knock off—on that one."

Mrs. Voight eyed Jim. "It's so early—and such a beautiful night—"

Jim rudely stretched. "Got to turn in. I get up at six-thirty. Well—"

People began to rise. Curiously enough the three who had precipitated the departures sat in their places.

There were good-nights.

They waited till the porch was empty. Then Jim and Herb bent down simultaneously.

"It's Dr. Galt, all right," Jim said.

"Stabbed—" Herb whispered.

Frankie was trembling. "Let's get Mr. Howard—right away."

They went into Mr. Howard's office. A clerk summoned him from his bungalow. Ten minutes later a Captain Spencer from Los Angeles joined them with one of the Paradise Canyon officers. Spencer was a small, wizened, very tanned person with a pleasant voice. The men walked to the porch and pulled down the shutters by which it was enclosed during the summer. They then drew the blinds along the inside windows.

The Los Angeles policeman got down on his knees and looked at the body for a full five minutes. Then he grunted, "Lend me a hand."

Jim and the local officer aided him in carrying the body to a divan. Dr. Galt's eyes were shut. He had not bled much. They turned him on his face. Protruding from his left shoulder was the handle of a knife. Frankie looked away, shaking.

Spencer said absently, "Now—what about the idea that this man shot Poling?"

"He could still have done it—and be killed by someone else," the local officer said.

"Yeah. He could have."

Frankie spoke in a high and jittery voice: "How did he get here? Why did they put him under that table? Suppose—he'd rolled off when—!"

Spencer said reprovingly, "I'm afraid you'll have to leave, Miss Bailey. A murder is invariably ugly and unnerving."

Frankie made an effort to control herself. "I have to stay. You see—I talked with Dr. Galt—yesterday afternoon."

Spencer raised his eyebrows. Everyone else was thunderstruck. He said, "Do you want to dictate your story?"

"No. I'll tell it. As often as you like. It isn't much. You already know that"—she gestured expressively toward the body—"he is—was—one of the most famous surgeons in the Middle West. He saved lives. He didn't take them."

"Miss Bailey—please!" the captain said.

"I'm getting to it. I knew he was hiding out, staying away, for some decent reason. And I imagined he'd be near here. Maybe watching us all. So I walked up on the mountainside yesterday afternoon alone and stood in plain view of half the desert for an hour. I didn't see him coming till he was almost beside me. We sat down and talked. He said that missing Mr. Preston so narrowly had alarmed him. He said he had been afraid of murder even then. He'd heard a shot, earlier in the morning, while he was hunting. He wanted the rifle right away—to clear himself.

"While he was hunting for his gun, he saw the riders find Mr. Poling. So he slipped down there and learned that a .30-40 rifle bullet had killed him. Then he knew he had to find his own gun so he could show it wasn't the one that had been used. He hunted all day. He told me that the posse looking for him sometimes came within a few yards of him. But he couldn't find his rifle. Every rock was like every other. Toward five he worked his way back along the mountainside—till he saw me. He asked me to say nothing to anyone—for the time being." She said to Jim, for no reason, "I didn't like Dr. Galt much. But I was relieved."

Spencer sniffed. "Very praiseworthy of you. You didn't suggest, by any chance, that if his yarn were true he could come in any time? If his gun hadn't been used, and was on the slope, it would eventually have been found—and cleared him."

Frankie hesitated. "It wasn't to clear himself that he was staying out in the desert."

"What do you mean?"

"He told me all about hunting for his gun. Then he said that there was a great deal more happening in Paradise Canyon than the mere killing of a riding master. Those were his exact words. He started to tell me. He said he hadn't been hunting lions—exclusively—at any time this season. He'd been investigating. Whether he would have told me what he was investigating or not, I don't know. A crowd of people rode over the Rim Trail just then. He ran."

"I suppose you can get some of those riders to testify to spotting you on the mountainside yesterday?"

Frankie's eyes burned. "Do you think I'm making this up?"

The captain turned from her to the body. "I don't think you are." He bent over. "The knife is precisely the sort served with my chops here this noon. Stainless steel, pointed."

"I wonder," Jim said slowly, "if it could be the one that was on my plate when it was stolen last night?"

"That's what I was wondering. Will you mind letting me take your fingerprints, Mr. Preston? Just as a check." He paused. "Whoever did it was able to carry a hundred-and-fifty-pound man from wherever it was done to here. Or drag him." He turned to the manager. "Can you close off this porch?"

"It would be awkward, under the circumstances. It was bad enough to have Poling shot. But this—and under a table where twenty guests had been playing games all the evening!"

"I'm very much afraid you'll have to. Before any more persons muss up the room we'll send experts through it. Take a day, anyhow."

"Very well—" Mr. Howard was beaded with perspiration.

Herb Willet spoke for the first time. "Can we go?"

"Certainly." The captain addressed Mr. Howard: "I'll want to interview everyone who was on duty around here last night—late, I mean." Then he said, "You can go, too, Mr. Preston. I doubt if we can take fingerprints at the local jail. But tomorrow, when the experts arrive—"

Jim nodded. He went out into the lobby with Frankie and her fiance.

Herb said, "I'll take you home, Frankie. Good night, Preston."

IV

The tall, bony man walked off with the girl, out the door, and into the garden. As he went, Jim found himself speculating on whether or not Herb Willet could carry a hundred-and-fifty pound man.

Frankie walked slowly. Neither she nor Herb spoke. When they were within a few rods of her bungalow, he led her into an arbor covered by bougainvillaea.

"You're getting stuck on that swimming guy," he said. "Falling in love with him."

"That's—"

"Ridiculous? Look, Frankie. In trouble, a woman turns, not to the man who can help, but to the one she wants to help. Tonight when you had looked under the table, you turned to Preston."

"I wasn't going to say it was ridiculous. I was going to say that this was no time to discuss such a thing. If I do like him—what then? Dr. Galt—"

"Quite. Dr. Galt lies yonder with a steak knife in his heart. But I only wanted to hear you say—admit—you found that fancy diver attractive." There was a long pause. "A man," he continued, "gets sick of being thought of as a jackass."

"Herb! I don't think of you as—!"

There was a sudden vehemence in his voice: "Will you marry me, then? Tonight!"

"Certainly not."

"Oh. Right. Silly of me—"

Jim, who had followed them, pressed his body deeper into the black shadows of the vine. Frankie's admission of interest in him was submerged in the recesses of his mind. The thing that occupied his startled attention was the change in Willet. For a few moments he had been direct, emotional, nearly violent. Perhaps he had detested Dr. Galt for pursuing Frankie. Jim wondered if Frankie had ever flirted with Poling, the riding master. And he wondered if, by any chance, Herb had been out on the desert on that fatal morning.

Herb and Frankie left the arbor.

At noon, the next day, Jim was palely facing Captain Spencer and two unintroduced men from Los Angeles.

"Your fingerprints were on that knife, Preston," the captain said, after staring at him for several seconds.

"Then it was the one swiped with my supper."

The policeman ignored that. "You never saw Poling alive?"

"Never. Alive or dead."

"You haven't any idea who tossed you in the pool?"

"None. My back was turned."

"Nobody had been near you?"

"Only Sam."

"I've talked to Sam. He didn't hear anything, either." He eyed Jim a moment. "Sam's fingerprints were on the knife also. So it was the one on your plate, all right."

"I thought it would be."

Spencer thrust his face very unexpectedly into Jim's. "Suppose I told you, Preston, that I'd learned you did know Poling? That I'd found out what you had against Galt? That the fingerprints on that knife—yours—were in the position of a stabbing hand, and not a hand that is cutting meat?"

Jim was scared to his roots. He realized, with dread, that he was a stranger in this part of the country. But he looked back steadily at the policeman. "I'd say you were a darned fool."

"And I would be." Spencer glanced impatiently at his assistants. "But it was worth trying. I might tell you that I have investigated you, and your record's perfect. I might add that your fingerprints were in the carving and not the stabbing position. Smudged. By a glove. The murderer probably tried to leave your prints on the knife—as much of them as he could—and still use the thing." Spencer looked sleepy and irritable. "You're bright," he said presently. "You tell me what it's all about. Usually I look for some piece of junk that will tell me which one of several people killed the body. This time I have a mountain of junk—horse, saddle, bullet, knife, a letter "G" traced by a dying man to be a help and acting only as a hindrance, the plate your dinner was on—"

"You found that?"

"In a culvert on the golf course. Sure. We hunted for it."

Jim's eyes suddenly widened. "Look. Did you pump Dr. Galt's stomach to find out if he ate the meal?"

"To—what?"

"Well, maybe he stole my food because he was hungry, and ate it, and somebody stabbed him while he was eating—with his own knife. Or maybe the murderer deliberately snatched my plate to get the knife. You could tell—"

Spencer grinned at Jim, and then turned to one of his men: "Call the undertaker and then send Dr. Cable over there. Have 'em report at once."

They sat in the office and waited. It took a long time. Finally the report came back. Spencer answered the telephone. When he hung up, he said, "Empty. So your plate was swiped to get the knife."

"I wonder where the food went?"

"Probably down the culvert. Water runs through it, you know. It's the stream from Blind Canyon. But what does that prove?"

"Nothing," Jim said thoughtfully, "except that the man who killed Dr. Galt was plenty ingenious. He knew Galt was hanging around the hotel. He knew he was going to kill him. So he threw a coin in the pool to get me to the edge to swipe my dinner and make it look as if Galt himself had stolen it, but really to get a knife that had somebody else's fingerprints on it."

Spencer answered, "You find me a motive, and I'll get the murderer, no matter how slick he is. I think we ought to look into the private lives of the renowned doctor and the riding master, very thoroughly. And then of everyone who knew them. How about that Willet, for example? He's a queer duck. Didn't Galt chase his fiancee?"

"I don't know," Jim answered. "These people live a bit differently from any I've known."

Spencer chucked. "You ought to see how they live in Hollywood! Well—thanks, Preston. Keep your ears open. And thanks, also, for the idea of finding out whether or not Galt had eaten. It's interesting, but it doesn't do us any good to know he died hungry."

Jim walked to the employees' dining-room. He did not feel hungry. Sam appeared soon after he sat down. "The soup is thin today," he said. "The stew is good. I recommend the veal, though. Did they give you a third degree?"

Jim grinned. "Bring anything. Yeah. We both signed that knife with our fingers."

Sam nodded pleasantly. "I'm lucky. At nine I go home."

"Where do you live?"

"On the desert. Near Marble City. I got a house. I've worked for the hotel for ten years, and saved. Bought me a little home and car. And my break was being away. Captain Spencer worked for three hours this morning on the boys who stay at the hotel. They came out sweated through."

Jim laughed. Sam went out, and came back with breaded veal cutlet and vegetables and salad. Jim had been thinking. "You say you've been here for ten years?"

"Since the place opened." Sam's amiable face became sober. "And I've seen plenty. Not only in the picture crowd."

"That's what I was figuring. You probably know the Farnham-Bailey people pretty well. You probably knew Dr. Galt and Poling."

"I did." Sam moved closer to Jim. "And if that cop hadn't torn into me the way he did, I could have told a lot."

Jim pretended only moderate interest. "Such as what?"

"Take Miss Bailey. Now, she hates her stepfather."

"Does she? I've noticed that she always calls him Mr. Farnham."

"That's it. She doesn't like that big guy. Take Mr. Willet. He hated Galt. I think, personally, that he's nuts. Always following people."

"Really? Who?"

"Everybody. I've seen Mr. Farnham go past my place on the desert on one of his hunting trips maybe thirty times. And, like as not, soon afterward that Mr. Willet would tag along on his trail. He'd follow Galt, too. And he'd ask questions of the help, plenty of questions."

"About what?"

"About the other people here. He's a screwball. He's engaged to Miss Bailey. Why doesn't he marry her? Why'd he chase Miss McKay last season?"

"The movie actress? Did he chase her?"

"They got to be mighty good friends. I tell you, Mr. Preston, if I was that cop I'd want to know where Willet was the other morning. I'd ask him so many questions he'd get dizzy."

"Why didn't you say all that to Spencer?"

"I did—some of it. But he was so tough and loud he got my goat."

"Suppose I dropped a bug in his ear?"

Sam shrugged. "I was thinking of going back to him, anyway."

Jim went back to the pool. Galt's body was going East after the inquest, the second in four days. The verdict of that inquest was pretty sure. Person or persons unknown. People came to swim, and remained to whisper to each other.

In the middle of the afternoon Mr. Howard dropped over and privately asked Jim to do all he could to divert the hotel guests. People were checking out. The Los Angeles papers were playing the murder in banner headlines. Reporters were arriving on chartered planes. Jim contributed what he could by diving until he was weary. Frankie didn't show up. But, late in the day, Herb Willet strolled down to the pool. He waved languidly at Jim. He took off his beach robe and lay down in the sunshine and stayed there until the other bathers had left. The opportunity to talk to him alone was welcome to Jim. Nobody had questioned Willet. So eventually, Jim walked around the pool and sat down beside the knobby, prostrate form of Frankie's fiance.

Willet said, "Hello, Preston," and closed his eyes wearily.

Jim looked away, his earnest face strained with anxiety. "I was thinking about Dr. Galt," he said presently.

"So was I—not surprisingly."

"Any guest at the hotel could have stabbed him," Jim continued. "An outsider would have had trouble getting into the grounds."

"True. The fence around the place. And the watchman."

Jim felt the excitement of his ambitious undertaking. "Any guest. Take yourself. Suppose you'd wanted to do it."

Willet smiled superficially. "Suppose I had. Take me. How would you work it?"

"Well—suppose you hated both Poling and Galt, for private reasons. Suppose you knew Galt went out often before daylight with his .30-40. Suppose you got one like it—waited for a morning when Galt was out and Poling was riding. Shot Poling."

"Wait up, there. What if Galt came in with an unused gun?"

"What was to prevent him from reloading it—or even swabbing it out?"

"Right-o. You're smart, Preston."

Jim wondered exactly what Willets' continuing and slightly impertinent smile meant. "All right. You find out that Galt lost his gun—a pure accident—but a break for you. Galt is out in the bush. So you locate him. You pull a fancy trick to get my steak knife. Later that night, when Galt is prowling around here, probably to get food, or maybe to get you, you stab him. Somewhere near the porch. Then you see the night watchman's light approaching from somewhere out on the grounds. So you heave Galt onto the porch—just to hide. While you crouch there in the dark you notice the table shelf. You put the body there. Then you go to your bungalow and turn in."

Willet inhaled smoke, blew it out, and looked up. "That's about how it happened, I venture to agree. Now, Preston, why did I do this bloody business?"

It was time for Jim to use his facts. He looked up at the sky and said idly, rapidly, "You did it because you're jealous. Because Frankie flirted with Poling and Galt. Because Galt came here every winter and tried to take her away from you. You did it because you're psychopathically jealous and suspicious of everybody near you. You're unbalanced. Because you are even jealous of me. You charged Frankie with falling for me only last night—when she hardly knew me. Because, Willet, you're a homicidal maniac, and it's been growing on you for years, and the fact that Frankie won't have you for a husband has finally touched you off. Don't get up! Don't move! I'll clip you if you budge!" Jim spoke with abrupt alarm, for Willet was grinning at him in a manner which, under the circumstances, was manifestly insane.

"All right," Willet said; "I did it. Now. How do you prove it?"

Jim stared at him. He had neither proof nor witnesses to this confession. "I'll just ask you to come over with me to see Spencer. You can tell him."

Willet began to laugh. He sat where he was. Presently he said, "See here, Jim. I didn't do it. I said I did just to make you see one thing: you'd never be able to prove it, short of forcing a confession. But where did you find out all that stuff about me? I imagine you tagged Frankie and me the other night." His face clouded for a moment. "But the rest of it?"

"Never mind," Jim said. He was watching Willet closely, unsure of whether the man was sincere in his amusement or skillfully evading him.

V

Willet's expression gradually became confidential. "Look. I'm older than you. Five or six years, anyway. I like you. I think I understand you. I think I know what it must be like to take all the bilge and insult from people like these and to be a mere hired man, when all the time you're a first-class engineer."

Jim stared.

"I have been investigating. And shadowing people. You included. And now I guess I've either got to give up my line of inquiry or take you in on it. I much prefer to do the latter. It would involve your silence, at least until the air cleared."

"I can't promise it," Jim replied.

"I don't ask it—till you hear what I have to say. It's this . . . Four winters ago I met Frankie. She's a swell kid. Sincere, even-tempered, good-looking, normal—flirtatious, if you like. I love her. I don't think she loves me. Anyway, though, we became engaged. At that time her mother had just married Farnham. And Frankie didn't like Farnham especially. He's dull and domineering and aggressive. Very well. The Farnhams were planning to take Frankie to Florida for the winter, and I, naturally, was going too. Well, suddenly they switched plans and came here. So I did, too. I couldn't figure why Farnham wanted to go to the desert. He doesn't ride well. The hunting's nothing extra. I wondered about it frequently. Then Dr. Galt showed up, and has showed up every winter since. Apparently because of Frankie. But do you think a man of his attainments and temperament would give up a big practice for months every winter because he was hopelessly crazy about a girl? I wondered about that.

I wondered, when I found out about it, why Howard worked every winter as hotel manager, when he's worth a couple of million."

"Is that the truth?" Jim asked with astonishment.

"It is. All right. Here were three important and wealthy men hanging around here season after season for no really good reason. So far, so good. Arlina McKay hung around so much she lost two fine contracts in Hollywood. And Mrs. Voight stayed here one winter when her brother died in Chicago and when her mother was ill to the point of death. I figured that there was some attraction I wasn't getting."

"I can't agree," Jim answered. "I think that's your imagination."

Willet nodded. "So did I. But—for four seasons Farnham has kept a hundred thousand dollas in cash in the safe at the Paradise Canyon Hotel. Galt has a letter of credit for seventy-five thousand every year he comes out, though he spends, at the most, only a tenth or a fifteenth of that. Mrs. Voight keeps a tremendous account in the local bank. So does Howard. Quarter of a million. Miss McKay, also—"

"Why?" Jim asked.

"I don't know, but I've guessed. Galt, Farnham, Howard, Mrs. Voight, and Miss McKay—all have a fortune on tap, in cash. So, you might think they were all prepared to buy something. What? Well—they were all horseback riders and hunters. They all kept scouring the landscape. I followed all of them at one time or another, and, from the way they habitually behaved when they thought they were unobserved, you'd guess that they were hunting for a lost object. Now, Jim, what in the world is there in these millions of waste acres of sand and rock that would make—"

"Gold!" Jim exclaimed softly.

Willet looked at him thoughtfully. "So. Am I crazy? Or—is there something going on here that involves not my jealousy, which is real enough, but five rich people who have been waiting and hunting for years, unknown to each other, for something they stand ready to buy the minute they find it."

"You mean, they're trying to find a mine, or something? And when they do—"

"They'll be all set to buy the land it's on from the owner. I think that each one of them is convinced that there's a tremendous fortune somewhere out on that desert. So they want to be ready with cash—when and if."

Jim said, "Did Poling keep a big account, too?"

"I could never find out about him. If he, also, was on that gold hunt every winter, and had available cash, he kept it at his ranch or buried somewhere."

"Why did they always hunt in the winter?"

Willet gazed at him. "I wish I knew."

"Why didn't you ask pointblank?"

Willet got up and pulled a chair close to Jim and sat down. "That's not hard to explain. First, I merely marveled. Then I followed Farnham. Saw him ride out and stop and stare all over the desert, and come back without firing a shot, saying the hunting was lousy, but fun. Then I observed that other people were doing the same thing. So I entered the hunt. I didn't know what to look for. I don't think they know. They never refer to maps. They just tool along on foot or horseback, staring everywhere. Howard, by the way, has tried all sorts of mechanical ore locaters. If you don't believe this story, I'll show you where he caches them, out in the sand. I enjoyed it. I was near Frankie, outdoors, and I learned a lot about the desert. Sooner or later, maybe even this winter, I was planning to get them all together and blow the whole business wide open, just for fun, at a dinner or something. Then—Poling got killed. You see?"

"See what?"

"I connected that instantly with this gold business. This patient, secret hunt. Then Galt. I thought it meant—"

"That somebody had discovered the mine."

He nodded. "So, I kept quiet."

"But—you can't!"

"Why not? I'd like to see the murderer caught."

"You've got to tell the whole thing to the police."

Willet looked grimly at Jim. "I don't want to. You can compel me to, of course, but see here. This murderer's clever. Don't you suppose he has a peach of an alibi ready in case of need? And suppose the papers get hold of my yarn? Why—the desert would be crowded with thousands of people overnight. Do you have the faintest idea of what a gold rush is? To let this story out would mean that hundreds, at least, would break their hearts and lose their last few dollars."

Jim was silent for a minute. Then he said, "You have a car?"

"Sure."

"Would you mind showing me that cache of Howard's?"

Willet grinned. "Good going! I stuck it in deliberately. If you had swallowed the story without any proof I'd have been disappointed in you."

They drove through town. They turned into the desert on an unpaved road. It petered out in divergent streams of horse tracks. Presently they were driving on hard sand and gravel, dodging cacti and mesquite and sage. The sun had dropped behind San Fernando. Willet took his bearings from a slag pile and a distant canyon. He stopped the car. On foot, they proceeded through the lavish colors of sunset to a small dune. At its foot, in the dry brush, were half a dozen packing crates, bleached and empty. Jim looked at them. They were addressed to Howard.

"Dig about there," Willet said, pointing with his toe.

In five minutes Jim dug a carefully wrapped instrument. Its manner of operation was as undecipherable as its function.

"An electric diviner," Willet said. "Works with dry cells. All these gadgets are phony."

They stood side by side. Jim suddenly and shockingly wondered whether Willet had brought him there to kill him. He looked at his companion's face. But Willet was staring toward the color-drenched clouds. Jim felt weak with relief. The guy was sound, after all. Suddenly a dazzling thought occurred to him.

"Tell me, Willet—Herb—did any of those gold hunters ever lie down?"

"Lie down? They crouched. A man standing on the desert is pretty conspicuous. So they were continually dismounting. I never got near enough to see them lying down. Why?"

"But they could have been lying down?"

"Sure. Farnham and Galt were always squatting behind something or other. Maybe lying. I couldn't say. But—why?"

Jim didn't reply. His eyes ranged along the rocky miles of San Ferdondo's slope. "I believe your whole story," he said finally. "And I'll help you on it. I'm sorry I tore into you this afternoon."

Willet smiled. "That's all right. Darned amusing. And nervy. How could you have known I didn't have another knife? We were all alone."

"M-m-m. That's what I was thinking just a second ago."

Willet laughed heartily and slapped Jim's shoulder. "All right. Now— we've got to watch day and night, and do a lot of first-class thinking.

If we don't get anywhere in a few days we'll have to tell the police. Where do we begin, do you think?"

"Let's talk to the desert rats. All of them. Pump them about the old legends."

They started back to the car. "Another thing —" Willet said, and paused awkwardly.

"Yes?"

"Frankie. She's more or less excited about you."

Jim was embarrassed. "She's a pretty fine girl. But I hardly know her. And —"

"I just wanted to say — I'm pretty fond of her. But I want you to know also that she probably doesn't love me. And if she ever does fall for anybody, that guy'll have to become either my best friend — or my bitterest enemy."

Jim didn't say anything. Herb Willet had been too earnest for a reply. He looked now toward Jim, meeting his eyes with an expression that was friendly but deeply concerned.

"Forget it," he said finally. "You know how it is."

On the following day, at the second inquest, the verdict of an unknown murderer was given.

In the forenoon of the day following the inquest, Jim learned accidentally that Mr. Howard was going for a ride. Wanting urgently to see one of the "gold hunters" on the quest, Jim closed the pool, under the pretext of cleaning it, borrowed some riding clothes from Herb, hired a tranquil nag, and rode out in the wake of the hotel manager. Mr. Howard took what seemed to be an arbitrary direction, although it was probably one in which he had not previously searched, and went over the country slowly, often dismounting to examine the terrain.

Jim returned to the hotel at two-thirty, weary and hungry. He took a shower, started refilling the pool, and went to the kitchen for something to eat. The chef was in an irritable mood, so he asked for his friend Sam. The chef said that it was Sam's day off, or that the day before had been, and if people wanted to eat why didn't they show up at mealtime? Jim started into town for food, and found Sam asleep in a chair in the sun on the employees' porch. He had a newspaper over his chin and chest and had been snoozing for so long that his exposed face was sunburned, but when Jim woke him he amiably rallied cold chicken and iced coffee.

Mr. Howard didn't get back from his search until four o'clock.

Mrs. Voight left in her car for a trip to Los Angeles. She said she was going to remain there for the week end. After she had gone Herb dropped over to the pool.

"Mrs. Voight," he said, "had a camping outfit in her car when she drove away. Don't you agree, Jim, that she's probably not going to L.A.?"

Jim said, "Did it ever occur to you, Willet, that the hypothetical person who may have located the hypothetical mine, may be intending to kill his rivals one by one? Poling, then Galt. I followed Howard to have a look at just what you'd described, and I half expected all the time he was scanning the country-side that a rifle would crack and he'd fall from his horse. If Mrs. Voight is really going to camp out somewhere and make a furious effort to find the missing mine, she's doing it at a mighty unhealthy time."

Herb nodded. "I suppose she is."

Together they watched the sun go down. At last Jim said, "I have one idea—maybe foolish. I'm not going to explain it now, because it isn't ripe. But if I need help I'd like to feel free to call on you."

"Anything. Any time."

"Buy a raincoat."

"A—what?"

"I've got a raincoat. I'll lend it to him." Frankie spoke from a spot behind their chairs. "What's the idea, Jim? What are you planning?"

Herb grinned at her. "A hunt. For ducks. Jim says they sit all over the Salton Sea in rainstorms. Want to join us next time it pours?"

"I'd love to," she said. "Anything to get away from the glooms. And now it's worse. My stepfather broke his arm this afternoon."

"Where?" Jim asked casually.

"Oh, out walking. He said he was restless this morning and went out in the baking sun to walk it off. He came in all bandaged up."

Herb and Jim looked at each other. Their eyes were expressive. Perhaps Mr. Farnham had broken his arm. Perhaps it was not a break. Perhaps it was—a bullet wound, for example.

VI

That evening Jim went into town and he met two of the oldest living inhabitants of the desert. At the cost of a few drinks he was overwhelmed with stories of the gold rush. A giant nugget lost, a mine in a cavern, a mine that ran under a graveyard, and a river that ran underground — so many stories that Jim realized it would be impossible to sift from them the one which was being investigated by the guests of the hotel.

On the day after, Frankie came to the pool to swim and stayed all the morning. She and her mother and Herb invited Jim to have lunch with them, and Sam served it on bridge tables beside the pool. The sky was bare of clouds, the sun blazing hot, and Jim had the first real opportunity to talk to Frankie, as well as to consider his own feelings about her. Their meeting on the night of his arrival had been an enchanted adventure. In the hours of alarm that had followed, she had often looked to him for courage. He had expected that, and it had made him proud. And now, all day, talking to her, lying in the sun, diving for her, playing in the water, he could see glimpses of a deeper radiance in her gray eyes.

He was in love, and he had never been in love in that way before. Over his possessive and complex desires hung the shadows of death, and between him and the girl stood a man whom he liked increasingly as his acquaintance continued.

When the long gorges in the sides of San Fernando filled with blue dusk, Frankie left reluctantly, and Jim was sad at her departure. Any distance between them would, from now on, make him feel purposeless.

Captain Spencer walked up to see him. "Want to chew the fat a while?" he said. "Asked you to keep your ears open — remember?"

"Sure. But nobody's said anything hereabouts that would interest you."

"M-m-m. Nice day. Hot." He sat and viewed the panoply of desert twilight. "Haven't picked up a thing, eh?"

"No. Have the police?"

"No."

"Why don't you start something? As far as I can see, all the cops do is eat and sleep and draw their pay." Jim grinned. "Isn't there any routine you can use in things like this?"

Spencer yawned. "We haven't been loafing all the time. Like to ask you a couple of questions, as a matter of fact."

"Sure."

"Why'd you follow Howard out on the desert yesterday?"

Jim was surprised. "How do you know I did?"

Spencer sighed. "I was right behind you."

"Oh."

"And where'd you go with Herb Willet the other night?"

"Out on the desert again."

Spencer's head moved imperceptibly. "I can take you in, and ask you all this, you know."

Jim pondered. "I wouldn't have anything to say if you did hold me."

"I know it. I just hoped you'd help me out—because I also know you have some sort of hunch."

"I tell you what—I have. I admit it. But it's too daffy to give you now. If I get hold of anything that clinches it, or helps it make sense, I'll spill it immediately."

Spencer was silent for longer than Jim had been. Finally he said, "Why do all these people spend their winters out there with the tarantulas, Preston? That's what you've guessed, isn't it?"

"You know about that?"

The officer was gently sarcastic. "I haven't your brains, of course, but—your friend Mrs. Voight is out there now."

"I thought so."

"In Alto Grande Canyon. And Farnham's broken arm—isn't broken."

"No?"

Spencer fished in his pocket. "Here's the bullet the doctor took out of it." He flipped it to Jim. "A .30-40. Same gun that killed Poling. Farnham offered the doctor a thousand bucks to substantiate his broken-arm story. The doctor hurried to me." He rose. "Sure you don't want to tell me what your hunch is—yet?"

"Positive."

"Or why you want Herb Willet to buy a raincoat?"

"You listened in on that!"

"From the chlorinator shed." Spencer began to walk away, slowly and peacefully. "I'm giving all of you plenty of rope. That's my routine—in such cases."

Jim thought that he laughed, but he was not sure. . . .

Two days later the weather changed. When Jim woke up, it was pouring. Jim went down to the lobby in the elevator. The night clerk was eating his pre-retiring meal.

"When'd the rain start?" Jim asked.

"About one."

He went to the phone and called Herb Willet's bungalow. "I think it's going to pour all day, so that lets me off duty at the pool. How about that duck hunt?"

"I'll be ready in a quarter of an hour. Pick you up in front of the hotel."

"Better meet me somewhere else. Say, the caddy house on the golf course."

"Oh. Right!"

Jim put on old clothes—and an oil-skin coat. He tramped through vertical sheets of rain to the deserted caddy house. A car slid up, and for a moment he was frightened. It wasn't Willet's sedan. Then he saw Frankie at the wheel. He hopped in, dripping.

"The barnacle gathered I was up to something," Herb said. "She stuck. It's just as well. My car wouldn't start."

Frankie, in a blue raincoat, turned from the wheel. "Where do we go? And what are we looking for?"

Herb winked at Jim. "A gold mine," he said. "Which way do we go, Jim?"

"North."

Frankie turned into the main road. Jim looked back through the rain. No other car was leaving Paradise Canyon on their trail.

"You don't mind," Frankie said, "if I'm faintly amazed? A gold mine?"

Herb chuckled. "All right, darling. Let me explain. Our young friend, Mr. Preston, is a gentleman of considerable intelligence—"

"You can skip that. I know it."

"And—an engineer."

"Engineer!"

"An honor graduate. Now—for reasons we haven't time to detail, he and I feel sure that various persons hereabouts have been gold-hunting for some years."

Frankie was vastly excited. "So that's it! That's why my stepfather insists on the desert every winter!"

"Exactly. We are at the moment assuming a lost mine. Our bright young friend knows that the hunters have no maps. He knows they hunt only in the winter season. Why, he has said to himself, do they hunt only in winter? If they never refer to maps there must be some other way of locating the treasure. If they hunt only in winter, it must be locatable only in winter. What, he asks himself, happens in winter and not in summer, spring or fall? It rains, says his massive mind. But are these people looking for a stream? No. Then what? How about an underground river? Suppose they are not looking, but listening? I didn't get the brilliance of the hunch, even when he asked me if I'd ever seen any of the searchers lying down, ear to the earth, till he told me to buy a raincoat."

Jim replied diffidently, "It's a loony idea, but—"

"Loony? It's genius! You are absolutely right! Our friends have scoured the local desert listening for a subterranean gurgle that will, according to some antique yarn, double or maybe quadruple their already ample funds. By golly! They're looking for the Golden Gregg! The mine in a lost cavern!"

Jim said, "I think so. Don't you suppose that's what Poling meant by the "G" he drew on the sand? I've been wondering, if he had lived a few seconds longer, whether he wouldn't have marked down two "G's" and an arrow or something."

"You think he found it?"

Jim nodded.

"But where are we going?" Frankie asked.

Herb replied to that question. "Ask the professor. He's an engineer, remember. That doubtless means something of a geologist. What is the compass bearing, anyhow, Jim?"

"I'm not sure. But I've taken a pretty good squint at the mountain and the land around here. I'd say there were two spots in this neighborhood where you might expect an underground river. One's below Red Water Canyon. And one's right under the west pass."

Frankie was shaking her head affirmatively. "And we're going to cut across to Red Water?"

"And get out," Jim answered, "and slog."

They got out. And slogged. For an hour. Then two, finally four. Their feet became heavy with wet sand. Rain ran down their necks. The visibility was so low that it was difficult for Jim to reconstruct the theoretical path of a possible underground watercourse. When they wandered any distance from the glistening side of the mountain, it was lost to view. When they finally gave up, they could not locate the car.

And it was while they were scrambling through the wet brush hunting for the car that Frankie suddenly stopped dead still and then threw herself down in the mud.

There was no doubt of it. The sound was sonorous, liquid, eerie, and it made the ground tremble a little. She yelled.

Herb ran up from one side and Jim from the other. They dropped to the earth. They listened. Herb rose.

Frankie said, "Now what?"

VII

Jim looked through the rain toward the mountain to take bearings. Then he grinned. "Maybe we're right. Probably nuts. But, assuming we're right, we can assume that at least one person found this spot. According to the Golden Gregg yarn, there was an entrance to the cavern. Whoever found this place may have found the entrance and, if so, probably covered it. Shall we carry on?"

Frankie wiped wet hair out of her eyes. "Carry on."

Herb smiled. "Got any ideas about where to look?"

Jim nodded. "That's easier. Can't be far. Water's worn this spot thin. We're standing on a dome. Look for piled-up rocks or recently cut brush."

Jim, himself, found the opening—a crack in an exposed ledge, three feet wide and about two feet high. A barrier of stones had been built in front of it, and the stones had been covered by transplanted cacti. Jim called the others. He had rolled away the rocks when they arrived.

They all regarded it without speaking, awed, afraid. Jim took a flashlight from his pocket. "I'll go in," he said.

"Me, too."

He shook his head at Frankie. "Not today. You two watch. It may be impossible to explore down there with so much water. I'll see."

She grabbed his arm. Her voice was suddenly imploring: "Please wait! Suppose—"

"Suppose there's a man in there," Herb said. "Yeah. Better wait."

Jim hadn't thought of a possible occupant. He knelt. "I'll take a quick look, anyhow. If I'm not back in ten minutes get the cops."

He went in. His flashlight showed a rapidly widening tunnel with a dry floor. Within fifty feet he could walk upright. A sound overhead startled him. He shot the light up. A bat whizzed past his ear. The tunnel dropped. The floor became rocky. The water sounds grew deafening.

Then he rounded a turn. He stood at the edge of a cavern too vast to be plumbed by his light. Its floor was white sand. Great, shining stalactites hung from its ceiling. Through its center a black river roared in a deep channel. Near the river were some rotten planks and rusted pieces of metal. Fresh footprints marked the sand from the place where Jim stood to the debris, and the sand itself glittered with myriad minute fires.

Jim faded back into the shadows. He filled his pocket with the sand. He went back the way he had come. Only then was he terrified. He began to run.

When he emerged into the daylight he found Frankie crying on Herb's shoulder. She shouted when she saw him, and threw her arms around him for a brief, relieved instant.

Jim said tremulously, almost hysterically, "It's it. The Golden Gregg! There are ruins of a sluice down there. And the sand—" He held out a handful.

They bent over it. "Are those specks gold?" Frankie whispered.

"Yeah," Jim said.

Herb looked at him. "You know where this is, don't you, Jim?"

"Oh, sure. We'll find it all right. And we better cover it up exactly as it was."

"I mean—this is on Poling's ranch."

They stared at each other. Then they covered the cave mouth carefully and hunted until they found the car. They started back toward Paradise Canyon.

"It looked inexhaustible," Jim said.

"M-m-m," Herb answered.

"The sand's rich."

"Wasn't thinking about that."

"Oh." Jim gazed at Frankie. His face was depressed and speculative.

Herb saw the expression, and said gently to the girl, "Look, Frankie. It's going to be tough on your stepfather."

"My stepfather!"

"I hate to say it. But he was looking for that mine. So was Galt. Your stepfather had a date with Poling the day he was killed. Suppose it was to buy Poling's ranch and not to arrange a trip. Suppose Galt found the cave that morning, and Farnham was hiding in it."

Frankie slowed the car. "I can't believe that!"

"Farnham's a tough, quiet, acquisitive man. And remember—I know why you don't like him—"

Frankie shrugged. "Just because he is beastly to his employees doesn't make him a murderer."

"No. But—"

"We'll let the police decide that, anyway—won't we?" she said.

Herb turned. "Think we ought to tell the cops—yet, Jim?"

"No."

Frankie said angrily, "You've got to! You can't hide all this information!"

"Just for a day, or two—" Herb's voice was reserved.

"If you don't, I will!"

Herb ignored that. He said to Jim, "I'll talk to Farnham. I think the best way will be to give it to him quietly—"

No one spoke again.

Jim was thinking. Farnham? It certainly looked like Farnham. But there were others: Howard. Mrs. Voight. Arlina McKay . . .

It was late afternoon. Dark. They drove under the archway that led to the grounds of Paradise Canyon Hotel.

"You change," Herb said to Jim, "and come over to my bungalow. I'll sit on Frankie. And I'll have some food sent over. I'm starving."

Jim went to his room. He had a hot shower. He put on dry clothes. His face was set, thoughtful, grim. In the lobby he saw Mr. Farnham. His heavy form was relaxed in a deep chair and his eyes were on the pages of a novel. Jim ran through the rain to Herb's bungalow.

Herb was still bathing. Sam brought in and set up a bridge table. Jim talked through the open bathroom door.

"Farnham's alone in his house now."

"Good."

"I just passed him in the lobby. He was getting a terrific stack of bills from the cashier. I wonder what for?"

"Great scott!"

"Yeah. And he ordered his car. Going to have it call for him at the bungalow in half an hour."

"I'll get a wiggle on."

Sam brought in a tray of covered food and a portable heater. Herb came out and tipped him. He and Jim sat down at the table. Jim was watching him attentively. "I think—" he said.

Two minutes after Sam left they had run through the rain to Farnham's bungalow. There, in the dark living-room, Herb had seated himself. He was listening to a muted radio. Farnham had not come over from the hotel. Jim was hiding behind a portiere.

Then the door opened. Footsteps approached through the murky hall. Sam came into the living-room. He was no longer wearing his white waiter's uniform. And he was no longer a waiter in deed. He held a revolver in his right hand. Jim jumped.

But he missed. A moment later Sam was whispering tensely, "Up! Up! Both you guys! Now! Get over in the corner there!" He started toward them slowly. "I'm going to knock you both out. I gotta!"

The front door creaked again. More footsteps. Frankie switched on the light. She saw Sam covering Jim and Herb. Sam's face grimaced and he whipped his gun toward her. "Come here!"

She stood, paralyzed, beside the switch.

"Come here! Now, look. You're tying those guys up. Then you're coming along with me. In your car. Get it?"

Frankie nodded her head.

Sam was panting. "I'm on the spot. I'm leaving. You're going with me. If anything happens to me it'll happen to you first. See? Now. Work fast. Use those portieres—"

There was an instant of stiff pantomime. Then a shot snapped it. Sam's gun fell to the floor. He cried out and grabbed his wrist. Captain Spencer walked into the room, grinning . . .

Two hours later, in the presence of Captain Spencer, Jim, Mr. Howard, and a stenographer, Sam had finished his confession. Sweat-soaked, nursing his wounded wrist, he sat back in his chair.

Jim spoke: "If I can't be of any more use, Captain, I'd like to go to dinner. They're waiting for me."

"Go ahead. And—thanks. Thanks plenty. If you ever need a job—"

Jim grinned slightly. "Don't thank me. If you hadn't showed up when you did—"

"What did you expect me to do after I found you and Willet and Miss Bailey were missing?"

Jim's grin widened. He went out of the room and through the garden. The rain was only a thin sprinkle and a fresh breeze was stirring. Soon it would be clear. He entered the Farnham's bungalow. He was enthusiastically greeted. A long table was spread with silverware and china, and only Jim was needed to complete the party.

They sat down. But nobody was eager to eat. Farnham put the question that even Herb had been impatient to hear answered:

"How in the name of creation did you come to suspect that waiter?"

"It went like this," Jim answered a little wearily. "When I was taking a shower this afternoon I got the water too hot, and it nearly burned my face. That reminded me that I'd seen Sam with a sunburned face a few days ago. It dawned on me that the thing was odd, because Sam's a busy person. He couldn't have had time to sleep on the porch long enough to get a bad burn. His chin was under a newspaper, and hadn't been sunburned at all. I thought—suppose he was faking sleep and faking the burn. How, I wondered, would a guy burn his face in the sun, and not his chin? It struck me that about the only way it could be done would be to wear a false beard all day."

"But why would he wear a beard?" Mrs. Farnham asked perplexedly.

"That's what I wanted to know. I recalled that the chef said that the day before had been Sam's day off. Look: if Sam had been out on the desert all day in a false beard, and was working the nap-under-a-newspaper to alibi his partial sunburn, it meant that Sam was in on the whole business. Then I thought a lot of things. In the first place, Sam was the one person nobody had investigated who could have done both murders. He lived outside the hotel grounds, so no one could have checked up on him the morning Poling was found. He went home at night at various times, so he might easily have been around here when Dr. Galt was killed. Then, he had just left me that time when I was pushed into the pool. I thought of the ten years he had spent here. And I wondered if he hadn't possibly lived a double life, by establishing himself—disguised as one of the desert rats—around town nights, and if he hadn't used that disguise when he went hunting for the mine. As a waiter, he could pretty well keep track of the other gold hunters.

"That was right, as it turns out. Sam had been hunting for that mine for four years. He found it. He had savings and he tried to buy Poling's ranch, but Poling liked the place and wanted to keep it. A few mornings ago Sam went over to Poling's and told him about the Golden Gregg and asked for a ninety per cent cut on all the profits. Poling said no. He got on a horse and started to town. Sam shot him, on the way in, from ambush. Probably he figured he could buy from Poling's estate. Then Sam drove away to take a look at the mine—and got there just as Galt was coming out. Galt didn't see Sam. Galt had stumbled on the cave when he cut back to hunt for his rifle. Captain Spencer found that gun, by the way, long ago. He knew Galt had not killed Poling. But he kept quiet. Spencer's pretty tricky."

Jim drew a long breath. "Anyway, I figured Sam was the murderer. He knew he'd have to kill Galt. Sam hid on the grounds here, and stabbed the doctor when he slipped in late at night. When I came over to Herb's place this afternoon, and Sam was there, I just yelled into the bathroom a few hints that would make Sam think that you, Mr. Farnham, were about to do him out of a chance to get Poling's place, and the Golden Gregg. Then Herb and I waited in your bungalow for Sam to appear. Only—I guess I'm not much of a murderer-catcher." Jim paused. "You see, if he'd gotten away, by using Frankie as a hostage, he could have dropped her and left the car, and turned himself into a bearded hermit whom everyone around here knows by sight. In other words, Sam would have vanished; and the killer of Poling and Galt would never have been caught."

Herb broke the long silence.

"The nerve of the guy! Killing a man with a knife that actually had on it his own fingerprints! If anything would confuse suspicion, that would."

Jim nodded. "Sure. That's why he went to such pains to get it. He's inventive. As a matter of fact" —he grinned again—"there's been a lot of smartness used here. Spencer, for example, told me that you'd been shot, Mr. Farnham, and hadn't broken your arm. Did it just to jar me. He knew I knew something. He even showed me a bullet and said it had been taken out of your arm."

Farnham chuckled. "Barking up the wrong tree."

Herb turned toward the big man: "Tell me one thing. How come you started looking for the Golden Gregg?"

Farnham looked uncomfortable. "It seems foolish, now. And almost criminal. But remember when Mrs. Voight was getting up a gold-panning party a few days ago? Well, I went on one three years ago. By George! They were all on that party—Howard, Miss McKay, Mrs. Voight, Galt, myself—and Sam was in charge of the victuals. Funny I never thought of that. Anyway, there were about twenty of us in all, and it was pretty exciting to see the yellow sheen in the bottom of those pans. The stream-bed we worked—or, rather, played in—had water in it only during the rainy season, and nobody knew how it was fed. Underground springs, the guides said.

"Then, that night, we had entertainment. A cowboy played a guitar and an old-time prospector told stories. Among his stories was the one about the Golden Gregg, how it was found by a prospector who heard the gurgle of water, and so on. Well, it occurred to me then that the underground springs where we were camping were the outlet from the cavern that hid the Golden Gregg. The gold we were panning was just a waterborne sample of the gold in the cave.

"I made up my mind to do a little listening out on the desert for underground water. So, evidently, did five other people present that night. When I got started I couldn't quit. I began to be obsessed with the idea that somewhere out in the desert were millions, maybe hundreds of millions, in gold. Of course, I guessed that the same thing attracted Galt here each winter. Once or twice we hinted toward it, but we never really discussed it. Then, when he was killed, and Poling, I naturally felt—"

"Let's not talk about it any more," Mrs. Farnham said to her husband.

"Let's not," Frankie agreed.

At nine o'clock the rain stopped. Frankie grew restless. Finally she said, "Jim—take me for a walk."

Her mother looked at her protestingly. Jim's heart beat hard. He turned to Herb questioningly.

The tall and bony man smiled—sadly, perhaps, but gamely. "Go on, children. I'm tired. And you have my blessing . . . By the way, Jim, I'll want you to sign some papers tomorrow."

Jim was looking into Frankie's eyes. "Papers?" he echoed. "Papers?"

"Yeah. The reason I was still bathing when you came over to my bungalow this afternoon was that I'd been getting off some wires. I had my lawyers buy Poling's ranch—at least, they've already got an option. It's in your name—and mine."

"What!"

"Sure. You found it—for your half-interest. I bought it—for my half. And you'll have to be in charge of operations. I don't know enough about engineering to fix a tire." He walked up to Frankie. He took her hand. "Have a swell walk," he said softly. "And look: I'm leaving Paradise Canyon tomorrow or the next day."

"Leaving!"

Mr. and Mrs. Farnham looked on with surprise. Jim turned his head away.

"Yeah. Got to rush to Florida. A guy down there has turned up eleven new ligulae that I don't have in my collection. So it's up to me to push out in the Everglades pronto and catch up with him."

"Oh," Frankie answered. Suddenly she kissed Herb. Then she took Jim's arm. They hurried out into the night. There were tears in her eyes. Across the gardens a breeze blew, from the rain-freshened vegetation, the scent of jasmine. She took Jim's hand.

DEATH WHISPERS

THE HIGHPORT HERALD
HIGHPORT, NEW YORK
600 CENTRAL AVENUE

Albert L Watson, Chief
Police Headquarters,
Central Avenue at Spring St,
Highport, New York.

Dear Chief Watson:

For more than a month the matter described in the attached document has haunted my conscience. I have considered calling on you and explaining it in detail. I am, however, a somewhat retiring person and that idea has distressed me. I do not talk well and I am uneasy when cross-examined.

On the other hand, since the thing involves two deaths and since one of them was murder, I feel that the police are entitled to the whole story, although, as you will see, there is nothing left for the police to do.

My conscience, my respect for law, and my notion of my duty as a citizen, are among the reasons which prompt me to write this out. I'm afraid there is another: an exhibitionistic desire to set down a remarkable series of events—an adventure rare in the life of persons like myself—which culminated when the whisper of death was very close to me.

So here is the thing which rankles my conscience and still prickles my skin. I trust you will file it away where it will be forgotten. But, because it has been placed in proper hands, I shall sleep better.

Yours very sincerely,
RALPH BARRINGTON WALKER.

Chief Watson read the letter, polished his bald head with the heel of his hand and muttered, "Crank!"

Lieutenant Quag, who was sitting nearby, failed to hear. "What'd you say, Chief?"

The bald man held up a typewritten script—seventy pages of it—and yawned. "Some dope thinks he solved a murder, I guess. He's written the cops a love-letter about it. Imagine!"

Then he began to read. For a few minutes his expression was one of sour amusement. Presently it ebbed line by line and was replaced by deep concentration. He leaned over his desk on his elbows and wet his thumb to turn the pages.

"Interesting?" the Lieutenant asked.

His answer was a grunt followed by a command. "Go out and get me some sandwiches and coffee. I'm havin' my lunch here."

Much later, he turned the last page, whistled vaguely for a moment and then put the typewritten pages in a large envelope and wrote, "Permanent File" across it. Lieutenant Quag returned just then. He had been looking for a man who had turned in eight false fire alarms.

"Still readin'?" he asked. "Thought the guy was a nut!"

The Chief sucked his teeth. He took out the script and slid it across the desk. "You read it. Then we'll burn it. Some sap might find it in the files and give it to the reporters for a Sunday supplement feature. Go on! Read it! It'll make you realize what a dumb bunny you are!"

So the Lieutenant began on the first page:

> To whom it may concern:
> My name is Ralph Walker. I am an editorial writer on the staff of the Highport Herald where I have been employed in various capacities for eight years. I am thirty-seven years of age and a graduate of Princeton University; I majored in English, minored in Psychology, and won a Phi Beta Kappa Key in my Junior year. I live at 980 View Avenue and am recently married. My interests have been largely scholastic and my recreations more in the nature of hobbies than games or athletic sports. I am, in other words, an introverted individual and wholly satisfied with my present occupation.

Lieutenant Quag looked up at his superior. "This egg likes himself," he said sardonically. "And all this high-fallutin' language is too much for me! I—"

The Chief frowned. "I said, read it! He can't help it if he's smarter than you are!"

Quag shrugged and went on:

> During September and the early part of October I became inadvertently aware that what had passed as a natural death was a murder. I was able to determine, eventually, how the murder had been committed and by whom. I was also the instrument of final justice in the matter, although that act was outside of my intent. Other lives were in danger. Mine was. And, through the whole episode, I was stone blind. Literally blind.

I had undergone an operation for a somewhat rare ocular affliction and my eyes were under bandages.

"What is the guy," Quag asked, "a mind-reader?"

The chief became impatient. "Look, Lieutenant. He's an editorial writer. He can't help that fancy writin'. He's also one of the smartest lads in this burg and he's got more guts than a train-load of panthers. I've half a mind to telephone him if we get stuck down here. I mean, when we get stuck. Now. Read that. And shut up. It's your assignment for the day."

Quag nodded.

He, too, soon became absorbed in the narrative:

I was operated on late in August. My doctor had explained, before the operation, that I would have to wear bandages on my eyes for six weeks. Inasmuch as I was then a bachelor, living in a small apartment on Crenshaw Street, I made arrangements for a trained nurse to care for me when I returned from the hospital and I prepared to sit out the weeks of darkness at my home. However, good fortune changed that.

Tommy Riker, the young millionaire, is a friend of mine. We had been in college together and, though our modes of living are widely disparate, we had kept up a long and pleasant contact. He planned to be in Europe in September and October and when he learned the nature of my prospective confinement, he insisted that I use his apartment during his absence. He pointed out the cramped size of my own place, the fact that he would have to pay his two servants while he was away, the more or less mythical desirability of someone on his premises to care for them, and the fact that his quarters would be cooler than my own.

His arguments prevailed. Thus, two weeks after the surgery had been performed, I was moved into his luxurious suite. Tommy's place consisted of eight rooms on the top (fourth) floor of the Croyden Arms Apartment on Pine Boulevard. The building was old but substantial and remodeling had made it very comfortable. There was a terrace overlooking the street (though I couldn't "look" at anything) and a wide rear porch with outside stairs leading to the ground. When there was a breeze at all, it blew through Tommy's spacious rooms, and there I set myself up with his two colored servants, Wesley and Minerva, and Miss Straton, my firm and rather prissy nurse.

I was in no great pain either then or afterward, but I was probably a difficult patient in spite of that. To be deprived of sight is a terrible ordeal. For the rest of my life I shall admire the forbearance of the blind. I have become interested in projects for them. Of course, my state of mind was made more irritable by the fact that I knew I would see again, and was impatient for the day to arrive. But I disliked the blackness intensely, and it was some days before I became resigned to weeks of it and began to try to find a certain diversion in my affliction.

That "diversion" took the form of a normal enough "game", considering the ennui of the hours. It consisted, simply, of trying to substitute for sight all my other faculties. The blind play that game constantly—because they must. I did it to while away time. Miss Straton disapproved of it and belittled my efforts—which only intensified them. I am, I fear, a very stubborn individual.

It began, one afternoon, when I was sitting in my bed in the master chamber, which fronted on the Boulevard. "I see," I said to my nurse, that the cops arrested Tim.

I could feel Miss Straton look at me. "Tim?" Who's that?"

"The peddler. The fellow who hawked flowers along the street."

There was another pause—one that disconcerted me. "Why do you think that?" she asked.

"Easy. First, why do I know his name was Tim? I heard Mrs. Baylin ask him his name when he came up the back steps a few days ago. She bought zinnias, incidentally. Two dozen. Second, I heard him complain that he couldn't get a license—for some reason I didn't hear. Third, his voice broke off in the middle of one of those strident yells of his, and his horse started to run. A police whistle blew a second later. I imagined that he'd seen the cop and taken off. Finally, for two days he hasn't come past. So—I conclude he was arrested."

"I see," Miss Straton said. "That's clever—but it's wrong." She seemed pleased at my error. I am stubborn—but she is contrary in that quick way of obese middle-aged spinsters. She also seemed to be acting under some slight stress, so I repeated, "Wrong? How so?"

"I'm not supposed to tell you things that will upset you," she answered finally. "But I guess this won't. Apparently nothing does. He was hit by a truck and killed. It was in the papers last night."

I sat there in a vexed mood. It was too bad the fellow was dead. To me he had been, merely, a loud cheerful voice. But I also felt annoyed because my deduction had failed. And because she was pleased by my failure. It increased my sense of utter incapacity. And it made me determine to repeat the performance successfully. Miss Straton had taken a sniffy attitude about the thing. There had been a sniff in her voice. She disapproved of me anyway, I felt sure. Part of her duty was reading to me, and she did not share my taste in reading matter.

That fact had emerged even at the hospital. "You're a sick man, Mr. Walker," she had said one day. "You shouldn't ask me to read all this stuff about wars and threatened wars and crimes and vice investigations. It's upsetting."

"Maybe it upsets you," I'd answered. "But not me. I'm an editorial writer. It's my business to know what people are doing—not to live in a world of wishful thinking." I had mulled that over and told her we'd read a novel instead of the newspapers. I picked out *The Grapes of Wrath*. It didn't mend the situation between Miss Straton and me.

Anyway, the flower-hawker was dead and that ended that. I was supposed to sit in Tom's apartment thinking of sweetness and light until my month was up—and my nurse was bent on keeping me from learning the truth about anything—if the truth happened to be unpleasant. She regarded that as her duty. And she did her best to prevent me from knowing about the death in the other apartment on our floor.

The death of Robert Purvis.

She failed badly—and I used her failure as my revenge.

Mr. Purvis died in considerable agony on the afternoon of September 16th.

The apartment next door was a reversed duplicate of the one I'd borrowed from Tommy. It shared our back porch and our terrace over the street—although the back porch was open, but a high cement wall separated the terraces. It was occupied by Mr. and Mrs. Duval Baylin, their two grown sons, Clarence and Duval Junior, the Purvises, who were Mrs. Baylin's mother and father, and temporarily, by Lynn Baylin, who was a cousin to the boys and the Purvises' granddaughter.

Lynn was twenty. She was staying with her relatives in the interim between a summer as a camp counselor and the opening of an art school. The two Baylin boys were some years older than she. Mr. and Mrs. Baylin were rather young to have sons of their age. Grandma Purvis was about sixty-five and her husband was sixty-nine when he died.

I knew that, and a great deal more, after I had been in Tommy's apartment for a week. They were friendly people—boisterous, even. They came to visit me on the day of my arrival and every day thereafter. They were flatteringly fascinated by the fact that I was a writer. They regarded me, even, as a minor celebrity. Mrs. Purvis and her daughter,

Mrs. Baylin, vied with each other to prepare delicacies for me, and, since cooking was a hedonistic rite in the family, I was given many handsome additions to the excellent fare provided by Wesley and Minerva.

I knew that Grandfather Robert was wealthy and that he had retired. I knew that Clarence was struggling in the brokerage business, Duval Junior in the grocery business, and that their father was cashier in the Keevley Bank.

I knew that the Purvises had come from Minnesota and that Duval Baylin, Senior, had been born in Wisconsin. I knew that the old gentleman's mother had been a Finn. I knew that the whole bunch of them skied, snow-shoed, skated—and curled. At curling (which I realized vaguely was a kind of bowling on ice with a super-top that looked like a tea kettle) it appeared that Grandmother Purvis herself had held no less than seven County championships. I knew that Grandfather Purvis, like his Finnish ancestors, loved to spend interminable hours steaming out in hot baths. I could hear the water run.

I knew that Duval Junior was one of the best amateur mandolin players I'd ever enjoyed—if not the best. I knew that Lynn could make an unforgettable chicken pie. I knew that Clarence stuttered a little and that Mr. Duval Baylin Senior was a famed poker player. Some of that information had significance later on. Some did not. I knew they liked animals and sports and the movies. I knew they laughed easily and frequently—and I liked them for it. They were gay and gregarious—and no one could have wanted better neighbors during a siege of blindness—although I did disagree with their taste in radio programs—and I had to listen to their selections, because they liked everything loud and forthright. Excepting, perhaps, Lynn—who was as friendly as they, but less violent about it.

I knew, moreover, that Lynn's parents had died when she was twelve and that she had worked hard to help with her education, although her grandparents deplored her independent struggling and had constantly tried to persuade her to let them assume her financial burdens. Above everything else, I knew that Lynn had the most appealing voice I'd ever heard—and of that I shall say more later on.

My knowledge was ramified by the myriad other details you unconsciously garner in talking to people who are liquacious and extroverted. They enjoyed talking about themselves. They were fond of each other. Healthy, robust, merry—they represented tens of thousands of other American families, and I, who had dealt in life with so many exceptions both good and bad, was fascinated by the norm. I suppose I talked to them and questioned them extensively for that very reason: it was fun to learn about people who were just "average" and not criminals or politicians or statesmen or in the public eye for any other reason.

Into that family came death.

My nurse thought I was asleep all during the night of Grandfather Purvis' agony, because she had given me a grain and a half of barbiturate.

The reason for that was another minor feuding between her and me. Late in the evening — perhaps at eleven-thirty — when I'd been "officially" put to bed and the building and the street had quieted down, I'd rallied myself for a cigarette. I lay in my bed smoking and listening to Duval play his mandolin. He was on the terrace and evidently alone, because I couldn't hear even a murmur of conversation. I put out my cigarette after a while and tried again for sleep. But the smell of smoke roused me and I rang for Miss Straton.

"My cigarette must have rolled on to the floor," I said, "and probably I've burned a hole in a thousand dollar carpet."

I didn't feel happy about that possibility and she was far from happy over the fact that I'd rung for her. "This just proves it," she said petulantly.

I agreed that I was a lummox.

"Not slovenly," she answered, "but so set on showing me how bright that journalistic mind of yours is that you imagine things! If there was any smoke — it drifted in from outside. A smouldering trash fire, no doubt. You haven't dropped a cigarette — and this rug is perfectly all right! You've got the fidgets! I'll give you something."

So I was even more irritated. I lay awake trying to think of some way to win my argument about blindness and the analytical mind. I heard Grandfather Purvis' groans begin at about two-thirty — and I knew the time because I'd prepared for my siege in the dark by buying one of those expensive foreign watches which, when you press the stem, musically denotes the time in three-tone rings for the hours, quarters, and minutes. I heard the doctor come at six — and a taxicab later. I caught the sound of the meter flag being racked down and perceived the brief pause for payment.

It was silent on the Boulevard at six. I knew that the doctor had sent for something or somebody and a taxicab had been used to transport it or him. Because I did not know Mr. Purvis especially well — he had visited me only twice — and because one does not necessarily identify a night emergency with death, I went to sleep—and Miss Straton did not waken me until nearly noon. Then I had my breakfast, my bath, my alcohol rub, and I said nothing of what I had heard during the night simply because Miss Straton said nothing. I wanted to gather some further information—and spring it on her.

I did so. The household adjoining mine was abnormally quiet, even for daytime, when all the men save Grandfather Purvis were normally at work. I didn't hear Lynn singing when she washed the luncheon dishes. I didn't hear Ella, their cook, scold the cat. I heard, on the other hand, numerous murmurs and footfalls, which suggested that the men were not at their offices. I heard the automatic elevator that serves both apartments shut and bang a score of times.

The afternoon was hot and sunny. I had learned to "feel" the sunshine—and the edge of a shadow. I could feel it, even, in my bath—for the sun sometimes filtered through a dusty skylight over the tub. I had myself wheeled out on the terrace. At about four o'clock I heard Mrs. Baylin come out on her side of the cement wall. She was weeping. It required less than a second to identify her voice. Most of us know most of each other's voices anyway; we recognize the majority of telephoners with the first word. When you are blind, that voice identification becomes a habit of great acuity. Mrs. Baylin was weeping quietly but with anguish. So I knew that her father's nocturnal seizure had been fatal.

By and by somebody came out and tried to comfort her. But she was inconsolable and commenced to blame herself in a sobbing invective of which I heard fragments: "I feel that it is all my fault! . . . I peeled them—and I've always been afraid of them so I was very careful! . . . I know them well, too . . . and I know that Death Cup the doctor mentioned. . . . I couldn't have missed one in the mess . . . but I did!"

That made things pretty clear. Death Cup—Destroying Angel—Deadly Amanita. A poisonous mushroom. People frequently mistake it for the edible kind. I wondered why Mrs. Baylin felt so sure of her rightness about the matter. And, indeed, her assurance was the basis for a great deal of anxious wondering in her family later on.

Oddly enough, in spite of the grief next door, I felt elation. Invalid psychology, I suppose. I was ready for Miss Straton when she wheeled me back into my bedroom.

"It's too bad," I said quietly, "that old Mr. Purvis is dead."

She was startled. But she made a guess. "You heard them talking just now?"

"Well—yes. I also heard him last night. I heard the doctor. I heard Mrs. Baylin crying. So I knew he had gone. I heard her mention Death Cup—so I know it was mushrooms."

She murmured assent. "I tried to keep the news from you. As part of my duty."

"But I figured it all out. You see—there's something in what I said. You can figure out things—!"

She was disgusted. "Well—of the attitudes to take!"

I thought that she was probably right. "Anybody else sick?" I asked.

"Duval Junior was—for a while. Not very. There must have been only a few bad ones in the batch. It's a shame!"

"Yeah. It's a shame. It's always a shame. Thirty people a year die of it in New York City alone. We've had a dozen cases in Highport. People are such nitwits. They picked them, I suppose—"

"I don't know."

"Probably. They rush out into the woods and because of some old wives' tale about—'if they peel they're safe'—they bring home a load of death and cook it—and die." I realized that I was writing aloud an editorial about "Don't eat mushrooms!"—so I shut up.

I heard the undertaker come, and I knew it was he when a coffin bumped hollowly up the rear stairway.

After supper Lynn came over to see me. She sounded sad and possibly anxious. I couldn't be sure. I knew she had brown hair and blue eyes and was about five feet six—Miss Straton had vouchsafed that much. "Mousy brown," she had said about Lynn's hair. I suspected she was pretty, simply because my nurse had been so grudging about her description. But I could only suspect from her voice that she was worried. Not just sad. Worried.

We made the customary observations at such a time. I said the old chap had seemed extremely nice. She recollected a scattering of little things he had done—how he'd whistled for her to dance when she was a child—butterballs he'd brought home—the monkey he had given her. He sounded like a sort of idealized grandparent. The kind you would yearn to see, if you were eight years old.

After a while I stopped her reminiscences and switched her to talking about herself and her plans to study art. It revived her, somewhat.

"I'm no good," she said. "But I love it. So I hope to learn enough to be able to teach."

I've often admired that facet of human nature—the side that is willing to teach a subject in which it cannot create. It's unselfish. After an hour or so, Rafe and Chan showed up: two youngsters from the city room of the *Herald*. They came breezing in and Rafe called ahead, "Hello, Barry, you old cockroach! How's being in the Black Hole today? Webbon told us to look in on you when we picked up the obit! So we—."

They broke off. "This is Miss Baylin," I said. "Mr. Teague, Mr. Collever. Reporters. Bum ones."

I had another scrap of evidence about Lynn's looks. Both boys paused and their voices hushed. If she had been homely, they would have ploughed over their callous reference to an obituary.

Lynn said, "Hello," and "How do you do?" nicely.

Chan apologized. "We didn't realize you were here, Miss Baylin. Sorry."

The chin of her spirit was up, though. "I understand. Have you been over to talk to my family?"

"Not yet."

"Then—maybe I can give you what you want. It'll save Grandma and Aunt Alice a lot of pain. I suppose you have most of the information about Grandfather Purvis in your—your morgue."

"Yeah."

"I wouldn't put myself through that," I said to Lynn.

But she did. She answered their questions—even about things that were pretty hard to discuss. Her grandfather's will, for example. "I really don't know—exactly. I'm sure that he divided it among all of us. We've always understood that. There were a few other people—Mr. Laidlaw—who was his oldest friend. He was here for dinner last night. And Ella, I suppose. She's cooked for them for ages. And a couple of pet things—like an astronomical society he was interested in, and his college."

"Have any idea how much it is?" Chan asked.

I squalled at him. "For God's sake—!"

But Lynn answered. "About three hundred thousand dollars, I believe. He said something like that—a while ago. There's never been any secret about such things in our family. We've all shared everything. And Grandfather has helped every last one of us—plenty of times!"

Rafe asked a question I could have socked him for. I would never have let him into my room if I had even thought of the possibility of such a question: "Don't suppose anybody could have slipped him that mushroom?"

There was a little pause. Then Lynn said quietly, "Good heavens, no! We all loved him!"

After that, I sent them away. I was furious. But I was also alarmed—by a very small thing. Lynn's pause. They hadn't noticed it. But I had— because I couldn't see, so every other sense was strained for invisible indices of mood and meaning.

She got up after a little while. "Better go back, I guess. I'll drop in tomorrow."

"Don't feel that you have to."

"I'd like to." I could hear her moving toward the door. "So they call you Barry? That's much nicer than Ralph! Goodnight."

I lay there. She had turned over in her mind the question about the possibility that the toadstools had been administered. And it had upset her. It was enough to upset anybody.

Because I write editorials, I frequently think of people *en masse*. I consider them statistically. After Miss Straton turned out my light—a click that made no difference in what I could discern—and went off with my evening paper—I began to think that way. I couldn't help it. They were nice people—friendly people—sincere people—for all I could tell. They had been hospitable to me, and thoughtful. They were my neighbors. I had counted on them to help pass the dull hours of darkness. And one of them was dead.

I knew that under the surfaces of many such homes were elements which belied serenity. Fears, worries, debts, problems, jams, ambitions, and frustrations. I knew, furthermore, that there were fifteen thousand murders in the United States which the police would like to solve—and couldn't. I knew that by various inferences, thousands of others had been committed and gone unrecognized. Even a tenth of three hundred thousand dollars is a lot of money—especially in view of the fact that people have killed deliberately and coldbloodedly for less. For much less. For a few dollars; twenty—or a hundred.

It was hard to imagine murder being done by any one of those people. But, because of my training and my way of thought, I had reason to believe that under various circumstances a large proportion of all people is capable of killing. Indeed, I knew it to be a fact. I tried to arrest the unpleasant foraging of my mind by telling myself that I could do nothing about Robert Purvis' death in any event. Nobody could do anything about it. It was undoubtedly just what the world presumed: a miserable accident. But the thought stuck, and it was a long time before I went to sleep.

I woke up sometime after midnight—not with a start, but slowly. I had a feeling that my awakening had been caused in part by some external agent—although I slept fitfully enough anyway in those days—but after a while, I realized what the agent was. The still warm night air was faintly tinged with the aroma of bacon. Nobody was cooking bacon in my apartment. So—it undoubtedly came from the Baylins'. Nothing abnormal about that. They'd been up most of the night before. The day past had been bitter and distressing. One or more of them had probably eaten lightly—or eaten nothing. But hunger had at last asserted itself and he or she or they had gone to the kitchen to fry bacon and probably scramble eggs.

With that thought, I wooed sleep again. But I could not sleep for the reason that I was not satisfied with my conclusion. It explained what was happening, undoubtedly. It left something else unexplained. Something remote and forgotten. I struggled with the feeling that gave me, and abandoned my effort at last. I was on the verge of sleep when memory shook me awake.

It was the memory of a trifle. That scent of cooking had come to me at night on another occasion. When? Two nights before. Of what sort of cooking? Not bacon—but something being fried—sautéed in butter. Mushrooms. I wasn't sure—but mushrooms have a very definite odor. What time? Eleven, maybe. I hadn't noticed. But the unusual circumstance accompanying that recollection of a scent and a faraway sizzling made me sit up in my bed. It had taken place at a time when there was supposed to be nobody in the Baylin apartment. That was the catch—the flaw—the oddment.

Lynn had said they were all going out. But there was a better check than that. Miss Straton had neglected to give me my preslumber medicine—a sludge of milk and vitamin-containing gruel. She had found me awake at ten and gone to the kitchen to fix the beverage. We had no milk, it appeared, so she had stepped across the little hall to borrow some. Only—no one had answered her knock—so I had been compelled to take the stuff with water.

As I lay in my bed I could remember Miss Straton's words: "I tried to borrow some milk—but there's nobody home. I think Miss Baylin mentioned that they were all going out."

However, somebody had been in the apartment an hour later—and I was sure the elevator had not come up. Sure—because its arrival with the first of the returning Baylins disturbed me again that night, and kept me awake afterward as, one by one, they came home. Somebody had been in the apartment cooking something. Probably mushrooms. Cooking them—furtively.

That was what my thought amounted to. And, of course, I thought next that in order to poison one individual, you'd have to put the poisonous mushrooms on his plate. You couldn't add them to a stew or a sauce that would be served to everyone. You would have to prepare a separate toxic dose and hide it—in say, a dish on the ledge under a dining table—then add it unobserved to a single portion. That picture flashed into my mind. If you were smart, you might give yourself a tiny dose, so you would be ill enough to divert any possible suspicion from yourself. Duval Junior had been sick.

I thought of Duval—nervous, quick, intelligent. I didn't know what he looked like. Not even the color of his hair and eyes. I would have to ask Miss Straton. Suppose, however, a hypothetical murderer had realized that, if deliberate poisoning became suspected, his own illness would be regarded not as an "out" but as an indication of possible guilt? To prevent such an occurrence, he might have given the lethal dose to his wealthy grandfather and the slightly poisonous one to—anybody but himself. It was a step in reasoning that would be difficult to make believable, and probably impossible to prove. But that step might mean that to imagine Duval had done such a thing was stupid imagining.

Such thoughts were undoubtedly horrible. But I was not horrified. People believe they would be, in similar cases. They assume they would hesitate a long time to call a casual acquaintance a killer on such flimsy evidence. And they do hesitate—if the nomination must be public. But I am enough of a psychologist to know that all of us have a corner of our minds reserved for a far franker and more sinister regard of our fellowmen than we would care to admit. I imagined murder in the apartment across the hall with the detached shamelessness of a small boy picturing himself slaying Indians. I was wide awake and astonished—but I was not horrified. Horror crept into my mind only when, presently, I reflected that Lynn might be a party to the deed, or might become involved in it.

I should also truthfully confess that, by that time, I was sure Robert Purvis had been murdered. I never doubted it for a moment again.

As evidence, I had only the flimsy belief that, two nights before, somebody had sneaked back into the Baylin apartment and cooked some mushrooms in butter. I added, after thought, two more points: the fact that Lynn was contemplating he same idea—and a hazy recollection of the dish-washing that had followed the midnight cookery. It was extremely sleazy as memory—really not even a decent impression—of water running and running in the kitchen—pouring into a pan from a faucet. That would be the murderer erasing the traces of poison—washing away the muscarine or phallin nervously, no doubt—afraid that the next food cooked in the pan might make somebody ill, or afraid that suspicion might lead to chemical analysis and analysis might lead to him.

I decided that cheerful deep-voiced Grandfather Purvis had been assassinated—and the thought fascinated me. I lay there wondering if I could figure out who had done it. And I asked myself who had been on hand.

His wife, Emma, a hearthy woman, a good cook, and very kind. What else was she? I didn't know.

His daughter—Mrs. Alice Baylin. A woman much like her mother.

Mr. Baylin—the bank cashier. Educated, affable, quiet, a baseball fan (his radio had hammered the World Series into my brain) and sympathetic. It was Mr. Baylin who had put an elastic band on the red end of the push-button on my bedside light. "Then you can feel whether it's on or off," he had said. "Seems to me if I was blind, I'd still want to know whether I was lying in the light or the dark."

There was Duval, whom they called "Junior".

His brother Clarence.

Lynn—my companion and the daughter of Mrs. Baylin's dead sister.

Ella, the cook and family retainer.

And Mr. Laidlaw, whoever he was. "Grandfather's oldest friend," Lynn had said.

Inasmuch as I liked the Baylins. I leaned at once toward Mr. Laidlaw. *Probably an old futz.* I thought. Pressed for funds. Had envied his wealthy friend Robert for decades. Polished him off.

Of course, it was difficult to conceive of a mere friend of the family slipping into the apartment, secretly preparing a dish of death, and pouring it on his friend's meal a night later. Still—it was possible.

The thing I needed to know was, who needed a few thousand dollars badly?

I smiled when I thought of that. Who doesn't need a few thousand dollars badly? Almost any one of us can change a wish into a need at a moment's notice. And most of us are in debt, in the sense that we are buying on installment plans, that we are obligated for rents and premiums, that we owe taxes, and consequently have, in one way or another anticipated our earnings. A large percentage of us is in serious debt, with borrowings owed and no way out in sight. A small fraction of us—but a fraction that runs into hundreds of thousands (I was editorializing again)—needs money for purposes which cannot readily be revealed: to pay blackmail, to replace defalcations, to square ourselves with gamblers, and so on.

It was more likely that everybody in the Baylin ménage needed several thousand dollars fairly badly than it was that no one of them ever wished for more funds. Of course, there is a long leap between wishing for money and being willing to kill for it—a leap which, in my mind, passes beyond the borders of sanity. So, even if I did learn anything about the financial status of the individual members of the family, I would have to apply my knowledge with a grain of salt. To need money was not to be liable to condemnation—in spite of the fact that most murders are for profit.

I thought of that—and then I turned to a consideration of the act itself. My picture was pretty clear. Somebody who knew that the Baylins were going to have steak and mushrooms. say, for dinner, had provided himself with a handful of toadstools, cooked them on the night before, put them, surely, in a sauce like Ella's sauce, hidden them in a handy place, and covertly intermingled them with Grandfather Purvis' portion. While a plate was being passed—or while some incident diverted the general attention. It wouldn't be very difficult. Dangerous, maybe—but not difficult.

Miss Straton knocked and came into my room at that moment. "I saw your light still on," she said reprovingly. "It's well after midnight. If you're having trouble in going to sleep. I'll give you a sedative."

I thanked her, and she fiddled with my pillows and bedclothes— pulling my sheet so tight that I knew I would have to struggle for some time after her departure to free myself. An idea had come into my mind. My nurse and I had been feuding for some time over what was right and wrong, what the President should do, and whether or not the human race had depreciated several hundred percent in the last twenty years. The theory I had just evolved would be a shock to her. I took a considerable pleasure in shocking her—just as she did in reproving me or catching me in an error. My theory would be perfectly safe with her: Miss Straton was sometimes irritating—but her fundamental character was solid iron. She was professionally close-mouthed. She had morals and ethics. But I had an additional motive: if I were to occupy the remainder of my career as a blind man with the investigation of a thus-far imaginary murder, I would need help. I would need eyes. Maybe she would refuse to lend hers—but I could try. So, I prepared to let fall my bolt.

"Miss Straton," I said, "I was awake because I have something on my mind."

"Oh?" she said—rather disparagingly.

"Yes. I think that Robert Purvis was murdered."

Then, with great anticipation, I waited. I could imagine her words: You newspapermen! Always thinking the worst! Your minds in the gutter! The Baylins are such lovely people—and you suspect them—!

Only—that wasn't her answer. She spoke, finally, in a low and tense voice. "You think that, too, do you?"

To say that I was startled is to give no adequate notion of my reaction. I suppose that, up to then, my speculations had been unreal. Miss Straton's words suddenly filled them with a stony and frightening actuality. I gasped. "Then you—?"

"Why do you think so, Mr. Walker?"

I explained. In detail.

Again, she paused. "Yes. I smelled that cooking, too."

Oddly enough, I, who had taken the whole thing so calmly, was outraged at her calm. I said, "But—good heavens, Miss Straton! If you've been thinking a horrible thing like this—why haven't you—?"

She interrupted me. "I am a nurse, Mr. Walker. I'm accustomed to horror. I could tell you not one, but a dozen stories—like this. If I chose, that is. You needn't pester me, though. I don't choose! I am just as sure as you are that he was killed."

"Then—don't you think we ought to do something about it?"

"Evil," she answered sanctimoniously, "will out."

"It will not! Not unless somebody 'outs' it! Did all the 'cases' you just referred to lead to just punishment?"

"No. But—in this instance—there is a difference. I am quite sure that the Baylins themselves suspect the truth. Miss Lynn, tonight, for example. Her manner was worried. If you could have seen her—"

"I'd like to see her," I said. "We can skip that, though. I know she was worried. Are the others?"

"I'd say they were. Quite anxious. You notice—they're quieter—"

"That's natural. With a death—"

"Yes. But the way of that quietness isn't natural. The way they look at each other—and the way they talk—or don't talk—"

I thought about that. It is a grim situation when a group of people begins to know that in its midst is a murderer. A situation calculated to break down morale, shatter loyalties, destroy nerves, and bring to light the worst in all the natures involved. Suspicion of murder: Maybe Duval did it. Clarence. Dad. Lynn. How did Mother behave that night? Has somebody got a secret and did that somebody kill to protect it?

My sudden picture of life in the Baylin household was a shocking one. I said something about it to Miss Straton.

"I've seen it before in other families," she said with a voice that was implacably disapproving. "It's not pleasant. If I were you, I'd simply forget what you've been thinking about and let nature take its course. It's always wisest."

That sort of bromide angered me. "Sure," I answered. "And what's nature? Isn't human nature designed to interfere with the rest of nature? If you let nature take its course, it'll include letting my nature find out all I can about the Baylins."

"I was afraid of that," she said.

"And I may want you to help me."

"I'd rather not, Mr. Walker. It's outside my duties—"

"You're scared?"

That touched her quick, as I had known it would. "I'm a person of religious convictions," she replied—and by her manner she intimated that I was not—"and I dread neither man nor the devil."

"In other words, you haven't a public conscience. If you saw a man robbing another on the street, you wouldn't bother to run for the police?"

"I mind my own business."

"And help nobody. Right no wrongs. Do no good deeds. Let the rest of the world go hang."

She melted a little. "If I see a way I can help them, I'll help, Mr. Walker. If I can be of any real use to you in the same cause, I'll try. Only—I'll be the judge of that usefulness. Do you think you can sleep?"

"Oh, sure. Like a baby."

She went out, with the over-pronounced silence of all nurses, and I knew I had eyes to use in the days ahead. Shrewd eyes, even if what they observed was sometimes colored by a most righteous brain.

Lynn called on me in the morning.

That wasn't usual. She knew it was my habit to "work" in the morning. The publisher of the *Herald* had given me full pay for the length of my operation and convalescence. He had insisted that he would not expect any copy from me. But, after a week, I had been filled with the urge to tell my readers what was what, and he had arranged to have a stenographer sent to Tommy's apartment. Each day, after Miss Straton read the papers, I dictated two or three editorials. Some of them, I found later, weren't at all bad—considering that I was flat on my back and couldn't see a light bulb at two paces.

Lynn came just as I was finishing up a piece about political skul-duggery at the state capital. A favorite theme of mine. I have never understood how states manage to keep going in view of the net brains, personality, motives, and veniality of their representatives. There is a mysterious and wonderful quality about democracy—as there is about man himself.

"You're wearing black," I said. I don't know how I knew. I will never know. I was simply certain—abruptly—that she was in black. Telepathy, if you like. It would have been useful to me later—but it served me only that once, and then merely to tell me the color of a woman's dress.

I heard her breath catch. "Yes. The funeral is—this afternoon."

"I see."

"Grandfather would have wanted it that way. He hated the whole thing. I mean—"

"—the panoply of death?"

I presumed that she nodded—without realizing I couldn't see. "He was a sweet old thing. He had so much common sense. We'll miss him dreadfully." She paused. "All of us."

A man is a fool. I was listening to her voice—listless now, with undertones of worry. That lovely voice. Musical and husky. Probably the sirens had voices like that, and they used them to lull and deceive. But I could think only that such a voice was meant to inspire and to reassure. It hurt me to catch the trouble in it. I believe I said that I have become interested in blind persons and their problems—since my malady. They have told me that you can judge character more surely by a voice than by a face. But I don't think I was busy at that time in appraising the girl's character; I think I was—merely—in love with her voice. So I did something impulsive and potentially dangerous. I noticed that pause between her statement that they would miss their grandfather and her additional phrase: "All of us."

I said, to my own confoundation, "Don't you mean, Lynn—'all but one of us'?"

Then I lay there—because she was saying nothing. That is one of the formidable handicaps of blindness—that wait for responses—in the dark, without the clue of eyes and lips—a wait to know whether an answer will be full of hate, or fear, or relief.

Lynn whispered, eventually. She whispered, "Yes."

Then I was startled. My self-centered preoccupation vanished. The full force of her admission went through me in a series of waves. This girl suspected what I had abstractly—almost lightly—assumed to be true; and she had shared her suspicion with me! For an instant that latter fact gave me an intense feeling of pleasure. She had confided in me— willingly and courageously. But after my first pleasurable reaction I had two others: perhaps her confidence was only the product of fear—fear and her comparative strangeness in the rest of the group; or perhaps it was swift and clever act to find out how much I knew and how much I guessed—an effort to cover up for herself or for somebody else. I think I would have given all my savings at that moment for one look at her eyes. And even then, I might have been deceived. People are seldom what they seem.

I didn't speak at all. So, after a long time, she said, "I've wondered— how many other people would be thinking the same thing."

After that, I had to decide whether to make my statement seem like an insulting speculation, or to take her into my confidence. There were no alternatives. And I chose the latter course because, as I have said, a man is a fool.

"I don't know," I answered.

"It's a terrible thing to think of!"

"Yes it is, Lynn."

"To sit there—looking from face to face—wondering. And to watch them look from face to face—and at you—wondering about you."

"If you don't want to discuss it—"

"I'd rather," she replied, after a moment. "I think I came over here to do exactly that. I think I was losing my grip—in the house—and I felt that I had to talk to somebody. You're detached, and calm—"

"That's an undeserved compliment."

"But you are. I've got to decide whether to just forget it—or to try to do something—"

"You could go to the police—"

"Yes. I've thought of that. But suppose I was wrong? Suppose it was an accident? Then—think of the appalling mess—the shame—the everlasting cloud that would hang over everybody! I couldn't do that."

"The police can be discreet, if the occasion warrants it."

"Are you sure? The answer is, you're not. Nobody is. If they turn up something that they think is 'leading'—their discretion may very well fly away. People forget that the police are just human beings."

"So—?" I said.

Lynn touched my shoulder—put her hand on it—and leaned near me. "What makes you think—the thing I think?"

I told her about the cooking of mushrooms. She didn't interrupt me. When I'd finished, she said, "Then—it's true."

"Not necessarily. Somebody could have cooked a few because he was in the mood for mushrooms. With scrambled eggs, say. And there's another—outside—chance. It could have been somebody who sneaked in that night—though you'd think a person not belonging to the family would have done their infernal cookery elsewhere. On the other hand— it would have put suspicion on the family if it was ever discovered. I've been mulling a lot. People are afraid of detection these days. Smart people. And justifiably afraid, in most cases. The person who cooked toadstools—if we grant somebody did—might have done it in the apartment because he knew the family would be out and because he thought that if it came to a showdown and the poison was found on the pan—the blame would surely be fixed on a member of the household. It's a pretty fancy idea—"

"Anything that any of them did would be—pretty fancy."

"What do you mean by that?"

"They're bright," she answered. "Full of ideas, and information, and ingenuity. Anything they did would be tricky. That's another reason I felt so hopeless. More than likely somebody did kill Grandfather. And more than likely it would be impossible to prove it."

She had been talking with increasing nervousness. I put my hand over the hand on my shoulder. "Look," I said. "Either we're going to discuss this more—or we'll quit right now. It's up to you. If you want to go on, there are questions I'd like to ask. If not—let's stop now. I've got some Chinese checkers with two sizes of marbles and I can play a sort of half-decent game that way. You can bring the board and turn on the radio—"

"Ask the questions," Lynn said. "I can't stop thinking about it. And I can guess what they'll be. Who needs money badly? Who knows anything about mushrooms? Who had the chance to come back here the night before the murder? Who had the chance to put poisonous mushrooms in Grandfather's dish? Am I right?"

I was surprised. "More than right. Well?"

"The answer is—to everything: everybody."

"Meaning what?"

"Well—take the matter of money. Mind you, Barry, I haven't been poking these questions at people. I wouldn't dare. I've just been piecing together what I've heard and learned and inferred since I've been here in Highport. We all knew that Grandfather's fortune would be divided among us. That was never a secret. So you can't get anything from that fact. Now. Take me. I want to spend three years in art school. I need the money for that. I've been working my way this far. It looks as if lack of funds and a job might keep me from going on. That wouldn't be a motive for killing a person I love—to me. But it might look like it to somebody else. See?"

"Not really," I said.

"It might. I know. All right. My uncle—Mr. Baylin—has been worrying fearfully about money for weeks. He's had two salary cuts. He's pretty bitter about it. I've caught him in fits of abstraction so deep he jumped like a cat when I spoke. Why? I don't know. Before Grandfather died, I've found myself wondering if he was in some kind of financial trouble. Some sort of jam. Maybe you'd wonder why—if he was in trouble—he didn't go straight to Grandfather. And it's hard to explain. Grandfather was a kind man. But he was also terribly straight-laced. I don't know anything about banking—but I presume it's full of temptations. Of near-shady chances to make profits. And if my uncle had taken such a chance and lost—he simply couldn't talk to his father-in-law about it. If you understand."

"I do. That's just a suspicion, of course. But it might include—I hate to say it."

"Yes. My aunt. If Uncle Duval had told her about—the trouble I'm assuming now—then she would have a—"

"Motive."

"Yes. A motive. There are other things. Grandma Purvis is an old darling. Liberal and rugged and gay. She's also an old rogue. Grandfather was crazy about her—and disapproved of her all his life. Grandma had a passion for horses and betting—like thousands of other women her age. It gave her a terrific kick. The whole family knew about it—except Grandfather. She managed to sneak away and see a few races every year—on one pretext or another. Shopping expeditions to New York—and club conventions. As far as I know, she was a restrained better. Two dollars—or, at most—five a race. But—I don't really know at all. She was acquainted with a score of bookies. She knew the times of every horse in every trial for years. We thought it was terribly cute. That is—till now. I don't believe for a minute that she could poison her husband. And yet—her betting doesn't seem so innocent now. Suppose she was in one of those conventional sordid messes with a bookie? Or something?"

Nothing could be said about that. Lynn was giving me—not motives, but the possibility of motives. Not fire—but smoke.

She hurried on. "I never did trust Clarence. It's silly, I presume. I remember when I was sixteen he took me home from a dance once and kissed me. He insisted that cousins could marry and it was all right. The point is, I didn't want to be kissed, but he kissed me anyhow. It was kind of—nasty. I know nothing about his business. He's a broker. I've heard him say, a dozen times, 'Money's scarce. You've got to get it by any method you can—and what they call "legal" today spoils the game.' Things like that. Junior—that's Duval—bought a grocery. He was terribly enterprising in college. He managed all sorts of things. But the grocery business is difficult. He's been on the verge of losing his store for a long while. It's worried half the fun out of him. Ella—the cook—has nourished a dream to own a cottage and a garden—all her life. Last year she made the down payment on a bigger plot and house than she can afford. That's an old story—"

"Yes," I said. "What about Mr. Laidlaw?"

"I don't know. He was a very old friend of Grandfather's. Interested in astronomy. He's been around for as long as I can remember. We've almost forgotten he isn't a relative. He's a tall string-bean sort of man with a deep voice and eyes set way back in his head. He gave me the shivers when I was a kid. Now—I like him. He's tremendously well-informed. An encyclopedia. He lives on some sort of income—"

I stopped that line of discussion. It was getting nowhere. Or, rather, everywhere. "Any mushroom experts in the family?" I asked.

Lynn chuckled ruefully. "You only need a handbook, don't you? Cooking is a family hobby. They've all tried to outdo each other getting up midnight snacks and so on for years. Grandfather has—had—a place on the Rhode Island shore—a summer place. We've all been there—often. A hundred-odd acres. At one time or another, we've studied birds and flowers and insects and—presumably—some of us—mushrooms. I remember gathering edible ones with Junior and Clarence and their mother when we were kids. From the old pasture—"

"And who could have come home to cook them the other night?"

She hesitated. "I figured that if it wasn't an accident somebody must have cooked them sometime. The ones we had were sautéed—in butter—as usual—and my uncle served them on individual filets. Heaps of them. I imagined that somebody had fried the poisonous ones and kept them ready. Maybe in wax paper in his pocket. Or her pocket. And put them on when we all went to the window."

"Went to the window?"

"Yes. Think back. You must have heard the parade that went by about seven-fifteen that night? The night Grandfather ate the things? A calliope and red fire and so on—for the commission election?"

I remembered. I nodded.

"Well—they're inveterate parade-watchers. We all went out on the terrace."

"Who went last? And who was first to go back to the table?"

"I don't know."

"Try to think!"

"Barry, don't you believe I have tried? It was all just confused. People jumping up. People straggling back. We'd already been served. Suppose somebody had poisoned his own plate? It wouldn't have taken a second to switch plates. There was only candle-light. It could even have been done without the parade—when the plates were being passed. I've thought and thought—and I can't see anything that indicated a thing!"

"Who sat beside him?"

"I did—on one side. Mr. Laidlaw on the other."

"And—about—who could have come home to cook those things?"

There was resignation in her voice. "Mr. Laidlaw had a key," she said. "He was using Grandfather's library. He could have come in. We were all out that night. Alibis are so silly, anyway! The guilty person always has the best one, doesn't he?"

"Sometimes it seems best—at first."

"Very well. Let me think. My aunt and uncle were at the movies. They went late—they said—about half-past nine. Down to the corner theatre. Uncle Duval got bored by the picture and went out. He told me he walked along Main Street and went into a shooting gallery and came back to pick up my aunt. My aunt says she sat in the theatre. Junior," she frowned in thought, "had been going over his stock at night for two nights and coming home very late. He says he did that. How can you prove he was downtown alone in his store every minute?"

She stopped again—and went on impatiently. "Clarence was 'out with a blonde.' Was he—or could he produce a 'blonde' who would say he was with her all evening? It was Thursday, remember. Ella's day off. It was hot. Ella mentioned casually that she'd been in Revere Park down at the river—alone—that evening. Grandmother talks about 'her last evening' with Grandfather. She says they took a long drive together. Well—they often did. But Grandfather's dead, and he's the only person who could have proved it. So you see? If somebody did come home and prepare that poison—it could have been anybody. And if somebody else had walked in—all the cooker would have had to do was to take his 'feast' to his room—and dispose of it."

"Suppose," I said, "the person cooking the toadstools had been caught by somebody who asked for a portion of the delicacy?"

"Simple. You'd just agree to serve it—put it in a glass dish—drop the dish—and throw everything away because there was broken glass in it. That—or a number of other things."

"Where were you?" I asked it curtly.

I could hear Lynn draw in her breath. "I—was—like the others. Doing something perfectly ordinary—normal—but something I can't prove. I know a man—a sculptor who lives here in town—and he was going to meet me in the lobby of the Highport Plaza for dinner. Late—because he was working. You see—we all dined out—or 'picked up' something to eat—because Ella was out. I got to the hotel at nine. I knew he wouldn't be on time. He never is. He had me paged around ten. He told me to eat and he'd come later. So I did. I had my dinner alone—and I dawdled over it. Then I got another message and he said he couldn't make it. So I went to the movies, too. Alone. I got back after twelve."

The inadequacy of her alibi didn't seriously bother me. I found myself thinking about the sculptor. A man for whom she would wait a whole hour in a hotel lobby because 'he was always late.' A man, therefore, whom she knew well and whom she liked. I didn't say anything at all. If I wasn't jealous, then the word has no meaning.

I was surprised when she said, "You see? Even you don't accept that! It's true—but—I was afraid—when you started asking where we were—you'd doubt my story!"

"It was the Death Cup," I said, deliberately changing the subject. "At least, according to what Miss Straton read to me from the papers. The Destroying Angel—which is common, looks like the edible kind of mushroom, has no odd taste, and is full of phallin. That poison usually doesn't start to work until so much has been absorbed that it's too late to use first-aid measures—or any others. It's easy to find. Doesn't take a lot of it. If Duval got a taste, he got a mighy small one—whether he gave it to himself—!"

She said breathlessly, "I've thought of that—!"

"—or some clever person gave it to him to throw any presumptive suspicion his way. It's a frightful death—"

There was remembered horror in her voice. "His groaning woke me. We thought he was having a bilious attack—for a long time. He's had a good many. Then—we thought it was a kidney stone and we got a doctor—and the doctor didn't seem to realize for quite a while. It was daylight when he said, all of a sudden, 'Have you people served mushrooms?' "

"Daylight—and too late. Funny." I mused aloud. "Toadstools are a sort of mediocre method for murdering anybody. People react differently. There are antidotes to some. Whoever did it, granting somebody did, couldn't have been absolutely sure that Mr. Purvis would die."

"No."

"Did you all know—on Thursday—that you were going to have steak and mushrooms for dinner?"

"Yes," she answered. "You see, Duval Junior brought home the mushrooms. From his store. Prize ones—and fresh. He showed them to—most of us, anyhow. And he probably told the rest. You must realize by now that all the Baylins are pretty keen about food."

"Yes—and gratefully. Though I must say I'll feel wary about accepting any further culinary tidbits."

"I doubt if they offer any more. They're sensitive."

Maybe I smiled at that. I'm not sure. But at any rate. I heard her stand up quickly. "I thought it would make me feel better to tell you all this," she said rapidly. "But it doesn't! You just lie there, as if you knew more than you cared to tell! I wanted to get it off my chest! But you make me feel half-guilty myself. If you could know what living is like—right through this wall—with everybody looking at everybody else, and listening, and starting to ask questions that are never finished, and sitting in chairs staring at space—! Aunt Alice was so sure the ones she peeled were all right! It's awful! I know I can't stand it much longer! But you just lie here playing arithmetic with us—"

"I didn't mean to hurt your feelings," I said. "I can imagine how it must be. And I think you were very clear-headed and enterprising to ask yourself all these questions and get so many answers. It made the perplexity greater—but at least it showed nobody could walk up to someone and say, 'You did it.' "

"It probably showed"—she had gone to the door—"that the whole dreadful tragedy was an accident—and whoever came home and cooked mushrooms just sampled Junior's basketful for his own pleasure and is scared to death to say anything about it now."

She pulled open the door so forcefully I could feel a draught of air. "Goodbye."

I sank lower on my pillows. I'd made her angry—and there was nothing I could do about that. I couldn't even follow her to apologize. "I'm sorry," I said.

Her voice was calmer. "I am, too. I'll drop in this afternoon, when I don't feel so impossible!"

She went then, leaving me to ponder the mass of information she had given me.

They all probably needed money—as I had more or less guessed. Not one of them had a good alibi for the night before the death. They all knew about mushrooms, presumably, and they all knew that mushrooms had been bought for Friday's dinner. A fine business. I wondered who Mr. Laidlaw was—and decided to find out.

But I had no chance to investigate then. Miss Straton came in. "I guess," she said with testy vigor, "you have a pretty good idea of who did away with her grandfather!"

That flabbergasted me. I didn't know whether to be madder because she had been listening to us or because she had come to such a conclusion. Finally, instead of showing my sentiments, I said calmly, "How do you know?"

"She was too quick at explaining how a person could have gotten out of the fix if he'd been caught frying the mushrooms—the poison ones!"

I grinned. "She's bright—that's all."

"And you should have seen her face when you asked her what she had been doing the night before the killing!"

"You weren't just listening," I said, "but also looking through the keyhole."

Miss Straton sniffed. "Keyhole nothing. I went out on the terrace from the living room and stood behind the portieres!"

"That's one of the handicaps of being blind," I said. "A person has no privacy—that he can be sure is private."

Sometime after I'd made that particular statement, I had occasion to recall it.

The day passed. Lynn did drop in, but only for a moment. She seemed still to be in an unsympathetic mood toward me. I took my afternoon sun bath; Miss Straton wheeled me out on the terrace and left me there until I felt the cool shadow of the cement wall that separated me from my neighbors and called her to wheel me in. I phoned Chan down at the *Herald* and, on the pretext that I'd met Laidlaw and he interested me, I got what information was to be had in the office. It wasn't much.

Sullivan Laidlaw had been a lawyer in New York City for some thirty years, with a stodgy corporation practice, and after his retirement in 1936 he had moved to Highport, his boyhood home. He was known around town fairly well, respected, even liked; he played good bridge, had brought some minor fame to Highport by discovering a small comet, lived well but not ostentatiously, and so on.

Miss Straton brought my dinner at seven and cut my meat. I tormented her some about her suspicion of Lynn. But I was sure of nothing and rather annoyed that I had learned so much without discovering a single significant fact about the "murder" of Robert Purvis. After dinner, in an obviously disapproving manner, she read some more to me from *The Grapes of Wrath*.

Finally I tired, not of the book, but of her voice and attitude. I sent her away. For a time I listened to the sounds of traffic on the street—the floating voices of human beings, the quivering rumble of a passing truck, the peculiar noise of a kid on roller skates, and the swing and thump of the radio in the Baylin apartment.

The radio had been switched on and off a half dozen times that day. There had been periods of excessive quiet. Periods of chatter. I'd heard Ella serve iced tea on the terrace—and strained my ears unsuccessfully to hear more: the street had been too noisy.

Now I was listening again and after a time I did hear a singular sound. A sharp report—not like a gun—but startling nevertheless. It was familiar but I could not place it. Presently it came again. And again. Then I heard Mrs. Baylin call loudly enough so that her words were understandable, "Junior! Quit that!"

And I heard the young man's protest. "I'm killing flies!"

"All the same—quit!"

That had been it. The smack of a folded newspaper against a wall. It had worn on Mrs. Baylin's nerves—just as the radio had worn on the nerves of other Baylins that day. Their humdrum domestic dissonance was changed drastically from what it had been during my first weeks at Tommy's. The house didn't sound the same. And no wonder. They were frightened.

I made a conscious effort to relax. I was tired. I hadn't exerted myself— but the September heat and the nervous strain after weeks of idleness had fagged me out. The Baylins were afraid, I kept thinking. Afraid that the old man had been killed. Afraid that one of themselves had done it. Afraid to find out the truth, because it would bring shame. Afraid not to find out—because that would leave a possibly dangerous person in their midst. Afraid, I suddenly realized, to do much looking, because to look might mean to discover and to discover might put another person in the same peril.

That was why Lynn had talked to me—a comparative stranger—rather than to anybody on the other side of my wall. Suppose she had accidentally confided in the murderer? Then she, too, might have followed her grandfather. That ended my relaxation for a long time. It was an element I had not considered. A policeman hunts a man-killer with a drawn gun. An editorial writer, apparently, doesn't even have the brains to imagine the presence of that sort of danger. Not that I was in danger. But Lynn might be. And, presumably, seven other people besides. I think the feeling of fear began to reach into me then. Not fear for myself—but fear nevertheless. A feeling of dreadfulness. A feeling of murder done, and a murderer smiling and talking and eating and driving cars on the boulevards and yawning in the sunshine. A feeling of unnaturalness and doubt.

I felt more helpless than I had, when that emotion took the first frail possession of me. I considered letting my interest drop. I tried to persuade myself that such a course would be wise. I didn't actually believe that I could do anything in any case — excepting, perhaps, to entertain my mind in its void and to help Lynn, since it appeared that she wanted assistance of sorts. A confidant, at least.

If it was a crime at all, I reasoned, it was in that category of crimes which are seldom solved. Any one of eight people could have done it and, short of finding circumstantial evidence, which a blind man could scarcely hope to do, there was no way of leading up to an accusation. So I began the familiar hours of my night-grind. I went through the old courses: listening, piecing together what I heard, thinking about my job and my writing, plotting plays that would never be produced (or even set down — which is a favorite diversion of mine) and occasionally pressing the stem of my watch to learn that it was eleven-fifteen, twelve thirty-four, and one-twenty.

The Baylin apartment became silent at last. The street quieted.

It must have been after two when I heard the first of the sounds which ultimately resolved things. I sat up in my bed to listen better, strained my ears, held my breath. It was a purposeful sound — a bafflingly familiar sound — and one that escaped identification by a hairbreadth. I suppose, in my state, any unusual noise would have attracted my excruciating attention. And this one was not only unusual, but furtive. Moreover, it came from the house next door — or from the terrace of that house.

I sat still for several seconds — perhaps a minute. The sound went on — a grinding bumping sound, a sound that involved weight and energy. As I listened, I could almost name it for an instant or two — only to have it become hopelessly meaningless. Finally — although it was against my doctor's orders — I climbed out of bed. I found myself frightfully weak. But I tottered to the French windows that gave on the terrace, got my bearings from the portieres, and went out into the darkness. I could hear quite clearly then. The noise came from the other side — from the terrace itself or one of the rooms fronting on it.

I assumed the Baylin apartment was like mine: the living room on the outer part of the terrace and the master bedroom on the inner; an interior corridor explained that architecture by leading from the entrance vestibule to the living room. I suppose the point of that design was to put the living room on the airiest corner of the apartment building.

However, although I could hear the noise better, I was still unable to identify it. Somebody was doing something on the Baylins' terrace or in one of the two front rooms. I stood in the doorway on my jittery legs for a full five minutes before the noise came for the last time. After that, I heard quiet footsteps make their way across the terrace—apparently to the front wall. Somebody stood there—evidently looking down at the street. By and by a match was struck and I smelled cigar smoke. I stayed long enough to be sure it was coming around the high cement wall which separated our terraces. I didn't want to be fooled by a chance whiff of cigar smoke from the street, four stories below.

I was pretty sure that only Mr. Baylin smoked cigars.

The next day was a scorcher. The heat had been building up for nearly a week. I slept late, and when I took my bath at eleven-thirty I could again feel the sun burning down through the skylight. Miss Straton, because of the temperature, permitted herself to be more than usually short and Lynn did not come over.

However, Clarence "looked in" on me on his way to his office.

"We've kind of deserted you during our trouble," he said. "Anything I can do for you?"

He sounded normal enough. "Thanks—guess not. I'm sorry about your grandfather. He seemed to be a pretty fine chap."

"The best. Well—if I can shop for you—or anything—ring me up. Incidentally—I think there's some kind of cards with raised pips on them we might use to get up a bridge game—?"

That was like the Baylins. They were a thoughtful inventive family. I didn't tell him that I liked chess—and hated bridge. I just thanked him again.

Clarence's visit was a sort of social signal for the rest of the family. That afternoon Mr. and Mrs. Baylin dropped in to see me, and in the evening, when Lynn came over, she was accompanied by Duval Junior. I was sure that she had tried to come alone—and that he had come with her either to tease her or because he hadn't realized that he would be *persona non grata*. I think that the Baylins were all genuinely interested in my vocation; in fact they stood a little in awe of it. Anybody who had worked on a newspaper for as many years as I had would have been amused at such a reaction—and perhaps with justification. All men have editorial opinions on all subjects—and all women, too, these days. The trick is—to be articulate. My job is not so much a sign of brains as of a special skill—a skill in my case hard cultivated.

Duval Junior tried to strike up a worldly conversation about the European situation. I think he must have seen laughter in Lynn's eyes, however, because he soon abandoned the effort. We talked about the heat for a while and then, because we couldn't help it, about his grandfather. He made one rather startling bit of discussion. While Lynn was describing the old man's virtues—some of which were rigid enough to be obsessions—he interrupted to say casually, "Yeah, he was a good man. But even so, it wouldn't surprise me if more than a few people thought he'd been knocked off by that Amanita."

It's easier to dissemble when you have only your mouth and your hands to worry about. There was a marked silence, of course. Then Lynn said, "Why do you think that, Junie?"

"His dough."

She said, "Nonsense!"

And I could almost feel him shrug. "Sure, it's nonsense! But—just the same—it's something everybody in the family has thought—more than once in the last few days. And I bet you have, too, Mr. Walker!"

"Well," I answered, "the human mind being what it is—some such notion drifted through mine."

"Yeh," he said. "You have a few little strips of fried whosis in your pocket—and you toss it in on a plate of the real thing—and—there you are!"

"I wish you wouldn't talk that way," Lynn said.

His answer was boyish. "So do I! But it goes whizzing around in a fellow's bean. Anyhow—it's too late to find out a thing by now. And I don't believe there's a Baylin in the world who goes in for that particular kind of psychosis. Some dumb mushroom farmer just probably made an error of one spore—and it happened. I'm glad it wasn't more. I had a colic that made knots out of me for a couple of hours!"

That day passed, too.

And the next.

Then I heard another noise.

It, too, came at night. Very late at night. And I heard it neither well nor for long. I immediately identified it as the sound of someone walking on the roof. Rather, I should say, moving on the roof—carefully. In socks, perhaps. Or barefooted. I had no reason to connect the sound with the

Baylins or with the death of Robert Purvis. I was not even positive that it was a noise of human origin. It might have been a cat. It might have been the movement of some object along the tar and gravel under the gentle pressure of the breeze which was blowing. And yet—if I had not heard the sound—

I've often thought that. It would have made incalculable differences in my life. But I did hear it. I heard it because I was there—and wide awake—nervous and apprehensive—sick, in a way—and listening all the time. I didn't have much to do besides listen.

So I cross-examined Miss Straton the next day.

"Could a man get up on the roof?" I asked.

She said, "What for?"—which was like her.

"I don't know what for. I want to know if it could be done."

"Well—I suppose so. From the little hall where the automatic elevator and the stairs come up. It seems to me I remember a trap door overhead."

I asked her to look at the trap door. She protested. "You're still thinking about what happened to Mr. Purvis?"

I said I was.

She clucked disapprovingly. "Well, for my part, I think if there was any foul play—that young lady is to blame. It showed in her face the other day. And imagine—coming in to visit a gentleman the way she did night before last—in shorts!"

I laughed. "Was she in shorts?"

"Red shorts," Miss Straton replied. "Crimson. You should have seen them!"

"I wish I had. Now—go and look at the trap door."

She came back—on a new tack: "If I were you—I'd forget the whole thing—the way the Baylins themselves are doing. Just—stop troubling your mind. There's a trap door, all right—but it hasn't been opened. Not this year, anyhow. The last painter who went over it, painted it shut—which is the way painters do everything, these days! Nobody's opened it—and that's that. I'd just stop keeping myself up nights, Mr. Walker—"

"How about the back porch?" I asked.

"Did you hear anybody on the roof?"

"Maybe," I said. "And maybe not. Could a person get up by way of the back stairway? Is there a roof over those stairs? Does the roof connect with the apartment roof? Could an active man—?"

"An active man," she said, "can go most anywhere. I'll look. But you'd be better off to stop thinking about all this!"

While she was away I thought to myself that her state of mind, and the state she rightly or wrongly attributed to the Baylins, was typically human—and foolish. I could recall a hundred newspaper campaigns which I'd helped start to right some civic wrong. They had made a great furore for a little while. The citizens had been "up in arms." Then—after an arrest or two—after a minor improvement—the whole thing had been forgotten and the original wrong had continued pretty much unchanged. It's as hard for human nature—in most cases—to keep being afraid as it is to keep being angry. The Baylins had endured their days of terror—vague and nameless—and nothing had happened, so they were busy forgetting. Grandfather Purvis was dead and buried and they would miss him—and probably there had been a bad mushroom in the batch after all.

People like to follow the lines of least resistance—whether those lines are parallel to the facts or not. It's an addle-headed way of living.

Miss Straton came back grumpily. "An active man, you said. Well—as I said—any active person could do it. I could do it myself—if the house was on fire. You'd have to step on the porch rail and pull yourself up on the ornamental iron work and swing a leg over the coping around the roof. But if I were you—"

I pointed out that she was not me.

A full week after Grandfather Purvis' death I discovered the origin of the first noise I'd heard. It was an accidental discovery. And yet, I like to think of the contributory factors in all accidents: I stumbled on the agent of the sound but I knew it was an agent simply because I'd remembered that night-noise and because I was still subconsciously trying to figure out what had caused it.

I'd persuaded my doctor to let me do a little standing up and walking around. For that purpose, Miss Straton had cleared the furniture from my half of the terrace. Tommy's apartment was so filled with junk and clutter which he'd collected from the world's ends that it was hard for a person who could see to move in it without colliding with Chinese gods, trophy antlers, porcelain vases and the like. My room, for example, was a modest museum of primitive fighting tools—maces and krisses and boomerangs and spears—about which Miss Straton's opinion was picturesque and frequently iterated. So we had turned the "front porch" into a void and there I could walk safely. The wall on the boulevard and along the building's side was shoulder high, and the wall separating Tommy's high verandah from the Baylin's was higher still, so that there was no danger of my falling over and into the street.

I was out there in the afternoon, fumbling my way around the perimeter of the enclosure, following the wall-top with my hand, when I discovered that on the wall where it came flush with the house sat a large, decorative cement urn. The wall had been widened to give it a base and I felt over the thing with some amusement at the taste and aesthetics of architects in the early part of his century.

The ornamental gadget apparently had animal heads on it and, after a moment, I clung to one to keep my balance and to rest. While I was clinging, I unintentionally rocked it a little. The urn was off center, or there was a pebble under it, or the base was uneven. For a moment I was terrified by the thought that I might overtopple it and send it crashing to the ground below. But a quick examination of the base showed me that it was actually quite well situated—and only a bit wobbly. At the same time, I realized with a sort of slow astonishment that a sound like that of the urn grating on the wall was what I had heard some nights before.

Obviously, there would be an identical urn on the other side of the house. And somebody had come out there late at night to rock it. I fiddled diligently with my urn. By pushing hard on the thing—and at the same time rocking it as much as the irregularities of its base would permit—I could make it "creep" along the top of the wall in any direction I chose. Therefore, somebody had been cautiously moving the Baylins' urn that night. Why?

Because something was hidden under it? I tried tentatively to lift it. Of course, I was weak. But the thing must have weighed a couple hundred pounds—and its base was shoulder high. Probably the person had not been trying to get under it. Just to move it. To move it where?

I thought hard until Miss Straton came out and insisted I'd had enough exercise.

The solution didn't come to me until that evening when Lynn dropped in to see me. I think, now, that I was stupid not to have seen at once what my discovery implied. But she gave me an additional link—a link I might conceivably have missed—at least until my eyes were unbandaged.

For a while, we amused ourselves playing a game which she suggested. It was a pretty silly game—and a rude one. But it was fun—and it showed that the incubus of the past days was lifting from her. "I read about the game somewhere," she said. "You dial a phone number. One you make up. Then—when somebody answers—you try to keep him on the wire as long as possible. With chitchat. Your opponent keeps time on how long you talk—and the person who keeps somebody talking longest, wins the game."

It seemed like a good idea. I've thought, since, that if the staff of the *Herald* could have seen me endeavoring to hold angry house-wives and delicatessen keepers on the wire, there would have been much amusement. But I was bored and we played for a full hour. Lynn won, finally, because she learned that one of her victims was reading a book on gardening, and they talked about flowers, soils, and fertilizers for fifteen minutes.

"I hear," she said afterward, "that you're up and around."

I told her how we had stripped the porch.

"Why don't you go down to the garden terrace? It's very sunny. You could get a good tan. And there's a wall that keeps people on the street from seeing you. Grandfather had a comfortable chair down there, and he used to love it."

"I didn't know there was a garden," I said.

"Not much. A few draggly dahlias—and some shrubs. It's down below the front porch terraces and it gets more sun—"

Then—a bell rang in my brain. Below the front porches. Underneath the urn that I'd heard moving. "On your side of the building," I asked, "or mine?"

"Our side."

"Right under?"

"Yes. But what difference does that make—?"

I grinned. "I thought Miss Straton could drop me caramels."

"Well—she could. They'd bean you—"

I was thinking furiously. Nobody could have wanted to push an urn over at night. Not unless they had desired to destroy Grandfather's chair by smashing it. Which was silly. Then why move it? I'd ruled out the wish to look underneath it—but now I considered that again. And while I played with the notion, I had another. Perhaps somebody had been returning it from an abnormal to its normal position.

I wanted to be positive of the geographical situation.

"It sounds nice," I said. "I suppose that when the sun got too hot, he could pull his chair over against the house in the shade?"

"That's right."

"I might try it. Though I'm not sure I want to be tanned from the cheeks down—and on the forehead. And ghost pale between. When the bandages come off, I'll look like a Blackfoot medicine man in warpaint—or something."

She laughed—and we went on talking. About people and problems and books and mankind in general. She was a smart levelheaded girl. Her politics were a little more liberal than mine, but then, she was conservative in spots where I wasn't. She had a great deal of purposeful imagination and the character with which to pursue it. The hard effort of her own life had given her a great deal more strength than is possessed by most young women.

She was serious only for a moment that evening—when she was on the point of leaving me. "Barry, are you still wondering over—what we thought about Grandfather?"

"Some," I confessed.

"Don't you think we were hasty? Don't you feel that we invented things?" An urgency crept into her voice. "Haven't you about given up? Or have you found out anything that might keep you believing it was—?"

For some reason, I felt that Lynn was pumping me. That she wanted a bulletin of the status quo in my brain. It was only an evanescent hunch—a fleeting accent of over-interest. But I, who was on the verge of telling her about the urn, smiled instead and said, "I haven't found out a thing. How could I?"

I could almost feel her discontented shrug. "I don't know. There's something rather formidable about you—lying here day and night—listening—and thinking. Especially thinking. You're very subtle. You have a lot of ingenuity. And I suppose you know your ears are terribly sharp."

I grinned. "That's from taking bird walks when I was a Boy Scout."

"I'm not kidding."

"Neither am I. There was a time when I could identify about a hundred birds by the songs, squeaks, whistles, and croaks that birds make. But it hasn't done me any good. Why? Have you heard anything?"

I thought she hesitated. "No," she said. "Not a thing. Well—good night, Barry. We had fun."

She left me.

I shouted for Miss Straton and had myself packed away for the night.

Grandfather used to sit on a terrace—four stories down. When it was too sunny, he backed his chair against the wall. Right under that urn, I was ready to swear. Somebody had joggled it out so that a push would send it crashing down on him. And then, after mushrooms had killed him, somebody—that same somebody—had come out on the terrace in the small hours and jiggled and yanked it back. Why? So that its off-balance position would not be seen. So that the preparation to do murder by dropping the urn would be erased.

It was as clear as that.

I felt up to the push-through switch of my light, found the rubber band, and put myself in darkness—as if it made a difference. I had a few more questions in my mind. Had anybody else besides Grandfather Purvis used that terrace down below? Did anyone beside Mr. Baylin smoke cigars? Because whoever had rocked back the urn from its suspicious position had lighted a cigar afterward.

I considered the other furtive sound I'd heard. The possible footsteps on the roof. Perhaps the person who had placed the urn off center had planned to push it down from the roof. With a long pole. Perhaps the nocturnal visit to the roof had been to take away the pole and thereby to destroy the last evidence of a method of killing which had never been used. It was, at least, a good theory. Grandfather sitting in the shade in the late afternoon. The jardinere killing him. The accident attributed to the wind, or to the slow displacement of the thing by the vibrating passage of trucks on the street through the years.

Certainly the mushrooms and the cement vase seemed like the ideas of one person—of a person bent on committing a murder that would look like an accident. And either method might have succeeded. One had. It was therefore necessary to destroy all traces of the other.

I lay quietly—listening, because I always did, and I made up another editorial.

Murder, I thought, was actually an easier crime than theft. It was only the terrifying associations—the essential horror of murder—that made human beings hesitate to embark on its grim course. Valuable property is always strongly protected. Human life is not. Human beings die easily. A few minutes without air kills them. A few minutes under water. A blow that cracks the thin skull. A wound severe enough to let out the blood. A fall to the earth from a relatively low height. And there are ten thousand toxic substances which will destroy a man's life—whether he eats them, or breathes them, or gets them in his blood, or absorbs some of them through his pores. Thousands of men are killed each year by accidents. And thousands of events may be staged to make a murder seem like an accident. As man grows older, his hold on life weakens. Stepladders kill the aged. Falls on stairs and in bathrooms—

My mind was alive and at work.

Here was a murderer who had prepared a cunning method of achieving his purpose. He had used the natural facts surrounding his victim to destroy him. An urn unbalanced above a favorite chair. A basket of mushrooms brought home for a treat. And—since he had prepared two different ways of killing—might not he (or she) have made ready a third and even a fourth? Or a dozen, for that matter?

My thoughts ran over the accounts and confessions of other killers which I had read in my own newspaper. There was a familiar note in many of those tortured narratives: "First I thought I could fix his car so that the exhaust would kill him—but he always got out so quick, I gave that up. Then the idea came to me of setting fire—" So it went. "I tried arsenic on him once and he got sick but he didn't die. So I arranged that trip to the lake and we hired a row boat and went up to the end where the woods are—"

On and on. Not one plan—thoroughly worked out and wickedly executed. Two plans. Five. Efforts that were failures and that nevertheless did not arouse the suspicions of their victims. "When it didn't work—I went to the hardware store and bought—"

It was grisly material. A fearsome notion. But it filled me with a furious new urge. I began to think of the poor old guy and the web spinning around him. His most natural act might have been dangerous. His bath, for example. The old dodo had loved his after-dinner, pre-bed bath. From my own bathroom I'd heard the water running. The splash of his descent into it—and even the comfortable grunt which went with it. Sometimes he went to sleep in his bath. I'd heard Grandma Purvis call to him—jiggle the door-handle—waken him—chide him. A most natural event.

And yet he bathed—slept sometimes—underneath an old and dusty skylight—as I did myself.

There had been footfalls on the roof not long ago. Were they on another errand of erasure? Removing, perhaps, not a pole to topple the urn—but something else? A heavy weight on a rope, for instance?

I could see the setting with my mind's eye very clearly: the old man snoozing in his tub; the lift of the skylight—perhaps on oiled hinges;

the fall of a heavy weight—a weight dropped with the accuracy of a plumb-line; perhaps, even, by a murderer who had measured the drop from the square opening of the skylight to the head of the tub with a plummet so he would know exactly where to hold his weight. Perhaps he had measured from the urn to the chair below with the same bob.

I went on imagining. The skylight up—the weight falling. The old man might groan or splash and then lie still. It wouldn't take much of a weight. Twenty pounds, maybe. Or thirty. It could be dropped a good nine feet, I thought. The murderer would pull back his deadly tool with a rope. Hide it. Climb down the back porch roof support and tread the steps carefully—unseen and unheard. Enter by the elevator and front door later on—his alibi established with care.

Suppose there was a sound? A loud moan? An intense splashing—due to reflexes? Then—it would take whoever was in the house a long time to break down the bathroom door. The more I thought of that, the more clearly I saw how easy it would be. The murderer might even descend on his rope—or on a rope ladder—and fix the body to suit his scheme. Or—if the weight had not sufficiently accomplished its purpose—he might strike other blows. And afterward set the stage so that the most thoughtful observer would say, "Grandfather must have slipped here—and hit his head there."

Countless people—old and young—have died in the same way—by accident. Life insurance companies have statistics on it. Home accidents. Thousands every year. Rugs that slipped. Steps that broke. Urns that fell. Soap and water and tubs—and a body no longer agile.

Who would look up and wonder if perhaps someone had entered by the skylight? Nobody. Nobody at all.

I was so intensely gripped by my mental images that I did not realize until that point how flimsy my speculation was. I hadn't solved anything. Indeed, Robert Purvis had died in his bed from poisoned fungus—not in his tub from a blow on the head. The bath tub scene was my own invention. It was a killing I had committed myself. I had no more than a hint that the murderer of the old man had any such a notion in his mind. The hint of footfalls on the gravel roof.

I relaxed a little, and laughed at myself. I thought, as all of us think at one time or another, that I would make a pretty good criminal myself. It is a perversely entertaining thought. We read the details of, say, a gigantic theft which misfired, and we believe that we would have foreseen the circumstance which led to failure. "The fools!" we say. "They should have buried the license plates!" Or, "Morons! Why didn't they change the tires on that car!"

But out of all that tense reverie, I had one positive idea. I had canvassed the ways of detecting the hypothetical bearer of the poisonous mushroom and found them blind alleys. Too many persons could be suspected. Too many had the opportunity. But someone was removing the traces of unused schemes to kill—and that someone might be caught. At least, further scrutiny might lead to his identification. Maybe it could not be proved that he had committed the crime itself—but to catch the man who had walked across the roof, or who had juggled the urn back into place, would be to put him "on the spot."

I turned on the light again, sat up in bed, and lighted a cigarette. During my siege of being blind, I hadn't smoked much—but that night I chain-smoked for hours.

The notion of a killing in the bathroom stayed in my mind. I was by that time persuaded that there had been somebody on the roof. Of course, I had never seen the roof, but from what Miss Straton had told me about it and from the general plan of such roofs, I was sure that there wasn't much up there. The elevator kiosk, maybe, and the paint-stuck trap door from the common hall; a couple of ventilators, and the two skylights. The murderer, who thought in such terms as dropping an urn, might also have gazed down into the bathroom at the old man and thought of dropping some other object. It was so easy.

In searching for possibilities by which to recognize the murderer through his efforts at clearing up his preparations, I fell to wondering about the object he might have planned to drop—granting always that he had such plans. I say I fell to wondering. It was not teleological thought. I was so carried away by the fact that there had been a death, a murder scheme, and a man on the roof—that I pursued my idea of his reason for being there almost against my will.

It had to be something dropped. He couldn't descend and club his slumbering victim; the descent might awaken him. He couldn't shoot or slab; that would not look like an accident. And he counted on the resemblance to accident in every hypothetical case. Also—he would have to retrieve the thing he dropped. Perhaps he had planned to go down into the bath to get it. But more than likely, he would have tied a rope to it.

He had probably stored the weight and the rope on the roof—ready in case the mushrooms failed or in case the urn missed—or both. Or in case he decided the bath tub slaying would be safer than the toppled urn. A rope was easily disposed of. He could have carried it in his shirt. But the weight. He couldn't have thrown it to the ground—it would have made too noticeable a thud. Not a brick or a flatiron. Too light for certainty. A cement block? A rock? There was a danger in that—the danger of blood being absorbed—the difficulty of hiding so large an object, the chance of its discovery and the subsequent analysis of virtually ineradicable stains on it. A grate stolen from the furnace? It was summer—and nobody would look into the furnace for months. But a grate was unwieldy. He would want a concentrated weight. A twenty or thirty pound weight that would surely kill—one that could be hauled up, and cleaned, and put back in its place, or perhaps buried. Objects of that sort are rare—in city apartments.

It was natural that, having lost myself to such an extent on pure speculation, I thought of a curling stone. The Baylins were all curlers. It's a winter sport—and nobody would look at his stone in September— granting that they had stones. Some of the stones were iron. Iron ones wouldn't absorb blood—and could be cleaned. The things were fearfully heavy—and they had handles suitable for tying a rope to.

I became perhaps abnormally curious about my idea. Did the Baylins have such "stones" in their apartment? Had any of them been moved? Was any missing? Was it possible that the murderer had followed my scheme even to his choice of an instrument, and then, either confidently or carelessly, left upon a stone fingerprints, or a strand of rope, or even a scratch from the gravel on the roof? Such evidence, if it existed, would not be conclusive. But it would give me enough to turn over to the police—and they could go on from that point.

I had decided on the police. I was positive that there had been a murder. I shared the common human feeling that a murderer on the loose was a dangerous man. I made up my mind that, with any further corroboration at all, I would phone the Chief of Police and ask him to listen to my story. I did that with the full knowledge that even Lynn might have been the guilty person. She'd spoken of trying curling. Lots of women curled. She was evidently husky enough. She had nerve. But I made up my mind that one more step might best be taken by me before I summoned the police.

I set out to get that step taken the next day—after a bad night and a late unsatisfactory sleep. Miss Straton was pouring coffee for me when I told her.

"I want you to do me a favor," I said. "A big one."

"I'd be glad to, of course."

"I want you to search the Baylins' apartment—some time when they're all out."

"What!" She said only that one word. But it nearly blew my hopes to pieces.

It took me two days to persuade her to do it. She was an honest woman; she told me that at least a hundred times. She wasn't going to start spying and peeping on other people. When I threatened to fire her and hire a nurse that could be persuaded—she stymied me by offering to quit. When I told her in careful detail my reasons for wanting her to make a raid next door—and what I wanted her to look for—she launched on a two-hour harangue on the absurdity and folly of my idea. She thought of scores of things that were wrong with the theory I held—including several I hadn't considered myself.

I finally resolved the deadlock—partly by wearing her down and partly by insisting that she was performing a great human duty. If she did what I asked, we might right a great wrong. If it came to nothing—no harm would have been done. And if we didn't make a try—nobody ever would. Time was precious. Each day made our chances less.

"Also," I said, "I'll give you a hundred dollars."

She said that an offer of money, under the circumstances, was an insult. But when she brought the curling stone to me, she reminded me that she had earned her money.

I imagine Miss Straton made a pretty jittery burglar. She picked a Thursday night when Ella was away. The family had gone out to dinner. She had long since learned that Ella kept the back door key under the mat—so gaining an entrance was no problem. She was gone for about an hour—and I sat in my bed in a state of extraordinary suspense. I knew that she was not likely to be caught: the banging of the elevator mechanism would give her ample warning of anybody coming up, and she could slip out the back way. But I had undergone numerous alternations of expectation and disappointment before I heard her come toward my room, panting and walking awkwardly.

There was a thump beside my bed.

"Here it is," she said. "The only one I could find. It was in Mr. Baylin's closet—with the guns and fishing tackle—in a carton on the floor. And I certainly earned my money. I was that terrified—!"

I was sitting up—breathless—swearing because I couldn't see. I hadn't dreamed that she'd bring the thing to me. But there it was. "Look at it! Is there dust on it?"

"No. It seems recently wiped."

"Turn it over! Any scratches that might have been marked on it by gravel on the roof?"

I heard the heavy thing turn. "No. It's clean. Polished."

"You used gloves? And you were careful not to touch the handle?"

"Yes. Though it's a mighty lot to lug. It's iron."

"But you think somebody's had it out of the box lately?"

My nurse snorted. "Did you ever seen a maid that would lift a weight like that to dust under it! I'm certain it's been out! It must weigh a hundred pounds!"

"Sixty," I said. "All right."

"I'm hot and sticky," she said. "I'll wash. And I never thought I'd see the day when I robbed a house! You may be right about what you think—and you may not. But that stone, as you call it, ought to have been covered with dust—this city being what it is. Everything else in the closet was! How that young woman could have pulled it up on the roof—! Though they do say that passion gives extra strength to people—!" She must have seen my grin—because she went down the hall muttering.

I heard the elevator crash and hum and I knew the Baylins—or some of them—were coming back. Miss Straton had just comfortably made it. And I was exultant. Somebody had taken the stone out. Somebody had polished and cleaned it. That virtually cinched my elaborate hypothesis. The stone had doubtless been standing for an unguessable time on the roof—ready—in case of need. My pleasure in my coup was so great that I was completely thunder-struck when, instead of hearing the Baylins' door open, I heard my own burst in.

Lynn called, "We're visiting you!" and there were footsteps.

That was an error in my situation. I hadn't thought about the possibility of a friendly break-in. I groped once for the stone—but I couldn't tell exactly where Miss Straton had put it down—and I didn't want to be seen swinging my arms around in the air. I did some fast thinking while their feet moved toward my bedroom, and I was trying to look my chipperest when they entered—Mr. Baylin first. Again, I was wishing I had eyes to watch them with.

"How are you, Walker. It's the whole gang. We brought our ice cream up here to share with you. Thought you'd enjoy the treat."

"Great," I said. I was listening to everything at once. "Tell Miss Straton to break out dishes—and make coffee! She's in the back of the house somewhere."

It was Clarence who saw it first—or, at least—who spoke first about it. "Look here! A curling stone."

I nodded—sure that they were turning from the stone to me. "Yeah, just roll it out of the way. Under the bed, will you? Miss Straton found it there—and wanted to know what it was."

I heard the stone mover—and Duval Junior's grunt. "Like Dad's. Exactly. Probably the same make. Didn't know Tommy Riker was a curler."

"He takes a shot at everything." I answered. "Look at the walls around this apartment!"

It wasn't much of a joke—but they laughed. Miss Straton had heard them enter, of course—and she was standing in the hall—nickering. Looking frightened, too, I was sure. I called to her and repeated the request for plates. Mrs. Baylin went into the kitchen to help.

Duval had finished putting the stone under my bed; I'd felt the joggle of the springs as it rolled beneath me. Anyway—it was out of sight. Maybe they would believe me.

It was a merry gathering, but I sat there, sweating. Trying to look carefree—from the cheeks down. I was glad they couldn't see my eyes. Because my eyes must have been preoccupied, to say the least. I was wondering what the next step would be. Maybe even the murderer was fooled. It was possible—but not very probable.

We talked through the ice cream. Lynn gave my coffee to me. "There are cigarettes," I said, "pointing to my bedside table. "And I can dig up cigars. You care for a cigar, Duval?"

The young man said, "No thanks. Never use 'em."

"Clarence?"

"Same here. Only Dad smokes rope."

Dad.

Would he go across to his apartment soon—and look in his closet—and find his stone was missing? Then what? I wished that they would leave. I wanted to think. I had to think. It was a bad *faux pas*. Unless—of course—my imagination had betrayed me—and the stone had merely been taken from its box and given a cleaning. A loving cleaning—such as a man might give to a prize fishing reel. Was I crazy? Or was it

Mr. Baylin who had rocked the urn back into place that night—and then lighted a cigar? Had he killed his wife's father?

They gave me no time to ponder. Not until we had passed two hours together. Not until we'd had more ice cream and listened to a long story from Mr. Baylin about a man who had let loose a squirrel in the bank and an anecdote concerning his grocery store from Duval. Not until Mrs. Baylin had teased me about her niece's interest in me. Not until after eleven o'clock.

Then they said prolonged goodnights—and the door finally closed behind them.

Miss Straton trotted to my bedside. "They saw it!"

"I said it was Tommy's."

"But the one—!"

I begged her to let me think out what to do next. Probably by having tipped our hand, we had given the guilty person time to tighten his alibi—and nothing else. But neither of us mentioned what both of us feared. I suppose it seemed too outlandish—too fantastic—after that pleasant visit. But I know that Miss Straton slept all night on a day bed which she pulled into the hall—that is, if she slept.

However, I didn't call the police. Twice, before I gave up and tried to sleep, I reached for the telephone. And both times I said to Miss Straton, "I just can't do it! They'll think I'm crazy."

It was morning when my theory was confirmed.

Tommy's colored couple was in the kitchen. Miss Straton had gone to the drug store to get a prescription refilled. I suppose the presence of the servants and broad daylight reassured her—and her reassurance was unconsciously caught by me. Certainly I did not think of demurring when she spoke of the errand.

And, after she had gone, I was not frightened by my solitude. I was accustomed to it, rather. Indeed, it did not seem like solitude. Traffic was bumbling busily down on the street—and the Baylins' radio was going full blast. It was a windy day—and though I hadn't felt for the sun, I was somehow sure the sky was bright and blue. Maybe the smell of the wind, or the lack of humidity in the air had supplied the information. But it was fine weather, I knew, and I sat in my bed framing over and over possible methods of telling a police officer what I suspected in such a way that my telling would convince him.

But each time I recited the thing, I gave myself the answer I thought the policeman would give: "You're out of your head! You've just been sitting here playing Sherlock Holmes because you have nothing better to do. The old gent got a bad mushroom—and you've invented the rest of it."

That's what I thought.

I was reaching for my tenth cigarette that morning—when I knew abruptly that there was somebody in the room. It wasn't by light and shadow, because I was insensitive to such factors. Or by sound. I had heard nothing. My door into the hall had been blown shut—and no one had opened it. The French windows that opened on the terrace were wide, however. The person had come through there.

I stiffened. I was sure I was being watched. That the intruder knew I was aware of his presence. That he was a little puzzled by my awareness.

Tommy's rugs were thick. I heard no sound for several seconds.

All that, I have set down calmly. But from the moment of my realization, I had been in the abyss of terror. Only one human being would enter my room silently, and stand silently. He would come only upon one errand. To get the stone. To do away with me—because I knew so much.

My tongue stuck to the roof of my mouth. I felt the hairs rise on my neck. My heart thrashed like a loose piston. I shivered. It would be a blow—or a shot—or a stab. I didn't know which way to turn my head.

"Who is it?" I said finally—in a startlingly shrill voice.

There wasn't any answer.

"What is it?" I repeated.

I heard, then, a faint clink of metal. That confirmed the horror. I knew—or guessed—what it meant. One of the many hideous weapons was being taken from the wall. I thought of yelling—but I was utterly incapable of making a loud sound. I did not hear—but felt—footsteps coming toward me.

Then—convulsively—I jumped out of my bed. I sprawled on the floor. But I crawled rapidly until my head hit the wall. Feet came after me—swiftly—quietly. I pushed along, my shoulder against the wall, until my hand hit the corner. Then the bed again. I scrambled over it. I heard him—or her—going around it.

I stood up—wet, and shaking with a palsy.

"Give me thirty seconds," I whispered.

There wasn't an answer. Just—silence.

"I won't yell," I said.

The feet moved. I ran—in real blind man's buff—and for my life. I tripped on a chair and took a header. Then I thought—foolishly—that I had to see, bandages or not. I tried to yank the dressing from my eyes. But I couldn't. The adhesive was too strong for my queasy fingers. I was sitting on the floor. I expected the blow at any moment.

I gasped, "Wait!"—and thought of a way to make him wait. "It won't do you any good to kill me," I said.

I could "feel" again, that a raised weapon was being lowered—or held back. It had been very close. It was not over. "No good!" I repeated. "No use at all!"

There was a long agonizing silence. I sat still. I wasn't being killed. My attacker was thinking.

"Miss Straton knows!" I continued. "She stole—the stone!"

Then somebody whispered. "What a nit-wit!" the voice said. It was hoarse, contorted, but recognizable. Duval Junior's.

"No good, Duval!" I repeated. "It'll just add to the thing already on your conscience!" I waited. "Why did you do it?"

He talked almost to himself, at first. "I won't take it! I won't stand it! There's a way! Must be! When she comes back—!" Then my question filtered into his brain. "Why? Because I despised him! Because he found out how I ran my business and made me pay back to people every cent I've earned for two years! Because he was a self-righteous old holier-than-heaven! Because he persecuted me even when I was a kid—about stealing—and telling lies! He spied on everything I did!"—He broke off again. I heard his breath, coming and going. Then he spoke. "You think you're smart, eh? It'll still work! You—then her! And over the wall! Double suicide! Don't move!"

I'd tried to stand—with the vague idea of lunging for the door.

"Double suicide!" he repeated. He began to chuckle. I could sense his approach. "You—and she. Crash—in the street!"

"You poor fool," I said. "I wrote the cops! Every detail! Last night!"

"I don't believe it!"

"You will—when they walk into your apartment—and take you out to electrocute you. Or when you're running—across the country—with your name on every radio—and every human being looking at your face—and no place to hide! Money spent—cars chasing you—motorcycles—the whole world! Three murders instead of one—!" I pointed at the place where I thought he was standing.

He whispered. "Yes. That's it! Murder and suicide! You killed her! Jumped! A blind man—!"

"—when you can't sleep at night," I went on frantically. "When you don't dare ask for anything to eat! It's all in the story I gave the cops, Duval! The urn out there on the porch. The skylight over the bathroom. The mushrooms—and all about how you studied mushrooms—!"

I stopped. I couldn't think of anything else. I sat there. He was silent—thinking again. Seconds passed. I heard my breath coming through my teeth unevenly. I am not a brave man; I have never pretended to be. And I sat on the floor in my personal darkness as craven and quivering as the greatest coward. I waited—and waited. I heard the curtains move in the morning air, and a sound that was generated inside of me, which grew louder and louder—a humming roar. I knew that my senses were slipping and that, somehow, maddened me. "Go ahead!" I said rabidly. "Hit me! Throw me over the wall! Kill her! But in the name of mercy, get it over with!"

There was silence.

"Get it over with," I repeated. "Don't let me sit here—dying a thousand times!" I began to weep. Then I cursed and raged.

But he made no sound.

He wasn't in a hurry. He was waiting. Waiting to hit me. After hitting me, he would wait again—to kill Miss Straton. And after that, he would throw my body out over the terrace rail. And go home across the roof—when he'd put back his weapon—and wiped the prints from it. He would be at home to meet the cops: No—I didn't hear any signs of a struggle; no, I can't imagine why he killed her; they seemed friendly to me.

It was fiendish—like his other ideas.

I broke completely, then. My senses went. I didn't cry any more. I sprang at him. Once—twice—a half dozen times. Groping in the room—falling over chairs—trying to get my inadequate hands on him for one last frantic tussle with—anything but silence and his undoubtedly amused dodging from my crazy leaps. Finally I was too weak even for that. I fell the last time and lay there, begging him to get it over with.

How long I stayed in that position, I do not know. Perhaps for three or four minutes. And still the blow did not fall. Instead, I had a sudden sense of something else amiss—of a new element in the situation. I wondered if one of the servants had heard my falls and looked in—to be confronted by death. But it couldn't be that. There was no sound at all.

And that was it. No sound. Even the traffic had stopped. It was still on the street—absolutely still. I could hear other streams of traffic in the distance—sounds usually inaudible. I thought that perhaps I had been struck—and this was the first stage of death. Then I heard a police whistle—sharp and shrill and not far away. I sat up a little—stupefied and without thought. A siren squalled in the distance—low and feline; presently in drew near. Next came a further sound: the remote but crescendo clang of an ambulance bell. And I understood. I was alone. Duval Baylin Junior had jumped over the terrace wall and killed himself.

No postscript is really necessary to this document. I need not say that I promised silence to the Baylins. The fact that I am now married to Lynn is in itself an explanation for that. I think Duval was mad.

As a child, he had never been "persecuted" by his grandparent any more than his brother Clarence. Both boys, of course, had been subject to frequent harsh correction. He, evidently, had magnified that treatment. It is not exceptional to find in a bright and vital family line a single individual whose brain is weak or vicious. His father told me—later—that he had been afraid of Duval's mental health on more than one occasion. Mr. Baylin was the one who had replaced the urn on the terrace wall, too. His explanation was that he had noticed the "coincidence" of the unbalanced urn and the site of his father's chair below, and that, afraid the "coincidence" might lead somebody to suspect that the mushroom poisoning had been deliberate (as I had), he had been at some pains to replace the urn.

Mr. Baylin may believe that explanation. But I think, from the first, he was appalled by what he suspected, and when he noticed the position of the urn, he guessed the reason for it. However, it was his son. Instead of reporting his observation, he rocked back the urn, furtively, at night. The death of Duval Junior almost broke his heart—in spite of what the boy had done.

Mr. Laidlaw, I have had the pleasure of meeting. He is a delightful old gentleman and still totally unaware of the sinister nature of the tragedies which were visited on his friends, the Baylins. Lynn's nervousness on the night we analyzed the alibis of her family—the nervousness which led Miss Straton to suspect her—was due to a quite irrelevant cause. She had been afraid that, by telling me she had planned a late dinner with a sculptor, she would make me angry or arouse my disapproval. For Lynn had fallen in love with me—who was without eyes—just as I had fallen in love with her—who was only a voice.

She has a wholly unwarranted respect for my intelligence. She believes the police everywhere ought to be instructed in what she calls my "method" of crime detection: looking not for clues of a completed murder, but for clues having to do with abandoned attempts at the murder of the victim.

By examining Duval Junior's books, we easily found traces of the swindle which his grandfather had compelled him to redeem. It was a financial peculation by no means as imaginative or as ingenious as the death traps with which he had surrounded the old man.

About the eventual restoration of my sight, only one fact seems important. My ghastly half hour in Tommy's apartment set back my convalescence. Lynn aided in nursing me — with increasing tenderness. I arranged with my doctor to have Lynn be the first person upon which my unbandaged eyes would fall. I shall not try to describe that sight, except to say that her hair was golden — instead of "mousy brown." That description had been a bootless and prudish effort on the part of Miss Straton to keep me "from thinking too much about her."

My victory over my nurse was, of course, complete. She is now on another case. I hope it will be long and remunerative.

Anent my wife's respect for my mental ability, I have a confession to make. I have not yet made it to her — but I hope I shall find the moral strength to do so. It occurred to me only recently that my hideous half hour, and the threat to Miss Straton as well as myself, might have been avoided if I had been a little cleverer. I could have put the solemn finger of suspicion on Duval much sooner. I had the material.

The one element of Grandfather Purvis' death to which I had not given great attention was the method by which the poisonous mushroom had been added to the edible ones on the old man's plate. I had thought that such an addition would have been simple. A dish hidden under the table. Concealment of the fatal slices in a napkin. I had even thought of looking for the instrument of administration, but I had abandoned such a project because I was blind and bed-pent.

I had not cogitated any more about it. If the stuff had been in a dish, the murderer would have washed it at some convenient time. If it had been in a napkin, he would have washed it also, or otherwise disposed of it. Burned it, perhaps. That idea came to me long after the event — and when I thought of a burning napkin I also thought of a burning handkerchief. A handkerchief could have been whisked across the old man's plate — and the deed thus done. And then I remembered the night of the poisoning—when I'd smelled smoke and sent for Miss Straton, thinking my rug was smouldering. It hadn't been my rug.

In all probability it had been Duval Junior's handkerchief, burning to ashes as he sat alone on the terrace playing his mandolin. If I'd had the apperception to guess that—! But hindsight is always more accurate than foresight.

Lieutenant Quag finished reading the document and looked argumentatively at his Chief. "You may not recall it," he said, "but I was the one who picked up young Baylin's body. I thought it was suicide then—and I still think it was suicide!"

The Chief stared at him with unbelief and indignation. "That's what the newspaper fellow said!"

"Oh," Quag replied uncertainly. "Oh. I hadn't thought of it from that angle yet. Yeah. So he did."

Chief Watson called upon his gods to witness the incompetence of his minions. It was an irreverent exhortation.

TEN THOUSAND BLUNT
INSTRUMENTS

Because she had no patience with what she regarded as a weakness in herself, she went into the big room. *A tolerance for weakness—for—timidity, especially—should be reserved for other people,* Gail thought. There wasn't anything new about her phobia. She'd felt it when she was a kid—on her first trip to a museum. She had felt it in college when her geology class went to Belvidere Hall to inspect the fossils. She felt it now.

Outside, the early winter afternoon was dim with foreknowledge of night. There was light, ample in its way, in the gigantic chambers of the American Museum of Natural History. But the electricity threw shadows. And the windows let in a diffusion of darkness, a murk that emphasized the wrong things and made the reassuring ones indefinite.

Gail entered the Jurassic Hall as if she were pushing against a barrier, and stared willfully at the monstrous skeletons of the dinosaurs. Her skin prickled. Her mouth was a little dry. She tried hard to analyze the cause of this panicky, meaningless sensation: the bones had no flesh; eyes did not roll in the bowl-sized sockets; these horns, teeth, jaws, and articulated vertebrae had been dead—in the earth—for millions and millions of years. Perhaps that was the incubus: the millions of years.

"Hello, beautiful!"

The voice did not startle Gail. Rather, it steadied her. It made her remember that people—men and women and children—were moving calmly through the haunted chamber of dinosaurs. The corners of her lips twitched. She turned. It was a boy in the uniform of the Army Air Force. Second looie. He had a nice, Middle-Western face—open and tanned. Or maybe, she thought, it was the voice, not the face, that had prairies in it.

"Mashing is undignified," Gail said. "It's not for officers."

211 Ten Thousand Blunt Instruments

He grinned. "Kind of dead in here." It was kind of dead. Horribly dead. Thirty-million-years dead. Gail nodded.

"I thought—maybe—you'd like to go to a livelier place. Where I've been the last six months, blondes—green-eyed ones—are scarce."

"I'm sorry, Lieutenant. But in about ten minutes I'm due back at work upstairs."

"You mean you work in this mausoleum?" He didn't believe her.

"In it," she said. "Not for it. I work for the War Department. They send us up here, occasionally, to find out things, I'm a researcher."

"Oh." He thought it over. "Well, in that case, far be it from me to interfere. I don't suppose—later on—?"

"I'm putting in day and night on this assignment, Lieutenant. Sorry. And I haven't any blonde friends—with or without green eyes. I don't know anybody at all in New York."

He sighed exaggeratedly. "Me, either. Well—win the war, sister!"

The young woman's eyes were bright, a shade overbright. They fastened on the wings spread proudly on the boy's breast. "You win it, Lieutenant! Good luck—and good hunting, when the time comes!"

They separated, each feeling that New York was a little less huge and inhospitable.

She walked up the broad stairs, beyond the last floor on which the public was admitted. The quality of light changed and its quantity diminished as she entered a shabby interior corridor along which were offices of some of the executives and scientists of the Museum. At a door marked, "Dr. Horace Jordan, Zoology," she paused and braced herself again—but not with fear, this time. She was amused, wistful, and perhaps a trifle maternal. She turned the time-stained knob.

Dr. Jordan was bent over his desk as usual. And, as usual, maps were spread out upon it and the green-shaded droplight was burning. His thin, sensitive face was concentrated, but the squeak of the door lifted it. He smiled politely, but his eyes, which were brown and luminous, had no extra shimmer of welcome for her. " 'Afternoon, Miss Vincent."

"I missed you yesterday." Gail hung her coat and umbrella on the hatrack. To do so, she had to walk around three tables which were a crowded chaos of books, specimen jars, rolled maps, bones, piled photographs, and dusty collecting cases. Dr. Jordan's office, like so much of the Museum, was big, venerable, and dark.

He watched her. "I went over to Jersey. My sister's place. I'd left a lot of junk in her cellar—junk from the African trip I made in '38. I got out some notes, and last night, at home, I sketched this map for you. The country beyond Ujiji."

The country beyond Ujiji. It was a romantic phrase. And there was, Gail thought, a good deal of romance in Dr. Jordan and his life, even though he hid it behind a scientific manner only moderately tempered by his use of slang. She knew that, as far as she was concerned, she would gladly put down all her chips if he gave even half a sign of noticing that she was a girl—as well as a researcher. But he didn't.

It had been that way for Gail almost from the moment she had spotted him, months ago, standing uncertainly in the colonel's office in the War Department in Washington. At that time, she had known only that he was a famed zoologist, a formidable hunter, an authority on vast stretches of the Dark Continent, and a well-born New Yorker—things everybody knew. But she found out afterward that he was a great deal more that she admired in men: shy but resourceful, modest but willing to take responsibility, reticent about himself but a fascinating talker on a myriad of other subjects. And she had liked his looks, his intentness, the attention he paid to what was said, his smile, which was the shy kind, too, but merry, and always waiting to be evoked.

"In *Who's Who*," Gail once said to a girlfriend, "his biography sounds tough and dashing; but he's one of the gentlest people you ever met."

Looking at him now, Gail felt that, and more. She could fall in love. He couldn't, probably. He was an habitual bachelor. He was in love with his absorbing and sometimes dangerous work. He wasn't a ladies' man. He didn't even like her, especially. He was always a little impatient, as if he hoped her assignment would soon end and he could return to his own labors.

"This"—he pointed with a fountain pen—"is what I was talking about. I marked the altitude here. You can see—the valley's flat for about forty miles. You could put plenty of airports there—which, I take it, is what the War Department is coyly interested in."

Gail flushed slightly. "It's on the new flyway for India—"

"Exactly. It's grass—easy to clear. Hard ground. Pinsch and Felton were there in '28 and I queried them. They say the drainage is superb and the rainy season short. Ten months of ideal visibility. A road could be pushed through from Ujiji. The army engineers who built the Alaska Highway, for instance, would think any such chore was a cinch. No tsetse flies here, either. I checked that with Ralston. I'd say, in all the parts of Africa I know, this would make the best permanent installation for air transports and for military ferrying."

Gail peered. "Railroad's been moved, up by Ujiji."

"Lake level changed. Yeah. Condition of the railroad is only fair. But good enough."

"The War Department will be grateful," the girl said.

"The War Department," Dr. Jordan replied, sitting up straight and grinning a little, "could have gotten all this and much more information a great many years ago, without bothering a busy scientist who is in the middle of a job and who has been moved by sheer patriotism to consider his favorite stretch of country in terms of military airports."

"The Department didn't have the funds years ago," Gail replied defensively.

"It wouldn't have cost anything. It was all on file."

"Where?"

"In Berlin." He chuckled.

"Oh. How do you know?"

"Because the Germans have been getting ready for this war a long time. Only a few miracles like the Battle of Britain, the Russians, and the victory in Africa, have kept all this territory" —he pointed to the map— "from becoming an Axis airport on a main Axis flyway. They were there surveying and inspecting in '38 when I was."

"I'd better hear more about that." Gail hurried to the small, tidy desk which had been assigned to her. She picked up a notebook and some pencils, and came back to sit beside the zoologist. "Colonel Frain'll want to give the information to G-2."

He yawned. "Okay. But it's just a few years late. When I was there last time hunting my zebras and so on, this area had two other parties in it. They claimed to be Boers. Maybe they were Boers. I dunno. But I do know that they pretended to be hunting game and they had more scientific equipment than guns, by ten times. And one of them had a habit of humming the 'Horst Wessel Song' when he was preoccupied. So they were Nazi Boers—if they were Afrikanders at all. They were doubtless doing, not very obviously, some leg work for the German geopolitician. They quarried around, too, and left the district governor with the impression that they'd found oil-bearing shale. They think a long way ahead, those Nazis."

"The War Department'll appreciate that too, Dr. Jordan."

His eyes, brown, steady, but almost always abstracted, showed a brief and surprising trace of anger. "Sure. Now. But in '38, when I went to Washington and tried to tell 'em our potential enemies were already preparing to carve up Africa, they booted me out of the place. Said I was a nut."

"Yes. We have been very blind in this country," Gail said soberly.

"Oh, well." He shrugged. "Let's get on with the work. The sooner—" He stopped.

"The sooner we do, the sooner you won't have a lady researcher nagging you." Gail smiled.

He said, "Exactly." He described the "Boers" who had been advance agents of Greater Germany.

Gail finally made herself stop thinking that a girl could fall in love with a man like that, if he were just a little less like that. A little more human. The afternoon steeped itself in successive shades of darkness until, some time after the closing bells had sounded on the floors below, it was night.

"I've got a dinner date," Dr. Jordan said.

"I'm going to slip out later."

"Then you'll be back?"

"Yes. If I may, I'll copy those notebooks you brought from Jersey."

"Sure. Anything. I'll be in later, myself. But I'd like to do my own work for a while, if you don't mind."

She smiled. "Okay. The War Department'll give you a recess, Doctor. . . ."

When she returned from her solitary supper her footsteps echoed through the great, darkened halls. Some were open. Metal gates had been pulled across the entrances of others. The stone floors rang faintly with the pacing of the guards. In limitless penumbras she could see curled mastodon tusks and leg bones as high as herself. She shivered, and hurried toward the higher floors.

Lights shone in some of the offices. Old Dr. Weber was working with his door open. Fat Dr. Pinsch and fatuous Dr. Felton, the geologists, were talking earnestly in the latter's room. At the far end of the immense corridor Gail could see the gaunt frame of Dr. Beal as she fumbled with her key. Gail had left the light on in Dr. Jordan's place, not because she was afraid of falling over the objects in it, but just because she was afraid, always, at night in the old building.

A few big flakes of snow had left drops of water on the collar of her coat. She shook them off and went to work under the truncated cone of yellow that fell downward from the green shade.

An hour later Dr. Jordan walked briskly down the hall. He looked, Gail thought, positively jaunty. But the personality which had been his at his "dinner date" seemed to melt as he entered his office. "Hard at it, I see," he said. Without waiting for an answer, he stripped off his coat, put on an apron, and began to rummage through a bone heap on one of the far tables.

Another person, she thought, might have told her about the dinner. She went on copying, quietly. At ten o'clock, or thereabouts, he crossed the room. "Going to slip down to Akeley Hall and check some data."

She didn't notice how long he was absent. When he came back he made a few jottings on a pad; then he put on his coat and hat. "Don't stay all night," he smiled. "I must admit, you're the hardest-working female I ever knew! But they tell me that around three a.m. the dinosaurs start walking."

It was a purely accidental statement, meant as a joke, but she felt her flesh crawl. "I'll quit in a little while, now."

He nodded and said, "Good night, Miss V."

She worked on for a while, until a voice came through the door, which Dr. Jordan had left open. "Hello, bright eyes!"

Gail looked up and laughed. "Hello, Henry."

Henry Grant, the man standing in the doorway, was young, thin, and very blond. Like so many of the men who worked in the Museum, he seemed overzealous and underfed. He was a technician whom she had met soon after reporting for work—a boy from the Middle West—and, in a casually amiable way, he had been doing his best to improve his acquaintance with the girl.

"I'm busy," she said.

"That excuse is going to wear out, some day. I'm going home. I stopped by to see if you'd let me take you—and have a snack on the way."

She shook her head. "Not ready yet, thanks. Try again."

"Don't think I won't, lady! Getting along all right?"

"Well enough. I have to interview everybody in the place who's ever been in Africa, just about."

He laughed. "That's a pretty big job. You'd better change your mind and come along."

"Not tonight, thanks."

"Okay. 'Night."

She rose, when his footsteps had receded, and pushed the door shut.

He hadn't been gone long when there was a knock. Gail finished a sentence, and said, "Come in! Oh . . . Dr. Weber . . . Dr. Jordan's left for home."

Dr. Weber, against the light filtered from the hall, seemed more ancient, frail, and other-worldly than any of the great institution's staff. His thin, silvery hair floated above his gnome-like head; his eyes, bird-brilliant, changed from an expression of keen anticipation to one of childish disappointment. He held a coffee can, rusted so that the label was blurred, in both hands. "I thought I saw him a little while ago," he said uncertainly. "Down in Akeley Hall. I was in the Gallery, looking at the lesser koodoos."

"He was there," Gail answered. "But he's gone."

"Marvelous exhibit," the old man went on. "They all are. I like to look at them at night when there's nobody around. It reminds me of the days when I worked in the field myself."

Gail felt a thrust of impatience at age, at the thoughtlessness of age and its minute preoccupation with its own affairs. But she knew that Dr. Jordan liked the old gentleman and that his earlier days, also, had been excitingly romantic—from the scientific stand-point. She was tired, she realized. She closed her book. "I like to look at the koodoos, too—and the lions and tigers and the elands—everything."

He came into the office. She saw, then, that the weight of the coffee can was considerable for its size. Dr. Weber's arms were shaking.

"Why don't you set it down?"

"Yes. Yes, I will. You don't know his home phone number?"

"Dr. Jordan's? I think it's in the book."

"M-m-m." He put the can on the desk beside the maps. "Still—it will keep, I suppose. I took care of things. I wonder how much young Horace knows about mineralogy?"

Dr. Weber tipped the coffee can. She could see then that it was full of glittering, yellowish crystals, the size of Brazil nuts.

"I wonder," he repeated. "This is rock he brought me from Africa. Said it was curious and so he chipped me some samples. That's like the boy. Thoughtful, always. Impulsive, too. Because it's really a very common substance. Quartz. SiO_2—that is, with a mineral impurity that gives it the yellow cast. He'd kept it in storage some place, he said, until yesterday. Meant to bring it to me before."

He took a short pipe from his pocket. Its bowl had been burned down, so that it was irregular. She noticed his hands were shaking.

"I wish Horace were here," he continued, fingering the pipe. "Because I've really got to know —!"

"Know what?"

"Well — how much he knows about minerals. I'll tell you. He wanted an analysis. Well, we'll give him one. Be a joke on him if he really thought this stuff was anything — anything novel. Got a sheet of paper?"

She gave one to him. Chuckling, he wrote on it in large characters, "SiO_2." He put the paper on the doctor's desk and the can of rocks on the paper. He said, "Are you interested in minerals?"

"I'm afraid I don't know much about them."

"Pity." The old man walked toward the door. "Beautiful things, some of them," he said.

She heard his feet move slowly down the hall. She tried to return to her work. But after twenty or thirty minutes of effort she decided she was too weary. She put on her coat and her pert hat and went down the long, forbidding corridor. She rang for an elevator, and Ivers, one of the guards, finally came up in it.

Out on Central Park West it was cold and windy. The trees across the thoroughfare were a shrieking chorus, against the dimmed-out backdrop of the buildings of Fifth Avenue, beyond the Park. She caught a bus and rode chillily to the small mid-town hotel where her expense allowance maintained her in modest comfort.

Gail Vincent was the last innocent person to see Dr. Weber alive.

His "disappearance," although noted on the following day, was the occasion for only minor alarm. Toward the end of a morning that had been busy for Gail and Dr. Jordan, they were interrupted by the Museum's vice-director, Dr. Thomas Evans. Unlike many of the scientists attached to the institution, Dr. Evans was well groomed and worldly, a fairly tall man with large, intelligent gray eyes and a taste in tweeds. He came in smilingly, apologized for disturbing them, asked Gail if the Museum was serving the War Department well, and plumed himself a moment over her enthusiastic reply. Then he said he was "somewhat concerned."

He sat down on a table edge and swung his legs. "We can't find old Paul Weber. His housekeeper phoned that he didn't come home last night. In the old days you might expect that Weber had bounded off to Tiber and had forgotten to tell us. But he's been sticking to routine for a good many years. Under the circumstances, I worry about him."

"He was here last night," Gail said. She told the vice-director about the call.

Evans turned to Jordan. "Were you in Akeley Hall? Did you see him?"

"I was down on the main floor, counting stripes on zebra legs. There was somebody up on the gallery. I saw a light on in—"

"He said the lesser koodoos," Gail said.

Dr. Jordan nodded. "About that spot." He smiled a little. "Old Paul loved to saunter around the Museum at night. Of course, he concentrated on the Hall of Gems. It was his own creation, somewhat, wasn't it?"

The vice-director nodded again. "What about this business of the can full of quartz?"

"Right behind you."

Evans tipped the can, and the collection of yellowish crystals clattered on the table top.

Dr. Jordan picked up the sheet of paper on which was lettered, "SiO_2." He showed it to Evans. "This is Paul's notion of a joke, I guess. I saw the stuff in an outcrop—up Ujiji way. Being a zoologist, not a specialist in minerals, I had a vague idea it might be interesting, and I thought of Paul, so I hammered some off and put it in this can. When I came back, with a big collection of animal specimens, I forgot all about these stones. They got sent over to my sister's place in Jersey and stored, and I came across them only day before yesterday; so I lugged 'em in to the Museum. SiO_2 means plain quartz, which was Paul's gentle way of telling me I had been wasting my time."

Dr. Evans said, "Anything to add, Miss Vincent?"

"Well, yes and no. He was terribly anxious to get in touch with Dr. Jordan last night. He considered phoning him at home. Then, for some reason, he decided not to. He said it would keep, or something of the sort. He seemed—well—excited."

Jordan shook his head. "Haven't the faintest idea why the old boy would be excited. Unless this stuff is special, after all."

"I'll have it looked at." Evans began scooping it into the can. "Meanwhile, we're running through the usual routine. Hospitals, and so on. The thing that disturbs me most is that he apparently didn't leave the building last night."

Dr. Evans added, "None of the guards let him out. Of course, it's possible that he went out unseen. There was a meeting here—a lecture—until after eleven. He might have gone out with the people who attended."

Dr. Jordan said quietly, "You've started a search here?"

"Naturally." Dr. Evans walked to the door. "I'll keep you informed. Meantime, I'd prefer that this remained confidential. No use setting up a hue and cry over what may prove to be, at worst, the normal sort of tragedy that overcomes us all in the end. I called on you two because Henry Grant told me he'd seen Paul turn in here yesterday evening."

Dr. Jordan sighed. "Golly, I hope nothing's gone wrong. That's a noble old boy, Evans. Wish we had more of 'em in this world. I owe Weber pretty nearly everything I am and do." He explained, casually, for Gail's benefit: "He was a friend of my father's. Got me interested in nature when I was a kid. Took me camping. Saw what was just a kid's interest in living things, and made the most of it. Slanted me toward biology. And chaperoned me into this berth when I'd taken my degrees. He's one hell of a nice old gent!"

"He is," Evans agreed. "And I'd hate to have anything happen to Paul, myself. For that reason. And for the Museum, too. I don't like inexplicable events in my organization. . . . You don't remember anything else, Miss Vincent?"

Gail said she was afraid not. Paul Weber had walked away from the office at some time close to eleven o'clock. That was all she knew.

She and Dr. Jordan went back to work.

On the following morning, Thursday, they learned that the Bureau of Missing Persons had been notified. The matter rested there for the entire day. By then, word of the disappearance of the mineralogist was spreading via the grapevine that exists wherever there are human beings. An exhaustive search for the old man, performed by the guards and other employees, had yielded nothing whatever. He had been in the hall outside the office where Gail worked at some time near eleven, and then he had vanished. . . .

He might not have been found for months. As it happened, chance gave an entirely new face to the problem of the missing man. At a quarter of six, on that second day of his absence, Gail and Dr. Jordan were hurrying to finish up a report on edible game in a place called Nobanzi.

The afternoon had become night because of heavy overcast. A few snowflakes were falling and the wind was on the increase. Most of the Museum staff had left.

Suddenly, the low, hurried dictation of the zoologist was broken by a sound in the hall. It was a gasping groan, audible because their door was ajar. After it came dead silence.

Jordan's pencil stopped on a page of his notes. "What's that?"

Gail, transfixed for an instant, rose and rushed to the door. At first she thought the long corridor was empty. Then she saw the figure of a man, a hundred feet away, leaning against the wall. She ran toward him, followed by Jordan. He passed her before they reached the leaning man, and said loudly, "Good lord, Taylor! What's the matter?"

Taylor was short and portly and bald. He had turned as pale as paper. In the muddy light that suffused the corridor, a diamond dust of perspiration glinted on his cheeks, his brow, and his bald head. He merely pointed a shuddering finger in a rubber glove.

The object at which he pointed was a long, waist-high box, painted a battleship gray. There were five or six such boxes in the corridor, and Gail had noticed them before, but only casually. The hand-lugs of this box had been turned, and its lid removed. It was brimful of an opaque, brownish liquid from which rose a reek of carbolic. Not a box, then, but a tank. A tank filled with preservative.

Gail had a horrible hunch, and so did Dr. Jordan. His face also paled and grew tense. He cast his eyes about in the passageway, stepped to a heap of shelving, picked up one of the boards and began to stir the dark fluid. Something stuck briefly above the surface—a huge hand, covered with fur. Gail gasped.

"Gorilla," Jordan said sharply. He prodded again. He lifted above the liquid, for a mere split second, another object. There was no mistaking the dripping awfulness of it. He let it fall back.

He turned to Gail. "You okay?"

She gathered herself. "Yes."

"Take Taylor into my office. I'll go for Evans." He addressed the bald-headed man. "You've had a bad shock, Taylor. Go into my room and sit down."

Dr. Jordan was very calm. Very collected. He kept his lips firm. He was thinking—thinking swiftly. He wasn't afraid. But he had room for emotion, and he expressed just a little of it: "That—that"—he gestured at the tank—"that old man was my best friend, in a way. I—I loved the old guy! And whoever has done this to him is going to pay for it. I am going to make him pay!"

Gail knew that he would if it was humanly possible. She thought that she wouldn't want him to feel any other way about it. He was brimming over with a decent and bitter passion. She glanced at Taylor and back toward Dr. Jordan. He was running up the hall.

Gail took the limp scientist by the elbow and led him along to Dr. Jordan's door. No one else had as yet appeared in the hall. Gail put Mr. Taylor in a chair and went back to make sure of that fact. Down the long passage she could see the open tank. And then, far beyond, a door closed. Martha Beal, the biologist, walked toward Gail without seeing her, turned at a side passage, and vanished.

Gail closed Dr. Jordan's door. She poured a glass of water for Taylor.

"I'll be all right," he said. "I was just terrifically startled."

"Of course."

Minutes passed. She heard Evans and Jordan walk past—and walk past again, later, in the opposite direction. Under her ministrations, Taylor was beginning to recover.

Finally, the two men came in. Evans was haggard. Dr. Jordan seemed more abstracted than usual. But he said, "Still okay, Miss Vincent?" with the trace of a smile.

"Yes. And Mr. Taylor's better, I believe."

Taylor unfolded a clean handkerchief and wiped his forehead. "I was stunned—"

Evans lighted a cigarette with a wavering match. "This," he said nervously, "is a pretty terrible thing! It'll make headlines. It'll reflect all sorts of things—on me! A museum should house science, sense—" He realized how incoherent he sounded and made an effort to control himself.

"Well, Taylor, what happened? How come you were poking into that tank?"

"I was doing an article on comparative anatomy. Anthropoids. There were a couple of points about gorillas I wanted to check, and I knew we had this one up here. I phoned Shollt for permission, but he'd gone. I felt sure he wouldn't object, so I simply came up, opened the tank, and reached in. I got"—he broke off and drew a long breath—"what Jordan did. I suppose you observed"—his voice rose as he addressed Jordan alone—"that there was clear evidence of a hard blow on the head?"

"We've phoned for the police," Evans said heavily. "That's all we can do for the moment. They'll want to question you, Taylor, first, no doubt. You'd better pull yourself together for it. I, naturally, will explain that what you did was mere routine. Quite all right." He dropped suddenly into one of the desk chairs. "But who on earth would murder Paul Weber?"

"The police," Jordan said softly, "will want to know who could have. I mean," he continued, "who was here the night Paul vanished? You were in your office, Evans. I was. Gail Vincent, here. I saw old Pinsch around that night when Weber disappeared. Felton, too, of course. They're inseparable. Henry Grant looked in here. So there's Grant—"

"That's futile speculation." Evans stopped studying his own thoughts. "There was a lecture that night, remember? A hundred-odd people attended. Tickets were a cinch to get hold of. Anybody who came to the lecture could have sneaked out, ducked the guards, and hidden around to waylay Paul Weber."

"Point is," Jordan answered, "could and would just 'anybody' have known we had preservative in these tanks and where they are and how to get into them—let alone how to transport a body to them?"

The talk went on. A police car wailed its approach out on the cold street. Dr. Evans went to meet the men, and brought back a sandy-haired, blue-eyed man of middle age.

"This," the vice-director said, "is Lieutenant Grove . . . Dr. Jordan— Mr. Taylor—Miss Vincent, from Washington."

Lieutenant Grove let his eyes examine each of the three. Then he got out a cigar, bit it, lighted it, and said, "All right. Shoot."

They told him, in turn, all they knew about Paul Weber's activities on the presumptive night of his murder. Grove listened carefully. At last he said, "I think, Dr. Evans, we'll have to begin with the usual methods. Comb the place. Try to find the weapon of assault. Try to find, if possible, the exact place where he was attacked—"

Evans stared at the officer. "You'd be able to clean up that job in about ten years."

The policeman frowned. "My boys on Homicide are trained—"

"I'm not impugning them. I simply mean that the enormousness of the plan you outline hasn't occurred to you. The weapon, for example. I'd say—and I imagine the casts of the wound will bear me out—that it was the usual blunt instrument. Curved, but not round. The skull fracture is plain. Curved like a chair arm—like the surface of a mastodon rib. At a guess, there are ten thousand such blunt instruments in the Museum.

"As to the scene: Weber liked to roam the Museum at night. It's fairly well guarded and most of the exhibition halls are closed off with gates. But keys could be stolen—manufactured. The guards could be dodged. On this floor, the fifth, there are offices and labs. On the sixth, more labs, the department of experimental biology. There's a big basement with a cafeteria, machine shop, paint shop, carpentry shop, restrooms, nurses' rooms, the heating plant, and a pipe maze nobody understands except the man in charge.

"There are various staircases and many elevators—one that'll carry whole elephants. Has to be. The four floors under this are exhibits—thirteen of the total twenty-three acres of floor space, Lieutenant! And then there are some higher rooms, and the building interconnects in such a way that you can get from one part to most any other by way of the roof. I've been here, myself, for twenty-two years, and I'd say, at a guess, that there's a good ten per cent of the floor space here that I don't know a thing about! So, you see—"

Grove whistled softly. "All right. I'm convinced. We'll just have to do the best we can. Now . . . on the night Weber disappeared—Tuesday—the following people are known to have been here." He consulted a memorandum book. "You, Dr. Evans. You, Jordan. Taylor—you weren't here? You, Miss Vincent. Felton and Pinsch, geologists. Henry Grant, a technician. Martha Beal, biologist. A medical man named Garrison Lombardo. The guards. From what I've gathered, I take it you're all surprised that Dr. Weber was murdered."

It was, oddly enough, Taylor who first answered. "Astonished. He has spent his life here. Privately wealthy, and sometimes eccentric. Opinionated and possessed of a temper, yes. But a magnificent scientist. He's a widower—has been for a decade. No children. The shocking part of this whole business is that—well, Paul Weber simply wasn't the kind of man who—who gets—"

"—who gets murdered?" Grove finished.

"Yes."

"In an individual case," the lieutenant said, "you never know what the type is until the thing's done. Maybe Weber hadn't an enemy, but somebody hit him with something, and hid him away in a gorilla storage tank, where—"

"Weber did have enemies, of sorts," Evans said uncertainly.

The policeman turned. "Who?"

Dr. Evans frowned. "I am not making accusations, you understand. Simply telling facts. In a professional way, Pinsch and Felton were bitter enemies of Weber. It began—oh—before my time. Maybe a quarter of a century ago, when Pinsch and Felton were young men. They quarreled about the manner of the formation of the Atlas Mountains—"

"Ye gods!" The man from the Homicide Squad was disgusted. "We can't start checking back on old technical feuds!"

"This was different. It got into a lot of scientific journals. In the end, old Paul Weber more or less won the argument. Only, by the time he won, he was so sore at Pinsch and Felton he took pains to try to show them up as fools. Then they had a battle in the newspapers about water-supply sources for New York City. That was in the nineteen-teens. It was a geological argument, but it ended up with Pinsch swinging on Weber at a mass meeting; and Weber—he was in his early fifties and wiry—swung back and knocked Pinsch off the platform.

"Later they argued over the air-carriage of loess from the Gobi Desert and a lot of other topics. Felton sued Weber, once, for libel. Weber sued Pinsch, once, for slander. The thing has calmed down in the last decade, although they seldom speak and always take pains, when referring to each other in monographs, to use the most slurring terms that the form permits."

"Felton and Pinsch," supplemented Jordan, "are a fairly ornery pair. You never know how deep that sort of thing goes, either. Weber may have been up to some new insult or trick—may even have wanted to rope me in on it. I never cared especially for the two geologists, and the old boy knew it."

"I'll see them," Grove said thoughtfully, "and take you along, Dr. Evans."

The vice-director nodded. "One more person ought to be considered."

"I thought of her, too," Jordan murmured.

"Martha Beal. She and Weber were in love a long time ago. Engaged to be married. She was his technical assistant, one of the first women to be employed in that capacity here. The engagement broke off overnight, nobody ever knew why, and she moved to another department. Ever since, she's hated old Weber. Martha Beal is a very intelligent, shrewd, hard-working woman. She might have cracked—"

"Easily," the lieutenant agreed.

"She'll be number three on my list." He turned to the vice-director. "I'm going to have to have somebody here, Doctor, as a liaison between me and my men and you and your staff. Somebody who knows the Museum and the personnel and can be trusted."

Evans smiled a little. "Jordan?"

The zoologist looked at Gail. "I've already been deputized to the U. S. Government."

Gail said, "I suspect that as soon as my colonel reads the papers he'll wire for me to come back to Washington."

"Which," said Lieutenant Grove, "in view of your importance as a witness, the New York Police Department might oppose."

Evans smiled more openly. "In which case, Jordan—"

"In which case, all right! I loved old Paul. I'll like finding whoever did that to him!"

The police officer walked to the door, where he stopped and turned.

"Incidentally, what is your work, Jordan? What, for instance, were you doing down there on the main floor of Akeley Hall night before last?"

Jordan's eyes flickered. "I was standing in front of a stuffed Hippotigris with a flashlight. I was making a comparison of the legstripe patterns on the Equus burchelli and the grevyi."

Lieutenant Grove stared, and then snorted. "This is a fine job for a cop!"

Evans opened the door wider. "Jordan's talking about zebras. Come on, Lieutenant. Taylor? Coming?"

When they had gone, Dr. Jordan creaked back his desk chair and looked thoughtful. "Where do we start?"

"Where do you start?" Gail smiled a little. "I never had anything to do with crime."

"You're a researcher, a gal with scientific training. You've been G-2-ed, and FBI-ed. That lieutenant from Homicide—Grove—won't ever get anything out of this."

"I wouldn't be sure."

"He won't. He's a good fellow, and bright, too. But he isn't a scientist. This business goes back to obscure things that happened long ago. It involves people, ideas, situations that Grove doesn't know anything about. No police officer does. It involves a knowledge of the Museum. For instance, nobody would dare transport Paul's body to this floor late at night. It would be too conspicuous; somebody might be working here.

"The body had to be carried up here at a time and in a way which wouldn't be noticed. And there's one good way—those zinc-covered roller tables we use to carry big specimens. We wheel them around continually. We cover them with sheets so as not to discomfit the visitors. Now, pretty nearly anybody could roll such a load into an elevator, roll it off on this floor, and wait his chance to open the gorilla tank and put the body in.

"The lieutenant wouldn't understand that. He'd think we would remember, because, in his mind, the rolling table would have a human corpse on it. But, in ours, the business is normal. See what I mean?"

"Of course." Gail thought a moment. "If he was killed while he was wandering around on the floors below, he probably would have been hidden overnight—there are simply millions of places—and moved up here later on."

"Right."

"What do you intend to do? I mean, how will you start?"

"With some dinner," Jordan answered. "Join me?"

Upon their return they put into action the plan they had devised. First, Gail sat under the green-shaded lamp and described, step by step, Dr. Weber's call on the evening on which he had last been seen.

Jordan listened carefully and asked a few questions. But when she had finished he shook his head. "I don't get it. I mean, what excited him. . . . Let's go to Akeley Hall."

A policeman stood outside. He let them in. Dr. Jordan turned on a flashlight. A few bulbs were burning, far overhead. Otherwise, the vast panoply of African habitat groups was dark.

"I stood here," Jordan said, "and counted those stripes." He shone his light on the leg of a zebra. "I knelt to do it. There was somebody up above on the gallery. His back was toward me. I didn't even look, directly. I was concentrating and in a hurry. There was a smell of pipe smoke. I'm sure of that, now that I'm here. Paul's, I think. So he was up there when I was here— just as we both thought. He may have gone back again. Let's look it over."

They left the lower room and went up to the gallery entrance. It was unlocked. It was dark in the gallery, but not too dark for shadowy visibility. Gail was not afraid—only the dinosaur bones had the power to intimidate her—but she moved closer to Dr. Jordan.

"Old Paul," he said, "if it was old Paul, must have been standing right here."

"It's so real," Gail said, "that you can almost smell the African air."

"The fellows who made it would appreciate that compliment. . . . Now. if we assume Paul came back again we might imagine his attack occurred somewhere around here. Of course, we have no way of knowing exactly, or even approximately, when he was killed. I daresay the fact that he was put in that preservative will prevent even the police examiner from determining the hour of death with any accuracy. . . . Shall we look around?"

Gail found herself searching painstakingly along the floor. Dr. Jordan had provided her with an extra flashlight and she used it, but without any feeling of effectiveness. Hundreds, probably thousands, of strangers had walked through the gallery since the night of the mineralogist's disappearance. She searched the floor, the protective rail in front of the glass, the molding beneath it, and the railing around the edge of the vast balcony which overhung the main chamber.

Then she stopped, pushed her flashlight close to the foot of the railing. "Here's something!" she called.

Dr. Jordan came hastily.

The pool of light held on the railing-base. In it were a half-dozen spots, smaller than pennies, and dark. "I thought—" she said.

The zoologist bent low. "You're right! Blood!" From his pocket he took a penknife. He hunted for an envelope, and produced an electric-light bill. He removed the bill and carefully scraped into the envelope a couple of the dry blemishes. Then, with great care, he examined the gallery for a distance of a few yards.

"I don't know much about blood," he said. "Human, that is. But plenty of people around here do. Martha Beal, for example."

"Under the circumstances—" Gail began.

"Under the circumstances, she might be exactly the right person."

They went back to the spot where they had found the blood and knelt over it for a final scrutiny. Gail was very conscious of Dr. Jordan kneeling there close to her. She thought that the sense of urgency which Dr. Jordan's nearness gave her was the kind of emotion men had—one perhaps not suitable to a girl.

He glanced up in time to see her looking at him. He blushed, so she knew he had interpreted her expression correctly.

He went on looking at her. "It's pretty swell of you," he said evenly, "to come here with me on a job like this. You're the kind of person, Miss V., that a fellow—"

He didn't get any farther. Gail saw a figure loom up behind him— suddenly and silently. She lost track of her bewildering feelings in the second it took to snatch his arm and pull him away. She half screamed, "Look out!"

Dr. Jordan jumped toward her and past her, like a cat. He spun and came up standing. Then he said, shakily, "Oh! It's you, Ivers! Lord, you scared us half to death!"

The Museum guard was big-boned, Irish, and somewhat amused at the havoc he had caused. "I've got on sneakers," he said. "Dr. Evans, and the cops, too, told me to keep a sharp lookout. I heard somebody muttering in here. So of course I gumshoed in."

"The next time you gumshoe around me," Dr. Jordan said, "you're likely to get slugged."

Ivers apologized. "I'll remember. Made me nervous, what happened to Dr. Weber. Make anybody nervous. Not that I cared for him—"

"What was the matter with him, Ivers?"

"Fussy. Nosy. Always prowling around at night. Always getting us to open things up for him."

Jordan shrugged. "Okay. . . . Come on, Miss V. We'll hunt up Martha Beal." They walked from the gallery. "Irritation," he said to Gail as they waited for an elevator, "is not a motive for murder. But I suppose one of the guards could have killed Paul—if there's a fiend among 'em."

They went up to their floor and walked down the familiar corridor again, Gail still shaken from her fright at the looming appearance of Ivers, and from the emotions which he had interrupted. There was a light burning in Martha Beal's office. The door was open. But they had not reached it when Gail felt a repetition of the alarm which had accompanied Ivers' sudden materialization.

She had passed a space between ceiling-high specimen cases which lined that part of the corridor and, after going by, she had found herself entertaining the notion that somebody had been pressed back, hiding, in that space. It was just an impression—a sense of whiteness where a face might have been. She halted.

Dr. Jordan went ahead, and peered into the office. "Martha?" He turned. "Not in."

"I think—" Reluctantly, uncertainly, Gail made herself walk back. Martha Beal was pressed between the towering cases as stiffly as a mummy.

Dr. Jordan saw her, and said, "Good heavens!"

The woman stepped out of the recess. "I hoped you wouldn't notice me."

"We wanted to talk to you," Gail stammered.

"Exactly. And I wanted privacy. Well, you found me, so come in."

Gail realized that there would be no more explanation than that. The woman was going to let them think what they would. She couldn't have been hiding for long, Gail reflected. Around her workbench were the paraphernalia of an experiment left unfinished.

Miss Beal was tall and very gaunt. Her eyes were a washed-out shade of blue. Her hair had been dark red once, but it was now raddled with gray—long, knotted, and untidy.

About her was a curious aspect both of desuetude and fanatical energy. Her present expression was so rigid that Gail barely returned her look and deliberately let her eyes stray to the wilderness of material in the room. There was everything, she noted, from shrunken human heads to headache remedies—from big brown bottles of acid to old shoes, a party hat, and a boomerang. It was a room in which Martha Beal not only worked but also had her principal existence.

Dr. Jordan, meanwhile, had been introducing Gail. Both women merely nodded, at his words. "I called here, Martha—or we did—because we wanted you to do us a favor."

"Naturally."

"It's about Paul. You've heard that—?"

"Yes. I heard."

Dr. Jordan was disconcerted. "The police," he explained haltingly, "asked us to do what we could to help. Miss Vincent and I were about the last people to see Paul alive. In my office, in her case; in Akeley Hall, in mine. We've been looking in Akeley Hall, and we found—" He told her about the blood.

She sat silent until he had finished. Then she said, "And you want me to examine it for you? Make sure it's human? Type it, if I can?"

"I'm sorry to trouble you, Martha."

"Why?"

Dr. Jordan flushed. "Well, I know—"

"You know nothing!" Her eyes gathered bitter light and darted from the man to the woman. "You speak to me of Paul with emotion, with grief! What do you know about either one? The emptiness of both have been the fullness of my days! And now it's going to be a public topic! The police will dig it up, drag it out of me like a confession drawn from the victim of torture! I loved him!

"Yes, I was mad about him! He was the only man I ever had a chance to be mad about! I saw him everyday, every hour. He appreciated me. My mind. We laughed at the same things. I let myself think that he was falling in love with me. And I made him think so. He wasn't, but how could he know that? I was ugly, even then. Unfeminine! Finally I was so sure of myself I gave him a chance to break the engagement. Casually, easily, because I was testing the strength of the false thing I had created. And he broke it!"

Martha Beal began to weep. Gail did not move. She wished she was somewhere else. In a moment, however, the disturbed woman went on:

"I hated him, after that! I fed myself on hate and anesthetized myself with work. And only tonight, when that talky, attractive woman in ichthyology told me about the discovery did my hatred begin to die down." She stifled the last vestige of a sob. She pushed back her hair.

"Give me the blood!"

Dr. Jordan reluctantly handed her the envelope with the transparent window. He nodded to Gail.

"Don't go," Martha Beal said. "I can give you the first part of the report in no time."

They sat uncomfortably while she tapped out the brown powder, added a drop of liquid, and dexterously adjusted a microscope. "I can tell you Paul's blood type," she said in a low, heavy tone while she worked. "There's nothing about Paul Weber I can't tell you. He gave an emergency transfusion here once. He's Type Three." She peered into the eyepiece. "This is blood—yes. Human. The rest will take considerable time."

Dr. Jordan was standing, at last. "I'm sorry, Martha, that we were the cause of bringing all this up."

She didn't say a word.

They went out.

In the hall Dr. Jordan wiped his forehead. "More than I bargained for. I wanted to see her, but—"

"She's a little unbalanced about Paul."

"Just a touch."

"And that business of hiding. I thought maybe you'd ask her—"

"People don't usually ask Martha much. They wait to be told. But it's one to file and consider. One for Grove. Gosh! When I saw you seeing her, I felt my spine wilt!"

He opened his office door.

Inside, sitting at his own desk, was the lieutenant. "Been waiting for you two," he said. "Have some questions to ask. Incidentally, congratulations on finding the bloodstains!"

Jordan bristled. "How in the name—?"

"Just routine, Doctor. Number one, of course, was to check the places where the victim was last seen. My men collected a couple of blood samples while you were having supper. Number two was to keep an eye on the people who had last seen the deceased, although they were supposedly working for me."

Jordan grunted. "At least, we know where he was when he was attacked."

The lieutenant shook his head. "Maybe. Even probably. But we don't know. As a scientist, you'd doubtless say we did. As a cop, I say that all we know is that a few drops of somebody's blood got spattered at the bottom of the railing a couple of days ago. The cleaners missed them. The murderer, if he wiped up after the crime, also missed them. But several hundred people went by there. The blood might have come from a kid who cut his finger."

Gail said, "Better tell him about Martha Beal."

They told him.

He thought it over. "What was your feeling, Jordan?"

"That she'd do anything, if she wanted to."

"That's the impression I got. . . . Miss Vincent?"

"She's a bizarre sort of woman. She embarrasses you, deliberately. A little bit out of her head. She'd been crying. At first, I thought it was for Paul. After she talked I realized it was from self-pity."

"That's what women usually cry from," Grove said cynically. "I ought to know. . . . See here. I want to ask you—" He fished a piece of paper from his pocket. It was scribbled with notes that ran in all directions, as if they had been written against his knee and against walls. "Question number one: What sort of suit was Felton wearing Tuesday?"

Jordan said, "Good lord! That is a question! Brown, I believe."

Gail laughed. "Blue. Blue serge."

Grove glanced at her. "The point comes up because I've been questioning the guards who see people leave here. I asked them to try and remember anything peculiar about the people I mentioned. I got a zero, except that one of the guards said Felton was wearing a gray suit and stood around a while, apparently because he hated to go out in all the weather. I tried to check that point, but I got various answers. Pinsch couldn't remember what his pal wore. I haven't asked Felton himself, yet. Somebody else said black. But we've got gray, blue, black, and brown."

"I'm not positive," Gail said, thinking. "Not when I try to visualize it."

"It goes to show," the lieutenant interrupted, "that people's memories aren't worth anything when you pin them down. A point you both might bear in mind. . . . Next: What do you know about Dr. Lombardo? He was around here Tuesday night."

Gail shook her head.

Jordan reflected. "Garrison Lombardo's a popular lecturer. Audiences are crazy about him. I was never very friendly with him, myself. He's an M.D., you know; they're rare on the staff. Specializes in tropical diseases. I was going to take Miss Vincent in to see him next week.

He can add a lot to our dossier on Africa for the War Department. Only, I was going to warn Miss V. that the eminent specialist has an eye for ladies."

"You can skip that," Gail said.

Grove grinned and looked at them inquiringly. "Okay. But you know nothing about his personal affairs? Didn't you know, for instance, that he's a gambler? That there's a rumor out he's lost thirty thousand dollars and is being hounded for it?"

"No," Jordan said.

"Do you know if, by any chance, Paul Weber has mentioned Lombardo in his will?"

"I suppose he mentioned all of us, more or less," Jordan replied. "Funny, I hadn't thought of it. Paul was pretty well fixed, you know. He located a lot of mines in his earlier days. He was as good a businessman as he was a mineralogist. And . . ."

"Well?"

"Come to think of if, Paul might have made a special bequest to Lombardo. Lombardo once saved his life. In Africa. Lombardo was studying tsetses, and heard that a white man was very sick in the jungle. He went in, and found Paul dying and nursed him around."

"M-m-m-m," Grove said. He referred to his list. "The next question: Grant."

Jordan shrugged. "I know still less about him. He's a technician. Trained in the Middle West, St. Louis, or Kansas City. Good man. Been here two or three years. Keeps his mouth shut, and minds his own business."

"What kind of technician? Would he have access to the gorilla tanks?"

The zoologist grinned. "Lieutenant, you mustn't get thinking of those tanks the way the newspaper headlines do! To us, there's nothing gruesome or dramatic about them, any more than there is about handcuffs to you. . . . Sure; Grant would know about the tanks. They were merely equipment. They weren't locked."

Grove answered the grin with twinkling eyes. "Okay. We cops have found out a few things, though. Grant, for instance, has been in court twice since coming to Manhattan."

"What for?"

"Street fighting."

"That youngster! Fighting?"

"In Yorkville. Before Pearl Harbor. He got into tangles—"

"You mean he's a Nazi?"

"He was fighting pro-Nazis. He started one minor riot by heckling a Bundist soapbox speaker."

The policeman smiled at the doctor.

"You're on our blotter, too, I discovered."

Jordan glanced at Gail and flushed darkly. "It was an impulse."

Grove addressed the girl: "Imagine! Same charge: assault. He was let off with a caution."

Gail stared incredulously at the scientist.

He was still red, but he grinned. "Did I hang one on that guy! It was at the zoo here in the Park. Some ignorant busybody told some kids that a raccoon was a panda. I corrected him. The oaf argued with me. One thing led to another. He swung, and I flattened him, and he began yelling for help. He charged me with assault and I countercharged, and it came to nothing in the end."

The lieutenant folded his page of scrawled notes. He pushed back the doctor's chair. "Well, I'm tired and I bet you two are. . . . Did you bring that gorilla to America?"

Jordan frowned. "I dunno. I brought one for Shollt. It might be the same. Why?"

"Felton, I think it was, said you did. You did bring back a terrific load of stuff?"

"Yeah. I usually do."

Grove was at the door. "You birds get your stuff through customs easily, I take it?" He waited for Jordan's nod. "Be a marvelous chance for smuggling."

Jordan's eyebrows lifted. "It would. Matter of fact, I've had offers."

"Offers?"

"Well, one offer. Last trip. Chap in Freetown, a Britisher, tried to persuade me to cart home a lot of ivory. It was undoubtedly ivory taken illegally, though he told me the old cock-and-bull story about getting it from the place where elephants go to die."

Still the lieutenant did not leave. "Where'd you put that can of quartz?"

Both Gail and the doctor glanced at the cluttered table upon which the coffee can had stood. Jordan said, "Guess Evans came for it. He said he was going to have it examined."

"He didn't. I phoned him while you were talking to Martha Beal."

"It was there when we went out to dinner," Gail said.

The lieutenant's voice was troubled: "That's what I thought. Somebody walked in between eight and nine, and took it. As usual around here, it could have been anybody. . . . Good night, Jordan. 'Night, Miss Vincent. If I were you two I wouldn't stand in any dark rooms with your backs turned!"

Jordan pondered after the policeman had departed. Presently he took a key ring from his pocket and crossed the gloomy office. A chest stood under windows which overlooked the frozen Park. He unlocked it. "This is a rather nice case," he said modestly. "It belonged to a friend of mine, long since gone to his reward. Before that, it belonged to a rajah. Teak. For guns. I keep a few here—the old problem of no room at home. Want a look-see?"

The guns shone dully under a layer of dusty grease. Dr. Jordan picked out a medium-sized pistol and wiped it with waste. For a few minutes he worked expertly. He took cartridges from a box, inserted them, and dropped the pistol into his side jacket pocket. "You never know," he said.

They walked from the night-hung building together, for which the girl was glad. Jordan tried to take her mind off the doings of the long day.

"Where's your home, Miss Vincent?"

"Washington."

"Family live there?"

"I haven't any family. Father died before I can remember. Mother ran a millinery shop in Detroit. She died four years ago."

"I see. Can I drop you? I'm taking a cab."

"Thanks."

Gail arrived at the Museum at a quarter of nine the next morning. It was an unsettled day—raw, with an indecisive threat of cold rain or wet snow. She ached a little from nervousness and lack of sleep. All night long she had kept wakening to mull over the events of the day before.

At the museum, she hurried from the elevator down the hall and turned into the office corridor. She banged squarely into somebody who had been making a turnabout, ricocheted, and looked up. It was Dr. David Felton. He had been pacing in front of the offices—pacing so anxiously he hadn't paid attention to her quick feet. That was all very plain in his manner. He began muttering apologies. His smooth, black pompadour was rumpled. He gesticulated. "Sorry. I've been waiting for Jordan."

"As a rule he doesn't get in till around ten." She took out her key and unlocked her door.

Dr. Felton was behind her. "I thought he might, though, today. I—er—maybe I'll wait."

He was wearing a gray suit today, she noticed automatically. Whatever kind he'd worn on the suspected night, it was gray now. Gray, mussed, and with a hole burned in the trouser-leg—by nervous smoking, no doubt.

Felton sat down. "Awful. Awful thing! I wasn't precisely a friend of the deceased, but to think of him wandering as usual out there in the gallery! And then clubbed to death!"

He rose and began to pace again. Gail wondered how he knew Dr. Weber had been killed in the gallery. It was not common knowledge, so far as she was aware. She eyed him, and he seemed to blanch under her scrutiny. "Won't wait, after all," he said curtly. "Thanks just the same!" He hurried from the room.

Gail sat down at her desk and thought that over. Presently she rose and followed him. He had gone back to his office. The door was shut. She could hear him on the telephone. His words weren't discernible but they sounded worried. She wondered if his colleague, Dr. Pinsch, were in the building. His office was a few doors away. She walked toward it, and Pinsch's voice came through the glass panel distinctly: "Of course not, Dave! Keep your shirt on!"

The voice inside the office lowered; Gail leaned against the door to try to catch the words. But she could hear nothing.

Then the door flew open, she lost her balance, and was forced to lunge into the office to regain it. Dr. Pinsch held the knob, looking angry and a little frightened. He was a small, fat man, sharp-eyed and sharp-tongued. He had stepped aside to let her stagger through the door. He said, "Well?"

Gail tried her best to dissemble: "I was coming to call on you. I have a list of things to ask you and Dr. Felton—about water tables in the Ujiji country."

His expression became crafty. "And another list to ask us about the murder of Paul Weber? I've already heard you and Jordan are stool pigeons for the police. I can't say that the staff appreciates it. It's surprising—in Jordan. You, coming from Washington, might be expected to be listening through keyholes."

Gail faced him. "All right! I was listening. Not because I work for the Government. But because I'm willing to help find out who killed a nice old man. You should be willing, too."

Dr. Pinsch grinned wryly. He pushed a chair beside his desk. "Sit down. Evans said you'd be interviewing me one day. Which is it—murder or geology?"

Gail said, "I'm embarrassed."

"You should be. Caught people usually are! I was talking to Dave. Dave Felton. He's frantic at the moment. The police called on him last night. As they did me. They have every reason to think that both he and I detested Weber, because we did. They have no reason to think we did away with Weber, because we didn't. But their attentions have seriously perturbed my friend. . . . And now we'll discuss Africa, if you wish."

She listened, and made the proper answers. He had covered up as neatly as possible for the telephone call and for Felton's nervous condition. She also thought that he would make an unpleasant, dangerous enemy. There was no way to tell exactly how his lifelong feud with Weber had affected him. It had enraged Dr. Felton. But Dr. Pinsch was different. For one thing, he was brainier.

She accepted his material, promised to come back when she had digested it, and left him as soon as she could.

Henry Grant and Garrison Lombardo had also been in the Museum that night. She knew them both. Her researches into the private counsels of Felton and Pinsch had been interesting; so she decided to continue.

Henry Grant's office, on the sixth floor, was unlocked and deserted. Like the other shops and labs, it was odorous and crammed with miscellaneous apparatus: chemicals, armatures on which specimens were mounted, fossil rocks, imitation trees and flowers, and wooden bases glued together and held by clamps. Henry was a super-repair-man, as well as a taxidermist of a highly specialized sort. His coat and hat were in the room, on a hook; in his coat pocket was a copy of a magazine dealing with natural history. It had a pterodactyl on the cover.

A woman in a smock glanced in at the door, said, "Where's Mr. Grant?" and answered herself: "Down working on the deep-sea exhibits, isn't he?"

Gail said, "I'm sure I don't know," and went down to the main floor.

There were not many visitors in the exhibition halls as yet. The room which depicted life under the sea had been roped off. From behind the barrier came sounds of hammering. Gail ducked under the rope. In the faint, bluish light which represented sunshine fathoms below the surface of the sea, weird animals "swam" overhead and on all sides: sharks, turtles, and a gigantic manta ray.

Henry saw her and stopped hammering. "Hello, bright eyes!"

"Morning."

"Studying submarine fauna? Is the War Department planning to tell divers what to look out for along the African coast? Or are you working for the Navy now?" He laughed, and then coughed.

Gail smiled. "I came to see you."

Henry jumped down from a perch behind the manta ray and put his hammer in a toolbox. "Good! Time for it, too."

"I came on account of Paul Weber."

"Oh." He was disappointed. "I thought you were going to wheedle me into buying you a cup of coffee in the cafeteria."

She shook her head. "Some day—"

"Your 'some days' don't show up often." His good humor was strained by his chagrin. "I don't know a blooming thing about Paul Weber. Hardly said ten words to him since I came to work here. And the police have already investigated me. Why bother about these old dead men, bright eyes, when there's us lively young fellers around?"

"He was a nice old man. Dr. Jordan was mighty fond of him."

"Jordan, eh?" Henry said speculatively. "You falling for teacher? Jordan's hardly your type. Too stuffy." He coughed again.

"He is not!"

"All right. He is your type, then. And I'm not. And I'm busy."

"You didn't see anybody Tuesday night after you looked in on me?"

"No, Miss Holmes, I didn't." Henry was peevish. "Frankly, no. I went home. I caught a cold. I had to wait half an hour for a bus. As I told the police, I worked late on the so-called night in question. Some kids had knocked a slab of fossil rock off a pedestal, and Dr. Evans buttered me into staying overtime to mend it, and I did. But I didn't see any killers sneaking up on old Weber and I didn't see any ghouls hauling his body up to the tank."

"Oh, all right," Gail said. "You don't need to be snippy."

"I'm not snippy! I've got a cold. And I don't like pretty-girl busy-bodies going around asking questions. Why do you bother your head with things like—? . . . Lookee. When I get over this cold and you get over your crush on Jordan, suppose we take in a movie?"

"Sure. You just decide what movie and I'll go meekly. I'm going now, in fact."

"So long, bright eyes!" He coughed.

There was still Garrison Lombardo, the M.D. Like Dr. Pinsch and Dr. Felton, he was on her list of staff members to interview for the War Department. Henry had been disappointing, but Dr. Lombardo might add something to the material she had collected from the two geologists.

He received her in a courtly manner. He would be delighted to put at her disposal any information he had about tropical medicine. The Ujiji country was fascinating from a clinical standpoint. It was refreshing to find that so charming and attractive a young lady had given her services to her country in this terrible emergency.

She took careful notes as Africa was discussed. He paced the floor, smiling, showing his white teeth, delicately brushing back his curly hair and fingering his mustache. She led the discussion away from African diseases to the topic of Dr. Weber's murder by such easy stages that Lombardo seemed unaware of the change.

His eyes rolled expressively. "What a loss! And what a terrible thing to do! The poor old man!"

"You were here?"

"Unfortunately. And the police have already discovered the fact."

"I suppose you didn't notice anything?"

"No. No, I didn't." He sighed and shook his head. "I didn't see Paul that evening. As it happens, though, I have what the police might consider an adequate motive for wanting him dead. It is a personal matter. Such minds, the police have! He was my friend. But they insist that I might have destroyed him. Could I—would I—kill my friend and also sink him in a tank of preservative? It's unthinkable! The trouble is"—he smiled broadly—"I also had what they call an opportunity. I was not in my office, on Tuesday, for quite a while."

"Oh?" Gail said.

"I was stealing."

"Stealing?"

He nodded solemnly, and then laughed. "Imagine how unlucky! That night of all nights I decided to commit a small theft! Why? Because I dearly love my nephew, Angelo. On Sundays we build model airplanes. Last Sunday we were ready to paint our newest one. My nephew calls this one a dilly. Four feet over-all, with a gasoline motor! We needed aluminum paint, and, unfortunately, we had none. I thought it would be difficult to obtain because of the war and priorities. So I promised my nephew I would steal some from the paint shop in the Museum."

Gail found herself smiling. "And you did?"

"Of course! I merely worked late, as I often do, anyway. I went down to the paint shop. The man who takes care of the furnaces was pottering somewhere. I heard him but I did not see him. I stole — in a bottle, some varnish — in a bag, the powdered aluminum. I have an absent mind. I left it somewhere here and remembered it only this morning. Now, when I looked, I find it had been taken. The police, I suppose."

"You told them?"

"Of course! Otherwise they would think I had been killing my friend."

Gail rose to go. Dr. Lombardo rose, too.

"You've been very kind —"

He bowed. He came around his desk. He looked at her with a too-luminous light in his dark eyes. Gail backed a little bit, but he merely held out his hand. "Charming!" he said.

So she held out her hand. He seized it, kissed the back of it, and a moment later kissed her shoulder and her cheek.

He was talking. "You are so beautiful!" he said. "So often, every day, I have gone out of my way just to catch glimpses of you. So ravishing. I distress myself with it. Now I distress you with it — and I cannot help it!" He had taken her chin in his hand before she realized that she was going to be in the midst of a very long kiss in a very short time.

"Just let go of me," Gail said quietly, "or I'll hang one on you."

Dr. Lombardo persisted, with ardor. So Gail hung one on him. Possibly he had expected to be slapped, at the worst. He had certainly not expected a fast jab from a tight and quite competent right fist. He let go, embraced himself, and swore softly.

Dr. Jordan was sitting on the chest under the window, smoking a cigarette. He said abruptly, "Where have you been? I —"

She told him in some detail: Felton, anxious and rumpled; his call to the deceptive Dr. Pinsch; the offhand Henry Grant; the grandiloquent medico. She left out the part she still felt in her knuckles.

He shrugged. "What have you got for all that running around, though?"

"I've got a concise picture of the Ujiji geology from Dr. Pinsch. And a list of the diseases in the area from Lombardo. He's not so very dangerous, really. Just — ultra-male. And I've also got suspicions. I'm practically sure, now, that Felton and Pinsch know something. They're hiding something. And they're in it together. Henry Grant's too nonchalant to be guilty of anything —"

"There's a woman's intuition!"

"—and Dr. Lombardo's guile isn't dangerous — to men."

Jordan shook his head impatiently. He came slowly to his feet. "Let's call on Martha. She's just doing over what the police will do also. But she should be finished."

Gail followed Jordan around the "L" in the hall to the distant door of the woman scientist's quarters. Again the masculine voice boomed, "Come in!" Again Gail found herself staring around at the incongruous disorder in the room that had served for so long as a working place, a living area, and a dump heap for the trivia of existence.

Martha Beal was listless. "I worked with the sample," she said. "It's Type Three. Paul's type. Not necessarily his, I realized. But it does seem likely that he was struck down in the gallery."

Jordan thanked her. "I guess I was over-zealous last night, Martha. I shouldn't have asked you to do what I did. I was unconsciously unkind. And the police did it all ahead of me. No doubt they've analyzed their samples, too."

Gail did not want to look at the crumpled, ugly, beaten figure. She kept staring at the room. She had a feeling that it was vaguely different from the way it had been on the evening before. Something had been moved, altered, replaced, or taken away. She couldn't decide what it was. And the room did not smell so strongly of chemicals; its morning scent was fresher and more familiar. Those thoughts barely reached the level of registration , for Dr. Jordan was already rising.

Martha Beal leaned forward and said, "Whatever you do, Horace, find the murderer! All last night I lay thinking—"

"I know. All last night a good many of us lay thinking, Martha."

"—and I knew how wrong I have been! I loved Paul. He never loved me. I have clung for thirty years to a chimera, a lie, to self-deceit. He was a good man. He was good to me, even, not to assent to a marriage that would have been a tragedy. You were his pet—his protégé. He must be avenged."

They went out.

"Love," Jordan said, as they walked together through the building, "is every bit as dangerous and wounding as it is rewarding."

Gail answered "Yes" in a small voice.

He glanced at her, opened his mouth, and said nothing. They sat down in the office again.

"Whom do we work for now?" she asked. "The War Department or the police?"

He broke away from an abstraction. "Police," he answered. "I'm wrought up over this business. I don't think I'd concentrate very well on African flatlands. Would you?"

"No. Any ideas?"

"None. Only a plan. I think we ought to put down everything we've seen, heard, thought, suspected, guessed, and wondered about. Make a complete dossier on what happened to Paul, like the one we were making on the Ujiji country."

She smiled. "Even with maps?"

"If maps are necessary. Sure. Begin, not at the beginning, but with right now, and go backward. Put down all you observed about Martha, and all I did. All about Felton and the others. About Evans, Taylor, the guards, the whole business."

"It'll be quite a job," she said.

"Better than hoping we'll think of something, or that Grove will send for us."

"Then let's do it."

The rest of the morning was spent in compiling data. They filled two yellow blocks of ruled paper with their penned notes. Each of them tried to enter every observed detail, every inflection, every mood. They ate lunch hurriedly, in the basement cafeteria. They took advantage of their presence on that floor to look into the paint shop. They re-explored the gallery of Akeley Hall.

At three-thirty, when they had virtually completed their stock-taking, Evans phoned to request Dr. Jordan's presence at an emergency meeting of the Board.

Gail sat alone in the gathering gloom, studying the yellow pages. Occasionally, as she read, she made new entries on the margin. The account left glaring blanks. They didn't know for sure where Dr. Weber had been killed. Or where—or if—his body had been temporarily concealed. They didn't know what had been used as a weapon.

Gail thought about the matter of a weapon in connection with her suggestion that the murder might have been impulsive rather than planned. If the latter, the weapon would have been brought, and disposed of. But if it had been an act only momentarily premeditated, the killer would not, in all likelihood, have had a weapon on his person. He would have used something in the vicinity. He would have seen Dr. Weber enter the gallery and gone off to seek a tool. Gone to seek it in the Museum, a place where, as Evans had indicated, there were ten thousand blunt instruments.

Gail left the office.

The immediate exterior of the gallery was empty. But the place connected with other halls, with passages and corridors, with stairs, and the heavily ornamented staircases. The choice of weapons, even within a half-minute's walking distance, was considerable. Every available foot of wall space, in some areas, had been used for exhibits. And since many of them were of no intrinsic value, they were not attached firmly or kept behind glass. Maces and battle-axes, halberds, poleaxes, broadswords, American Indian war clubs, Australian boomerangs, small meteorites, petrified wood, tile from a Roman bath—each, in its way, suggested grim assassination.

Gail kept ruling out the ones that were impractical and the ones that would not satisfy the contour of the wound in the dead man's skull—a broad, curved depression.

With a sudden prickling sense, she realized that one of the weapons displayed on the wall had a familiar connotation. For a little while she could not place it. Then it came to her: the boomerang. There had been a boomerang somewhere—somewhere—and she remembered. Everything, Gail had noted, from shrunken human heads to headache remedies, from brown bottles of acid to old shoes, a party hat, and a boomerang! There had been a boomerang in Martha Beal's office on the night before; this morning Gail had sensed a change. The boomerang was gone!

She returned to the stairhead where the Australian weapons hung. There were three of them—dark, angled, polished. Upon two, was the inevitable accumulation of dust. The topmost, just within Gail's reach, was not dusty. On the contrary, it shone with the luster of a fresh coat of varnish. Gail, coming closer, realized that it was the smell of varnish which had obscured the chemical odors in Martha Beal's room that morning and given it a recognizable freshness.

Gail re-entered the office. Dr. Jordan had returned from the Board meeting. He was sitting by the window, staring at the dismal coming of night. When he heard her, he stood up, electrically, only to have whatever he was going to say quenched by her flow of words. She finished dramatically: "I suppose she could have learned to throw one, somewhere. I can imagine her, standing across the gallery or in the big room below and hurling that thing at him."

Jordan stared. "It wasn't thrown, Miss Vincent—if it was used at all. Thrown, it hits edgewise. I know. I was struck, once, in northern Australia. Waited a month for a boat and about the only amusement was boomerangs. Edge-on, a boomerang makes a terrible wound, but a narrower one than the one we're dealing with. This one, and I'll agree you've probably found the weapon, must have been used flat-side-on. As a club."

"Hadn't we ought to call Grove right away?"

"In a minute." He sat down again. "The Board meeting was stupid. A few of the city's richer men tried to blame Evans for letting a murder happen in these holy premises. He was politely 'scandalized' and 'helpless.' I sat, thinking of other things. Thinking of our list. And I thought of something rather interesting."

Gail said, "I'm sure Lieutenant Grove—"

"—ought to have all the facts we can possibly gather. What I thought of is that Felton doesn't smoke."

Gail looked blank.

"I mean," Jordan went on, "you mentioned that he was untidy. You said he'd burned a hole in his suit—smoking. But he doesn't smoke. It isn't much. But put it with the possibility that he may have worn a blue suit in here on Tuesday and gone home in a gray one. The one he wore today. Then what? Then something else burned that hole. And what did that? Well, the mind jumps naturally to the thought that he may have scorched his gray suit at the time he was burning up his blue one."

Gail sat down abruptly. "Of course! Then you think all three of them—"

"I don't think anything yet. Two of them could easily be acting to cover up the third. Let's just add this to our notes."

He sat down at his desk. He took out his fountain pen and prepared to augment their collection of data. His pen had run dry. He shook it impatiently and unscrewed the top of his ink bottle. He thrust in his pen, pressed the valve lever, and frowned. He said, "Funny," and took out the pen. He tilted the bottle. Then, to Gail's surprise, he reached for an empty glass specimen dish and poured the ink into it. There was a clinking sound, and then with a blotter he fished out of the dish what looked like a glass pebble of good size.

"Some sort of stone," he said wonderingly. "I hit it with my pen point." He walked to the sink and washed the stone, disregarding the ink that stained his fingers. "Looks like a chip of that quartz, only it isn't yellow."

He held it up to the light. Both of them bent forward intently. "Sparkles," he said. He carried the dish of ink to the sink, dumped it, and washed the dish. Then he took the stone between his thumb and fore-finger and drew it across the glass side of the vessel. It left a long scratch.

"I'll be back," he said. "Wait."

While he was gone, the telephone rang. Gail answered.

"Hello, gorgeous. It's me. Henry. Sorry I was churlish this morning."

"That's all right. You have a cold."

"So I do, darn it! Have you solved the crime and won the war yet?"

"Not quite yet, on either one."

"What about that movie date we were discussing? Seriously?"

"Seriously, I'm too busy. But, seriously, when I'm not, I'll let you know. My social life is thin these days. Nil, in fact."

"Okay. I feel better. And, look. About Tuesday night. I didn't see anything. Not really. I saw Pinsch and Felton, though, and they were talking about Weber. I remembered it after you'd gone. They were looking for him, I think. Maybe the police should know about that item. You tell 'em, will you? Cops irritate me."

"Sure. Where are they?"

"Down on your floor. . . . Well, phone me before I pine away."

Dr. Jordan hurried back into the office. She told Henry she'd call soon, and hung up.

"Who was that?"

"Henry Grant. Trying to date me."

For a moment she thought he was going to show signs of jealousy. Instead, he said, "Talented kid!" and jumped excitedly to the matter in hand: "It's a diamond, all right! Uncut. Smith says it's worth about twenty thousand, as is. So I guess we'd better not take more notes or gather more facts. We'd better get Grove!"

But Homicide reported that Lieutenant Grove was out, was not expected, and could not be reached. Dr. Jordan left his name and an urgent request that he be called as soon as Grove reported in. Then he tipped back his chair and said, "Miss V., who'd hide an uncut diamond worth twenty thousand dollars in my inkwell? And why?"

"I don't know. It's crazy! I'm losing my mind, I think. Can't we do anything?"

"One thing: Supposing, still, that Felton burned up a suit of clothes — obviously, in our supposition, because it was bloodstained — he must have burned it here in the Museum, since he went out in other clothes.

Where would he do it? If there's one thing the guards do look out for, it's fire. The only place I can think of is the incinerator."

"You mean—we'd better look there?"

Jordan grinned. "I mean we'd have to sift the ashes in it on the chance something didn't burn entirely and the further chance that it hasn't been cleaned since Tuesday night. Are you game? It's a dirty job and one I'd hate to be caught at by the wrong person, if we're on any track at all."

Gail nodded.

Even Jordan wasn't sure of his route. He dodged quietly through the cellar. The workmen had gone. Overhead, the exhibition floors were empty of visitors. It was nearing six.

The incinerator was a small, kiln-like structure in the quadrangle behind the main building. Jordan had provided himself with a segment of old window screen and a coal shovel. Enough light fell from the windows of the rooms in use to make it possible for him to shovel the smoldering contents of the incinerator into two large empty ash cans. He rolled them back into the cellar. Gail was shivering from her vigil just inside the door.

Together they began the job of sifting the two cans of charred debris and ashes. They recovered paper clips, bits of broken glass, some bottles, and two tin cans. And then, in the mess, Jordan saw something that made him say, "Hold it!" Gail stopped shaking the screen. Jordan plucked out a hook-like object about an inch long, made of flat metal.

"What is it?" she asked.

"Felton's tailor will know for sure," Jordan answered slowly. "But somebody's tailor sewed it into somebody's trousers, for a clasp, at the waistline. There'll be another metal piece here, a narrow one, for an eye. This is the hook. But we can let Grove's men go on hunting from this point. It would be quite a coincidence—wouldn't it—if somebody else had just happened to have been burning up a pair of trousers here in the last few days? No sign of fabric, though. A thorough job. What do you say we wash up, leave our restaurant telephone number, eat, and come back and wait for Grove in my office?"

The lieutenant put in an appearance at nine o'clock that evening. He was brusque and patronizing until they had finished a long, joint recital. Then he looked from one to the other and whistled softly. "We could use you two permanently," he said. "Now, lemme get the picture. You think all three were in it?"

Gail interrupted, "Four, I just thought. That is, if you didn't pick up the aluminum paint Lombardo says he stole for his nephew."

"Pick it up? Us? No."

"Then Dr. Lombardo was lying, after all. He didn't steal paint for his nephew. He went down to get something to put on that boomerang so that no blood or fingerprints could ever be found on it. Varnish. He just brought along the powdered aluminum to make a good story. Because he said he never did take it home."

Grove thought a moment, after she had clarified that statement. "You think Lombardo and Martha Beal, Felton and Pinsch all worked together to do away with the doctor, then? They all had reasons, at that! Hate, for the woman. Hate and spite and an old feud, for the two geologists. Desperate need of money, for Lombardo, and an expectation that he'd get some through Weber's death. Lombardo, incidentally, needs the money, all right. He owes, not thirty thousand, but about five thousand, to a gambler who has ways and means of collecting. So you think—?"

"They took the boomerang off the wall," Gail said rapidly. "One of them followed Dr. Weber into the gallery and struck him with it. Dr. Felton carried the body to a hiding place and burned his bloody clothes afterward. Martha Beal took charge of the boomerang. Lombardo got some varnish for her. And Pinsch—well, he was probably there, since his partner was. They thought, after they transferred the body to the gorilla tank the next day, that they had plenty of time to work in. It might have lain there for months. So Martha didn't chance putting back the boomerang right away. Felton kept wearing the gray suit so that, months from now, nobody'd remember when—"

Grove held up his hand. "All right. All right. I'll see Felton's tailor in the morning. If that's the kind of clip he uses I'll start with Felton."

"You mean you aren't going to arrest anybody right now?"

Grove shook his head. "Just assign men to 'em all. I'll phone you in the morning. There are still a couple of matters I don't get."

The way he said that worried Gail. "What?"

"Where's the can of quartz? And where'd that diamond come from?" He looked at them intently. "I'd like to take it along."

Jordan handed it over. "We talked about this. I think, myself, the diamond was in old Paul's pocket."

"Why?"

The zoologist shrugged. "I couldn't say. Talisman, maybe. He liked gems. Something he may have carried around for years. Or, perhaps, something he had with him that he intended to present to the Museum. He's made a lot of gifts to the Hall of Gems. I think the people who killed him, searched him, and probably decided to plant that stone in my office just to throw off anybody who found it. Maybe they expected to steal it back later. I never lock the place. And I almost never use my ink bottle."

"And the quartz?" Grove persisted.

"Why don't the police do a little of the work?" Jordan responded.

Grove winked. "I accept that. All right. You'd better knock off and go to the movies or something. I'll call you tomorrow."

He did call. Gail and Dr. Jordan were on hand before nine. He telephoned about ten. He said, "The tailor says it's one of his. I'm sending for Felton now."

The rest of the morning passed—and the afternoon. Toward five, Grove phoned again. "I'm getting nowhere," he said. "That is—not yet. Felton's mum. I sent for Martha Beal. Her story is that somebody put that boomerang in her office. She doesn't lock hers, any more than you do. She says she didn't even notice it until just before you two first called on her. She examined it, thought for a while she'd brought it in some time and then forgotten it.

"Next—I'm still following her story, which could easily be true—she says she noticed blood on it, and got panicky. She says, rightly enough, there was plenty to make us suspect her. So she looked through the other offices for some stain or lacquer that would make the boomerang proof against examination, and found what she wanted in Lombardo's office. She was coming back with it when you barged down the hall. That scared her and she ducked between the cabinets. You spotted her, so she cached the aluminum paint before she came out.

"She got it later, scrubbed the boomerang, dried it, put on the varnish, dumped the aluminum powder down the sink, and replaced the weapon before she went home. I had to tell her only enough to get her started, and she spilled all that, including that piece about Lombardo's aluminum paint. Lombardo does have a nephew, Angelo, and he does make model planes with the kid Sundays. And there's a trace of aluminum powder in the woman's sink. So where are we?"

Jordan repeated the call almost verbatim to Gail. "It seems plausible—in fact, it couldn't be coincidence. She either told him the absolute truth or they're all extraordinary liars."

"What about Felton?"

"Nothing. Grove's keeping him. He just won't talk. So far, anyway, the threat of indicting him for murder hasn't budged him. He's staying in custody over Sunday. Well—?"

"We go home," Gail said. "I have a headache."

Sunday was bright and clear, and the longest day of Gail's life. She stayed in her room in her midtown hotel, hoping and expecting that she would be called. But her telephone did not ring once all day long.

Gail went to bed early and continued her daylong effort to divert herself by minutely reading the Sunday papers. But even the war news did not hold her attention. Once, a small item briefly registered on her consciousness because it mentioned diamonds: "Cartel Operator Sought," the paragraph was headed. "Konrad A. Zweissman, retired diamond expert and amateur explorer, at one time investigated by the Justice Department in connection with cartel activities said to be inimical to American interests, is being sought again by federal authorities. His last known residence was Catskill Vista, in New York."

The smallness and irrelevance of the item gave her a frantic feeling. She threw the paper aside. For a long time she considered telephoning Horace Jordan just to break the tense monotony of waiting. But she decided he would think she was being silly. She put out her light, finally. Friday's excitement at having accomplished so much became, by Sunday night, an almost unbearable feeling that she and Dr. Jordan had accomplished nothing at all. . . .

In the morning she dressed feverishly and hurried to the Museum. Dr. Jordan appeared an hour earlier than usual and he, also, looked as if he had spent a wracking weekend. They waited all morning, relieved somewhat by mutual companionship. Then, just before they left for lunch, Grove came. He sauntered up the hall, and threw his coat and hat on a chair.

"Well?" Jordan spoke impatiently.

Grove shrugged. "I've got Felton's story. Got it last night. And Pinsch has just corroborated it. Probably they're lying, but I'm darned if I can break it down! And I'd hate to accuse one of them wrongly. They'd raise unholy Ned! It's like Martha Beal's story—so simple you almost have to believe it. Stupid, maybe, but the kind of thing that stuffed shirts like Felton will do when they think they're in a jam. He said, when he finally sent for me, and he said it all without prompting, that he and Pinsch found Weber lying dead in Akeley Hall.

"Seems they'd gone to the old man's office, and from there around the Museum, hunting him. They knew he was in; knew his habits. They had some fresh geological debate to needle him with. That's why they were looking for him that night. They pushed into Akeley Hall. The gallery. And he was lying there dead, with a boomerang on the floor beside him."

"And you believed that!" Jordan was indignant.

"Wait a minute. Wait till I fill in. Felton saw, at once, that if he and Pinsch raised a hue and cry, they'd be suspected. He had near hysterics, at first. Then he insisted that they should remove every trace of the crime in order to keep themselves clear. Pinsch didn't want to until what he calls the 'sardonic side of making the old man vanish,' hit him. He thought of the gorilla tank, naturally. He made Felton do the heavy work.

"They wrapped Weber in a tarpaulin—and remember, they both told the identical story separately, though they've had ample time to prepare it. They hid the body up on this floor, in the blower-room, where almost nobody ever goes. They searched Paul. That diamond, they said, was in his pants pocket. They put it in your inkwell. One for you to ponder—and us cops if the thing was ever found. They put the boomerang in that incredible morass Martha Beal calls her office, thinking that she was an even better suspect than you or themselves—if, when, and as.

"Next, Felton says, they went down and burned his suit. It was easy. There was nobody in the cellar at all. Not around the incinerator, anyhow. Felton had had that gray suit in a box in his office for two months, since late fall. He'd taken it into town for repairs and neglected to carry it home. Says he detests to carry packages on trains—imagine that! They figured, after that, on at least a month during which Paul Weber would be merely a missing person. In that time, they thought, they could either dispose of the body or leave it where it was to create the havoc it did when Taylor found it. Only, he found it quicker than they were prepared for. Even that metal pants clasp would have gone out in the ashes on Saturday, though it seems they'd never thought of that. The only other thing Felton did, that he calls a 'mistake,' was to hesitate about going out on a cold night, late, in a thin suit. The guard noticed and remembered it."

Jordan said, "Well, I'll be damned!"

"Me, too! Of course, we're still holding him. It isn't legal to move murdered people around. But neither is it necessarily a solution to who killed Weber."

"What are you going to do next?"

Grove shrugged. "I wish I knew. Any thoughts?"

Jordan shook his head. So did Gail.

"I'm gonna eat," Grove said. He departed perplexedly.

And presently Jordan left for lunch. Gail felt in no mood to accept his invitation. She went out alone and had coffee and hamburger in a hole-in-the-wall. Dr. Jordan didn't come back after lunch, and Gail started going through the mail that had accumulated in the office for some days. It lay piled on the table nearest the door. In it was an unwrapped copy of a natural history magazine, presumably left there for Dr. Jordan. The current issue. There was a flamingo on the cover.

Gail began to look through it. Ordinarily it would have absorbed her interest. Now she jumped from one picture to the next, feeling frustrated, lonely, and disappointed in everything.

By and by it occurred to her that this wasn't the current issue. She looked at the cover again. The date was correct but, she thought, there was a pterodactyl on the current issue. She wondered why she had thought that, and recalled the copy of the magazine that had been in Henry Grant's pocket. He must have been reading an old issue. She asked herself why, because she had fallen into the habit, in the past week, of asking the "why" of everything. She decided to find out. It would be better to do even that than just to sit here.

In the library she found the file of magazines she wanted. The one with the flying reptile on the outside was two months old. She carried it back to the office. She leafed through it as she had the first, and she found nothing that seemed relevant. Defiantly she put it aside. For a long time she compelled herself to work on the notes about Ujiji for the War Department. When she ran out of will power it was growing dark again. New York City was wrapping itself in veil after veil of winter mist. It would be night again before closing time. She switched on her light, and once more examined the magazine she had taken from the library.

This time she decided to be more methodical. She began with the table of contents. She got no farther. One of the articles was entitled, "Semiprecious Stones of the Amazon Basin." Its author was Konrad A. Zweissman.

At first the name was tantalizing. She seemed to associate it with something that had happened long ago. But, after much frowning concentration, its relationship came back to her. She had seen the name only yesterday in the newspapers: "Diamond expert . . . sought by the Justice Department . . . cartel activities inimical to American interests . . ."

She sat rigidly. A new idea had leaped into her mind. The things they had neglected suddenly began to take new forms. The can of quartz and the man who wanted to smuggle ivory; the Boers who had actually been German agents and Paul Weber's excitement on the night he had come to see Jordan; the possible significance of the old mineralogist's last stroll through the Museum and his enjoyment of his joke.

Part of her thinking was logical, part guesswork, part intuition. But it began with Zweissman, the man who was apparently an enemy agent and wanted by the FBI. A man who was an authority on diamonds. A man who had sufficient prestige to write an article for a natural history magazine. There had been one diamond — large, valuable, uncut, inexplicable. Had it been in that coffee can of quartz samples? And, if it had, wasn't it possible that there had been more diamonds like it?

Ujiji was a long way from the Transvaal, where diamonds are found. But it was in Africa. Couldn't Nazi agents have gathered together a hoard of gems and entrusted them to someone who would get them out of Africa? Couldn't they have planned to send them, via America and Japan, to Hitler's war chest? So as not to risk them in Holland, the usual destination? Wasn't war coming soon to Holland? And wouldn't any such diamonds have to be smuggled? They would never get out, otherwise. And couldn't Horace Jordan have been made the unwitting victim of the affair?

Was the "Englishman" who sounded him out about smuggling old ivory, not English, but another German agent? Was he, perhaps, testing Jordan? And when he found Jordan uninterested, hadn't he nonetheless secreted his precious hoard in the can of quartz, where it would be magnificently hidden? Where even a customs inspector would probably not have made any distinction between the clear yellow fragments and the still clearer white ones?

Then what? Jordan, unknowingly, brought diamonds into America. Presumably, the agents on this side had a plan to intercept them. A paid agent "placed" inside the Museum. Or a staff member hard up for cash. Or a member secretly on their side. Somebody. Only — and Gail became certain she was on the right track — only, Dr. Jordan hadn't brought the quartz directly to the Museum! He hadn't stored it in any usual place, such as his home, either. No doubt his home had been carefully, tracelessly searched. But he had lacked room at home. He had sent the can of quartz, with some other things, to his sister's house in New Jersey, and there it had sat for three years, while baffled agents sought furiously for it!

It had reappeared on Tuesday—brought into the Museum by Dr. Jordan and turned over to Weber. Somebody had seen the coffee can, and, from that instant on, the old doctor had been in fearful danger.

Some time in the evening he had dumped out the quartz, had seen, perhaps at a glance, just what it was, and then—what lay beneath it. He had verified his discovery. Marveled over it. Come to see Jordan, maybe, at dinnertime, and missed him. Wandered around, excitedly. Carrying in his pocket one of the diamonds, with which to confront Jordan.

But Paul Weber had missed Jordan. He had written down the basic analysis of the yellow quartz as a "joke"—a joke, since he probably thought Jordan knew the different, colorless stones also were in the can but did not realize their worth. Then, having missed Jordan, Weber had gone out, leaving the can and the quartz—but not the diamonds. He had said, vaguely, that, "it would keep," and that he had "taken care of things."

If there had been many diamonds worth twenty thousand dollars apiece, that could have meant only one thing: He had hidden them. Certainly, he would not have left them lying about in his office. Perhaps, even then, he was worried. Perhaps he had seen a face looking in at him or had heard stealthy footsteps. But he had surely concealed the diamonds which Gail had hypothesized, whether he had been alarmed by anything or not.

Gail capped that brilliant piece of deduction by another. There was no place to hide jewels in the gallery of Akeley Hall. But old Paul had another haunt, one to which he possessed the key: the Hall of Gems. There, he was at home. And if the diamonds could be exquisitely camouflaged in a can of quartz chips, they could be concealed in the same way, and just as effectively, somewhere in the Hall of Gems.

Gail raced through the long, somber corridor. Her feet pattered on the stone stairs. She hurried into the Hall of Gems. The lights were on and the vast chamber gleamed like the cave of a genie. The extreme beauty of the place struck her. She began moving past the exhibits, searching intently. In the room were perhaps a dozen persons. But it would soon be closing time. A uniformed guard was already standing at the gate. She read labels: beryl, topaz, amethyst, citrine, which looked like the quartz in the coffee can.

Why, though, was Dr. Weber killed, she wondered? Then she knew. Even to be aware of the existence of the precious stones was to menace their delivery to Germany. He had known too much. Jordan didn't know. Weber had died, and the search for the treasure, concealed again by him, had been resumed. It was surely still going on.

She walked around a case filled with porphyrite and peered into its back. Nothing . . .

All that Martha had said, all that Felton and Pinsch had reported, and the absurd story of Lombardo—all were true. They had done what they had admitted, and nothing more. Tourmaline, jade, onyx . . .

She came to a large geode in a special case. She drew her breath and bent nearer. A geode, the sign explained, is stone within a stone, a nodule formed in a rock pocket by seeping minerals. Its interior, as a result, is filled with crystals, except for the center, which is usually hollow. This stone was about the size of her head. It had been sliced through, so that a "lid" could be removed. It lay in the case, like a jack-o'-lantern on its side.

In it, she saw the glittering, transparent arrangements of crystals that had "grown" toward the center. They were in parallel stalks about as thick as her fingers. Beyond them, in the back, where the light barely made them distinguishable and where no human being would ever have noticed their differentness, if that person had not been looking for it, were many more crystals. These were not attached.

The diamonds Dr. Weber had found could have lain in the geode for a century, undetected. It furnished a superb hiding place for them.

When she saw them in the shadow within the stone, masked by the crystal fingers of larger and therefore more spectacular prisms, she could hardly believe her senses. She—Gail—had figured it out and proved she was right! The myriad crystals which were part of the geode consisted, the sign said, of quartz, or SiO_2. So, perhaps, Dr. Weber's joke had included a sly hint of the hiding place of the gems, a hint which he could have interpreted!

The next thought that entered her mind was one that made her afraid.

Dr. Weber had found the diamonds. And died. Did the murderer know where they were now? Had he located them yet? Was he, even at this instant, in the Hall with her, watching? He had obviously stolen the coffee can from Dr. Jordan's office and found they were not in it.

Fearfully, she looked around. In the dull electric light the few remaining people seemed harmless enough. A warning bell and the urging of the guards would soon send them on their way to the elevators and the exits.

Gail left the Hall of Gems. She crossed the Hall of the Age of Man, with its towering mammoth. Beyond, were the elevators. One car closed its gate and started down as she approached. She would take the next, whichever way it went. People were already gathering. Then she decided not to take it. The chances that she was even now being watched were minute. But what if she were? Suppose the murderer had been one of the guards? The guard now entering the Hall of Gems?

She turned toward the staircase that led up to the fifth floor, and observed that Dr. Evans was standing at its foot, talking to another man. Near-panic seized her. Suppose it was Dr. Evans, and he had been watching her? She walked hastily into the room beyond. It was filled with fossil mammals. She could go on around to the north elevators. Dr. Evans, she thought, had every right to be talking to a man on the exhibition floor.

But her sense of normalcy crumbled steadily. She went on, almost at a trot, into the room that held fossil reptiles, the room that held her phobia, also. Beyond that were the cretaceous dinosaurs and, beyond them, a hallway.

The closing bell was sounding somewhere. A guard called to her that it was time to leave. She nodded; the man went on. Above her, now, towered the mighty piles of brown bones that had once been the frames of living animals—gigantic biological machines. The bell rang again. The guard's voice was far behind her. And the lights went out.

They flashed out in sections, but very rapidly. The last half of them went dark all together, as if a fuse had blown. Gail stopped stock-still. Coincidence? The footsteps of the departing visitors echoed ahead and behind. An iron gate clanged. Full of a new horror, Gail rushed toward the hall. Light from it silhouetted the ribs and vertebrae of the monsters. She felt sweat leak down her sides under her dress. For a moment she considered running back. She looked around—into the dim, cavernous vault behind her. She turned again.

The gate to the hall was moving. Then the guard who had his hand on it suddenly let go, and the hand vanished. Beyond him, she heard a mutter and a muffled cry of "Fire!"

An elevator door calmly opened. The last of the people in the hall entered it with a rush and it went down. A thin vine of smoke was swinging down the distant passageway.

She heard a low, bubbling sound, like a whisper, and, even as it started, she dodged. Something hard and heavy crashed beyond her and slithered on the polished floor. Gail knew then.

The gate behind her clanged shut. She was trapped. She screamed for help, her voice splitting the darkness. With an instinct that was repellent even as it made her act, she slid into the murk at the side of the room, out of the pale, uncertain light that shone through its middle. Now she could see the monsters dimly. They were like titanic cattle, staring and grazing in the gloom. Only there was no flesh on them and no skin. Swiftly, breathing with desperate care so as not to make a sound, she slipped off her shoes. The person who had thrown the missile at her was in the room. In her stocking feet she began to hurry along the bare, smooth stone floor.

Once, she distinctly heard the soft rap of lightly running feet. Then she heard nothing for a while. She moved around cases and skeletons, putting distance between her and the place where the tapping sound had originated. But the move only sent her deeper into the vaulted chamber, toward the end where the gate was already closed and locked. In the corridor there was still smoke and confused shouting. Sheer horror, she realized, was rapidly weakening her.

A cough, dry, low, and muffled, sounded briefly. The hair rose on the nape of her neck; she knew for certain—everything.

She tiptoed along. On a dais, between Gail and the hall, was the figure of another dinosaur, a horizontal ladder of enormous ribs with huge, flared horns. Gail ducked under the heavy silk cord that roped it off. She put a tentative foot on the great knee bone, tested it, and heaved herself up, like a child climbing into a tree. The thick, splayed bones, as big as a good-sized table, silently received her. She crouched on them rigidly.

The reek of smoke was now permeating the darkness. It wasn't like any Gail had ever smelled before. In the corridor men were shouting more loudly. From far away came the sizzle of an extinguisher. Below, on the floor of the chamber, was another sound—the same cough, muffled and horrid. Then Gail could vaguely make out a figure. It came forward in a crouch. The distant source of faint light shone hideously on the eyeballs for an instant. Afterward, it made a glint in Henry Grant's hand, the glint of a gun. He was coming quickly, but with caution, peering into every recess, and—she observed with a last desperate surge of horror— looking up into the colossal skeletons, too. He would not fail to see her.

The elevator banged again. Feet ran. A broad brogue came clearly to her ears: "It was a smokepot, Doc!"

Then Dr. Jordan's voice: "Get those lights on!"

"The boys are busy with 'em now."

Gail saw the figure below come to a halt. An ecstasy of fear welled in her. She did not dare to scream. It would give away her hiding place. Then Grant might not only kill her, but Dr. Jordan, also.

The gate was pushed wide open again. The guard said, "I think maybe that scream came from the room here—the one that went dark. Probably a scared tourist!"

Horace Jordan was coming in. She could see him clearly, silhouetted against the door. His voice was like broken glass. "Yeah, Kelly. If it was the girl I've been looking for the last half-hour, and anything has happened to her, I'm going to break you apart! She's the finest kid in the world! You shouldn't have left this spot!"

Her eyes darted back to Grant. She could see his teeth, now, faintly white; his arm was coming up. She knew what she had to do, then. Her voice was clear and loud: "Look out, Horace!"

The figure at the door dodged inside. Grant's gun split the darkness. Instantly, Horace Jordan's gun shot back. She saw Grant dive for cover in the deeper darkness. As he plunged, he fired again. The bullet ripped the great bones that concealed her. With the second flash came a second reply. For a few, infinite seconds, the two guns flashed in the dark. Then there came the sound of metal clattering on the floor.

The lights went on.

Grant was holding his arm, and blood was spurting from it. Dr. Jordan was standing just inside the door with his pistol in his hand. He blinked, glanced once at Grant, and started searching the great, skeleton-filled chamber for the girl.

"I'm right up here, H-H-Horace," she said, and then the dam broke and she burst into tears.

The zoologist ran. Gail half tumbled out of the thing of which she had been most afraid in the world. But she wasn't even thinking of dinosaurs. She was thinking of the way Horace Jordan had spoken about her.

He held her while she wept and shook. Behind them, the guards were taking charge of Henry Grant.

The doctor spoke, finally, in a wondering tone. "Horace," he repeated. "You called me Horace! And you're crying. Now, I must say, that's damn' human of you!"

Gail responded in a faint but determined tone, "Of course I'm human! If you only knew how human!"

She felt his arms tighten. "That," he said, "is what I aim to find out. I've been afraid for months you weren't real. The package was so irresistibly attractive, I couldn't believe that it held more than a mere brain. And brains, around here, are a nickel apiece! This is a lousy way to make love—and a particularly lousy place!"

She giggled. . . .

Dr. Evans was there in the familiar office, and Lieutenant Grove. Gail had been talking for quite a while and Horace Jordan was getting impatient.

"How does it happen," Evans asked, "that you were afraid of me, since you had figured out so much? I mean this afternoon on the stairs?"

"Because it was only figuring. I wasn't certain of anything. I thought it was Henry, because of that issue of the magazine. He'd been reading that article, I imagined. Or maybe he translated it. Or placed it. But I couldn't prove it wasn't you—or anybody."

Evans turned to Grove: "What about Grant?"

The police officer grimaced. "The FBI gets that baby! They always get the good ones! But he said plenty before they came for him. He's been in a terrible sweat, as you can imagine. I mean, he killed Weber there in the dark and raced back up to this floor to get the diamonds. They were missing. He made as careful and fast a search of Weber's office as he could, and then went back to do something about Weber's body. Remove the traces he'd left.

"But the boomerang he'd snatched for the killing was gone. The body was gone. The bloodstains, even, were gone. You can imagine the sort of days and nights he put in on Wednesday and Thursday! Then Weber's body was discovered, and Grant began to look frantically for the jewels. He stole the can, of course, and dropped it in the Hudson River on his way home, the same night. He came to the same conclusion Miss Vincent did, and located the geode. He says the diamonds are worth about four millions.

"He didn't dare smash right in. He made the smoke bomb to fake a fire at closing time, when things are jumbled, anyway, and the guards are busy with the public. He planned to touch off and blow some fuses, then to get to the geode. He was just checking things over when he saw Miss Vincent looking at the cache."

"Nazis!" Jordan said, with loathing.

Grove nodded. "He even beat up his own kind, to look like a good citizen. That I call low!"

Evans said thoughtfully, "Well, it's over. I'm glad. The Museum won't ever be able to repay its debt, Miss Vincent."

Horace Jordan rose with determination. "This sort of business," he said sternly, "can go on for hours. We all know what happened. I, personally, will undertake to pay a portion of the Museum's debt with one small steak—if there's one to be had. Mind you, gentlemen, I am not offering more steaks. One—only one. And then I am going to put the Museum in Gail's debt in perpetuity, if she'll have me. . . . Come on, Gail."

"Yes," Gail answered. "Yes to the beefsteak—and yes to the perpetuity!"

Ten Thousand Blunt Instruments

Ten Thousand Blunt Instruments by Philip Wylie, edited by Bill Pronzini, is set in Palatino by White Lotus Infotech Pvt Ltd, India. It is printed on 60 pound natural, recycled, acid-free paper. The cover illustration and design are by Tom Roberts, and the Lost Classics series design is by Deborah Miller. *Ten Thousand Blunt Instruments* was printed and bound by Thomson-Shore, Dexter, Michigan, and published in July 2010 by Crippen & Landru Publishers, Norfolk, Virginia.

CRIPPEN & LANDRU, PUBLISHERS

P. O. Box 9315
Norfolk, VA 23505
E-mail: info@crippenlandru.com

Crippen & Landru publishes first editions of short-story collections by important detective and mystery writers.

☞ This is the best edited, most attractively packaged line of mystery books introduced in this decade. The books are equally valuable to collectors and readers. [*Mystery Scene Magazine*]

☞ The specialty publisher with the most star-studded list is Crippen & Landru, which has produced short story collections by some of the biggest names in contemporary crime fiction. [*Ellery Queen's Mystery Magazine*]

☞ God Bless Crippen & Landru. [*The Strand Magazine*]

☞ A monument in the making is appearing year by year from Crippen & Landru, a small press devoted exclusively to publishing the criminous short story. [*Alfred Hitchcock's Mystery Magazine*]

MORE TRADITIONAL MYSTERIES IN THE LOST CLASSICS SERIES

Crippen & Landru is proud to publish a series of *new* short-story collections by great authors of the past who specialized in traditional mysteries. Each book collects stories from crumbling pages of old pulp, digest, and slick magazines, and most of the stories have been "lost" since their first publication. The following books are in print:

T.S. Stribling, *Dr. Poggioli: Criminologist*, edited by Arthur Vidro. 2004.

Margaret Millar, *The Couple Next Door: Collected Short Mysteries*, edited by Tom Nolan. 2004.

Gladys Mitchell, *Sleuth's Alchemy: Cases of Mrs. Bradley and Others*, edited by Nicholas Fuller. 2005.

Philip S. Warne / Howard W. Macy, *Who Was Guilty? Two Dime Novels*, edited by Marlena E. Bremseth. 2005.

Dennis Lynds writing as Michael Collins, *Slot-Machine Kelly: The Collected Private Eye Cases of the One-Armed Bandit*, introduction by Robert J. Randisi. 2005.

Julian Symons, *The Detections of Francis Quarles*, edited by John Cooper; afterword by Kathleen Symons. 2006.

Rafael Sabatini, *The Evidence of the Sword and Other Mysteries*, edited by Jesse F. Knight. 2006.

Erle Stanley Gardner, *The Casebook of Sidney Zoom*, edited by Bill Pronzini. 2006.

Ellis Peters (Edith Pargeter), *The Trinity Cat and Other Mysteries*, edited by Martin Edwards and Sue Feder. 2006.

Lloyd Biggle, Jr., *The Grandfather Rastin Mysteries*, edited by Kenneth Lloyd Biggle and Donna Biggle Emerson. 2007.

Max Brand, *Masquerade: Ten Crime Stories*, edited by William F. Nolan. 2007.

Mignon G. Eberhart, *Dead Yesterday and Other Mysteries*, edited by Rick Cypert and Kirby McCauley. 2007.

Hugh Pentecost, *The Battles of Jericho*, introduction by S.T. Karnick; afterword by Daniel Phillips. 2008.

Victor Canning, *The Minerva Club, The Department of Patterns, and Others*, edited by John Higgins. 2009.

Anthony Boucher and Denis Green, *The Casebook of Gregory Hood*, edited by Joe R. Christopher. 2009.

Vera Caspary, *Murder at the Stork Club and Other Mysteries*, edited by A.B. Emrys. 2009.

Michael Innes, *Appleby Talks About Crime*, edited by John Cooper; afterword by Margaret Mackintosh Harrison. 2010.

Philip Wylie, *Ten Thousand Blunt Instruments*, edited by Bill Pronzini. 2010.

FORTHCOMING LOST CLASSICS

Erle Stanley Gardner, *The Exploits of the Patent Leather Kid*, edited by Bill Pronzini.

Vincent Cornier, *Duel of Shadows: The Extraordinary Cases of Barnabas Hildreth*, edited by Mike Ashley.

Phyllis Bentley, *Author in Search of a Character: The Detections of Miss Phipps*, edited by Marvin Lachman.

Elizabeth Ferrars, *The Casebook of Jonas P. Jonas and Others*, edited by John Cooper.

Balduin Groller, *Detective Dagobert: Master Sleuth of Old Vienna*, translated by Thomas Riediker.

SUBSCRIPTIONS

Crippen & Landru offers discounts to individuals and institutions who place Standing Order Subscriptions for its forthcoming publications, either all the Regular Series or all the Lost Classics or (preferably) both. Collectors can thereby guarantee receiving limited editions, and readers won't miss any favorite stories. Standing Order Subscribers receive a specially commissioned story in a deluxe edition as a gift at the end of the year. Please write or e-mail for more details.

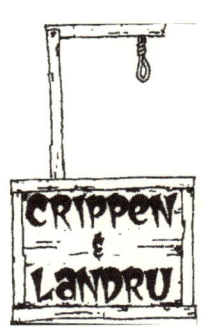